AXIOM

Book One of ARTORIAN'S ARCHIVES
A DIVINE DUNGEON Series

Written by DENNIS VANDERKERKEN
and DAKOTA KROUT

TABLE OF CONTENTS

ACKNOWLEDGMENTS

From Dennis:

There are many people who have made this book possible. First is Dakota himself, for without whom this entire series would never have come about. In addition to letting me write in his universe, he has taken it upon himself to edit and keep straight all the madness for which I am responsible, with resulting hilarity therein.

A thank you to my late grandfather, after whom a significant chunk of Artorian's personality is indebted. He was a man of mighty strides, and is missed dearly.

A special thank you to my parents, for being ever supportive in my odd endeavors, MDP for being a fantastic publisher, Jess for keeping us all on task, and all the fans of DD and CC who are responsible for the popularity for this to come to pass.
May your affinity channels be strong, and plentiful!

Last of all, thank you. Thank you for picking this up and giving it a read.
This AA1 is the beginning of a multi-book series, and I dearly hope you will enjoy them as the story keeps progressing. AA may start before DD, but don't worry! It's going all the way past the end of CC! So if you liked this, keep an eye out for more things from Mountaindale Press!

PROLOGUE

"Sir!"

A man in his early thirties looked up from the map he and a few others were pouring over and could instantly see that the messenger had serious and grievous news to give him. "What in the *abyss* is going on out there? Report!"

"Sir, the front line has fallen, the main Commander has been slain! There was... there is a *Mage* out there!"

Various sounds of consternation filled the tent, and a few people even ran to double-check the report. "Why in the world would there be a Mage here? There aren't even the most basic of *cultivators* in this fight! How could they *afford* a–"

"From what I understand, the Mage is killing indiscriminately. Sir! I don't know what to tell you. All I know is that command either falls to you or..."

"Don't tell me someone is bringing *him* this same message! As much as I don't want to be in charge, there is no way...!"

Even as he finished his statement, a powerful voice rumbled over the battlefield, "*Charge!*"

The bloodlust coming from the self-entitled voice was so thick that the warriors could almost taste it, and *this* group was right at the rear of the battle. "We've won, you backwater cretins! Turn and *fight!* Their line is broken! I said *charge!*"

The sub-commander barreled out of his tent and into the scorching sunlight that was the Soccoro Desert. Why there was a battle happening in this blasted wasteland, he had no idea. He simply followed orders and attempted to do right by his people... unlike his counterpart, who was only in the military for glory. Taking a deep breath, the sub-commander bellowed an order to countermand the words that had shaken the sand out of his tent. "Retreat! *Blast* that order. There is a *Mage* waiting out there! *Full retreat.*"

Sand and dust were present at the *best* of times in this wasteland, but the density and quantity today were on a different level. A sound reached his ears, a high-pitched **piiiiii... boom**. With that detonation, a massive amount of sand, soot, and various debris joined what was already in the air, choking the sub-commander in an instant. The sun was blotted out, and the world descended into a confusing and hazy blur.

"*Traitor!*" The snarl thundered across the burning sand and searing soot, burning deeper into the sub-commander than the sun ever had in this place. "Ignore him! For glory! For honor! For your King! *I said* charge!"

Next to the command tent, the sub-commander's eyes widened as a chance breeze pushed aside the storm of sand and soot and the battlefield was revealed to him. Death, flame, and destruction. Every man who entered the open space of the battlefield was starting alight and was burned into a pile of ashes in an instant. Even those who were *not* moving forward...

Boom.

A roiling wave of heat struck the sub-commander square in the back, and the taste of sand filled his mouth as he was shoved down into the ground by the invisible shockwave. His skin was shredded as the dirt, newly-made glass, and flaming splinters cut hundreds of lines through his armor. He stifled a groan and pushed himself up, his aching knee pulled to his chest as the toes of his boot sunk into brittle, half-glassed sand. A glance behind him showed that only a fireball remained of the command tent, and the lack of screams made his heart sink. Those were... his... ten years on the campaign trail; those were his brothers in arms! The only family he had!

He steeled himself; he would need to grieve *later*. If there *was* a later. For now, he needed to save as many as he could. Their loss was clear; the chances of victory were nonexistent. It was time to retreat, or they would suffer a devastating rout and be killed to the last man. There was no victory to be found here—not now, not after that *monster*, that *cultivator*, the one-man *army* arrived.

"Disengage! Disen-**hack**-gage!" His words somehow sounded clearly across the field, and he knew he would be obeyed by most. There was power in being there for the people that relied on you, and he knew that his opposite was not as beloved as he was. The people... they would run. Hopefully, some would even *survive*.

"Don't listen to *him*!" The next words to reach his ringing ears were accusatory. "I will chase you *down*, you *traitor*! I will chase you all down if it's the *last* thing I–"

A whistle of metal pierced the space where the words were forming, and the sentence abruptly ended with a very fleshy **hyuk**. It would have been a notable detail had a pillar of flame not engulfed the position in a cascading waterfall of fire and destruction. Loss. Total loss.

The newly minted Commander bellowed, "Get back to the bunkers!"

A cold feeling of dread permeated his insides, particularly his stomach when he realized... by giving an order, he had made himself a prime target. The Commander, the other sub-commander... this Mage was targeting command structure before all else. Panic fueled the muscles in his legs as he broke into a 'your-life-is-over' run through the billowing walls of hot sand. The cries and wails of the numerous injured littered the surroundings, the troops around him invisible in the artificial maelstrom of glowing orange and matte black. He had made the correct decision.

Boom.

A high pitched *piiiiii* sound filled his now-damaged ears, an infuriatingly sharp tone. It wasn't much, but it was all the sensory information available. Wait... had it gotten even *hotter*? Odd how that seemed so impossible at the edge of the scorching Socorro Desert. The panic of his current reality took grip once more, and his determined fingertips clenched into his palm, grasping the soil that he had been thrown into.

To his surprise, the flat rock he gripped was solid and cool. Without being able to actually *see*, there was still enough difference to inform him that he was now in the shade. He had gotten into the bunkers!

Hope blossomed as the poor excuse for a Commander forced himself to his feet. He took a few steps, then found himself falling into a deep hole that someone must have been using as a sleeping or cool-down area. As he settled on the dirt several feet below the bunker and tried to regain his breath, he realized that his dry throat was making each inhalation excruciatingly painful.

As soon as he could manage, there was no hesitation in snatching the waterskin—now considerably singed—from his belt. His shredded leather belt didn't survive this pull, falling to tatters as he pulled open the container and took a long pull. He did his best to squint his eyes open, at least enough to rinse out some of the caked-on foulness.

Though it did little to help the *pain*, it was still sufficient to restore a semblance of visibility. A jarring cry echoed down to him, so he pulled himself up to peek over the edge of the hole. Hope filled him for a moment as a duo of familiar figures burst into the underground space... but they were not the only things coming through the opening. Fire, prefaced by a sound like thunder heralding a storm, flooded into the space after them.

The air seemed to coil and writhe, producing a *horrifying* orange glow. The air became a swirl of ebon particles that danced in the air, and the only sound was the crackle of sand becoming glass in the sudden torrential heat. The sight of his men... his *family...* being swallowed by the flames was the last he remembered. He couldn't avoid the hail of rocks that erupted from the ground and shattered against the opposing wall, ricocheting straight for his head.

Darkness took him.

CHAPTER ONE

Thunk. The old warrior woke from a deep sleep with a pained jerk, his latent nightmares still sending the word '*traitor*' ringing through his skull. His forehead stung as his aged body awoke to the aching impact of a shelled nut. *Right* on a sore spot near the temple. It had healed over... oh, *decades* ago by this point.

Plink.

The communal gasp of several youngsters was the first sign of what was likely going to be a *taxing* day. A child's voice whispered frantically, "You *hit* him!"

Half-muffled replies from another tiny voice snapped in panic, "I didn't *mean* to!"

The first voice remained frantic. "You hit the *Elder*! You hit the El– *mlmm*!"

Any following words were muffled by the tight grasp of multiple hands, and a communal *shhh* hissed from several sources. The scuffle of feet moved with the unskilled stealth of a weighed-down pack mule as the small gathering of children tried to escape unnoticed. Fat chance of *that* happening.

Dry wood croaked like a grumpy frog as the Elder struggled to get off his resting place. One leg clambered over the edge of the bed, and a moment later, the other followed. A deep breath was held before the *hmmmpf* of effort pushed the aged wreck up and off the padded sheet. Trembling hands fell to his sides after the old man was finally upright—at least as upright as an almost fifty-year-old who spent most of his time horizontal and in bed could be.

Small crunches rippled and popped underfoot with every step he took. It appeared he'd wandered into... a mess of small shells. He pondered the unnatural addition to his floor, uncertain what to make of the situation. "Hmm. *Curious.*"

There was a slight stagger as a shell cut into his foot, but a few steps later, he was leaning on the window hole in the wall. This *particular* hole was 'mysteriously' missing the thin cloth that usually gave his home a touch of privacy. The Elder stuck his bald head through the window and squinted to find the missing cloth. Sure enough, it was floppily attached to the top of the frame and detached from the other three supports. The cover aimlessly flapped in the eternally soft breeze, the wind making his waist-long beard follow suit.

Barely a white puff floated overhead, the sky was its usual gentle blue. The beautiful sky was a common sight in this corner of the world thanks to a low annual rainfall. He realized right then that he must have overslept, as the sun was past its midpoint. Then again, as a member of the community not needing to perform any task concerning physical labor, he didn't give it a second thought. Nobody else did either.

As usual, it was a warm day—a pleasant one, even, as the cooling breeze took the weight and excess warmth right off his shoulders. A thumb and forefinger brushed along his upper lip, smoothing out a snow-white mustache that curved out past the sides of his mouth before sharply angling downwards. It was nearly a fourth the length of his equally colorless beard, and it served to distract from his wrinkled features, scars, and large, prominent nose.

"*Eeeeee*!"

A screech from the children allowed him to easily pinpoint where they'd scampered off to hide. When the Elder turned his still-waking gaze to meet them, they froze like wide-eyed rabbits before the alarmed pack sucked in a simultaneous breath... and scattered. Some dove behind shrubs, while others thought that thin, willowy trees half their width would conceal them fully. The last child mostly just dawdled in place—about to move left, then about to move right, then changing his mind like he was about to move left again. Distress was drawn on his face like a finely carved woodwork.

"Sprout*ling*." The Elder's voice was slow, full of depth, and held a parent's questioning tone. The inflection at the end of the word made the young child freeze. While the Elder's words had been forceful, his voice still possessed all the warmth one would expect of a doting grandfather. The tattered-robe-clad child panic-smiled, showing a *mostly* full row of teeth. His eyes darted around looking for help... only to see that the others had thrown him into the river and had left him to drown. They peeked out from their respective hiding places, motioning for him to stay quiet about their 'hidden' selves.

With no way out, the child swallowed loudly and attempted his best—completely *innocent*—response, "Y-yes, Elder?"

The Elder held a tense silence as he leaned his sharp-featured face forward out of the window further, beckoning the young child closer with a digit. Sharp eye contact was firmly maintained along with the 'come here' tug of the index finger. With much chagrin and a pinch of defeat, the young lad approached the window. Hidden children were watching with rapt attention, looking for a chance to flee while their 'caught' member dragged his feet.

While the sproutlings sought escape, the Elder had a cursory glance at the village. His small lodging was nestled near the center of the village, given that the 'center' was measured by proximity to both the bonfire ring and their haphazard attempts at an apple orchard. The lasting silence allowed quick deduction that the majority of adults in the village were out working the salt flats.

There was no loud whining in the direction of the apiary, so the caretakers were not currently working with the honeybees. The distinct lack of sizzling and iron striking bronze also added to the strong indication that young children—sprouts, or sproutlings in this village—were entirely unsupervised.

He'd actually have to get up today, and his inner lethargy bemoaned the very notion that such effort was going to be necessary. With a sigh and forced determination to get going with his day, he reached out with his thin, trembling hand and patted the sproutling's head after he'd approached. While the grandfather's voice was tired, it wasn't the kind of tired that came from freshly waking up and coping. It was the kind of slow, creeping drain that stuck with you at all times, regardless of what you did to try and work through it. His question was tender and soft. "Were you all trying to see who could get shells into an old, snoring mouth... so I would choke, wake up, and be able to tell my stories sooner?"

The small youth's eyes brightened with a mixture of wonder and surprise. How did the Elder *know*? He hadn't said anything, and they would have *sworn* that he'd been asleep when they'd come up with their devious trickery. The conflicted youth sputtered, "H-how?"

"Gather your friends; fetch me a pail of water. I'll be out to tell you a story after I've washed." He paused and clenched his fingers around the head of the sproutling to keep the child's attention. *Ever* so slightly, he tilted the young head up, so their gaze remained met. Chestnut brown innocence met the Elder's deep-set, dull blue eyes. "*Next* time, wake me *properly* when your caretakers are nowhere to be found. A nudge of the arm will do."

The young child beamed while trying to nod, clearly having already forgotten half the information. As the young one had not been held firmly, he slipped free and darted away to screech the information at the rest of the playgroup with glee. They made a massive cacophony before speeding off to the well like a poorly organized mob of energetic squirrels. The kindly Elder watched them bolt, then looked down at the floor behind him. The shells were small and broke easily.

He *did* have a tendency to snore or otherwise sleep with his mouth parted since he could never trust his nose. Since the children had never bothered him even when they had reached the pinnacle of boredom, this was a new experience. In fact, he had the sneaking suspicion that *someone* had put them up to this. He'd have the children clean the crunchy mess on his floor up later.

Staggering over to the center walkway, he patted an unstrung and *long* unused hunting bow hanging from a supporting beam. They had many adventures together, but that was all in the deep past now. From the edges of the beam, he picked up a simple, gray gi and white outer robe. The hanging robe was soft, made from the fur of those mountain animals. What were those called again? Alpacas? Popular beastie for cloth. "Shall we go wash? Al*paca* towel. Oh, ho-ha!"

His thoughts slipped before returning to the forlorn bow that had been repurposed as a clothing hanger. Well, *forlorn* was too strong a term. It hadn't been *that* bad in his many years here, spending his days on the edge of the known world. 'The Fringe' was what everyone called it, at least those who *knew* what a map was. Here, the social rules were considerably different, and education was *entirely* a personal ordeal—normally, an *ignored* personal ordeal. Being called 'Elder' still felt odd, but he'd gotten used to the naming conventions. In fact they were very simple—your name in the village was a derivative of your *function*.

Nostalgia struck him suddenly. He recalled arriving years ago, running from all the problems in the world. Had it actually been *problems* he was running from or merely regrets? His grip around the robe strengthened, and a tinge of discomfort bit through as he forced the thought to pass before reaching for his woven tabi and wood-carved sandals. This penchant to wander off in thought was going to be the death of him one day. Now that he thought about it... he had certainly been running from the regrets.

The Elder had to give up his name in order to be admitted by the Fringe. Now he was just 'the Elder'. It had been a rule as much as it was a ritual and one he recalled not trying to fight in the least. It wouldn't ablate the memories, but what lost soul did not appreciate the chance at a clean slate? When his arms were still strong, he had helped gather the salt from the flats each day after the thin tide that rolled over the flatlands evaporated, leaving behind only the substance that the town was named for.

Salt.

That had been long before he started deteriorating. There were people in the village who beat him in age yet still had more vitality and youth in them. While physically, he counted around the age of fifty, visually, he appeared several decades older. His position became more administrative as a result—check up on everyone else's tasks, keep stock of events, and humor the children. Or rather, *educate* them, as nobody else had the time or ability to do so. There had not been any sort of election or formal process to this.

He kept doing what he could, and the way people had addressed him simply shifted over time until they'd all called him 'Elder'. In this village, being *called* an Elder also *made* you an Elder. Being 'gifted' the title afforded you an automatic council position. It assigned larger responsibilities and decisions, such as speaking to the traders that came every few moons and keeping track of goods. His word relegated where the settlement grew, as such tasks were left to those who spent all their time paying attention to the minutiae.

The aged man stopped to squeeze the bridge of his nose and groan at the unfortunate recollection. The *traders*. That unpleasant conversation was *tonight*, wasn't it? Elder 'Switch' would no doubt muscle her shrill voice to the top of the pile again, making endless, *unreasonable* demands that only suited or benefitted her. How had she ever become a respected Elder in this town?

A pain in the shoulder snapped him from the vestiges of reflection. *Mmf*. He soothed it with a stern, thumb-pressed rub, drawing upon his limited knowledge of acupoints, being anything *but* quiet about his discomfort. When the mystery pain passed, he finished dressing and could already hear the panting breaths in the distance.

The *thudthudthudthud* of small feet accompanied a hasty beeline towards his small home. Was that *sloshing*? Why would there be sl– Ah! The pail of water. Good.

"I'm getting *old*," he mumbled while hitting the small of his back with the side of his fist, preparing his muscles as he lifted and moved the wooden plank covering the door. Shifting the rectangular weight to the side, a few of his stockpiled things fell to the floor. He stuffed the plank behind a spare cloth, logs, and other clutter he'd accumulated and stored over the years. An attentive moment was spent to safely store the fallen roll of vellum. Handwritten philosophy notes were priceless beyond compare... at least to an academic like himself.

Exiting his small home, he kept his hand over his eyes, so the light of the sun didn't stab him right in the face. His blocked vision aided in noting the smell of crushed posies and hibiscus that hung on the breeze.

"Ah, so Hibi is home," he spoke to himself, a small smile forming as he thought fondly of events to come. If *Hibi* was home, it meant that when For returned from the salt flats... he could tease the young man about the moon-eyes he constantly made at the girl. The current matter came first, as his slightly hunched form awaited the stampede coming right for him.

"*El~de~ee~er!*" screeched a mousy voice in the distance, though that distance was lessening in a *hurry*. Those little rascals were just so *fast!* With a curt nod, the Elder hummed his way forward and began his daily trek to the deeper salt-stream. One's health and cleanliness were important. He, as usual, didn't get far before there was a parade of activity underfoot.

"I got the freshwater!"

"No, *I* got the water!"

"I got it *first!*"

"I filled it after you dropped it!"

"I only dropped it because you *pushed* me!"

"Did *not!*"

"Did *too!*"

The Elder clapped his hands together. "You *all* got the water here, so you all did wonderfully. Put it in the usual place, would you?"

His tone was calm, passive, and weighted with pensive depth. The whirlwind stormed off, a wooden *tak* sounded as the bucket loudly hit a stone, and then the sproutlings raced back. "Elder, we get our question!"

"Yes, we get a question!" The children were all bouncing with big smiles, balled hands, copying his hunched posture. Sure enough, he'd told them before that if they helped him with something, they would get to ask a question outside of their adventure time. Which normally was generally nothing, but he tried to get lessons in between the many attention-demanding voices squawking over one another like a flock of tiny birds. He needed a solid breath.

"Very well. You did earn it. *One* question." The Elder paused in his calm stride and raised a single digit as little students fought to be heard.

"Why are leaves *green*?"

"Why can't we use leaves to color our clothes green?"

"Why does mum wash the color out of my robe?"

"What was your name before it was Elder?"

"I found a pretty leaf. Can I put it on your head?"

Several more questions whizzed past. It reminded him of the blather that happened closer to the evening when all the seamstresses got together and whispered that new gossip to one another. Of course, they whispered loudly enough for others to hear, and most things said were just to rabble-rouse, but everyone had to find joy somewhere. In the questions of the children though, one was out of place.

"What was my name before it was Elder? Now, now. You know that's not something one is supposed to talk about in the Fringe. Before I answer one of the others, what is the *rule*?" His tone shifted to a sterner, determined flatness as he kept a solid eye on the one who had chirped the question.

Serious engagement made the congregation fall silent and shrink away an inch. They knew better, of course they did. With a swallow, the mousy voice piped up, "Everyone that wants to live in the Fringe becomes *part* of the Fringe, and everything you were before is left behind."

The Elder nodded and dropped the stern quality; it was unnatural for him and took effort to uphold. "That's *correct*, sproutling. Now, while I have your attention, was it Elder Switch who put you up to that game from earlier?"

Embarrassed nodding did the rounds. The Elder sighed and rubbed his forehead. "That woman is rage *incarnate*."

The embarrassment of the group changed to quizzical frowns. They didn't know those words, so he explained, "She's always *angry*, particularly at me."

Clarification complete, he then turned to the young girl holding a very big leaf. "As for the question I'm answering. I pick yours, and yes, you can put the leaf on my head."

The Elder lowered himself down, and the smiling girl zipped up to place the big leaf on the Elder's bald head. He promptly got back up and struck a pose. "How is it? Do I look *beautiful?*"

He did a turn and a flourish, playfully taking the hem of his robe to make it sway from side to side as he took little, bouncing steps to match. A smile remained on his bemused face as he stood there like an awkward duck with the leaf on his head. The laughter and snorting giggles from the children made him not mind one *bit.* He didn't bother taking the large greenery off as he turned to continue his trek to the saltwater stream. At least the freshwater in the pail was going to quench his dry throat upon his return.

When the laughter was dying down, the Elder turned to look at them; dramatically and with much vigor as possible, he snapped back into the awkward 'look at my leaf' pose. As expected, back down into the land of snotty, ugly laughter the children went. One of his arms was poised above his head, oddly bent as he pointed at the leaf while his face scrunched up and eyes squinted. One knee was bent, while the other remained straight out and at a sharp angle. He couldn't hold that long, of course, so he released the pose and patted the new hat on his head.

"It's a *great* leaf," he mentioned as he wandered to the stream, giving them a light wave and an idea of where he was going to be when done with bathing. "Orchard. Bring your cups."

He stopped to look over his shoulder as a, "Yes, Elder!" rang out behind him. He gave a positive nod and the children charged off. "They're good little ones, beneath all their wide-eyed wonder and boundless energy."

The Elder mumbled the words to himself but couldn't keep the smile off his face as the sun uncovered from behind a single dense cloud and stabbed him right in the eyes. He recoiled from the searing assault with an *argh*!

It had gotten him *again* today. "You win *this time*, shiny sky orb. You win this time!"

CHAPTER TWO

Shkrack! A thin wooden cup crashed against the wall in the village longhouse, fragmenting into sizable chunks. The Elderly, bossy voice shrieked, releasing a spray of spittle as the sound of a long, thin piece of wood impacted with a **switch**.

"Ahh!" A screech of pain erupted from a young voice as they were hit by a sharpened switch. The wince was as deep as the injury, but the cowering young adult bore it as silently as possible.

"I. *Said.* Do it!" the curmudgeonly Elder demanded.

The young villager stammered in an attempted reply, "E-Elder, we can't just–"

His words were sharply cut off as the thin, freshly cut hazel branch swung and missed with a sharp **whizz**. "*I* am the only Elder in this village whose opinion *matters*. I am the oldest. I have been here the longest. I am *sick. And. Tired.* Of being told I cannot do what I want with *my* village. If I say we are accepting the new trading currency, then we are *accepting* it. If I say you work on the salt flats this year, then you *work* on the salt flats, and If. I. Say!"

Another **whizz** of the rod swinging past without striking the intended target interrupted the diatribe. "That *I* am the only Elder who matters, then you *will* live by that rule, or great hazel help you, I will strip each branch from that tree only to *beat* you with it until you're disciplined! I chased you as a bothersome little child, and I've had to chase you all the way to the age where we're supposed to name you, yet you can't even follow *simple* tasks!"

The hesitant reply came with a concerned tone, "Elder, the rule of the village is that all Elders must agree on a decision.

Otherwise, it can't be said that the village is sure—or united—about what is good for everyone."

He deftly dodged another wildly swung *whizz* from the ancient, enraged woman. "That tired old *relic* isn't fit to be an Elder, and I don't care what the rest of the village says! I will never accept him as my equal! *I* am the one that grew up here, and *I* am the only one who truly knows what is best! That lost-in-thought outsider has his head so high in the clouds that he forgets mid-conversation what *I* am talking about. That fallen log can't agree with me on the most *basic* tasks of how a village should be run, and he has stolen all my precious young sproutlings!"

She took a heaving breath and continued her tirade, "*My* stories are the true lore and history of the village! Not those flighty, made-up tales that blind oak keeps rattling off. It's affecting their young minds and making them deviate from what is truly good for the village! The youngest is even asking questions about things that have nothing, *nothing* to do with what he's going to spend his life doing! All those bothersome, pointless questions about *color?* There's nothing wrong with a lack of color! Our clothing is *functional,* and *I* have the softest robe. What else matters?"

The sneering tirade paused as the old crow of a woman leered, her dense brown gaze heavy upon the soon-to-be adult. "Tell the traders the deal is *accepted.*"

A deep sigh was all she got in reply. "A decision cannot be given if all the Elder in t–"

The crone shrieked as the violent whip of the fresh branch snapped loudly enough to scare some others out of the longhouse. "Get *out!*"

The young man's protest was silent and done swiftly with ink and vellum in tow. His arms were full of written documents that clearly weren't going to be delivered, and the man was sour about having been declared 'not an adult' and not deserving of a name.

"Grouchy old *toad*." His trembling voice was nearly audible as he stamped out of the building. Nobody cared that the longhouse was the most comfortable building to physically be in; by any other standard, it was the *worst* building to be in. Elders had privileges that other villagers simply didn't. People *had* to listen without interrupting when they talked, they could set the rules you had to follow, they could assign *names*, and they would determine the results of any disputes that became loud enough to make it to their old ears.

What you got out of life stopped being a matter of discussion, instead becoming entirely dependent on their ruling. They were *also* the only ones in the village who could *properly* write, even if most could decently read. Once a village had agreed on who was an Elder, the spot was *permanent*. They couldn't suddenly *not* be—as much as *some* very much desired it—unless an Elder declared they would discard the title and step away from the discussion table entirely. A few had done this, but almost always for the reason that *any* interaction with Elder Switch was beyond undesirable. Unfortunately, that also silenced their voices and opinions unless called upon, as it stripped them of privileges they otherwise had.

Only two Elders remained now, and one of them was a nosy outsider who had properly followed all the rules of the Fringe to be admitted. He had been brought up to the position by the virtues he freely provided to the villagers. Elder Switch, to the knowledge of anyone who indulged in gossip, *despised* her opposition above all else. Her regional purity clearly made her 'superior' in her own crone eyes, and she had not a single inhibition about being vocal about the matter. The whipping *switch* of the rod had even become so prevalent that it had been added to her name.

Elder Switch *seethed* as she sat alone, *sneering* at the small fire that reflected the burning, eternal smolder she felt inside. If something didn't go her way, it didn't need to *go* at all. She'd spent years and *years* solidifying her grip on the village. However, that sopping wet rag of an outsider had doused her rapid rise to power by simply *existing*! The slight left a sour expression on her face that could be seen just by glancing at her. Each of her heavyset wrinkles described the story of her long rise.

Plink. Old ears perked up when she heard a sound similar to a cup gently plunking on to a nearby table. Elder Switch sharply exhaled through her nose and started talking to the hidden figure who had just made its presence known. "*Gold.* It *will* replace salt as the main currency of the Fringe, and we *will* be the first to adopt it. I *refuse* to lose out any more to Lapis, that *pathetic* crag of rock-gatherers with their tiny, little village of color-loving savages. *Blue this, blue that, blue rocks, blue fabrics.* They're living in a blue world, and I don't *want* nobody to listen! To their attempts at sales, that is. I'm going to throw a *cup* at someone if I see that abyss-hued color. I *tire* hearing of how well it sells! Our Salt is a much more reliable and profitable village, and salt *must* remain the best-sold good of the region."

She swiped a piece of vellum from the little nook next to her, crumpled it in her gnarled fingers, and disdainfully threw it right on the fire. Switch derisively watched at the conflagration of the secret message in the hearth. "Lazuli has *no* place alongside Salt. The Fringe will be known as *my* salt region once the mapmakers come."

"Is the trader informed?" her impatient voice crooned.

A sharp, metal *plink* of a fingernail cleaning knife ceased its repeated activity. Words full of breathy poise and tact bled through a powerful woman's sharpened teeth, "Of course he is, *Grand Matron* of the Salt v– *Fringe Region.*"

The voice had altered its sugary words at the end, but the obscure figure slithered them forth with only the most minor of pauses. "The trader has all the gold ready; we only need the written documentation and the proper adoption. Once gold is the main currency, our bountiful services will be... *available.* My men can't do much with the sacks of salt your village is able to provide."

The obscure female continued her sales pitch with dark fervor, "*Gold*, however, will bring in an age of wealth the Fringe has never enjoyed before. All the comforts of the inland regions will start flooding into your coffers and homes. You will be the *first* to enjoy the tender warmth of a Beast-skin cloak—a robe of such refined quality, so unique in its singular presence that only the most loved, respected, and *honored* of Elders could possibly have one. Which, of course, can be none other than yourself, Grand Matron."

Elder Switch took a deep, serene breath with a toothy smile, half-lidded eyes nearly closed as she relished in the praise. *Ahhh*. "Yes. Yes, that's it. *That's* the feeling I love. Thank you, young one, for humoring a Noblesse such as I. Your presence is warming, and I am ever so pleased you've come with news. Are they *ready*?"

Switch snapped the last words before the figure in the back rose, only to take a serpentine step forwards and bow. The experienced raider was scarred; her dark-pitch black hair was tightly bound on the back of her head, while a few exposed knives covered her leather-bound frame. Her words had the same inflection of a slow-bleeding laceration as she drawled out the answer, "*Your* men just wait for the right moment, Grand Matron."

The obscure female sidled even closer. "We will remove all those who stand against you and secure your reign over the Fringe. Only your wisdom can lead it to the greatest prosperity, as you are the only one with the foresight to accept and understand the value of gold. Such insight is far too rare in the lands. Without you, Grand Matron, my men and I could have *never* come this far, and we *relish* the opportunity to repay you as soon as it arises. I, Hakan the Gilded Blade, will direct all my raiders at your guidance. The Reaper faction will guarantee that your plans see fruition, Grand Matron."

Elder Switch nodded, hands laced, feeling as though she was on top of the world. She shooed the raider out. "I'm pleased. You may go, young one."

Having been dismissed, a *thunk* of fist striking chest replied, and Hakan vanished into the shadows, slipping out into the almost entirely deserted village. Why sneak at night when you can walk in broad daylight without a soul present to see? A massive grin graced her face; after all, it wasn't frequently one found such a disgustingly *easy* mark. That dumb, old toad was just eating up her honeyed words. Hakan was *also* delighted to learn that her second mark, the Lapis Lazuli village providing blue pigment as a trade good up north, was such a sore spot she could use as a weapon.

The trap had been baited, and thanks to her additional ploy with the trader... the gathering this town was going to have in the evening would be *colorful* indeed. Soon, her blades would run her favorite color of red once more. Hakan could scarcely hide her delight as she noticed a huddle of children running about.

"I'll be back for you soon, my delightful *recruits*."

CHAPTER THREE

Past the bend of the nearest birch forest, a rather sizable caravan waited near a hastily hidden raider encampment. Lit torches hung from the cart's sides as several bulky, scarred men tended to the horses. Hakan raised a disappointed brow at the number of *her* men who were patting and paying attention to the hooded cart rather than the watch duty they had been *assigned*. The scarred force almost sounded like *babies* talking to the beasts. Hakan's reaction was so reflexive that she heard the slap to her forehead before she felt it.

They were children. Worthless, dumb, *children*. Still, this provided her an excellent 'teaching' opportunity. A thin dagger slipped from her bound thigh; her malicious grin returned to her lips as she silently charged at them with serpentine tactics an *adder* would find impressive.

Only the spooked jump and loud whinnying of the horses caused some of the lookouts to turn around, while the rest snatched reigns and attempted to calm the animals that had just experienced the chilled, discomforting warning of a rapidly advancing predator.

Shing. The slice of steel accompanied a shrill, unmanly scream as one of the scarred men gained yet another 'failure' mark on his face. He clutched it in panic, trying to keep the skin together while an unsympathetic boot crashed into his ribs.

Hurk! The airy sound exploded from the man who had just gotten the wind kicked right out of him.

"*Pathetic!*" decried Hakan as the swift *swip* of a bloodied dagger vanished back into a sheathe against the side of her thigh. "I leave you to safeguard the caravan from surprise ambushes, and you all just let me run right up to it? *Shame*! All of you, *shame*!"

Enraged, another kick beat the breath right back out of the fallen man's lungs, right after he'd managed to take a solid one. "Pick this *meat* up and send him to Needle. *Another* failure will mean him losing his head!"

Her deadly gaze snapped to a random member tending the horses, letting him feel a dab of murderous intent. This emphasized that this could happen to someone *else* if they failed to pay attention to their appointed tasks. Fear instilled itself into the actual caretakers of the animals, who were suddenly *very* invested in their tasks. The fright remained with them while the others hurried to jog off and warn the remainder of the raider camp.

This particular leader of theirs was impatient. Their supplies were short, and she wore her temper on her knife-clad sleeve. Scars tended to be added to people who failed to work according to the plan—or whatever Hakan *decided* was the plan, at least. Her voice hissed out her demands, "Where is Boro, the *traitor*?"

"You mean the *trader*?" a confused reply came from the bulky raider, who ducked for cover as a throwing knife flew through the air where his head had previously been. Her aim was *dangerously* accurate.

"Fetch my knife, and by the *abyss*, you'd better hope that my mood has improved when you return it, *recruit*." Hakan's words were a whiplash, and the scuffling movement told her that at least the burly recruit was rushing to retrieve her property. At least he was *trying* to be useful. "*Fool*."

The sound of flourishing robes and jingling accouterments invaded her aural space. "I am where I *always* am, mistress Hakan. Anywhere there's a *profit*."

Hakan sneered. Without looking, she could feel Boro wring his hands together with a greedy, half-lidded smile of his own playing across his features. Hakan could hear him do his customary bow of welcoming, the flourish of his heinously rich robes fluttering behind him as he performed a mocking greeting, "You *called* for me, Raid Leader?"

She detested how his willingness to debase himself somehow brought him prosperity instead of death. "The *pleasant* news is that the old toad has the hatred for Lapis that we thought she did. Is the *item* we discussed ready?"

Her impatience was clear, and Boro wasted no effort in smoothing over his response. "Ready, folded in a pristine box, and paid for. It must only be *delivered.*"

The trader folded his hands together to bow once more when he was close enough. "Mistress Hakan, you must grace me with your insight on why you believe a colored robe will force the hand of that old toad. I feel that Elder Switch, while... *unreasonable* at times, still would not go against the rules of the Fringe."

Hakan sharply turned on her heel and blessed Boro with an unnerving smile that ran from one ear to the other. Boro and the surrounding raiders felt an unpleasant shiver clench their spines at the sight. "Because, my dear trader who sees only glittering coin, it is not *what* is being delivered but *who* it is being delivered to. After what I heard today, my only regret is that I cannot be there myself to taste the very moment she snaps and betrays the community she serves."

Hakan's vigor slowed, and she took a deep, relishing breath as she imagined the internal torture that aged bat would feel. "We will have our coin. You will deliver the conversions, and then... then I add new prospects to my *family*. It has been *Far. Too. Long.* Since I've had unmarred faces to cut."

Boro's muscles cramped beneath his lavish robes as he shivered in horror, but he kept his footing. A single step would show weakness, and he knew that this blade-crazed lunatic would only relish in taking the opportunity to sate herself with his suffering. *Especially* since his face was an 'untouched canvas'. Not tempting Hakan, who saw herself as a bit of an artist, was a stressful prospect. One poor for the business, he thought. *Very* poor for business.

The deal with the Reapers was lucrative, so he held his ground. For many a season, he'd been 'in bed' with Hakan, converting the natural resources of a village into silver coin which the raiders could take and spend back at the very source that had handed it all out in the first place. Boro considered himself a monetary genius for creating the system, even if it left fewer villages to trade with once they had been... *expended.* The survivors added to Hakan's raiding party, and she only liked them young.

The rest? Well... Boro had developed a *learned* hatred of the smell of burning flesh and now purely subsisted on fresh vegetables where he could afford to do so. The occasional feast still had him indulge in meat after enough cups of fermented fruit in liquid form, but the constant experiences had soured his tongue. He shook off the disturbing line of thought. Salt would be merely *another* casualty in a long string of villages yet to come. That, however, was not his primary concern right now as he hesitantly asked what was bothering him, "Have the pursuers relented?"

Hakan's mirth vanished in an instant. Her smile bled into a frown, and her fingers curled around the hilts of considerably larger blades on her person. "You take this moment to end my pleasant thoughts, Boro?"

Boro said nothing and stood his abyss-blasted ground. He only repeated his question. "*Have* they?"

Silent for a moment, Hakan leered into the watchful eyes keeping silent in the forest, doing absolutely nothing as even the accidental sound of interference was grounds for flying daggers. Dejected, she spat on the ground and groaned an unpleasant *ugh*. Hakan flagged a hand at the general group for someone to approach and inform her. She didn't know the answer and was obviously unhappy about that.

An idea winked into her thoughts, and she stepped up to a decently sized hazel tree. Picking off a branch and stripping the excess, she decided that she preferred hazel over birch based entirely off the aesthetic from the swing. As Hakan waited, the scouting party came forth.

"It's not good, Mum." A wicked, loose snap of a switch struck the scout. It silenced him after a yelp, and that pleased Hakan greatly. Her voice *oozed* pleasure.

"Ooh, that's nice. I *like* that. The old toad may not be of great value, but I certainly appreciate her *style*." A few more wayward swings of the trimmed branch snapped through the air. "I'm not your *mother*. Someone give the report *properly*."

The wounded scout was sent off, and another took his place. Hakan considered striking this one just for the fun of it but noted it was a girl. She stayed her hand, having an extremely easy tell on the preference of who she preferred to hit. The lightly armored woman saluted before speaking. "Mayu reporting. The clerics are gaining ground every day. The loose ends we've left out are running dry, and they found one of the villages we sacked this morning. A messenger corvid came in with information that it was the third village we sacked while in the Fringe, and that's maybe a few days away."

"Per instruction of Raid Leader Majorca, we've sent a bird back to have them relocate camp to the second village we sacked. Both to throw the clerics off our trail, as well as to have them search in the wrong direction. We... will be *losing* that raid group when the clerics find them."

Hakan grit her teeth and quipped in irritation, "Well, that's not *too–*"

The raid leader's words cut short when she saw the urgency in her scout's eyes. There was more, and it was unlikely to be good. "What is it?"

The scout kept her spirit strong. She knew this was bad news. "The clerics received reinforcements. It's no longer the novices and common flock anymore. The... *weird* ones are here."

Hakan tensed with the intent to cleave someone. "Speak plainly, scout."

The scout nodded obediently, swallowed hard, and did as she was told. "Cultivators, raid leader."

Hakan's snarl was the definition of fury. "*Abyss.*"

"What do the clever ones think we have left to work with?" the leader spat, hoping there was more detail from the scout about this point. The scout took the hint and unfurled the vellum to read directly from the source. If someone was going to get punished for reporting this information, Mayu was going to send it straight down the command line to save her own scrawny butt.

"We have a handful of moons, at most, before they find this encampment. If we don't fully move camp within two moons, the other raid leaders have suggested a full withdrawal from the region. They said we have a lot of muscle, but not... enough."

Hakan's eyes were full of wanton fury at the report from her scout, fingers tensing and twitching around the wooden punishment tool. "Over nine hands worth of strong men and we don't have *enough*?"

The scout nodded at her leader's displeasure to confirm it—forty-five and a few extra was a low number for raiders.

"*Aargh!*" A muffled thud resounded as the raid leader angrily punched a tree to vent stress, still holding the switch in her off hand. Her eyes snapped to the trader as she spat out orders.

"Boro, go *today*. Pretend you're early and take all the gold with you–just keep it covered. We're taking the gamble, and we need the old toad to take the bait. I had wanted to do this *tomorrow*, but it seems time is against us. Take the package. Make *sure* to deliver it. Everything relies on that dumb, little box being opened at the right time. Can you wring your way into their ridiculous town meeting today? It will be in the longhouse. The building had preparations already in place well before I left."

Boro merely smiled with the calm demeanor of a practiced salesman having made a very expensive sale. "It *will* be done."

He bowed with a flourish, then fully took advantage of this opportunity to make himself scarce. A few of the people he flagged over quickly followed suit. While they didn't want to load up his cart for him, it beat out the possibility of a random stabbing due to inactivity. None of them liked being stuck under this raid leader, but there was no chance in the *abyss* anyone was going to defy her or tell her that fact.

Hakan waltzed deeper into the camp and slumped into a seat that had swiftly been vacated upon her approach. A cup of fermented juice was handed over with great deference. The raid leader sipped it, sneered at the taste, and longed for something more pleasant to think about. She pulled out a small, secret potion bottle and tipped it into her drink, shivering as she sipped the potent healing syrup. The image of the pliable, gentle, *playful* children in the Salt village came to mind. She whispered huskily to herself and closed her eyes.

"Soon."

CHAPTER FOUR

The children didn't know where the sudden, cold shiver running down their spines came from, given they were all plenty warm under the sun. Aside from the momentary discomfort, they gave it no thought as they gathered up fallen fruit into woven baskets like they were supposed to do. There were more than apples in the orchard, but some trees bore fruit they simply did not know the name for. Today, the group was in a hurry.

If they didn't bring something home by the time their parents came back from the flats, there would be scolding. On top of that, they only had time to gather until the Elder arrived. This signaled story and playtime, and they prepared oh-so-many more questions.

Trudging along his way to the orchard after having done the usual daily tasks that kept one healthy and clean, the Elder spotted one of his sproutlings sitting alone by a tree. The otherwise cheerful boy poked at fallen fruit with a stick, clearly disheartened. Detouring hastily, the Elder said nothing on his approach. Rather, the weary grandfather noisily grunted and sat down next to the depressed, grim child. This glum behavior was recently common for the boy, whom no longer had direct remaining family or parents.

He didn't like his life with the family that took him in, as they only had eyes for their own offspring and were particularly strict on him even as their doting was directed elsewhere. The sproutling muttered a half-hearted greeting. Replying with action, the community-minded Elder wrapped his arm around the child's head, pulling the lad into his robed side for a hug. Warm and supportive, the Elder brushed the flat of his hand across the top of the unhappy boy's head.

He didn't need to ask if the sproutling was feeling lonely; that was clear to see from the sullen expression and stick-prodding that didn't have a shred of effort put into it. The boy wasn't his actual son, but that didn't matter to the Elder as he kicked up happy memories to distract the boy.

"Did you know that your father had a favorite stick?" the Elder warmly chimed, keeping the sproutling held comfortingly. A wordless nodding was the only reply.

"He would swing it every day, loud and boisterous, saying he'd be the best at it while bouncing about the apiary. Your mother would scold him because he swung so recklessly and wildly that he frequently struck something without thinking. It made a few people quite upset, and one day, to no one's surprise, he hit a beehive."

The Elder mimicked the sound of a great number of angry bees followed by the croaked, pitched squeal of two young people bolting. "Oh, the bees were *mad!* Your parents both ran screaming down the hill with a whole *swarm* chasing them. Api, the apiary keeper at the time, was booming profanities at them as they tumbled."

"Do you remember how they avoided the swarm?" Another nod was felt in the side of the ribs. The mumbled reply was something along the lines of 'hid under the water'. The Elder approved, as that was correct. "Indeed, they had to share a reed to breathe and were so embarrassed about the whole thing they didn't speak in public for many moons. Until, of course, we started catching them together in the... ow!"

The child had soft-punched him in the ribs, face red and embarrassed. This little one wasn't any good talking about affection and wholeheartedly rejected it, though it made him hurt to do so.

"Hmm. Why don't I let you go then?" the Elder responded, following with a side-eyed '*hmmm*?' only to find the grip on his robe to be significantly tightened. The little red face didn't want to be seen crying.

"I don't have a home," the boy miserably admitted, only to push his face painfully into the old man's freshly punched ribs. A soft sigh and a reassuring set of pats to the child's back accompanied soft words.

"Grandson, you will always have a home wherever I am." He remained quiet as the young one hiccupped little sobs, but the Elder supportively held the boy regardless—not speaking, not judging, just being there for a mind that was experiencing grief and loss. The Elder knew those tears well and did not question nor tell the child to stop.

He watched the sparse clouds and the occasional wayward bird. As usual, he lost himself in thought faster than anything; he began to wonder why the sky sometimes changed color. At least, he would have, had the sproutling not stirred and sat up to wipe his red, puffy face with the length of the Elder's robe sleeve. "I will?"

With warmth, the Elder soothed, "*Always.* When you can't handle it anymore, all seems lost, and everything feels like it has utterly fallen apart. Even if everyone rejects you, nobody wants you, and the world feels like it wants to crush you on all sides. I'll be on my little hill, waiting for you to come home. It won't matter to me what you've done, what anyone says about you, or even whatever darkness holds you tight on the inside."

He then softly poked the child's nose with the soft love of a grandfather. "You can smash your face into my ribs and cry anytime. I will hide your face so nobody sees–"

A punch in the arm made the Elder jump.

"*Oww.*" He bent comically forwards and held his arm, deeply exaggerated since the actual impact didn't do much of anything. "Why so hard? You've left a bruise!"

The Elder pouted with overdone expression. His sniffling sproutling smiled a weak, triumphant '*serves you right*' and wiped his face using the Elder's sleeves. Satisfied that his little one felt a little better, the Elder scowled and stood up with an *oof*, still pretending to rub a devastatingly injured upper arm.

"Awfully strong for such a *little* thing," he muttered dejectedly with full intention of having the sproutling hear it. Which, of course, just grew the smile on the boy's face. Opening and closing his hand a few times, he reached his open palm towards the boy. "Come now. Let's go see everyone. You're part of the family, and you're important to it. Take part in the stories with everyone else."

The boy took the Elder's hand and walked with the surrogate grandfather as he trotted off, giving a silent, strong nod. It felt good to be included in the family.

The sprawling orchard was a chaotic food fight by the time the Elder arrived. A laughing chorus of splats signaled an important task was forgotten until one of the children let free a sudden, sharp, and throaty panic-inhale as their feet skittered to a halt. The old man had his eyes closed, and that was fine. There was, he guessed, a juicy peach stuck on his face. The half-crushed delicacy slowly dribbled down his freshly washed cheek, beard, and robe.

This was fine. His robe was undoubtedly stained. That too was fine.

With deliberate motion and breath, his head tilted while he kept a hold of the young lad that had been crying earlier. His free hand slowly peeled the fruit from his forehead with a wet *squelch*. He said nothing at first.

The Elder just squinted through the sap as children remained frozen in place. He looked down, and the concerned, puffy, red faced child locked his gaze. He was confused as the Elder reached down to hand him the half-smashed fruit. However, the Elder made the imperative quite clear as his commanding voice rumbled, "*Get 'em.*"

The fruit was taken gleefully. His youngster let out a war cry and did exactly so, storming off to resume the paused engagement. The Elder found himself alone, no longer hand-holding as the sproutling ran off and launched the half-smashed fruit with the full force of his strength. While missing the intended target, the peach became a fully smashed fruit as it spun wildly out of control and splatter-squished into the oldest girl's nose, who was promptly knocked to her butt as she slipped and lost her footing.

A gaggle of children ready to make a glorious mess of things made the area ring out. The war of fallen fruit was on. The Elder wiped his face clean with the bottom of his gi, unknowingly avoiding being struck by an overhead projectile while bent to wipe his beard off. A few deft steps later, he was tactically positioned behind a sizable tree. Entertaining as this was, he didn't have the energy for it.

He could already feel the tremble return to his hands, and if it hadn't been for the warm sun, the aged soul would be feeling quite chilly. So, the Elder sat, thinking of taking a rest while the pinprick shocks took their daily toll. The ruckus died down a little later when a sproutling came around the bend and spotted the grandfather's unmoving form. Sounding an alert, the sproutlings dropped their respective fruits and ended play as one of them loudly began trying to rouse their caretaker.

"Elder?"

Multiple children nudged his shoulder while the oldest girl spoke, "*Elder!*"

Blinking as he woke, he raised his head to see the faces of worried children. When had he fallen asleep? He could not recall. "*Hmm?* Yes? Is it storytime?"

He made a show of yawning and putting his hand in front of his face, but it was a facade. To his luck, not one of the children picked up on his obfuscation as the important word shifted their expressions—their worry turned right around and into enthusiasm.

"*Storytime!* I pick this time!" yelled the oldest girl, getting the ball rolling. She had noticed something was wrong with their pale Elder but didn't want the group to dwell on it. Her robe was a mess of fruity colors and sweetened smells that matched her cashew hair and striking emerald eyes, the clear dominant trait for this generation of sproutlings.

"No, I'm the biggest! I pick today!" snapped out the oldest boy, equally covered in a mixture of pinks, browns, and greens. The Elder could feel the communal scowls suddenly leveled at the oldest, and the commentary was scathing.

"Oh, like you got to pick the best cup *and* the best robe *and* it had to be your pail? You picked *enough* today!" The Elder's hand rose before another fight broke out as the kids spoke over one another, his voice sinking back to the usual landscape of steadfast patience.

"What's all this about cups. Did you not bring them?" The children looked around as their conversation was shut down, so the Elder moved it along, "Well, won't you fetch them?"

The youngest shot a sharp, challenging glance at the oldest and ran off. "*BestCupIsMine!*"

The rest of the horde followed him in a hurry. "*No, it's not.*"

When the tiny horde returned, they found the Elder doing some elaborate stretches. They watched him while holding a cup each, not interrupting. The eldest held *two* cups. Clearly, his strength had won out as the additional mud-marks on several robes were tell-tale of a scuffle. "I see you have two cups, sproutling. How did that happen?"

The Elder rose and observed the cup-holders, gaze resting on the oldest as he calmly questioned. The oldest, of course, beamed with pride. "I'm the strongest! They couldn't get them out of my hands. So *obviously,* I was going to win and get what I want!"

The Elder nodded in understanding. "Ah, I see. Might makes right, is it?"

The youngster's nod altered direction to a solemn *no* as the unpleasant memory of Elder Switch came to mind. A stoic, disappointed look developed on the Elder's wrinkled face as hands laced behind his back. Deep worry crossed the oldest boy's visage, the Elder eroding what the prideful youngster thought had been certain success. He held firm to his two uncertain prizes as the Elder's lesson began. "So, does being stronger and being able to make others do what you want make it the *right* thing to do?"

The sentence from the old man was clearly aimed at the holder of both cups, and the boy stammered out a guessed answer, "...Yes?"

A sigh with some depth left the Elder as he hung his head for a moment, and his wrist turned to motion for a circle. They all sat, and the lesson began. "The answer was *no.* Let's show you why."

He took one of the cups and placed it in the center. "Say we had one cup. Just one. This is the only vessel that can hold water for everyone to drink. Is it right to fight over the cup, so only you have the water, or is it right to *share* the cup and work towards filling it as often as possible so everyone has enough?"

He held up his hand, for now not wanting an answer. "People will fight over the empty cup because that's what people do. They get *scared* that there's only one cup. They fear that if someone else owns the cup, they won't get any water. That is, of course, easy to understand. If there was only one toy, you'd all want it."

A round of nodding went about the circle. "So, say you fight for the cup. The strongest is likely to win, yet by winning, you have gained something far more dangerous. Something you *don't* want."

A circle of frowning faces now hung to his words. "You've gained the cup, but you've also gained everyone's *animosity*."

He paused at the look of confused expressions. "Their feelings of anger, want, and judgment. That which you feel for someone you're unhappy with before you think about *why*. Hostile intent."

The scrunched faces faded as they learned the new words. "In *fighting* for the cup, you haven't *filled* the cup. The cup may even have been damaged and now be less able to hold water. Most of all, you have not filled the cup, and now only *you* can do so. Because *you* have the cup, it means everyone who cannot drink from it now goes thirsty—because of *you*."

The oldest was in distress thanks to this sentence and put down both of the cups like they were hot coals. He didn't want that on his conscience. Everyone else followed suit but mostly because they didn't know what to do. "When you took the cup, you did not *gain* the cup, so much as you have denied it from everyone else. Now, which is the cup you were all fighting over?"

They all pointed at the smoothest, most well-made cup. The Elder understood and nodded. "Which is the *least* desirable cup?"

That took a little longer, but eventually, the children settled on a wreck of a cup. Not surprisingly, the youngest had been holding it. The Elder took a cup from the middle and held it out to the youngest. "Swap these."

The youngest handed over his bad cup and was rather pleased about a higher quality cup being close at hand. The Elder then held up the worst of the vessels. "This is *my* cup."

"Why do you want the *worst* cup?" The oldest girl was baffled. Her voice reflected the silent question of the group.

"An *excellent* question, always a sharp mind on you." With the Elder giving her a compliment, her mood brightened, and her face lit up. "Not only will nobody want to take this cup from me, but I can fill it as often as I need! Now, it's no good for me to have an empty cup, and that's the point. *Filling* the cup is what gives it *meaning*."

Grasping the intent, the oldest girl's eyes went wide; she'd gotten it! The rest of her family was still catching up. Noticing her reaction, a pleased Elder looked to the oldest girl and smiled. "Your thoughts?"

All eyes fell on her as the conversation was shifted.

"Ah, well. Ermm... Ueh." Her eyes darted to the Elder, who was patiently sitting there, letting her take all the time she wanted. "So, if... if we fight over the cup, then we might be able to show which one of us is the strongest, but that doesn't mean we've understood what the cup is for or how to best use it.

We've just shown who is gonna get the cup if it came down to us all wanting it."

"If only the strongest one uses the cup, then it's not the best for everyone. He got the cup because he was only paying attention to himself, not what everyone else needed, but the cup can't be used unless it's full. It took a few of us earlier today just to draw water up from the well, so filling the cup isn't very easy. Who has the cup isn't as important as if the cup is *full*. It has meaning because all of us can now benefit from it?" She was rambling near the end, and the certainty of her words fell away like a landslide.

With hope in her eyes, she drilled her gaze into the Elder, who reached into his sleeve and pulled out the leaf from earlier, placing it on her head. "I award you one leaf of smartness."

Her hopeful glint turned to a glum glare, but the child who had given the leaf-hat before was a bundle of smiles—just happy to see that same leaf reused for something. The child who had spoken could say nothing when she saw the happy, little face, so she just wore the abyss-dratted leaf-hat.

The Elder then picked up a small stone and carved 'Elder' into the poor-quality cup. The children ogled the craft as they could not yet write. He turned it around and showed them the result. "This is my cup. My name's on it. However, it's an empty cup. I can leave it out in the open, and it will be fine since nobody wants it!"

He placed it down and got an unexpected number of frowns in return. The Elder, not quite following the reaction, meekly mumbled, "...What?"

The oldest boy broke the awkward silence, "I would want it."

A few eyes rolled, and the oldest girl began to snap at him, "Well, of course you would, you *always* want–"

"*No, no.* Not because I'm the strongest." He was fidgeting and waving his hands to rebuke her words. "If... if I had this cup, now I would wonder what makes it full."

The oldest was visibly becoming more uncomfortable, his presence shrinking. "I feel full after I've eaten, laughed a lot, and when I go home after a day where we get to play like this. Where we get to... *talk* like this..."

The Elder perked up as concern struck him. Oh, he was an old *fool!*

CHAPTER FIVE

Of *course,* the oldest was muscling his way through life! Everyone in his previous peer group was already off on the flats, and he had nobody his own age to talk to. Only the noisy children and the oldest girl counted as company, the latter of which most certainly bossed him around.

"I want this cup because it means the Elder comes to tell us stories. It means I laugh. Nobody else ever tells me *why* I shouldn't do something, only that I *can't.*"

The youth's discomfort only seemed to grow. "I have to *listen.* I have to do what I'm told. But nobody tells me *why,* and I have this feeling that turns in my stomach when I think about asking... so then I *don't.* I remember..."

Feeling small, his head kept down as unthinking fingers went up to a scar on the nape of his neck, which looked like it had been made by a thin and flexible striking tool. The Elder could deduce the source of the injury and that his boy wasn't quite done speaking. Given the turn of the conversation, he didn't want the budding boy to stop either. The youngest was about to interrupt but was halted by a single glance of the immobile Elder. The oldest lad had been trapped in a shell, and the old man wasn't about to allow for a circumstance that would hamper his son's progress in opening up.

"I'm not smart like," the oldest boy's head raised, and he looked at the oldest girl, "you."

To everyone's surprise, he then handed over the best cup, and the oldest girl took it with some apprehension. This kind of sensitivity was not normal for the burly lad. A stolen glance at the Elder had her holding her tongue. The Elder was calmly seated, waiting with a monk's poise to let this boy develop. His fingers were laced, and the children had picked up that little gesture was something the Elder did when he was waiting for more.

"I want the cup because it means we're *together*, and I have memories of us as a group. I love the memories... They're my dream stories. They keep me warm when the sun goes down and the *rest* of the family comes home." His tone turned morose. "Nobody in my family wants to spend time with me. They're all always so *tired.* I get told off more often than not."

The Elder nodded and found the right moment to give the boy strength. "My dear boy, you have something far more powerful than your arms."

Uncertain of himself, the oldest boy sat up more, his embarrassment continuing to stifle him as his eyes fell on the Elder. The others were horribly curious and kept stealing glances, and their Elder didn't leave them in suspense for long. "You have an *amazing* willingness and adaptability to *learn*, young one, even when the topic seems against you. You gave up an item that had great value to you. You have acted upon the lesson without fully grasping it, perhaps even without realizing that you had done so. Perhaps your greatest strength isn't coming up with something, but you have an amazing ability to follow a plan to its end."

A hand motion for a nearby leaf caused a train of tiny hands to deliver it into the old man's grip. The broad, green foliage was then ceremoniously placed on the youngster's head. "By sharing what you care about, you have shown that might isn't always what's right but also what the full meaning of the cup entails. Being around others fills *you* with meaning."

He moved his hands around to motion at the other children. "*They* are the water in your cup."

The oldest boy was confused. The oldest girl, however, went *red* in the face and tried to hide it behind the best quality cup. Their Elder let them think on it, as the remaining children were already developing terrible little ways to tease the oldest boy about this for moons upon moons to come. Picking up on their mischief, the Elder popped the nearest of them on the top of the head with a cup in quick succession. * *Thunk, thunk, thunk**!

It didn't hurt, but it got their attention. "There will be *no* discouraging someone to share freely. Do not punish the behavior you wish to see. You always want your friends able to express themselves." He felt he lost the thread of conversation and softly sighed, wrapping it up.

"Understanding and caring for another allows you the insight of seeing where they're hurting. *That* is what's right. If might helps you accomplish that for *everyone*, good. If might *prevents* everyone from accomplishing that, bad. If might is used to hurt everyone at the cost of only *one* person having the benefit... then Elder will be very upset and will cover you in mill powder."

The children *blanched* at the mention. The Elder never hurt them, but if they came home covered in anything *related* to the mill, their behinds would be red and bruised from the beating they were going to get. *Never* were they allowed near the mill. There was only one, and it was far too important a structure for the village. It was never good to even be playing around there. The punishment was severe, and being the talk of the town afterward was worse. A fury of nods quickly followed as the original topic was completely lost at the sudden thoughts of avoiding mill powder.

"Help me up." The Elder raised his arms; the small gathering of children did what they could. For being such a frail, old man, it still took all of them to help him stand up. "Ahh, well done. Well done."

He softly stretched his arms above his head while the sproutlings groaned about how heavy he was. The Elder dismissed this and gave the oldest boy a hug. While horribly embarrassed, the draw of an adult father figure giving him attention was too big a need to deny.

"They're going to rely on you, my child," the Elder whispered in his ear. "Take good care of them."

The oldest boy nodded as the light in his eyes brightened. He got it now. It hadn't been about a cup; it had been about *him*. He was the strong one, and how he used that strength was what mattered. The Elder let him go and brushed a hand over his head. "Good. Now. I'll take questions."

He stated it firmly, needing to turn around the somber feeling he had. Nobody expected the oldest to suddenly be vulnerable, and the footing was uncertain. Still, he felt pride. They made *leaps* each time they had a good chance to talk, develop, and express freely. They were clever kids, given the opportunity to be. Their minds desperately *craved* the information they were being so adamantly denied in the village.

Salt was a place of *work*, not one of inner growth. At least, it would have been, had the Elder not been there to make a royal mess of it all. A hand rose from the youngest girl.

"Yes?" The Elder quickly addressed it, attention fully turning to her.

"Why can't we have names?"

She asked it so simply, but that was a question he had hoped wouldn't come to pass. However, trying to play that one down while already feeling so out of place with the group was going to be dismal. A thought occurred... had she waited for this exact kind of opportunity to ask that question? A situation where it would be poor for him not to answer it? He studied her face, squinting in inspection as he leaned forward. Sure enough, her face remained as flat and emotionless as a practiced thief trying to swindle you. *Clever girl.*

Seeing as the Elder very much did appear reluctant, the sproutlings were all silent and attentive. They *loved* making him pause and being told things he wasn't supposed to spill. The oddness faded and attention was instead spent on his answer. More than one set of eyes were curious about why they had to be called 'sproutling' instead of an easy name like Elder. Or why Elder Switch had *two* whole names. The old man, of course, caved. "Oh, very *well.*"

The youngest girl quietly hissed, " *Yesss,*" in a dramatic victory pose, and the Elder surrendered his explanation, "This is a *complicated* one. There are some adults who don't fully understand this, *so* until you have a proper understanding... don't spread what I'm about to tell you around. If you explain it poorly, you're likely going to hurt people."

The kids caught on and listened with rapt focus, trying to stay ahead of the Elder as he stuck a finger up and began walking. Pacing, rather, but they all smiled as he was clearly about to devolve into a full speech and completely fail to pay attention to where he was walking. The last time he did this, he'd walked off a rock on the split hill and dropped straight down into the salt-stream mid-sentence. They had laughed for weeks.

"I'll start with the obvious. 'Hibi' is short for hibiscus. It is the main type of flower she gathers. This is part of her profession, thus why she is named as such. 'For' is responsible for the Forge—on the rare occasion he actually gets to use it for something, poor fellow. He's got such a gift with copper and bronze, but they need him on the flats."

He sighed, looked up, and realized that while the children were still hovering the Orchard was already a good distance behind him. His hands moved even if his mouth didn't. It was normal for him to talk with his hands, an old philosopher trait. The children often whispered behind his back on how animated he could get. He knew this and didn't mind. "A name is an *identity*, and identities are dangerous and powerful. Once something has an identity, it is difficult to think of it as something else."

"Chair." He paused to observe their expressions. "You all thought of what you consider a chair, and for all of you, it was likely roughly the same image. When you're given a name, that name comes with such an identity—an identity that is both liberating and confining. While it may become easy to refer to you, it has also taken away possibility."

"*Frankly*, that bothers me. Most people are simply not flexible enough with their minds to see things any other way, not once they've been told something is 'just the way it is'. A wall is always a wall. The possibility that it could be otherwise does not elude them so much as the thought *cannot* occur, or at least, that's my view. In this village, when you receive a name, you also receive the *task* that you're going to be doing."

"Essentially, for the rest of your life." He paused and heaved a great sigh. "It won't change, even if you're called to the salt flats, unless people start calling you Elder. What you get is what you're stuck with. So, it takes until almost adulthood for names to be chosen for someone. To my great dislike, it has nothing to do with what you're good at nor what you love to do in life. It's a designation. A *limit*. A calling you can't escape."

CHAPTER SIX

The Elder appeared both sad and angry at the same time, causing the children to move away and give him some distance. When he noticed the change in elbow room, he stopped pacing and forced his face back to a gentle smile. "You're not at fault, my dears. It's how the Fringe works. The rules here are *ancient*."

The oldest girl raised her hand. "Is that why you haven't given us names?"

The old man said with a little grumble, then he sighed and nodded. "I am an *Elder*. What I say is what goes, once I've said it. So, I must be *very* careful. 'Sproutling' is a word for something that is growing. To sprout is to come from the ground and meet the sun, the beginning of growth."

"You're named as such for that exact reason. When you're given a name, your growth *stops*. In this village, your identity is dependent on what you do. When you have a name, you'll become so busy that even if you *want* to do something else, your obligations to the village will keep you in that place." His hands made white-knuckled fists as he kept himself in check. "I don't *like* this tradition. I would give you..."

The Elder looked at the blue sky as if he were distracted by something. "Unique, *beautiful* names. Names that matched you not just for who you are but all the potential of what you could be. I see such promise in *all* of you. Such bright *splendor!*"

The children held their collective breath. They were dying to know what their names were in the Elder's mind. That's why, when the Elder turned to look at them, he felt his heart sink deep. He *could not* tell them. Well... only by *village* rules, and he wasn't *exactly* one to follow them himself all of the time.

Pensive sadness turned into a contemplative, sly fox beard-stroke that slowly grew as fingers groomed down the hanging length further and further. The oldest girl was almost giddy as she saw a plan forming just by watching the details move on the Elder's face.

The old fool was a great actor but a horrible liar. His face gave everything away. "Well, sproutlings... I believe that, while the village may assign you a set name, tomorrow is a day of rest. If we so happen to take a long stroll out of the Fringe..."

He mused cautiously, knowing full well that he would take them into a dangerous forest—a dense birch thicket that was only considered to not be part of the Fringe since a year's cycle or so ago, when someone had made a bothersome land claim with appropriate documentation. The Elder knew it was risky, and he was fairly certain the children knew it too... but nothing was wrong with extra hope. So he laid his cards on the table, expecting the clever bunch to come to the conclusion that while they *could* go, they wouldn't.

"I could tell you then!" the Elder declared with pep in his voice as he took the gamble. While yes, the glares were... *sour*, he held firm. Eventually, his children relented. They clearly wanted to know right *now*, but at least now, the Elder had set a condition. The little wheels could be seen turning behind their lustrous green eyes. Little *schemers*, the lot of them.

"In the *morning*," the oldest girl demanded, her emerald eyes speaking volumes along with the strong forward lean of her hunting posture. She was setting a time since *someone* was clearly trying to wiggle out of it. Her determined gaze made it clear she was going to hound him, and this time, there was no escape. The oldest girl had a good bead on the Elder's habits, and she knew that if he got the opportunity to sleep in... then by the *Celestials above,* he was going to take it. If he *did* sleep in, they wouldn't be able to wake him up even if they drew on his face with spare charcoal.

Then before any activity, he would clean at the stream. They knew he usually went late just to avoid the majority of the village, and it took *forever.* To the great, jaw-grinding *impatience* of the kids, he was just so *slow* about everything. To be fair, his popping bones sounded as if they hurt, so they felt bad about trying to rush him. They had once snuck about like clumsy cats, peeking in on him washing and found out why he tended to avoid washing with people around.

The sight that met them was... *unpleasant*–beyond just the fact that he was a wrinkly, old man. A carpet of scars swirled across the grandfather's back and upper body, like he'd been slashed by a hundred tiny knives in a twisting pattern that had sheared off thin, repeated lines of his skin. It looked healed *now,* but at least one of them had lost their breakfast.

Since they'd been breaking the rules when they made this discovery, they had a don't-tell pact and never brought it up. That would have given away their mischief, which absolutely opposed the Elder's wishes to wash without witness. After he'd cleaned, they found the Elder would generally sneak off to the apiary before attending his tasks for the day. When this secret was learned, the children had been *incensed.* How *dare* he scamper off to do something else when he could be telling them stories!

They would give him endless bother for this in the cleverest fashion their group could contrive, as anything cheaply put together, he'd disassemble without any effort. They'd learned over the many years that tricks and poorly put together plans were a path that led straight to *failure.* Finding patterns and uncovering hidden details from the most minute scraps of information was a skill the Elder had in spades.

So far, it was an ability they could not replicate. As *soon* as he was aware of one part of their trap, the Elder was already halfway done puzzling out the solution to the entire thing. By the end of the next few strides, he had the entire operation well-grasped and was ready to circumvent it. If their ideas weren't well-discussed, practiced, *ironclad*... then they had *no* hope of success. The Elder's perception had served only to make them even more deviously clever, which the oldest girl was convinced had all been part of that ancient philosopher's plan.

She recalled that in the beginning, he had them talk themselves into contradictory circles where their own boasts would be turned against them. That's where the seed of competition had been planted. They were going to *get* this old man, and they'd do it without breaking *any* of the rules!

But somehow, time and *time again*, he'd foiled them with the most mundane of actions. For instance, pretending to not notice something only to—by seeming accident—lean down and pick up the *exact*, most crucial part of their plan... and have one of their own walk right into it to expose the scheme for what it was.

Currently, a hush stifled the group as the Elder and the eldest girl stared at each other. The intense challenge continued far longer than most children could handle, a splitting silence that was becoming awkward from its duration. Even now, as the fidgeting began, the Elder said nothing about his bluff being called.

The old man heard a long, squealing growl and wondered what it was from. Then he noticed the children holding in laughter as the boisterous growl erupting from his stomach killed the delicate balance of tension. Ah. He was hungry. Yes, that made sense. The Elder gave his stomach a pat.

"Enough for today, fetch your baskets from the orchard and deliver them. Communal mealtime will be soon, and I expect that I will need to fill up in order to handle the evening talk." The children remained quiet. They knew they'd been told to not make a ruckus during longhouse-dinner today, and they didn't want to talk to Elder Switch either. That old bat didn't look before she swung, and they all knew it.

Some of the sproutlings looked suspicious, and the Elder thought something was odd. He decided now would be a good time to take stock of his surroundings, and it appeared they were on a hill near the stream. That was odd. Wasn't that the rock he'd stepped off a few moons ago the last time they went on a...? "You *rascals!*"

They had corralled him while he'd been distracted with teaching them about village identity! Half of them must have not been paying attention at all and had instead been purely preventing themselves from serene giggle fits as they'd led him to the same slippery location where he'd taken a tumble before.

At least this time, his lesson had stopped gently, rather than abruptly. Not to mention the part where he'd been soaking *wet*. The chorus of plan-foiled laughter careened away from him as they took off to do what they were told, most of them waving as he had no hope of catching up to them even if he gave chase. He couldn't outrun them, and the snotty, little troublemakers knew it.

"Tomorrow morning!" the eldest girl called out as she sped away.

The old fool had to rub the bridge of his nose. "Oh, old man... you've taught them too much. Look at those lovely little minds go."

He sighed and turned to walk home. "I'm awfully proud of them."

Holding his hands behind his back, he raised a brow and checked to make sure none of the children were following him. It was time for a detour! The beekeeper kept a fresh pot of honey-infused stew bubbling specifically because she knew he was likely to drop by after washing but before tending to his tasks for the day. He had a great weakness for sweet things. Easy meals that circumvented the trek to the longhouse were *beyond* enticing, thus he did so regularly. The Elder hummed an old tune as he thought about the conversations today and the inevitable *nonsense* he was going to have to endure in the evening with Elder Switch.

That old toad was trying something, and he'd have to find an appropriately sized stick to stab into whatever new malarkey she might be concocting. There was gossip that she was going on and on about changing the currency of the village from salt to *gold*.

"*Hmmm.*" Shifting the currency was a *terrible* idea for the peace of the Fringe. After acquiring a nice big bowl of lunch to take home, he discarded that line of thinking and rubbed his thumbs together into his back once he'd set the meal down on his desk. His mind wandered, as it often did. "I wonder if I have *notes* on identity."

He talked to the walls as he broke down the base components of how identity formed outside of the Fringe in both function and linguistics. Once comfortable with the rough verbal outline, he swiftly picked up a fresh vellum and flattened it over a second small desk. There was time before he really needed to make an appearance and enjoying spurts of enthusiastic energy like this was a rarity. So, perhaps, just a little bit of writing? Just a *little*.

It took him very little time to grind some fresh ink while he munched. Dipping a quill in the well, he couldn't keep the crafter's joy from his face as he began to scribe and mumble to himself. "What creates the *identity* of a thing? Does it begin with the application of intent and will? Consistent application solidifies aspects which, in turn, become recognizable. When enough aspects are recognizable, then their terminology can be shared. Shared identity creates *consistency.*"

"Consistency creates *order.* A set order allows identity to be recognized more easily. A thing *is* what it is, simply because we've all *agreed* that's what it is. It's the same value that we've agreed it is, not something else." The Elder looked over the starting notes of his secretly enjoyed activity, nodded, and lost track of time as the scribbles continued. Celestials above, he *loved* academia.

CHAPTER SEVEN

A coordinated hive of activity and gossip. Those were the only words that could be used to describe the bustling longhouse. Actually, perhaps a chicken coop—one where a fox was running around causing havoc. The lengthy center table was prepared for a minor feast, with enough room to seat the majority of important people who were called upon to speak.

The head of the table was occupied by a sneering, old woman currently whittling a fresh tree branch. She checked the flexibility of the switch by holding it up to her eye, snapping it gently before continuing her 'work'. The opposing end of the table sat empty. The seat had been *vacant* for the entire duration of the meal—which was nearing its end—and a certain old toad's patience was wearing thin. There were matters of *grave* importance to be discussed and agreed upon in *her* favor, and she was being *stood up*!

The longhouse was lined with tables which had one side pressed against the walls. This provided room for children—and people who did not wish to get in the middle of things—to sit and have their meal. This was a gentle way to cover for their pride; not having a seat at the long table meant you would *not* be heard even if you *did* wish to speak. On top of the already stuffed space, an extra wide table had been hauled in and pressed between two others so the visiting trader could arrange his wares.

That the merchant, Boro, had arrived a moon sooner than expected had been a saving grace to keep people occupied. As much as it was an additional disturbance for the poorly tempered crone, she held her salty tongue. While the village had some larger matters to discuss on trade, individual villagers were neither barred nor prohibited from using their personal stock of goods to barter, measure, and exchange for whatever Boro may have brought.

A considerable amount of the afternoon had been spent with at least a dozen people setting up a tool known as a 'scale'. It measured the weight of a person's salt or other goods; though the precise calibration required was a considerable undertaking in a place that wasn't known for the most level of floors.

The time-consuming task spawned a not-so-friendly recurring joke since the nearby area of work was named the flats—seamstresses quipped that the trader wasn't the sort of man who got his 'feet' wet after a day of hard work. An array of goods, clothes, trinkets, glassware, and other items were on proud display as the absolute *peacock* of a merchant shimmied his rump through the constant mess of questions and quibbles.

Boro was *prancing*, proud to show off all sorts of illustrious knick-knacks, toys, and cooking implements with a bard's flair. There had nearly been a riot during the sale of a cast iron cooking pot that came with its own sing-song story. The entire circus had put a significant delay on the evening's events, and it all served to work on Elder Switch's frayed nerves. The first snap of her newly carved switch was as crisp as ever.

"Where is that *blundering* old fool? *You*! *Boy*!" Her voice snarled as she looked for a victim. The fresh switch snapped, and ended up pointing at the youngest sproutling. "*Fetch*!"

The youngest hadn't been paying full attention and looked around to see if it was really *him* that had been addressed. Maybe he'd be lucky, and it was someone else th–

Switch! Accompanied by a pointed gaze in his direction, another snap of the rod made the sproutling's heart drop into his stomach.

"Wh-wh...?" he stammered out under the buzzing burden of ambient noise.

"You heard me, *boy*! Fetch the old *idiot*." Small gears slowly turned in his head. He jumped right up and sped out of the longhouse. A *tsk* could have been heard behind him had he bothered listening to it. Instead, his arms went into the air. He was *free*! Free from the longhouse, its noisy people, and stuffy air; he normally was not allowed to escape this early. The cranky Elder had given him a convenient way out—and to find one of his favorite people, no less!

The youth was skipping by the time he arrived at the A-frame home. Then he leaned his face right into the window and took a deep breath, preparing for some sanctioned noisemaking. Clearly, making very loud sound was the best way to get someone's attention when it was otherwise mouse-silent between sonorous snores.

The burst of noise never made it past his lips. Instead, a frown settled on the youth as he, somewhat deflated, decided to clamber through the sabotaged window instead of releasing a sonic attack. Who needs *doors*? His impact crunched forgotten nutshells and *popping* sounds came from underfoot as he hopped down. The home was dark, save for the moonlight beaming through the window and numerous scattered holes in the walls. He found the Elder seated and face down on a table covered in vellum, spilled ink, and a few broken quills. The young boy nudged the Elder in the arm.

"Elder. *Elder,* they're waiting for you." The boy jumped back with a stumble as the Elder jarred awake and bolted upright with a deep nasal inhale. A nasty *crack* in his back followed.

"Hhhmmm? Who is... oh... *oww...*" The Elder's clenched hand pressed to the small of his back. Eyes squeezed shut and his grimace was plain to see even with the lack of light illuminating his face. The old man sucked in a breath between his teeth and let a slow exhale release from his bulbous nose. "I've got this. I'm good."

When the pain of age had faded, he wondered where all his sun had gone. Thinking that would be an excellent thing to ask, he turned in his wooden chair but didn't get past the young boy sputtering out a stifled snort as the Elder's ink-marked face came into full view. Finger marks dotted his long beard and cheeks; obvious rubs to the forehead were deeply smeared. When the Elder looked down at his hands, he could see there were several dark patches.

Given there wasn't too much of a mess on his hands, the majority of it must have lined his face with the sublime skills of a toddler's art project. His writing digits were more smudged than the rest, along with the entire underside of his hand that followed to his wrist down from the pinky. The grogginess of slumber lifted swiftly enough. Physically, he might have been a wreck, but his mind remained sharp as he took stock.

Luckily for him, the old man's intellect tended to do the heavy lifting. "I take it I'm late for the meal *and* the village talk?" he weakly asked with a partial eyebrow lifted, hands hopelessly trying to wipe dried ink off on his stained robe. It was to *no* avail. The deep smudge was stuck to his hands until he bathed, and given he was likely already late, comfort would have to wait. "*Always* with the ink..."

The quick nods from the youngest were indication enough that he was correct. Packing the vellum and scroll-binding them in haste, he stepped with ragged swiftness from his premises. *Oh-whoo*. Trying his best to ignore the dizziness of getting up too fast, his hand solidly pressed to the left side of an aching hip. That's what he got for falling asleep while writing. *Again.*

Even with his favorite pillow under his butt, it wasn't quite enough to work in comfort. He stumbled on in the direction of the longhouse, and he would have made it too if the *thok... thok* of an axe falling to split wood had not reached his ears. That was odd... Everyone should have been in or near the longhouse, as work didn't go into the night for safety's sake.

Stealing a glance behind him, he saw the young man trailing on his heels. A sour expression hung solidly on the youth's face as he leered directly at the longhouse. No words needed to be said for him to express just how *much* he didn't want to go back there. The Elder vocally made a decision as he turned on his foot. "We're taking a *detour!*"

The young man brightened at the chance for more time not spent near stick-lady. It barely took two minutes for them to move around all the A-frame homes and arrive at an open space that held soaring stacks of chopped wood. The chopped lumber was stored and ordered in very precise and specific measures, each pile holding an even amount.

"Choppy?" the Elder called the inquiry as a very large, puffy-faced man came into view. The lumbering man didn't react, still just neatly arranging the next logs to be turned into firewood. Choppy's almond-shaped eyes were sunk in, and the other villagers tended to give him some space, as he 'wasn't all there' and the man didn't communicate well.

Sure, his face was flat and the lad had tiny ears in comparison to the rest of the villagers, but the old Elder held firm that when it came to handling the firewood, there was simply no one better. Since Choppy could not hear very well, the Elder beckoned the youngest to his side with a motion and nudged the boy behind his robe so no rogue splinters could fling his way. After getting the youngling out of harm's way, he simply sat on one of the larger logs, awaiting attention.

Choppy, being distracted, tired, and *hungry* was surprised when he turned from his work to see the Elder mysteriously sitting there. A crooked but genuine smile broke out on Choppy's elated face, and the Elder rose to open his arms wide in welcome as he got up. Choppy didn't hesitate to melt into the hug, still smiling as he tried to blurt out words to say seven things at once. All that came out was garbled nonsense.

The Elder patted him on the back, listening regardless but didn't release the hold. He was of the firm belief that it was the child who determined the length of the hug, as you just never knew how deeply they needed one. Sure enough, Choppy was in no mood to let go after having been avoided by the majority of people for yet another day.

"It's alright, my boy, it's alright. *Look*!" he said as he pointed to a large stack of neatly carved firewood nearby. "That one is new! So big! Good! I'm *proud* of you, my boy."

The warmth of a parent radiated from the Elder's hold as he praised the very much adult-sized child's work. The youth behind the Elder had shrunk away, his face contorted as he held the sides of his robe.

"Elder..." the youth whined out, not finding this particularly comfortable. The Elder, unlike the youth, felt no such pity. Choppy was genuinely doing his best for the village, and the old man again assured the man-child he was remembering that fact. The Elder lightly tugged on his upper back.

"Come eat. I can hear your stomach growling from my house. How about a nice big bowl of stew in the longhouse? *Hmm*?" Choppy received another supportive pat to the shoulder and began to move. Finding the opportunity, the old man hooked his arm around Choppy's to pull him along. The lumberjack was *elated* to be included, and while the mostly coherent noises he made didn't follow his actions, a strong step forward from the Elder made the two children fall right in tow.

For about... *two* steps. Until the youngest was also holding to the Elder by his sleeve on the opposing side, not remotely interested in being left out. The Elder blanched as he approached the longhouse, shaking his head at the sounds spilling out into the night. It appeared that Switch had blown her top.

"I don't *care* if he's not here! A *delinquent* Elder like him is not necessary for this village, and if he's going to *shirk* his–" The rusty-hinge squeak of the main door interrupted the words, and the old hag's eyes snapped to him. Everyone present could swear that the temporary reprieve was only so she could inhale her breath faster. They all knew that she was about to begin an entirely *new* outpouring of derogatory commentary. Some adults even had their hands over their children's ears in preparation of the onslaught.

"Apologies, all. It appears *someone* neglected to fetch our dear woodcutter." While his words were soothing, the glare the Elder gave the congregation was anything but an apology. His silent displeasure that the community would leave Choppy by himself to hunger filled the room. That *this* Elder was displeased as well only slathered additional guilt butter on the already burnt-toast emotions of the people present.

"Choppy has been cutting *so much* firewood *without end* that there is now an entire *additional* cord of it in his workspace! So, for the foreseeable future, everyone is to take double their ordinary amount."

His words set his proverbial foot down, and rather than walk all the way to the opposite end of the table, he chose to settle for somewhere near the middle so the children on either side of him didn't have to leave. This also gave people a way out of needing to retreat due to embarrassment.

"I believe that calls for a congratulatory double portion in an extra *big* bowl! Along with a nice pat to Choppy's back when you pass! After all, *thanks* to him, you'll all be *warmer*. I expect your appreciation to be loud enough for even *me* to hear it when you do so!" He slid into the seat and was more surprised to see all the silenced glances directed at him rather than the muttered acceptance of what he'd asked of them.

"Why is everyone staring? I said all of that out loud, correct?" The befuddled question hung in the air only to be answered by a shrill retort.

"*You*! *Are*! *Filthy*!" The accompanying sharp, wooden snap to the table set everyone abuzz once more.

The ink-marked Elder calmly laced his fingers, sat upright, and turned his face in the direction of the head of the table to lever his retort. His voice was filled with absolute *sass* as he spoke, "*Indeed*, Elder. Some of us do work that actually *helps* the village, and that tends to leave a mark at times."

A breathy, communal '*Oooh*' rang out. It seemed the main entertainment and debate of the evening had begun. Passersby interrupted the deep, furious breathing of Elder Switch with their soft voices, patting Choppy on the shoulder to leave some words of kindness and a crunchy piece of bread that had originally been a scrap they didn't finish.

Choppy cared for none of that, beyond happy to have more of this tasty, crunchy, delicious thing while inhaling huge spoonfuls of a stew that was a thick mixture of vegetables, poultry, and fish. Bowls were provided to the Elder and the youth as well, but per his instruction, one of the larger bowls had been used for Choppy, who had been alone all day with his work.

Elder Switch's ire was not something that was doused by a meager distraction, and she chose to negate his quip in favor of going on the attack. "You are *late*. You are *filthy*. Your face is smudged, and your robe is *unsightly*. How did you even get brown, green, and black on you all in the same *day*?"

She hurled the irritation at him and didn't give him a moment to sass a clever retort. "You have had the entire village waiting on you, and you ignored us in favor of having your head in the clouds! At least *now,* we can finally come to a proper agreement on things that should have been decided the *last* time the merchant was here."

"Things which were only held up because you could *not* be reasonable!" Her accusatory, gnarled finger stabbed at him through the air. Elder Switch looked like her eyes were going to pop out of their sockets from how large they had become. The spittle from her mouth had those nearby recoil to avoid an impromptu shower, though more from fear of sudden rod-lash than some paltry saliva. "Then... *then*! You get here long after the meal is at its best, and you bring two worthless saplings to the *grand* table to sit with everyone of import?"

The patient Elder slipped in a quick and determined response, "I *sure* did."

"No! Children do *not* get to sit at the long table." Stick swishing, the Elder needed a moment to catch her breath. The screech of her voice caused a now very *discomforted* youth to feel stiff, legs already shifting half-off the bench in preparation to make himself scarce and run.

The ink-stained Elder laid a shielding hand on the sproutling's upper back, giving a calm and steady reply against the shouting crone who was being painfully haughty, "I placed him at the table, and that gives him *full* right to sit here."

Sure enough, an Elder's word that one was allowed did very much provide precedence for them to take a seat at the long table. The youth was not required to leave, as per the rules.

"Not *him*," Elder Switch snapped. "The *other* one."

Switch believed she was cleverly quipping as she moved the goalposts of the argument to suit her needs. The patient Elder merely copied the previous movement and laid his hand on the back of a very voracious and distracted eater, still shoveling food into his endless tunnel of a mouth.

"No, no. *Choppy* has a name and is therefore considered a full *adult*. Pay *attention*, Switchy, you're starting to slip in your old age." The not-so-covert snort that went around the room was neither silent nor hidden. The majority of the villagers *did* cover their mouths, pretending not to notice the slight as Switch went red.

They could feel Elder Switch's eyes going bloodshot as the calm, simpering, and very much relishing-the-sass Elder began chomping away at a very needed dinner. The similarities to how the Elder and Choppy were eating brought a mercurial glint to Switch's eyes. "Well, at least it seems that you eat like your family."

The quip was *mean*, drawing a connection from how filthy he appeared to how messy the adjacent children were eating in similar food-scarfing fashion. The youth was eating fast, but that was more to get as much food in his tummy as possible before being dismissed from the big table on top of keeping his head down. People tended not to bother you as much when you had your head down.

Repeatedly knocking on his chest to get a big clump of fish swallowed down, the Elder nodded with a hiccup to Switch's words. "Indeed, I *do!*"

His spoon waved around, the motion indicating everyone in the longhouse. "What a *beautiful* family it is. Filled with strong people, good sproutlings, proud adults, and one *excellent* set of meal makers. Who made this *delicacy*, and may I *please* have another?"

Mmm. "Yummy!" He scanned around while lifting his now empty bowl. The Elder was scraping the sauce out with his spoon and eagerly swapped the bowls when one of the Mill workers came to trade it out. "Thank you, my sweet dear."

"You're welcome, Elder," muttered a big man—built from nothing but muscle—who nodded, *blushed* just a little, and silently had a better day. Then he returned to his table near the cooking pit, where he was teased and prodded by the others who worked in the Mill. That shining pink blush was just so *precious* on him.

CHAPTER EIGHT

Elder Switch was *seething*. Her vision snapped to various members of the village, each of whom felt their laughter die when their chortling was noticed by her strained, twitching eyes. Thankfully, Boro could still be seen fiddling about in the back, providing a necessary distraction. Forced to change topics, the room hastily returned to exchanging gentle pleasantries.

Using Boro's chatter as cover, people averted their eyes from the dissent-seeking pair of ancient, judgmental orbs, conveniently finding something else to quibble about. The merchant verbally *danced* his way through deals like a sommelier at the wine market. The trader occasionally sipped from a very costly looking, dwarven-made tankard as business once again slid his way. Ah, the volatile ups and downs of a local market.

Switch wasn't keeping her temper as easily as her academic opposition. Her fingers were clenched on her switch, knuckles tensing white from sheer grip. She was *not* losing hold of this village! She was *not*. The Elder felt horrendously *displeased* that she wasn't the main focus of the evening, and her words impatiently stabbed to the heart of the matter, "Since you're so *jovial*, Elder, we can get right into the discussion on the new trading agreement."

Boro perked up and excused himself from his current barter with the finesse of a practiced wedding crasher; his moment to shine had arrived. The ink-stained Elder drank some much-needed water after being halfway through inhaling his second bowl. He gently set the cup down with a relieved *aaahh*.

He nodded his agreement, using his already stained robe to wipe his mouth clean. The robe needed a solid wash as it was, so what was a little more paint to the canvas?

"Concerning altering the currency of the Salt village from its namesake of, well, *salt* to Gold. Is that correct?" he queried rhetorically, continuing to speak before Switch could intervene with a well-practiced speech announcing the virtues of the metallic currency. No doubt she would refrain from mentioning the myriad of personal benefits she would accrue. The unyielding words the Elder spoke were uttered with absolute finality. "I am *completely* opposed and have *no* intention of changing my mind."

A gagged sputter erupted from the back of the room as Boro promptly choked on his drink. So surprised to hear this unexpected non-starter to a negotiation that the potent alcohol had climbed back up and evacuated through his nose. So *rattling was* the burning sensation that he wiped his face with a luxury handkerchief. He otherwise *never* dirtied such a valuable showpiece.

Elder Switch was *mortified*, furious beyond her ability to convey. A scowl of disdain formed on her face, and she managed to voice a cracking whisper, "*What* did you just *say?*"

The people of the village for whom this somewhat mattered—and attended because they'd lost some sleep over the topic—exposed a strong sense of relief via deep sigh. The evening was now clearly going to wrap up, no immediate, sweeping changes were going to assail them overnight, and they didn't have to worry about learning some *arbitrary* new way to count and measure their hard work.

Boro embodied horror. His expression mimicked a living painting of panic as he shot the patient Elder a scathing look that could only be insultingly translated as 'the *audacity* of this dog'.

Luckily for the trader, he caught himself. Smoothing away his unsightly expression before anyone spun to see it... anyone save Switch, who had a full and unobstructed direct line of sight to him and whose raging, demanding eyes mandated immediate action. The action in question was demanded from him in particular, as he could quickly feel the blaming weight of 'the scapegoat' land upon his shoulders.

Boro swallowed and thanked the people nearby for their assistance during his accidental moment of inhaling when he should have swallowed. Presenting a firm and considerably less graceful step, he soldiered his way behind the merchandise table and threw delicate covers off a finely carved box. Since this ornate item had been purposefully covered the whole time, the murmuring of the curious crowd quickly picked up as the nosiest among them pushed to the front, eager to see this hidden-away treasure.

Many already guessed there had been some sort of container tucked away, and their curiosity *demanded* sating. With a quick appraiser's glance, Boro accounted that the inked Elder was preening his long, thin beard with the help of the youth next to him. They were having a great time swatting at the dangling hair to beat the crumbs out.

Picking up the box, the trader perched upon his table of wares, becoming prominently visible as he cleared his throat. He said nothing while awaiting permission to continue. Speaking to the village as a whole was a... *delicate* prospect. If one was not allowed by an Elder to proceed, it very much meant you were talking over them. That tended to make a lot of good customers *incredibly* angry. Elder Switch, hopeful that the trader had some sort of plan prepared, chimed her usual shrill tone, "*Speak, trader.*"

Boro performed a flourished bow and paced right into a practiced recital, "Blessed thanks for your permission, *honored* Elder. As you know, I was meant to be here after another moon had passed and so did not expect to be present for this eve's discussions. I humbly express my appreciation for being gifted your grace to attend such a lavish meal."

He held the box up and conspiratorially winked at the crowd—like he was about to let them in on a secret. "When I was last allowed to attend your banquet, I was provided payment in secret by several members of the community to acquire a suitable gift for their beloved Elder."

Boro paused to let the crowd simmer with gossip. Who had chipped in? Who *hadn't?* Why had the most knowledgeable gossipers of the town not whispered about this? This should have been top seamstress material! A few women leaned over tables to grab hapless men by the front of the robes, finding a probable answer to where some valuable salt had gone missing or other equivalent reasons that suddenly had an outlet to sate *questionable* home finances.

Switch settled and felt her heart rate dampen as she sunk back into her chair. Both hands sought comfort, tweezing the instrument of pain in her gnarled grip. *Yes. Good.*

The trader had something prepared after all, and from the sound of it, she was going to be bestowed the first of many promised gifts. She would delight in making a scene of it in front of the entire village, lording it over the inferior, ink-blotch Elder as the well-deserved prize it was. Her incomplete toothy smile dreamily spread. Her satisfaction was aimed at some of the previous Elders who had stepped down and might be on to her ploy.

A minority regarded her with respect, but most met her expression with *revulsion*.

Yes, my people, my conquests. Soon, I'll show you what you can all do for me, what I will expect from now on, Elder Switch's prideful thoughts swelled with anticipation. She was no royal, but right now, she felt like a spring princess preparing to be coronated. Ah, the joys of being the *true* leader of a village.

She was still lost in her dreams while Boro carried the eye-catching case past the side of the long table in her direction. Her eyes confidently closed with a self-assured smile as she leaned her head back, resting it upon the top of her chair.

Click.

The audible snap of several latches being undone was music to her ears as the people in the longhouse went silent. Dazzled children were among the first voices of drawn-out, breathless wonder to be heard. "*Wo~oaa~aaa...*"

The anticipatory '*oo~oo~oh*' cascaded with rough unity as the soft sounds of clothing being presented filled the longhouse. Boro's voice rang with a salesman's pitch, "After well over six seasons of steady work, the Fringe would like to extend this rich gift to its grand Elder, made in conjoined effort with nearby villages and the proud funding of generous souls. I present to you all, a product to be sold in the future by yours truly. A genuine *Lazuli* robe!"

Clapping hands rang out, and Elder Switch finally opened her eyes with the full expectation that her first act as Grand Matron was to accept this praise. Instead, her heart turned solid, an ice-block of hateful frost. Her blood chilled, lips stiffened, and jaw froze. She found no words could escape her mouth as she saw a calf-length, luxurious, *heavy* robe of mixed dark blues contrasted with gently reflecting shiny white trim.

Rope patterns twisted in a helix along the circumference of the sleeves, matching the pattern that passed down the front hem and followed the bottom contour all the way around. Near the neck, a white gold brooch was ready to pin the collar designs of the helix together and finish an otherwise broken pattern. The luster of the cloth was rich and resilient, not a single blemish, loose strand, or miss-knit to be found. This was obvious, as even the seamstress gossip train held their tongues as their eyes wandered over genuine art.

Switch's unaccepting eyes wordlessly denied reality. All watched as the Elder known for remaining collected rose from his seat. He was looking around at everyone in touched confusion, failing at finding appropriate words. Switch could see his face melting, overcome with emotion and disbelief. He covered his fallen jaw and parted mouth with a trembling hand, eyes watering at this gesture.

He could scarcely contain the tears as they streamed down his cheeks. The old man was moved; he could find patterns where others saw nothing, yet hadn't seen this coming in the *least*. Mill-workers helped the Elder get his current, filthy robe off his inner gray gi as he remained speechless, unable to properly cope with this gesture. His weak sniffling forced back attempts at a smile, expression trembling to a frown and back again.

Keeping face as an Elder for the village was required, yet he could barely control himself due to the surprise that had been sprung on him. The robe was *striking*, and it slid over his other clothing without resistance. Boro assisted in fitting the robe and synching it up with the finely woven helix pattern belt, explaining how to use the brooch to hold everything in place. The merchant announced the details over the supportive murmurs as they got the cloth fitted, bottom hem brushing the Elder's ankles.

"The majority is made from wind-attributed Beast-alpaca, that mountain animal afflicted with a coat of clouds. The lining, pattern, and hem are something a little sturdier. You'll notice the thread appears extra thick and a little shiny." When the Elder inspected the exotic threads, he found they were dense and thin. A seamstress hounding the cloth for details explained that the thickened appearance was an indication of the amount woven rather than innate finery.

Boro filled the Elder in before his questions could be voiced, "These come from a Beast-spider."

There were a few glances between people as the merchant kept on lauding to bolster future sales. They didn't know that last word, but the mention of 'Beast' had unsettled them. The Elder used his gi beneath the Lapis-blue robe to dab his face clean of tears and hurriedly filled the villagers in as damage control.

"Fear not. It is a *harmless* creature." While the Elder's mention set the crowd at ease, his admonishing gaze pierced straight into Boro. Wordlessly conveying '*Spiders? Really?*' The trader felt reprimanded—as intended—from that intense, parental leer.

The Elder's true reaction did not go unnoticed by the more perceptive adults. A normal spider wasn't a creature one wished to encounter in the wild, and he was lucky that there were almost none in the Fringe. The region *crawled* with their natural predators. Even the fish and bird they had for stew tonight would happily snack on any spider it found. Suffering a cold shiver, the Elder recalled some of the massive desert variants that would lurk in your shadow and follow along with you during travel. It had resulted in the development of some sinister rumors, and he welcomed *none* of those recollections.

Boro, being an intelligent man, caught the intended message and mimicked the Elder's response immediately, "Oh, yes. *Harmless*. Try touching the hem of the robe! You can feel the quality directly, and as I *only* sell the final product, you needn't worry about the *details*."

He waved the last part off with a playful, dismissive gesture. Like it wasn't a big deal. In truth, he was twisting away from the worst cringe of his life. The worth of that robe exceeded the net value of a full *third* of his inventory, and here he was just... *giving* it away for the sake of 'the plan'.

It wasn't the first time this robe had been used for this exact purpose, but each time it physically *pained* him to settle it on the shoulders of another. He was doing his utmost to save face, but every time he had to part with this prized object, he could feel the devouring greed within him utterly take control and shout envy with acid fervor. Did nobody know just how valuable *color* was outside of the Fringe?

This Elder *clearly* seemed to. Salt and Lapis were head-to-head in competition over regional exports, and the prices were low until the inner-realms market adapted. As of last season, Salt was no longer the victor in that contest. Being a skilled merchant, he would soon cut his losses and have this prized robe back. A dark, small voice in the back of his head piped up, 'Abyss *to the rules*!'

His contained fury built, and just then he had the misfortune to lock eyes with a still dumbstruck Elder at the head of the long table. Switch reclaimed her senses upon recognizing the alteration—snapping from the subtle shift in the trader's happy business smile to predatory sneer. Boro was elated when an exact match of his expression was returned to him. *Aaaah, there we go. There the truth is.*

The tiny voice deep inside him relished the dreadful demeanor of a person pushed over the brink, freshly broken, someone ready to pursue value and personal gain at the cost of anything else, whatever the sacrificial cost might be. The trader watched as his fabled prized possession danced around the room with a living bag of meat inside of it. Using its fleshy arms to shake hands and say kind words to other meat in even *cheaper* packaging.

Boro shook his head and held it on the side as the headache struck. His forehead was on *fire*. While there was no deep pain, he had to get this under control before that aggressive raider perspective did more than just sit at the forefront of green-colored thoughts. These were *customers*. He was a *merchant*. There would be smiles, business, and *sales*. He got himself out of his mindset by clasping his hands together with a **pap**.

"Who is ready for some *discounts*?" His thoughts wandered over to a few items in his inventory which could be left behind. He knew he'd get everything back later. Even with the distraction, his merchant gaze locked to the only colored robe other than his own in the longhouse. Boro flinched at the sight that awaited him.

The Elder was teasing a strong-looking lad, a little smile on his face as he whispered... When suddenly, the strongman took the Elder firmly by the front of that lustrous robe. In an instant, the strongman had pinned the Elder to the wall with a foundation-shaking **thud**. To Boro's surprise, the Elder did not retaliate. Rather, he just looked to the side and chanted in a sing-song fashion, "Oh, *Hib~iiis~cus.*"

The muscled man went red in the face. Swiftly releasing the Elder, he embarrassingly brushed freshly fallen dust from the front and shoulders of the rich robe. A rather tall and thin blonde bounced over. Flowers decorated her hair, and a well-fitted, if simple, robe stretched around her inviting features as she flounced into close proximity.

She was a *sight*, and it didn't surprise Boro in the least that someone who looked like they worked a forge felt infatuation for a girl exemplifying the smoothness of a finished ingot. To the trader's relief, the 'Elder's robe' was unscathed. Praise to its *quality*, no doubt.

The Elder tapped the forge handler on the shoulder and held his bulging arm firm as the big man was tugged down to whisper-level. Boro couldn't make out the first few words that they exchanged but could roughly make out 'Being honest... feelings... the path to accepting yourself'. Apparently, that was the *last* word that was going to be said on the topic. The grinning Elder waddled off to leave the two to their budding romance.

As the trader returned to his wares, the Elder clapped his hands together and announced a celebration dance. They would have an impromptu *bonfire*! This got a healthy cheer, and the parade of villagers who had all eaten plenty left the building with the subtle stride of falling boulders.

The day of rest was tomorrow, so there was no reason to *not* indulge. While festivities began outside, Elder Switch rolled up to the merchant table as the personification of a pissy thundercloud. The merchant remained seated with his hands steepled in a finger-pyramid. Given that his customers fled like swine to be slaughtered at the approach of Switch, he could speak freely, utterly ignoring the conventions and rules of the Fringe in doing so, of course. He spoke without being invited to do so, was curt, and entirely lost the suave, appealing tone his words normally contained.

"The vellum is ready to be signed, and the conversion to gold can be finalized. I have brought the requested currency in my hooded cart. She is filled with any... *needs* your village may have from this point forward." Lifting the document from his hanging satchel, he unfurled the vellum over the table. Switch took the nearby quill and began signing it without a word. The depths of her hatred were present in her every stroke. The offered quills even snapped *twice* before she was halfway finished. Her brisk lines were sharp and hard-edged.

Boro was a step ahead and provided replacement quills without a word. In a moment of coy bitterness, he decided to enjoy poking the hornet's nest. "This document must be signed by all the Elders of the village in order to be valid."

Her retort was salty, "The document is signed by all... *surviving* Elders of the village."

Switch didn't raise her head to meet his provocation, and her words chilled even him. She finished and rolled the vellum back up to bind it. "Seeing as it takes a few moons for this document to reach its intended destination, I am as certain as *gold* this will be true by the time that happens."

The laughter that erupted from the trader was raw and unfiltered, "**Ah, ahah, aaah*. Now I finally understand what Hakan sees in you. Of course. You are correct, Grand Matron."

His greedy hands readily accepted the signed vellum, seating it in a prime position inside his favorite satchel. "I shall go inform *your* men that they may come to collect payment and begin their work."

The sour Elder kept silent a moment. A pruned glare settled on the man as she gave a single, accepting nod. To Boro's great delight, she spoke bitterly as he began packing his unsold wares, "I look forward to finally being at peace."

His fingers took a moment to trace over the incredibly ornate, now empty box that had once contained *his* robe. It left a void within him. Boro felt that he had grasped a sensation the raiders had learned many moons ago. His acidic voice spat out a word, finally buying what Hakan had been trying to sell him all these seasons. The traitor's voice was as dark as his new outlook on the value of other people's lives.

"*Soon.*"

CHAPTER NINE

The bonfire dance was a total success. Excess wood that had been stuffing the storage site was retrieved from the mound with drunken enthusiasm. Of course, neatly chopped logs spilled out when a few zealous drunks pulled from the bottom of the pile instead of the top. Ignoring the fact that the stack would need to be arranged properly the next day, the villagers simply knew that a continuous feed made for *quite* the blaze.

"Oh no!" Most of the villagers were happy; Choppy wailed in panic and ran over to properly re-stack all the fallen wood. His well-organized towers!

Pots were improvised as drumming instruments, and an ad hoc tune was brought to life accompanied by offbeat laughter. The villagers just didn't know any better tunes or actual music. What they came up with wasn't fantastic or noteworthy, but the extra noise added to the good spirits people were already in.

The event provided an excellent excuse for some conveniently *misplaced* alcohol to resurge into availability, and it filled cups faster than even gossip could spread. The Elder gleefully fetched the cup with his status carved in on it but lost it due to being tackled by a horde of children that cried in defiance. They wrestled him en masse in an attempt to deny him the chance to get a sip of booze.

"No head-pain juice! Drinking that means sleeping *late!* You *promised!*" The old man couldn't quite remember *what* promise they were on about until he weakly laid face first in the grass. After both the kids and his cup were gone, of course. Face streaked with dirt, he was now *one* cup short of having enough cups to enjoy a drink with.

"Oh. Right. The forest." It was an unimpressive set of words that he *mumbled* into the dirt. Hit with the clarity of recollection, some help from an adult or two allowed the Elder to get back on his feet. Furious robe swatting ensued in an attempt to get the dirt and dry grass clumps off.

To an insulted seamstress's surprise, it took nearly no effort to get the robe clean again. She began fuming and threw her knitting needles on to the ground. Such a high-quality robe didn't *allow* the grass to stick to it, and if the ground had caused stains, they couldn't be seen in the bonfire light. How could she hope to compete with such work?

The Elder sighed in defeat. His zealous horde of kids was not going to let this go, so he decided right there to finish the rounds and provide cordial 'goodnights'. When he'd *finally* made it back into his home, his back was complaining and his spine was more difficult to ignore than a displeased murder of crows.

Setting the door panel back in place, he could nary describe the relief that being alone and laying down brought him. Prized and precious relaxation welcomed him as he flopped back into the floofy folds of his blankets and pillows.

Heavens did he enjoy being comfortable. His calm return to peace was interrupted by the appearance of several small heads in his window. The Elder nearly jumped out of his skin as a small finger pointed at him, and a hidden face whispered a message, "*First light.*"

The owner of the voice scampered off after passing along the notification from what *must* have been the oldest girl. A tired smile settled over his features, and the old man felt everything grow heavy just before he slipped into the darkness. Undisturbed by the ongoing sound and light of the festivities, exhaustion quickly won out.

Time for the best part of the day.

Peaceful, soft breathing. Rest was achieved, and the Elder secretly hoped he wouldn't have any bad dreams... as he began to snooze.

HAKAN

In the raider camp, Hakan's smile spread across her face with all the anticipation of a sadistic genie. She impatiently eyed the path of a much smaller trading caravan returning late in the depths of night. It was against custom for a trader to travel at night; after all... there were *many* dangers abound, such as raiders who could ambush you at any time!

The blade-clad torturer mockingly copied Boro's finger steeple as she watched the process of his attempted dismount from the cart, hungrily lusting for the large vellum that he proudly flipped from his favorite little bag. How did that huge thing even fit in such a small satchel? That just didn't make *sense*! He was twirling the document around with great enthusiasm, precious prize obviously attained.

"You *deny* me the enjoyment of my favorite activity when you provide such splendid results, Boro. How could you! I'm *almost* disappointed." Hakan's lusty words allowed her a flash of pleasure as the gaudy man flinched.

Boro merely dropped the vellum into her open hand. "Signed and without ever bothering to read the contents."

Hakan blushed pink and *shivered* from raw delight! "I adore this little plan our overlord put together. These backwater nobodies never even *consider* reading the fine print."

Her cheer was stifled when she unrolled the document and began to read, noting the lack of signatures. Hakan's eyes flared as hot as fresh-forged knives to the trader, who was a calm and collected bundle of confidence while he fondled his mustache. "Only... *one*?"

"Irrelevant without *survivors*. All that matters is that there is a signature the rest of the Fringe recognizes as an established Elder," Boro sneered. The merchant's countenance was slipping again, and he was visibly thinking that nobody would miss the walking *meat* in that village if it went missing.

Hakan gasped, hands on her lips at the realization that he'd *converted*. "You let it *in*! Oh, Boro! I almost want to ask what caused you to see the edge of the blade."

She didn't care for a response, instead looking back down to the vellum. She rolled the prize up, the signed land acquisition deed *more* than enough to satisfy her superiors. Enough for her to enjoy a personal journey of indulgence, most certainly. Hakan flagged down a messenger with the barest effort, handing over the important, bound document. "See that this reaches my Mistress."

Her words didn't *specifically* state that failure meant a slow death by flaying. It was well known that these small pieces of vellum held the weight of a thousand blades, and the saluting messenger gave it the appropriate care before leaving at speed.

Boro cleared his throat, and a dangerous amount of attention quickly fell on him. "My end of the contract is *completed*. I'll collect my reward and be on my way."

He gave a slight bow and turned to walk straight for his caravan... but Hakan halted him with a question. "Oh, Boro, *one thing* before you go?"

The raid leader smiled as the words fell from her lips. She spent an inordinate amount of attention on the details of one of her knives, a knife that hadn't been in her grip just a moment prior. Pausing in his stride to quasi-glance over his shoulder, Boro waited for her question.

Hakan *hissed* her message, "*Die.*"

"That's not a question...?" Boro had many concerns—some of them superficial, some of them self-serving. The concern that *currently* held his attention was the set of arrows protruding from his back. They had whizzed from the brush and stuck him deep with a meaty *thwack*.

The sensation of his knees collapsing to the ground was somehow *more* painful than the arrows. Agony raced across his back, and he finally felt the wounds burn. His tear-filled eyes asked *why*; they were wide open—shocked. Boro's jaw dropped and remained unmoving as the creeping poison numbed his tongue, extremities, and vitals.

This poison was truly nasty stuff, and Hakan delighted in the front row seat to savor what her new venom did to people. She even approached and clasped Boro's paling face with both hands, studying the man's death in *exquisite* detail.

Hakan's voice was a husky whisper as her fingers traced over his swiftly chilling skin as his breathing turned to gurgles. "How I *ache* that you can't scream for me. You must want to ask me a thousand questions! Did I have you shot because you're of no further use? Did I have you killed because a trader that knows the *lust* can no longer be trusted to work with my reapers?"

"Perhaps you were put down because all your goods and wealth are *finally* in a singular location, or... just maybe... did I have you slain for the *sheer joy* of seeing what this new venom does to a person?" Her voice lowered, moderating to the barest whisper; her words were meant only for the suffering man.

Shinn! The iron bubbling of his own freshly cut throat bleeding messily over the ground was the last sound Boro heard before his life came to an ignoble end, and Hakan was the only one to hear her words.

"It's actually just because I *wanted* to kill you." The pink flush of enjoyment grew on Hakan's features as she *gasped* and squeezed the corpse between her shaking fingers. This feeling was the single most *thrilling* fulfillment in existence, and she lived for it. Without further fuss, she stood. Mechanically dropping the lump, the executioner eased back into her cold, fluid, raid leader demeanor.

"Raid the dead man's goods. He has no further need for them." A messenger jogged up to the bloodied commander and saluted. The sadistic leader barely spared the short-winded girl a glance. It appeared the boys had become too frightful to deliver any news to her. *Good.* That set a far more natural hierarchy which she strongly valued over this irritating, contrived system of ranks. "Report."

The messenger spared no moment as the leader was short with her. "The village has begun a bonfire and is currently in the midst of celebrations. There's more activity than we planned for the night raid, and with that massive torch in the middle of their settlement, they'll see us coming before we're close enough to properly mount an assault. They're drinking and wildly roaming the village. Corralling them would be a pain, and it gives the prey we seek ample chance to run."

Hakan bit her gloved thumb with a *tsk*, mulling it over as she restructured her slaughter plan. "We strike at *first light*. All that alcohol will make them slower to act, and their poorly timed festivities will drain them. Our targets shall be considerably less aware than we were otherwise expecting. Trap them in their homes, and burn the entire thing down if they don't have suitable recruits that fit my tastes. Even then, kill those that resist and don't leave survivors. I want a messy and dirty *slaughter*, it will serve as yet another ash site for the mistress's wishes."

The messenger was giving her a worried look but didn't comment. Hakan grit her jaw as she didn't want to address this. "Yes, yes, the direct superiors won't be pleased that we're wrecking a potential source of income and profit. However, they're really not the main echelon I'm here to please. Not with *clerics* on our heels."

She hissed out the concern, "Speaking of..."

The aspect of sadism turned her full body to face the messenger, expecting a follow-up report. The scout girl was nervous and clearly hoping not to be asked this but now was quite stuck. The messenger's lips mushed shut as the grip on the inside of her gloves tightened. Leaving the raid leader waiting was a good way to regret any further living, so her lesser fear relented to a greater one. "They are coming our way. We have no word from the distraction group."

Hakan frowned hard on hearing that news. "None at all? *Nothing* about the cultivators?"

The messenger paled, her reply a crippled mess that lacked any confidence. "The best guess we have is that the special clerics are responsible, far ahead of expectations. Some of the men are worried that the big line of smoke coming up from the village is going to give them a direct target to aim for."

The girl stepped back as Hakan waved her off, irritated and not in the mood for more. "Bah. We need not worry. Morning will come, we'll snag the recruits, clean up by burning all in our wake, and leave for the main encampment right away. We'll be gone long before those cursed clerics find our reaped crops, so long as it's not the abyss-blasted Choir. The Phalanx Sentinels are slow, the Inquisitor Branch languishes, and there's *no* chance it's an order of paladins."

The stern movement of Hakan's hand dismissed the conversation along with the presence of those around her that didn't already have a task. The coy raid leader was terrible with orders she was required to follow and even worse with unwelcome pressure from superiors other than her *mistress*.

Being cooped up so long on the edge of a forest just waiting for instructions was not her forte. It made her hands itch, and that made the craving for potion prevalent. This assignment was looking less and less savory as she tried to find what was wrong in all of this.

"The *other* team is the distraction?" she spoke her bothered thoughts out loud, squeezing her gloves. "We have likely been lied to in the older reports. The supposed distractions are not in place. Nothing at all is interrupting the path of the clerics."

The fresh report was likely true, and the annoyances were headed right for them. "Other team is the distraction my *shiny rear.*"

They were being thrown to the wolves as the *real* distraction team. They'd been *assured* that they were going to be fine. Her teeth grit as the thought that it was her behavior and indoctrination of troops to her beliefs that caused this. What *else* would it be? It was not a secret she failed to play well with others—or even wanted to. So, if the upper rank and file desired to play little games with her...

"*Fine.*" She'd play little games with *them*, too. The vellum was on its way, and she'd take enjoyment in defying worthless orders in the process. That annoying scrap of leather was all that mattered to the direct echelon above her, but Hakan's lusts didn't pay attention to that layer. Not anymore. Not after today. After *today...* it was her and her band against the world, and she was going to spread her influence far and wide.

She'd abandon this *nuisance* called the Fringe and march right into dukedoms and bishoprics. The raid leader envisioned snatching them all away under the banner of her bloody dagger.

Wasn't there a castle in a grove that bordered the Fringe? Something for later, as she mulled over her short-term plan. Some new recruits, a party to her tastes, and she was all ready to go. Attack from the east via the trade route, preventing stragglers since the west just led to the seemingly endless flats, the local portion of which supported the production zone for the village. There was nowhere to run from there, as it led from the Fringe into the Unknown.

If things did take a turn for the worst, she had standing orders in place to part from the village in waves. The first wave would soak up incoming arrows and serve as a distraction for the second wave, which was to assist and charge until the arrival of the third wave. Her personal selections for the third wave, however, included no such orders. The third wave was entirely designed to take all the goods and glory and retreat from the field of battle, leaving the others to buy time or struggle to catch back up.

They'd take as many prizes as the wagons would carry! She'd had cages prepared and constructed, and they'd make a lovely box to carry her living treasures in, all packaged and ready for her to play with, to convert into *properly* raised adults. This new batch of children would be the first of many *personally* trained servants to carry her banner into future fields. That's why it was important to get them young, while they were pliable.

Anyone already certain of themselves would require breaking, and that just led to mutinies, betrayals, backstabbing, and other unpleasantry she no longer had the interest or time for. She'd outgrown the practice of making torture a sport, and now was the time for bigger, better, and bloodier raiders. When Hakan had fresh guards posted, she decided to take a few hours to catch up on rest before her big day. Dreaming of glory to come.

The *advent* of Hakan.

CHAPTER TEN

Crickets chirped in the dark when the kids snuck in through the Elder's window. They each hopped on to the floor, in turn shushing the next one as their feet crunched on the popping shells they'd thrown a day before.

The ruckus was *anything* but stealthy, and the Elder was long awake without moving a muscle or flinching an eyelid. He hadn't decided what scheme to pull on them yet, but at the same time, he *really* didn't want to get up. Any chance they'd forget mid-way and let him sleep? A firm nudge in his shoulder proved otherwise, his hopes shattered like the pleasant dreams he'd been having.

"Elder," a young voice impatiently whispered.

"*Elder*," it sharply repeated.

The old man just rolled over in his bed, away from the poking. **Mmmmjjmm** "No~o~o."

The half-asleep response drawled out in a haze to the attempt to wake him. An unamused voice piped right up at normal volume, "Who has the pail of cold water we got from the well?"

The oldest girl very plainly asked as the mousy voice— still outside—chimed up nonchalant conspiratorial banter, "I've got it!"

The old man found this *exact* moment the perfect time to yawn wide and stretch with dramatic flair. What was so awfully cozy? It was soft and smooth. Rubbing his hands down aching sides, he was reminded of the Lazuli robe he currently donned. Oh dear. He'd let it air in the wind for some time while he did the usual morning routine. "*Mmm*sproutlings."

He exhaled the word more than spoke it. "I distinctly recall *first light* being mentioned. It's *dark*."

Without missing a beat, the oldest girl clamped her hand firmly on his shoulder; he was, after all, still very much laying down. "No. First light is when we *leave*. Didn't you get my message?"

The old fool *did* recall a youngster pointing at him, but the contents of the late-night whispered conversation had been... *vague*. It was far too early to pull one over on him, but given there were... he counted breaths.

Five. No, *six* of the children here? The chances of him having a peaceful day were nil. Especially since they were going through with this *awful plan* that involved *effort*, being up, and walking. Oh, he didn't want to think about it anymore.

With a supported push, he sat up. A nagging pull involuntarily tugged at his lower jaw, eyes closing as a yawn loudly stated its presence. With a grunt and a rise, he long-stretched his arms above him. "Do I even have *time* to wash and eat?"

He asked flatly and as matter-of-factly, his face full of a matching expression. The female group leader chimed her confident voice up again—clearly she had put the other rascals up to this, "Pail of water all ready, and we've all got sacks stuffed with leftovers, and the occasional stick and rock. Because we liked them."

The Elder stood at attention with hands on his hips. "You're taking *innocent* sticks and rocks out that far? How irresponsible! What if something happens to them? What if they're lost or chip? *No no no*, none of that. I want all sticks and rocks on my table for safekeeping. They'll be here when you get back, and you can pick them up after."

He scoffed and redid his belt so it was tied in a way he was pleased with, already moving the door while not being snippy about the excess bag-weight. He had tried phrasing it in a way that would make them leave the unwanted encumbrances behind.

Sure enough, the kids didn't like the idea of losing their favorite rocks on a long trek and did as they were told while the Elder took off at full stride towards the stream. The old fool frequently considered this trek the most difficult part of the morning as the incline got steep on occasions, but today, it was made with *determination*.

The stream ran from the salt flats and surged inland, carving through the landscape in several locations. The awkward path of the water made a clean divide where a small hill *should* have been. It was exactly such a miniature cliff that was the slippery slope the kids kept trying to lead him across, so he avoided hills when he could. Taking the flattest and easiest route—even if that took the extra minute—got him there with minimal strain. Unfortunately, the stream wasn't deep enough on the flat side, so each morning, he had to wade inward a little deeper than he liked for a proper depth.

It took some doing with his body in the state it was, but nothing some strongly applied willpower couldn't push him through on. As an additional bonus, the cliff sides served as decent sight blockers, and it let him wash in peace. As expected, the zippy, little squirrels effortlessly caught up to him.

The pail was handed over, and the Elder yawned wide again, rubbing his eyes to glance in the direction of the apiary. Apparently, he was spotted doing so, as the eldest girl had her arms crossed and cleared her throat at him. Before he could question her, she just pointed at the bag of food currently at her feet. Why carry what you could put down, and why let the Elder make an excuse to wiggle away?

"We'll wait around here, Elder. In case you *accidentally* wander off." Her voice was ironclad, confident in this plan of theirs.

Resigning, he undid his Lazuli robe and gray gi where he stood and tossed the clothing over without folding them up. Old scars on him were plain to see, and they looked incredibly unpleasant up close. The oldest boy took the robe, but his eyes were locked on the injuries while his face contorted in phantom pain. The Elder was only wearing his pants, but even then, they could deduce some of the injuries went further down his sides and likely spread across the legs.

The children were speechless from seeing those scars up close for the first time, so the Elder broke that uncomfortable silence, "Let the robes air, maybe beat them with a stick a few times to make the fabric breathe. I don't know how well that robe handles much of anything yet."

The Elder was eerily thin, and his arm strained just from picking up the pail. While the old man didn't make a sound, the children gained a glimpse of insight on why everything physical seemed so difficult for the older people in town. With a body like that, the Elder looked so frail that even the youngest boy could test the old man's salt—and win.

This wasn't enough to force them to reconsider this whole venture when their worry met the iron will of the oldest girl. She was holding firm, so they did as well. It was just the six of them, less than she'd hoped, but the usual crew was here. No. Make that five; the third girl ducked out and was going home without as much as saying bye. Not up for more of this, which wasn't uncommon.

She did leave her sack, though, so more snacks for the trip. That left the oldest girl, the oldest boy, the youngest girl, the youngest boy, and the mousy-voiced boy. Good enough, they were the core group anyway.

They all heard the humming from their Elder as he waded deep into the stream where the depth of the water was significantly more noticeable. They could never discern what kind of song the humming was; they just didn't know it.

It was one of those things that came from *outside* of the village, and their curiosity craved answers. A few meaningful glances later, and all but the oldest boy who was taking care of the robes crouched and stalked closer to the song. They thought they were doing well!

However, as soon as the first face came around the bend, the humming had already stopped. The youngest girl took a step back, eliciting glares from the rest of the crew. When she turned around her caught expression very clearly declared. "We're *abyssed.*"

"I *so* look forward to hearing what reason you all might have to sneak up on an old man bathing. Especially when it was *specifically* asked that old man wasn't to be bothered." The Elder's voice was passive and flat, but it made all the children squeeze their eyes shut in defeat and copy the '*got caught*' expression. An old sigh was easily heard.

"I suppose it no longer matters; I can't keep my secret spot hidden for much longer. I just about can no longer reach it anymore. Is everyone present?" His voice sounded defeated, a wet cough breaking up the way he was speaking.

"No," the oldest girl replied in defeat. There was no point in trying to hide anymore as the old voice continued.

"Fetch whoever is missing, forget the bags, and leave your robes on the bank. What I'm showing you is under the water." Confused but interested, the scampering happened fast as the aged voice recovered. The oldest boy was involved in a hurry and just followed suit with robes and bags in tow. The group carefully stepped around the bend, since there was only so much bank to keep stable footing on while the stream sharply cut one of the hills in half. They found the Elder breathing steadily, deeply, and with repeated practice.

He interrupted himself when he saw the small ones, "Alright, *ask*."

His already tired voice got right to the point as he needed to use both his hands to lift the pail and drink. Warm salt water was great for bathing but not for drinking. Questioning gazes did the rounds, but they fell on the oldest girl, the de-facto voice for this little band. She gave in, unable to lie to herself that she did, in fact, have several questions.

"You hum this song that we don't know, and we wanted to hear more. But that's not the question I want to ask anymore." She steadied herself for the big one. "Are you... alright?"

Even a child could tell that he was having difficulty just breathing. He was out of breath, looked like he was about to fall apart, and was using both hands to lift a simple pail. The aged man pressed his thumbs into the inner rim of the small bucket to set it down.

"...No, my dear. I'm not." He wasn't looking at them; rather, he was steadily squinting into the water of the pail.

"The song is a lullaby that I used to... sing," he trailed off, mouth still moving to make the soundless words, "a long time ago."

With a stern breath, he put the container down and began wading into the water, stopping before the dangerous drop off approached as he wasn't going to finish his answer about the song. He pointed up to the ridge and asked a flat question, "Does anyone recognize where we are?"

Small eyes glanced, and the mousy voice chirped to life. "It's where you fell."

The Elder nodded. "I always *marvel* at your memory."

Warmth fueled his smile as he saw the small boy crawl out of his shell from the praise. "When I fell that first time you all *managed* to trick me, the current swept me away. It pulled me under and under, and when I came up, I was in a cavern. I could breathe, and it wasn't dark. What does that tell you?"

The oldest boy was pumped up with energy and wonder. "Secret Cave!"

Excitement replaced trepidation in the group, but the oldest girl narrowed her eyes. "How is a cavern *not* dark?"

The Elder peered into the hidden depths of the stream, searching for an answer. "I don't know, and I believe it's time to pass that torch on. Perhaps one of you will figure it out. Perhaps the children after you. Consider it a trade for the bad news I'm about to give you."

The oldest girl had a strong guess what this was going to be about and seared the wound early. "You can't make it to the forest, and you can't give us our names."

Hearts dropped all around. The attention was on the conversation between their leader and their Elder, who continued the chat, "I'm terribly sorry, my dears. I cannot make it to the forest. I expect I would make it about halfway, if my memory serves me right, as I just can't see how far it actually is. Your names, however. Well..."

The Elder raised his head up and smiled at his children as he stabbed his thumb at the water below him. "Nobody listens to what they can't hear. So... if I happen to be talking to myself while in an isolated corner where I can't be overheard... perhaps the Fringe won't be *listening*."

Chapter Eleven

Ideas bloomed in the sproutling's thoughts. The plan was straightforward: make it to the cave, get the secrets, get home before morning meals. The old man just watched them with a pleasant joy as they put things together. He'd given them pieces of the puzzle, and even without being exceptionally prompted, he could tell they were solving the conundrum. They had wants just like any of the adults; using those to teach them sharp thinking was just good sense.

"Can we make it?" the oldest boy asked as he stole a look at the deep water. It looked awful dark even as the first rays of sunlight struck it.

The old man nodded with certainty. "You lot? Certainly. Myself? Maybe a few more times before I can't hold my breath long enough."

Their Elder did some stretches. "Here's what happens. Once you're deep enough, the water is going to pull you. Specifically, it's going to pull you down, and you're going to get caught in a force of water that feels like you're falling sideways. That stream spits you out into a cave. You're going to feel like you're going down, then up; then you're going to hit the ground while water is rushing past you in a hurry. *Steady yourself there.* If you go further, you're back in the stream, and it will spit you back out over *there.*"

He pointed further to the next hill, the salt stream cutting that one in half as well. "It's only a tiny bank of space you'll have to move on—a wall to the left, crawlspace to the right. Crawl to the light, and you'll be in the cave."

A detail came to mind that he swiftly threw in, "Oh, don't eat the stuff that glows. Tried that. Couldn't tell what was real for a week. Do *not* recommend."

His voice trailed off and waited for follow up questions. The mousy voice called, "So... we just hold our breath?"

"Just hold your breath. There's no swimming against that current once you're that deep, so take a big one and keep your hands over your mouth once you lose your swimming direction. I would say it takes about... hmm. Maybe half a minute? To..."

He'd lost them. They had no idea what a minute was. "This long, I'll count in seconds."

He raised both his palms and moved his fingers one at a time until he'd moved every digit on both his hands three times. "Twenty to twenty-five fingers is normal, twenty if the pull is fast. However, so you're not surprised in the future, I've known it to take thirty. Thirty seconds is half a minute. A 'finger', if referenced directly, is one minute, and a 'hand' is five minutes because that's how many fingers you have."

The younger ones were afraid but couldn't stop the older ones who had eyes full of lust for adventure. The Elder noted their hesitation. "I'll go first. Ditch your robe. Just go in your pants. Extra cloth and weight really don't help."

He motioned at a spot near the pail for all the things to be dumped and dove right on into the darkness with a splash. The children could see him swim straight down for the first few lengths of a person, and then with a sudden movement, the Elder was pulled to the side and vanished into the black.

The youngest girl shuddered and was about to voice her concern as the oldest boy loudly plunged into the depths. Her words didn't ever reach her tongue as the oldest girl followed the Elder. She turned in borderline panic to the younger boy, but he was filled with determination and taking deep, steadied breaths.

He swallowed a big one and joined the other three. Now she was alone with the mousy boy.

"Maybe we... should not..." she almost whimpered the words as daring teeth were flashed back at her in a sizable grin. *Oh no.* He was going to go as well. No, she didn't want to be alone. The mousy boy took her hand and squeezed it.

"Together?" His expression one of confidence and excited wonder. Her hesitant hand squeezed in return. Fear melted away as something akin to butterflies in her stomach bloomed. She wasn't so afraid if she wasn't alone.

"Y-yes. *Together.*" In unison, they began taking deep breaths, and with a jump, they were gone in the stream as they swam to follow. The first gasp of air the youngest girl heaved as she broke the cavern's surface was met by a strong grip on her arm. It pulled her to safety as she sputtered. Hearing another set of gasps right behind her, she saw the boy too was snatched to safety. Holding their breath had been mostly successful, but at least two of them were hacking up watery coughs.

Support was ready for them. After a solid few breaths in the dim dark, they began crawling in the perhaps two-and-a-half-foot tall space in clear direction of some faint light. Once inside what looked to be a tall dome, they all pushed their backs to the wall, breathing deep and looking to one another with proud smiles. They'd all made it. Every last one of them. A round of chuckles went around the circle as the Elder managed a few words, "I would like to welcome you all to my little secret place."

The Elder raised his hands, motioning at the luminous, domed space. "It's safe to touch that odd glowing moss, but again, don't eat it."

Another series of half-laughs and chuckles did the rounds in memoriam to the courage it had taken to get here.

The euphoria cut to pure silence as the Elder declared five names, "Lunella, Grimaldus, Tychus, Wuxius, and Astrea."

Everyone fell silent when the dome began to shudder, worriedly looking all around them as the walls thrummed and tremored. After what sounded like the thudding hooves of a stampeding herd passed above, the dome fell quiet.

"Well," the Elder's voice rose with apprehension, "it doesn't seem like the sky is falling on our heads. I'd say we're clear."

The oldest girl snapped her head sharply at the flouting Elder as he'd spoken with such nonchalance. Her emerald eyes stabbed him with greater force than her words, but that was one of the traits that made her such a delight. "You said all of that and just *hoped* the Fringe was going to let you get away with it?"

"Yes, *Lunella*. I just believed." He sounded certain. In reality, he'd absolutely rolled the dice on that one and would *never* tell them so.

The previously tense and miffed girl gasped as her hands went over her mouth. Was that *her* name? She *adored* it and was now trying to keep it together as her swiftly overwhelming emotions bubbled and fluttered. She hadn't expected to *actually* get a name for several seasons. This had been her gamble, and it paid off *wonderfully*!

The old man crossed his legs and swatted at wet pants; blasted cloth always got unpleasantly cold when he lingered here long. He'd bear with it. Pressing back against the wall, he saw her heartfelt reaction and extended his warmth with a delighted expression. "Do you like it?"

Lunella nodded through her crushing emotions; it was *beautiful*. The mousy boy chirped up and nodded as well but was thinking about something else with some concern.

"They all sound so *strong*. Does... does the Fringe have enough room for that many strong names?"

The Elder **humphed** at the notion, arms crossing. "The Fringe can come *complain* if it's dissatisfied at this point."

The retaliatory look in his eyes softened as it fell back on the poorly illuminated children. "I won't be around for many more seasons. I have many fond memories of this village. It has some great places and sights, but they're not what I love about it. The biggest secret I have is that what I love the most is *all of you.*"

The kids felt fuzzy at the mention. "The joy you bring this old man with your clever little tricks and energetic playing around is a life of fulfillment I cannot describe. Watching you all grow has kept my heart beating. I might be a touch lazy, but waking up to find what trouble you're going to get into that day is a *hoot.* Your lives are what gave this old man the will to keep seeing just one more day."

He rubbed the sides of his arms to warm up a touch. "So, I thought, and I thought. If *I* was going to give the few minds who I treasure most in this world *anything*, it was going to be the best names I could grant. The lengths I wouldn't go to see you all healthy, safe, and in good spirits..." He paused to let out another rebellious **hmmpf**!

"Oh, the heavens would have to descend to rob me of my last breath before I would stop trying!" His hand softly laid on the head of the mousy boy next to him.

"Yes, *Tychus*. Your names are *strong*. They are filled with a purpose for you to choose and a depth of meaning that will likely take your entire life to uncover. With your names, I've granted you something *special*, something only the five of you have in the Fringe—a reason to live that *you* can choose. That's all I want you to do when I pass. Just *live* the way you want."

Tychus went wide-eyed. That had been the toughest sounding name! Why did *he* get it? He was small and unblossomed, an absolute *acorn*.

"*Tychus?*" He tasted the name.

"That's *you*," the Elder affirmed with a pat on his head, "and Astrea is next to you."

Tychus tensed as the girl next to him needed immediate support. Having been holding his hand this whole time, Astrea was firmly crushing his grip, equally unable to keep her emotions in check. For her, this was less because it was a social implication and more because she now felt solidly included. The weight of the designation pressed invisible on her sternum, and the pressure made a cool shiver crackle over her skin. She was going to get through it. They were all here together, and that meant the world to her. Having Tychus' hand to crush *admittedly* also helped with coping a little.

The oldest and youngest boys were nervously exchanging glances, voices trapped in their throats. The Elder motioned at the youngest first to dismiss their uncertainty. "Grimaldus."

Then the oldest. "Wuxius."

"Do you like them?" The boys still had no words as the Elder returned palms to his knees, an eyebrow raising. The old man honestly wasn't sure. They weren't making a sound, and that made it *terribly* difficult for him to get any details.

"They love it," Lunella replied as she was wiping wet cheeks with the back of her hand."

The boys then agreed in a hurry.

"Oh, eh... Yes! I just don't know what to say," chirped Grimaldus.

"I just feel really *heavy.*" Wuxius was nodding in firm agreement as he found his voice. "I just... It's so *solid.* I don't know what it means. The name just sounds like it's filled with more than I can get a hold of."

That statement was echoed by the others as well, and the Elder filled in, "Well, that's part of the point, isn't it? You'll grow up with this, you'll shape it, people will recognize your name based on what you've done and what you say. However, unlike a simple meaning, I've given you complicated ones."

His hands drew visualizations of his words in the air. "Another *secret* for you. Certain things in life may *look* complicated, but really, they're made from a large number of small things that are simple. Coming together, small things look like a big mess, as we're only used to seeing the whole. When you have a good grasp of the small things, the big one will suddenly make sense too."

"I've given you this weighty, unknown thing that you're probably not sure what it is or how to carry. However, little by little, you'll discover details that paint a bigger picture, and when you finally have all the pieces, you'll find the truth hidden in a small hole in the ground surrounded by people you love." The Elder's voice faltered, and he cleared his throat. He tried not to dwell on how cold and hazy he was getting. The chilled Elder did the usual handclap to clear himself of his thoughts and rubbed them together.

"Well, I'm freezing and starting to shiver; shall we go home and go eat?" His facsimile of a smile didn't get the expected reaction; the sproutlings had grown and were holding back sobs.

They had been so happy about their names a few moments ago; why the somber air? He had to relent and looked to Lunella since she was going to be the one to speak regardless. Sure enough, her tone was bleak as she asked with displeasure. "How long do you have?"

If it hadn't already been chilly, the old man would certainly have lost feeling in his fingers after this. They had assessed that the clock was ticking down, and he supposed it was better to give them time to come to terms with however long he had left. He maintained eye contact with Lunella and gave the dreaded knowledge with a clenched heart, "Maybe a season."

The kids winced and bit their tongues at this. He wasn't sugar-coating the pain and just hit them with bleak truth. The anchor of knowing was an additional weight they didn't want to carry, and it made them feel terrible. They didn't want him to leave either, but that *abyss*-cursed serene expression on his face told them he was content with the impending end.

Seeing them muck about had been a joy. These children were an alternate reality of a life he'd never been blessed with. What had been closest to this contentment had been ripped from him as a young adult. This world was cruel that way. Cruel and unrelenting in the wake of the eternal unknown. It was normal to fear and shy away from what you didn't understand. He grasped this well as he found his voice.

"I'll begin my final lessons shortly. I suppose as a preamble, I'd like you to keep hold of this. It's a bit of knowledge that I hold very close." He cleared his throat again, but it throttled in significant need of some fresh air. "You're going to make mistakes, and that's okay. You're going to fall, and that's okay. *Get up.* You're going to question yourself and wonder if you're doing things right. *That's good.* Keep asking! When you make a choice to go forwards, don't waver. Only one choice is worth making, and that's the one you should live by."

The Elder leaned in, hands strong on his knees, emphasis carried on the provided wisdom. "Everything is either a choice you *can* live with or a choice you *cannot*. There is no reason to second guess; merely pour all your effort and being into the world you wish to see around you."

His back fell against the wall, eager to end it as he felt finished with the conversation. "I would have felt such regret if I didn't grant your names. Though, one day you will find that the best names are the ones you've chosen and made for yourself. Regardless of how long I have, if you fall and stumble, I'll come for you. I'll *always* come for you."

With a push to the floor, he was up and ready to go. "Now, let's go get warm. All of you first."

CHAPTER TWELVE

The Elder knew something was off as soon as he resurfaced. A smell in the air... it was *wrong*. His first breath of what should have been crisp air instead filled his tongue with the flavor of smoke. His hearing picked the muffled cries alongside the crackling *whips* of wildfire. Something was *burning*, falling... breaking.

The crashing tear of wooden supports caused a puffy *scrumph* as the unstable home collapsing on itself hit the ground and oppressed the senses. It also ended *several* muffled cries. This experience turned what should have been a peaceful morning gaggle of hungover groans into tortured screams.

The Elder had been the last to come back up through the stream, yet could not locate a *trace* of his young group through smoke so thick it forced his eyes to swell. The children had gone ahead of him, so the expectation was for them to be present when he resurfaced. A high-pitched screech cut through the rumbling, ambient mess of fire-wrought sound. *No.* He *knew* that voice! "*Lunella!*"

With significant effort, he dragged his old bones from the stream and on to the dry bank, worming his way from the water with all the elegance of a landed fish. His lungs burned; nasty smoke clogging the thick air made it all the worse. It reminded him of times he'd rather never recall.

It seemed that as much as he'd run away from conflict, strife with its endless reach had grasped him again. Life would not let him go silently into the night; it was here for the pound of flesh it was owed—or rather, from the rebellious voices that were dragged further and further into the distance, those of his *children!* The surrounding blares of activity made it a nightmare to determine who was where.

Accented, foreign screams echoed from the apiary as the crashing buzz of a destroyed hive split the air. A panic-fueled cry screamed out, "Bees! *Bees!*"

It wasn't any adult voice the Elder recognized, so that confirmed outside forces were at play. Total, howling disarray and fear sirened from uphill, so the Elder moved as fast as his feet would take him—which was admittedly rather pathetic and frustrating. He was *useless* like this! That his heart rate caused his hands to shake was nothing new, and old mantras chimed with military repetition in his mind.

Keep steady.

Keep moving.

Stay alive.

His shambled pace brought him back to the pile of robes the children had ditched. Creeping, wet cold still clung to his skin, and the cold-sickness was going to get his claws into him before his age did if he didn't bundle up. So, on went the robes, while a sack was repurposed as an anti-smoke face mask—a trick picked up in a desert long ago. He looked ridiculous and couldn't *begin* to care as his mind laid the foundations for action.

The Elder couldn't assess the threat. The amount of smoke meant the majority of the village was on fire, so this was a *raid*. His priorities in this battle boiled down to survival and retrieval of the children. That second objective was going to be difficult in his current state if there was so much as a toothpick-armed *weasel* in his way. He'd told the kids to stay alive. With hope, they would cling to those words. That's all he wanted them to do.

Stay alive.

Just stay alive.

Anxiety was squashed under absolute need as he throttled his worry and self-doubt by the throat. A *season* to live? No, old man! A *day* was fine! *One day* was more than *fine*, so long as he could see the safety of the children! The *clang* of metal clashing with metal put a hearty and swift dent in the chances of that plan. Thieves were bad; thieves with weapons were worse.

However, there wasn't a sword in the village? The *clangs* repeatedly rang from the wood storage direction, but there wasn't a... realization struck him like a brick. "*Choppy's axe!*"

The Elder then crumpled inwards like a potato sack as a pain spread from his stomach. A slung rock had struck him at speed and taken the wind right out of him, forcing an unexpected *ooof*! The earthy slam to the ground wasn't so bad, but it sure *felt* like it was. He remained there, unmoving. A crass voice called through the dense, smoky haze that hung low. "Hah, got another one! That's two hands for me in the lead!"

The Elder held his stomach with both hands but couldn't move, just gasping in air that came difficultly at a soundless wheeze. "Looks like that one's not moving. I'm calling it *dead*, and a point for me!"

The same crass voice then gained excitement as it spotted moving prey. "Are those *runners*?"

"Yes, they are! Let's *get 'em*!" After a murderous laugh, the thudding impact of several boots promptly vacated the location. The vibration was so heavy that the Elder could feel it through the ground he laid immobile on. This pattern of footfalls felt incredibly similar to the... to the thrumming they'd experienced while in the cavern!

"*Abyss!*" It took at least a full minute for his breath to even out, and he was forced to hear the community around him burn to ash. The syrupy coughing of people choking to death filled nearby homes, only to be silenced as the buildings burned and collapsed down on top of them. Anyone who wasn't trying to run had attempted to hole up, and neither choice ended happily.

The Elder barely got to his hands and knees as a pained whimper cried from the logging section. It sounded like Choppy was in severe pain; pain that he couldn't understand. Infantile whimpers and sobbing, bubbling cries told the old man there was liquid in the boy's lungs. The familiar sensation of strained muscle twisted in the Elder's legs as he got up and forced himself to move on.

While he was certain an arrow whistled past his head at a certain point, he winced and ignored it. The old man found the woodchopper on his back with a face stained by pained tears. The Elder fell to his knees to support the lad, momentarily skidding to a halt. "I'm here, Choppy. *I'm here.*"

Firmly taking his calloused hands, the old man attempted to console his boy by being up close and personal. He could see the damage, and he knew the end was coming for this lad. A deep cut from the right shoulder raked down into the lung, but it hadn't been shallow where it vitally mattered. There was going to be no recovering from an injury like this, not even if the big man found immediate attention. The remainder of the woodcutter's short life was going to be agony.

The Elder knew Choppy wouldn't bleed to death from this wound; he'd choke on his own blood first—a fate he wasn't about to let the boy suffer. Choppy's good arm held the Elder firm as needing, glossy eyes cried for help as the boy stammered begging words, "*Gllrblpain*. Pain. *Glpain*. Hate pain. Pain."

This good boy had used his wood logging axe to fend off the invaders. A swift glance in either direction showed not one but *two* split melon heads. For all the harsh times the village had given this big lad, he'd always been *amazing* with his aim. From the angle, the axe must have gotten stuck in a spine. It seemed to be protruding from the slain raider, but the Elder had no time for that now. He slid forward and detested that he knew what to do.

A familiar, practiced grasp firmly took hold of the suffering boy's head, and the old man pushed a knee forward to press down on that wide chest. This was the kind of injury that left a man to suffer for as long as possible while still being fatal— purest suffering until the final gurgling took the agony to a crescendo, finally coming to an undeserved end.

"I know, my boy. I'm going to take the pain *away*, Choppy. I'm going to make it *stop* hurting now." The old man needed to suck in a breath, tearfully ignoring the bite of the smoke. "Hold me tight, *my son*. Hold me *tight*."

The Elder's voice was trembling, and his jaw was clenched shut. His eyes burned, and wet streaks lined down his cheeks. He had to do this for a prized child once *more*. His breath quickened, and his dry mouth swallowed to cope. The good boy did what he was told to do and clung tight. The psychological harm the Elder did to himself that next moment was unspeakable, as he shattered the happy illusion he'd built for himself over these many, many years.

The physical exertion was just... a simple...

Snap.

CHAPTER THIRTEEN

"Alright, recruit. *Once* again, from the start." Armored fingers drummed with delicate impatience on the extended table in the salt village longhouse. This entire *mess* of a report had more holes in it than his favorite cheese, and Head Cleric Tarrean had not been able to acquire said cheese for *far* too long. He shook his head and forced himself to refocus. The bags under his eyes were reminiscent of crescent purple moons, and *still,* he couldn't take the liberty to rest; duty demanded the task be seen through.

His faith would carry him, as it always did, but this whole endeavor had been a repeated set of annoyingly convenient events. *Bothersomely* convenient. He went over how he just *knew* his superiors would be reacting:

'Where are the *raiders*, Tarrean?'

'Oh, I don't know! We have this intercepted vellum with a *surprisingly* detailed troop placement plan. Well, now we've arrived at the abandoned settlement, *Tarrean*. Where are the wanted men?'

'It appears that they're just taking their sweet time walking right over to us without a care in the world! Sure, we're already occupying defensive emplacements and are the wolf waiting for lost lambs to walk into our open mouth. Those raiders never saw it coming!'

'Why, Tarrean, where are we supposed to go from here. The map isn't very clear.'

'Recruit, if you look in the distance, doesn't that look like an awfully *large* funnel of smoke rising into the sky?'

'Why, *yes*. Yes, Head Cleric, we should rush to that position post-haste!'

'Tarrean, are we *certain* these are the raiders we thought they were? The last group seemed exhausted and in retreat.'

'Well, recruit, there's an awfully *large* number of buildings on fire, people screaming, and sharp, metal objects being stuck rather deeply into what seem to be awfully *innocent* people.'

Head Cleric Tarrean snarled and slammed his armored fist on the table, startling the man giving him a report into silence. Whoops. He hadn't heard a word the man had been saying. To top it all off, this mess was in the celestial-rejected *Fringe*. As if the history of this place wasn't *enough* of a nightmare for the Church!

Tarrean *almost* wished he could have just a sip of wine again, but his vows prevented him from such pleasures. The bridge of his nose received another squeeze, the shining metal of the gauntlet not injuring the cultivator in the slightest. A circular *go on* motion of his hands restarted the report. Acolytes and a Keeper were seated around the Head Cleric, pouring over stacked documents. Their gear was far simpler than his, though most of them had a weary expression that matched his own.

A new day was already starting to rise from the horizon, and silence laid on the wreckage that used to be the prominent village of Salt. Beams of sunlight funneled through the gaping holes in the longhouse walls, and a collective grunt heralded eyes being squeezed together to cope with the sudden brightness.

The next recruit in tow cleared his throat; ready to give a near-exact replica of the report with differences based *entirely* on the viewpoint of where he was at the time. Acolyte Tibbins fingered through the vellum to find the beginning of his report, and everyone worked to hold in a sigh as it began.

"As mentioned in the other reports, we found the settlement under *raid* rather than under *siege*. A poorly organized force arrayed itself against us and flung itself on our spears. The consensus I agree with—the intention was for a series of waves to greet us and that the utter lack of coordination altered that to a loose stream of individuals charging into a defensive line. Our casualties were minimal, and according to Acolyte Jiivra's more knowledgeable report on the matter, entirely due to an uncommon venom coating the arrows our squad was attacked with."

"We caught the effects too late since the poison was crystal clear and just made the arrowheads look shiny, which caused affected troops to not pay attention. The majority of the village was on fire before our arrival, and it seems that the idea was to pillage and burn." Acolyte Tibbins drank some water from a recovered local cup and retraced his fingers to where he was on the report.

"Losses for the village are... borderline *total*." The young adult motioned a thumb behind him to the still figures lining makeshift resting spaces along the wall.

"Recovered individuals of note are two old people. The catatonic woman hasn't spoken and was found seated in frozen horror at the head of this very table. As of yet, we have not found an explanation for why the *longhouse* is one of the few buildings not burned to the ground. From the stains on the floor, we can easily put together that people were executed here, but the old lady appeared to have been spared. From the complete inability to communicate, we are guessing that she was made to watch the ordeal."

"This also led us to think that we could not locate the leaders of the raiding force because they were simply not part of the main assault and escaped during the confusion while our forces were tied down with consecutive attacks. Cowardly, to be sure, but there was no doubt of that. We did find carriage tracks, but any more effort on our considerably exhausted forces was essentially impossible. No chase was given."

He flipped a page, took a breath, and continued speaking, "The other individual of note was an old man in a dark blue robe. Keeper Irene found him still breathing next to the body of a deformed man that had a sizable gash in his chest and shoulder. It is the Keeper's opinion that the man was spared due to being partially obscured and having the appearance of someone already dead. His breathing was found by accident when she was prying bodies apart for proper death count."

"Based on the high quality of the cloth, we've concluded that this must be one of the Fringe Elders. So, per the plans of the ecclesiarch, he is likely who we need to speak with pertaining to the *greater effort*. He has as of yet not woken, and while basic aid has been provided, we have no idea what state he may be in when he wakes up. Acolyte," the young adult's eyes bulged, and he needed to take a strained breath as he saw his own name noted, "*Tibbins* is responsible for the wellbeing of the Elder until a positive outcome can be reached."

A pleading look was in the Acolyte's eyes, but his superiors were too laden with their own burdens to reconsider his plight. Defeated without any words, Tibbins continued, "Almost no bodies under burned and collapsed buildings could be recovered. The few we *did* find were indicative of having received crippling injuries rather than directly lethal ones."

He swallowed and rasped out more of the report, "Being burned in their homes was *intentional*. Consensus is that the additional cries of help would distract us from pursuit. To my great regret... I must report that this was a fairly successful ploy, and no actual adults were recovered. However, we found no bodies nor remains of *any* children. With the depth of the discovered tracks, we are of the opinion that the children were *taken* rather than slaughtered."

Vellum rustled as he'd gotten to the bottom of that section, needing to flip to the next page. "Temporary encampments are being erected, as our forces require rest. Morale is low from being so close to the scarred zone, though merchant intelligence indicates it has been locally renamed to the 'Salt Flats'. Updated documentation shows that history past a few hundred years has been entirely forgotten or *wildly* misunderstood."

"Is *it* still dormant?" the tired commander inquired, wanting *that* off his chest *now*, as he hadn't heard this part of the report before.

The Acolyte calmed his worries. "Yes, Head Cleric, the scar is not expanding. The current state of the flats matches the scriptures."

Relief washed over the group.

"Good. It would have been a *horror* if that dungeon woke up again. Can we safely conclude no deaths were on the scar itself?" A different, more wizened Acolyte nodded, *older* vellum embossed with golden text unfurled to compare with fresher notes.

"Yes, Head Cleric, that is correct. No casualties were incurred on the flats, so there is no chance of the calamity coming to pass." The Acolyte received a stern nod from the commander, who chuffed in reply.

"Excellent. While that is good to assume, we must be *certain*. Establish a forward base rather than a temporary encampment. We cannot allow the possibility for these raiders to let misfortune come to pass due to their *blithering* ignorance!"

Tibbins, you're in charge of making the Fringe Elder agree to let us stay here."

"I don't care how *inane* some of the requests may be; the rules are *twisted* in this place, and we need *both* verbal and written consent... as far as I'm aware. So, if he wants to ride a *pony*, fetch the blasted horse! *Don't* come to me with requests for permission; just get it *done*. Bill it to Keeper Irene, have it added to the expenses tally. If it's *truly* egregious you may ask or, better yet, decline. Still... make him happy with us."

The hand of the fifth Acolyte down the bench rose. The Head Cleric snarled at being interrupted, "What is it, Mandell?"

The heavy accent of the Acolyte gave away his centralized heritage. "Sir, I don't understand. Why would a purely celestial dungeon waking be a *bad* thing? The majority of us have major affinities that align! From initial reports, I thought this place would be ideal for cultivation in addition to our daily chants and prayer."

Irene turned to give the Acolyte a leer, but couldn't fault the young man for not knowing. Her tone was motherly, though cutting. "May I, sir?"

The request to her superior was waved off with a, "Do as you please."

Irene's chair *squealed* on the floor as she turned herself to face the recruit. "In ordinary circumstances, yes, you would be correct, Acolyte. Unfortunately, this dungeon doesn't operate under the common behavior we generally expect from dungeons. It does not align with the reports we cross-referenced from the Adventurers' Guild, and even the *scriptures* refer to what happened here in the past as '*The Great Scarring*'."

"This is why we've been referring to the salt flats as '*The Scar*'. This particular dungeon is strange in several ways." She lifted her gloved hand to keep count on her fingers. "The scriptures say that at least a hand's worth of centuries ago, a celestial dungeon awakened here. Not developed slowly; not came from the heavens. It just... *woke up*, and *pop*... it was there."

"Not only was no one ever able to locate the core, but clerics at the time couldn't figure out if it even *had* one. Instead of building in layers, applying clever traps, or adding what we've come to expect as the usual gambit of monsters, those aspects simply *never appeared.* This dungeon only did *two* things, beyond absolutely *ruining* hosts of armies and emptying entire coffers of nations."

All the Acolytes, while tired, had latched on to Irene's words with rapt attention. "The first thing—and the only *confirmable* thing that this dungeon did—was flatten every bit of area it could spread to. On this flattened area, sporadic amounts of highly desirable resources would slowly accumulate as the tides came and went."

"The tide—to this day—remains one of the great mysteries of the Fringe. There is *no* major body of water nearby, and the mapped rivers simply do not provide the amount of water that comes and goes as the scriptures describe. Over the next few days, we will be able to generate an updated account."

"One of the rare Mages in those days described the phenomenon as watching a great beast breathe during slumber. As people died by the droves over the pursuit of scarce, rare resources, the dungeon grew—and grew in *width* only. It snaked across the landscape, and wherever its rising waters touched... the earth slowly flattened to a very *specific* depth. In certain places, it split like the roots of a tree. Up north, the pattern seems designed more like an infection rather than any cohesive pattern, while down south, there's nothing but straight lines and right angles."

A hand rose again, but she was just getting to the point and was sure she would answer the query before it was asked. "The *second* thing the dungeon did—something we're still not *certain* about it actually being responsible for—is a phenomenon that we frequently see in celestial cultivators that don't keep a proper balance."

"Every warrior, *every single one*, who stepped foot on the salt flats... slowly lost their sanity and the ability to see reason. They began claiming the land and resources as *theirs* and seeing themselves as superior regardless of established hierarchy. They also gradually physically withered when they failed to be present on the landscape the scar '*owned*.'"

Irene pointedly motioned to the Elder in the blue robe. "Eventually, you end up looking like *that*. We actually have fairly detailed notes on the subject, which involves internal corruption problems. So, Acolyte Tibbins, please *do* take care to not let his corruption consume him before the Head Cleric has what he needs."

Tibbins nodded with a salute. This part was following orders; he could do that. Mandell still looked confused; he didn't feel his question had been answered. "While that is certainly unfortunate, why would that prevent this area from being a good source of Essence for us to cultivate with? Our prayer certainly provides, but why would already present celestial Essence *not* be beneficial?"

Irene had to think for a moment but was decently certain she had the answer. "It is *very* beneficial. Had there not been a hidden trap that caused people to lose their minds, I would agree with you."

She squeezed the tips of her fingers together. "The issue comes from the *interaction*. By taking, we also give back. Any Essence we fail to refine fully returns to the dungeon. Unlike in a common dungeon, Essence density here is *always* low. A place where additional Essence suddenly depletes because of, say, the presence of a dozen cultivating clerics? Well, that may awaken a cycle we *very* much wish to avoid."

"The scripture is also *clear* that the Core was never found. The scar is vast, and worst of all, the spread of Essence is *incredibly* even. So using the adventurer trick to follow the path where Essence density is thicker to locate the core is *unfruitful.*"

"Scripture says that the Mage in the area proclaimed the dungeon *dormant* rather than dead. Specifically, when its expansion fully ceased after years and years of the Church and the Guild deterring people from entry."

"The region isn't named 'The Fringe' due to some landscaping design. It is named such because this very scar brings someone to the *fringe of sanity.* Delusions of grandeur and grand heroism are recorded to have been declared by cultivators rapidly rising in rank. Their intent to do well and invoke the best for us all was devoured and overshadowed by this place. It is one of the *well-kept secrets* the Church does *not* want the populace to be aware of."

"Could you *imagine* the rumors? That a celestial dungeon, a gift of the celestial above, drives people *insane*? Makes them commit great acts of violence in the name of what they consider to be right? The Church prizes and relies on its relationship of goodwill, its values of great virtue, to remain in the hearts and minds of the people. The Fringe is one of those secrets that has been obscured with misinformation to soothe the minds of those who don't *want* to know. This place isn't on the map because the Church *does. Not. Want. It.* To *be* on the map."

She put her finger down hard on a fat book. "The scriptures complain for an entire *volume* of notes and complaints that not a *single* bastion or permanent stone building could be erected! If there was any semblance that something *important* was here, permanent structures would have given it all away. A *full chapter* is devoted to disgruntled scribes going on and *on* about how movement was constant and tensions were *always* high!"

"Not only did they need to keep themselves from venturing into the scar despite the glint of prizes clearly visible in the distance, but they had to keep everyone and *everything* else out as well. Why do you think we still haven't seen a single monster? Eradication was *widespread*. As you must have clearly noticed just by glancing, the scar is utterly *massive*. The manpower and coordination that took made fully devoted scribes complain. *Fully. Devoted. Scribes*. Were... complaining." She trailed off with a soft sigh.

"I have never seen a scribe complain about *anything* in my decades with the Church, and these are *written* accounts." Her finger repeatedly pressed down *hard* on the volume. The importance of her words was not difficult to discern, even for the tired. Irene leaned forward in Mandell's direction. "Do. *Not*. Cultivate. While. In. The. Scar. Near *might* be fine, but certainly not *in*. Is that understood, Acolyte? All of you, in fact?"

Mandell's stand and snap to attention was textbook. His chair screeched back, and in an instant, he was in the official salute position. "Yes, Keeper, sir!"

The others gave mumbled responses. Irene let Mandell be at ease and return to his seat, handing the reporting back over. "Acolyte Tibbins, please continue."

Tibbins had lost his place on his report vellum and scrambled to find his lines again. The reporting continued for another hour until a fresh recruit announced himself with the news that temporary camp was set up. The meeting was dispersed, and the priests went to rest as a guard rotation of the least exhausted was set up.

The camp was sizable. Four dozen clerics had been housed in tents with only a handful remaining in the longhouse as the construct was not considered structurally sound. As soon as the majority of them had acquired some much-needed rest, the *real* work would begin.

CHAPTER FOURTEEN

The Elder continued rising from the depths of the small coma he had been trapped within.

"You win this one as well, shiny sky orb." The old man kept his eyes closed after stirring from slumber. He had opened them only to find a ceiling he didn't often see. A spike of light sunk right into his sight, and the chorus of complaining voices was wholly unfamiliar. He *sort* of heard most of it but didn't pay real attention—he wasn't able to.

Illusions and ghosts played across his senses, and he instead vividly experienced the memories of past conversations as if hearing them for the first time. He knew all the words of the conversation; he heard the retorts and quips that would lead to some juicy gossip. The giggling of children came and went with the usual swiftness as they swirled across the floor, carried by a haze on an unseen wind. In short, reality fled from his mind.

The unwelcome was truth pushed aside, and the old man's mind found nothing but shards with no idea how to put it all back together. Why bother? His imagined conversations of warm nights and welcoming stew were rudely interrupted by words and flashes that suggested that the village burned down. A pang of discomfort struck the inside of his head, and the old man found it best to relieve the pain by remaining still. Swiftly, long-past conversations and warmth returned with the obscuring certainty of steam. The haze lazily veiled over once more and was welcomed dearly.

"*Losses of the village are borderline total.*" A hollow distortion of the speaking voice reached him. The pang of discomfort returned with greater strength, and the misty haze blew apart as a strong gust sundered it. The laughter in his thoughts wavered, the emotions and ability to express repressed as grief found no foothold on the shattered glass shards in his unwilling mental state.

No, no, no. He didn't want to be *here.* There was just nothing left.

"*The children were taken rather than slaughtered.*" These words rang like a gong through the empty halls of his mindscape, painting chaotic color over and over on unseen walls. *Hope* arrived on screaming wings. The Elder felt overwhelmed. Unreal, ghostly steps approached from the other side of his closed eyelids as again he sunk ever deeper into malaise. A fall ended when you hit the bottom, and for the Elder, that was in a space between madness and self-reflection. It was time to save his mind. It was time to give someone else the reins.

Dizziness struck even though his body was unmoving. The Elder's view altered drastically as he meandered through an imagined hallway of memories. The scenes replayed in sudden flashes, and he fully experienced the images and accompanying scents and tastes. They bombarded against his mind with each additional step. Another step, and another, and one last one were taken before the familiar and comforting rasp of a whetstone reached his ears.

Scrape

A large flame was centered in this stable mental space. Moving towards the burning representation of his will to live, the old man that came into view near the fire had a considerably stronger back—a younger back. *His back,* from many years ago. The large fire licked at the dry, wood-shaped memories in the center, burning through everything with all the time in the world, sampling the flavors of ancient happenings soon to be forgotten.

Many more figures surrounded the fire, and they *all* appeared as younger, more youthful versions of him. All of 'him' was obstructed in a partial or complete, snowy haze that obscured their individual features. They were the reflections of his old self, the blurring corruption on them a representation of aspects long forgotten and traits willfully abandoned. He wasn't those people anymore. Those identities. Not completely.

Scrape

The whetstone personality paused sharpening its weapon, prompting the Elder to step forth and join the circle. He seated himself on one of the many cut stumps as darkness and blackened doors surrounded him. He recognized the whispers coming from behind those chain-closed barriers. They contained all of his regrets. His many, *many* regrets. The doors strained and shook inwards, threatening to burst even as he watched.

"I didn't expect that I would ever use *this* philosopher's trick again," his wordless voice spoke to nobody in particular. He was talking to *himself*, after all. There was no need to explain himself. This place was purely to accept that once again, he'd *failed*. The little crevice in the mind was the best imagined space he could construct to cope and convince himself to try again. You didn't become a philosopher and *not* make tricks to protect yourself from infinite existentialism. When you come to the realization that you know nothing, your world has a tendency to fall apart. There had to be stability, even if it was fabricated.

"*I* can't do this anymore." The current perspective's hands folded together and tearfully sighed, head dipping low in shame. It took willful effort to right himself again. He turned on his stump and faced the next empty seat to relinquish more than a mere question. "Can *you*?"

Slowly and with deliberate intent, a copy of his current appearance formed on the stump. An exact replica of his current voice replied in kind, "I believe *I* can. *I* can find the way."

The original nodded and asked, "Where did *I* go wrong, old friend?"

The copy slowly stood, and the perspective shifted. Focus faded from the eyes of the original and instead saw from the eyes of the new copy. "Nowhere, *Elder*. You did everything right, and we all know well that you can make no mistakes and *still* lose. That's not a weakness or a failure. That's just life."

The abandoned original remained seated on the stump. His time was over, and his mind needed to go elsewhere to move on. "What will you do?"

The new perspective folded his hands behind his back, adopting a slightly hunched posture to answer his own question from the version which had passed the torch. "What we *chose* to do. What we learned over all these years. That we hold to the *ideal*. That we make the decisions we will *not* regret. That we always, *always* hold promises to those dearest to us."

He laid a hand on the Elder's shoulder. "It has been a pleasure and a *privilege* to have *been* you, Elder. I *loved* the life you gave us, free of what we were used to doing."

Another door sprung up and immediately revolted as regrets exploded to life behind it, only to be plastered against the darkness and fade into obscurity. "I am *no longer* an Elder, and I believe I am the first one that will *accept* the regret. Because in this breaking I've realized... *grief* is the price we pay for love."

The Elder nodded at the new perspective and laid out his last question. He was fading, losing active consciousness as the new mentality gained it. "What will you do?"

The fresh outlook rolled his shoulders behind him. "I am going to get my children back if it's the *last* thing I do. It is *high* time we break into the details of an old tidbit we weren't supposed to hear, *old friend*. We can pretend to not be aware of that conversation out there all we want, but those voices are openly talking about Essence. That means they are *cultivators*."

The new perspective shared a knowing look with the version of himself that had paused using the whetstone. "It is high time we discover how they live so *long* and attain that time for ourselves."

The whetstone version of himself smiled like a fox, turning the blade over to show regretful, carved words etched deeply into the other side: '*This good man never goes to war again*'. This version of him had his mind broken in a desert long ago. His doppelganger put the whetstone down, gave a small salute, and proudly closed his eyes. He fuzzed over and began to fade.

The new perspective was adapting, restructuring personality traits and priorities. Major components of the personality of that time were being rejected, obscured, denied. Similar to the personality present from the war, several others became blurry. A few vanished from the bonfire scene altogether as their values and beliefs were fed to the fire, never to be considered in a decision-making process again.

When the new perspective looked back down to the Elder, half of the old man was a sketchy imprint of what it had been. A younger, more vibrant personality had cleared up significantly. His haze near the beginning of the circle was almost fully cleared. It was both necessary and thrilling to possess the blind will to go always forward. "I retreat no more. I hide no further."

"I'm going to need a new name." With a powerful movement of the old man's hand, '*never*' was blotted out and erased from the blade. The new perspective turned and, with unwavering steps, strode away from the bonfire. His voice trembled, then gained an unyielding quality, the core trait from which the fiber of his being was now constructed. "*Again.* Again, we go to war. "

CHAPTER FIFTEEN

The mental space collapsed into kaleidoscopic memories behind him, and every step forward pulled forth ideals, beliefs, and remembrances. This path he now walked was a recollection of all he'd done and was again *willing* to do. Memories knit together, and the new perspective opened his arms wide, walking straight ahead as he took his first step on the path of pain. No more gates to lock his agony behind. Blackened doors burst through their chains, and a deep breath was taken as he affirmed himself.

"I am neither Elder nor old."

"I am the weight of all my experiences and the incarnate will of the path which I now walk."

His hand snatched out and grasped a recent remembrance, slowing only to place the memory of Choppy's death before him. The boy had never deserved that, and it hurt to keep it in mind. Sadness and a clutched heart squeezed the space of his surroundings. With the acceptance of impending suffering, he took a step into the memory to make it part of his being.

Crushing lamentation struck him immediately as he looked to the light, willing himself to leave the convenient lie his mind had constructed to protect his sanity. His real body convulsed, and his eyes snapped open. It was at least high noon by the time he came around, and aged fingers gripped the sheets as the first of many howls rang from his throat. His face was once again stained with tears as he immersed himself in loss.

Survivor's guilt beat him without mercy as he worked his way through the fugue that entrapped him. One last time, the old was relinquished, and someone new was born to carry the torch. He had never ascribed to the idea that a person always remains that same person. People change, *dramatically* even, in times of crisis. He could never understand why others couldn't grasp that this wasn't the slightest bit odd.

He'd seen it *countless* times after a war.

Great loss.

Great grief.

Great love.

It all *changed* people. *How* they thought and what ideals they held. *Who* they were, and how they saw the world. His physical outcry had several clerics by his side in an instant, ready to steady the uncontrollably weeping, old man.

Some had no idea what to do, and others ushered them out of the way as Keeper Irene waltzed her way through and violently waved the rest of the priests off. Her voice was brisk and cutting as she dismissed them. "Why are you all standing around gawking like a foolish bunch of art historians? Fetch me water and fresh cloth! This man is in *severe* shock and requires immediate tending. *Where* is Acolyte Tibbins? Isn't this *his* duty?"

Irene had the old man supportively weeping into her neck while the majority of the thin figure slumped over her shoulder. She clearly had a great deal of experience handling uncontrollably weeping children. Her attentive hushing resounded with gentle care, soothing what in her eyes was just another big baby. She found there to be little difference between the very old and the very young, having had to take care of both.

"Tibbins!" Her words were as welcoming as they were grateful, the bony burden swiftly handed over to the Acolyte. He was soon holding the inconsolable Elder upright. As soon as Irene was free, she gave Tibbins a strong '*it's your problem now*' pat on the shoulder and walked off. Irene might have been good at this, but that didn't mean she *wanted* to deal with it. She had *scriptures* to tend.

Nothing the Acolyte said or did appeared to have the remotest impact. Sure, he succeeded in making the old man drink down some water, but this was an ordeal the young Acolyte still needed to learn to deal with. It took several hours for the heaving to slow down. Only then did Tibbins again attempt to reason with the man, who he was currently convinced was completely out of his mind. Granted, he could not blame the behavior.

"My back hurts," was the first set of cohesive mumbles he heard from the bleary-faced, old man.

"Sir, my name is Acolyte Tibbins. Do you remember yours?"

The old man pathetically groaned in response, "*My back hurts.*"

Tibbins had honestly run out of patience. The taxing hours had taken the goodwill right out of him with the unexpected and unwanted nursemaiding. Still, the man was his charge, so he used those strong cleric muscles of his to lift the aged old log with all the difficulty of bench-pressing a feather. Tired eyes squinted through the sunlight as the old man saw a long set of tents set up in a familiar order. "Ah. *Clerics.*"

He recognized the orderly campsite immediately. It was *meant* to be memorable, after all—the place you run to when you're injured and trying to survive. Each was a higher quality than a common healer's tent. The tent he was carried into, to his great chagrin after his most recent thought, was an *abyssal* common healing tent. Still, the cot he was laid on was significantly better than some sheets on the floor with bedding crammed under it. This was a resting place for the sick and had a much greater degree of comfort to facilitate that rest.

"*Sir*, do you remember your name?"

The old man blinked, taking hold of the words. Recent memories were filtered and parsed. He was a new man after his mental shift at his campfire, so he needed something *new*— something he could hold on to that was neither the ordinary nor similar to any previous *unordinary* name.

"Art..." the old man pushed a hand into his face, kneading skin together, "...Orian?"

He was grasping for ideas based on something vague a womanly voice had recently said. Art... historian? It was always healthy advice to listen to a good woman, and thus, he pulled his ideas from the recent experience and released his face. Expression clearing, he extended a hand in greeting to Tibbins. "*Artorian*. A true pleasure to meet you, cleric but truly unfortunate *circumstances* for it."

A weak smile slowly built upon his aged features, his voice slowly blooming with confidence as it all came together. "Yes. It is decided. My name is... *Artorian*."

CHAPTER SIXTEEN

Head Cleric Tarrean was pleasantly leafing through *real* paper once more in his personal tent. Smooth, crisp, light paper. None of this awful *vellum* for him! When he could get away with finery, he *would*. His polished, ornate armor was a testament to that. Just file such ostentatious tidbits away under some kind of basic need, and you'd find someone willing to cave and sign-off on the expense document.

After all, *he* was the Head Cleric of this expedition! He *deserved* this! It was his right to display his rank proudly, a beacon of righteousness for the Church. As a *mighty* D-rank seven, he was the most powerful cultivator of his entire expedition-wing. Then again, he had also been bestowed with *two* strong affinity channels rather than the pitiful singular one most people could count their blessings to have.

Tarrean took a moment to relish in his continued good fortune. This mission had been tailor-made for him, clearly with divine guidance. His prayer was going to be extra juicy during the noon session to thank the heavens for their abundance. Yes, it was *good* to be Head Cleric.

This was an easy mission in the 'secret' category that carried sizable prestige. He was putting the final scribbled touches on the mission report right now. The majority of the expedition would continue pursuit of the raiders under the watchful guidance of Jiivra. She was always seeking opportunities to prove herself, and this was a decidedly easy one to allow her.

A handful of hand-picked priests would remain behind with him, along with the wounded, to tend to the local situation and safeguard their excellent forward base prospect. In the old age, building was not allowed here.

Such times had passed, and he had such *visionary* plans. Stealing a swift glance at the entrance flap of his tent and finding it secured and closed, he retrieved a piece of vellum liberated from the exhausted raider group that had just *walked* into their weapons. A proper and fully signed, mundane deed of land ownership. The *problem* was, it was signed by someone with very angry hand-script, and that was suspect. If he could not obtain an exact copy from the present Elder, then this document—while prized—was a fake.

Rules were *twisted* in the Fringe. Mana signatures didn't *work* here. It made for an exceptional *mess* in bureaucracy, a piece of land where one could not bind ownership with absolute certainty. He wondered if all locations near celestial dungeons had this problem but quickly shook that from his mind. Celestial and infernal dungeons were *too* dangerous. It was all too well known that they caused wars through their own, seemingly innocuous means. At least *celestial* ones did. He would not spare a thought on what a blasphemous *infernal* dungeon might do to a person.

Extermination was the duty of the day when that Essence type became involved. It bred necromancers, extremists, and... *ugh*, demon summoners. The Head Cleric felt a sour taste in his mouth, and he swiftly bundled the vellum. Back to his precious paper products! If the signature matched, he could outright claim ownership of a chunk of the Fringe. He would *obviously* do so under the protective wing of the Church, but he knew he was destined for grander things.

Tarrean snapped from his distraction, tapping his quill in the inkwell. Let's see. He and the few injured would stay in camp. Tibbins had been assigned *babysitting* duty; he had to stay. Irene was a *must* as Keeper and needed to stay to keep a proper tally of all the goods they were going to find and claim in this village. Jiivra, unfortunately, was getting her chance to be the bigshot; so, squad lead it was. Therefore, that thankfully meant she wasn't going to have a presence in the forward camp.

Did he need any of the others? He *could* do without Tibbins but had no interest in dawdling around a drooling, old fool. He *supposed* he could see to the healthcare of the injured, young priests. It would let them see his own magnanimous value, and their respect for him would rise if he personally attended to them. Yes, that was more than enough to hold down his small encampment.

By *himself*, he was more than a match for anything the Fringe might have in store for him. Without the common threat of beasts, his only real concern was raiders. Wouldn't you know it, that's exactly what the majority of his people were about to set out to take care of for him. His plans were falling into place *perfectly!*

Heavy supplies could be left behind as well; Jiivra always did like her fast attack tactics. She'd appreciate the mention in the report, at the very least. Yes... that would do. Scribbling down some details, the bump of a spear hitting the ground twice outside his tent flap reached his ears.

"*Enter*," the Head Cleric called without looking up.

Tibbins entered the tent, saluted, and waited to be addressed. The Head Cleric drew some finishing lines and then laid down the quill. He addressed the young adult, wondering why he'd been bothered, "Acolyte Tibbins?"

"Sir! The Elder of the village is awake and mostly lucid. Perhaps not quite *stable*–but lucid."

Tarrean clasped his hands together with a smile as he leaned back. "Excellent! You have managed to procure the needed documents from the Elder then?"

Tibbins squeezed his lips into a flat line. "There are a few problems, sir."

"A *few*, Acolyte?" Tarrean's mirth melted from his face like hot butter. He blinked at the younger man. "Not one, not two. A *few*?"

Tibbins nervously swallowed. "Perhaps... allow me to walk you through it, sir. It threw me for a *loop* when I heard it the first time."

Tarrean remained calmly in his seat, ready to hear what was likely going to be the start of a longer than wanted day. Tibbins followed suit, seating himself on the other side of the Head Cleric's desk. "When I tried to confirm if our man in blue was the Elder, he looked at me and asked, 'Would you like me to fetch him for you?'"

That received the appropriate eyebrow raise from the Head Cleric, so Tibbins continued, "So he gets up and fetches *this* cup from the longhouse."

The young man put the wood with the word 'Elder' carved into the poor excuse of a wooden cup on his superior's desk. "He told me, 'There you go. I've brought you the Elder,' and proceeded to calmly shamble back off to the medical tent without a care in the world."

Tarrean rubbed his temples, sighing deeply. "I... see. How... This might be the start to a set of a few more complicated problems. Did you get an answer as to who the woman was?"

At least this he was hoping to get a solid answer for.

"Yes, sir," Tibbins replied, but he still had that incredibly flat-lipped expression. More uncertain news. "In his exact words, 'She's *Nobody*'."

The Head Cleric now matched Tibbins' thin lip-lined expression. He rumbled with a wholesome and yet demeaning monotone voice, eyes locked firmly on the Acolyte, "*Tibbins.*"

"*I know*, sir, I know. I do have *good* news," the Acolyte quickly retorted, his hands waving frantically. Given that there was no response from his superior, he quickly filled the void, "When I asked if there's anything he wanted, all he asked for was some water, a pillow or two, something to write on, and to be told about cultivation so he could indulge in a fantasy while he slept. I imagine he saw the clerics and thought of their Essence as something akin to mystical powers."

"Possibly, he's *idolizing* us. I don't want to jeopardize a useful view like that, even if it is... deceitful." Tibbins did a poor job concealing that he disliked being a liar and didn't want to be one to a gentle old man in the last stages of his life. Tarrean—on the other hand—had a glint in his smile as it spread across his face.

"No, Acolyte, that's alright. *Indulge* the man. Tell him *everything*, and then more and *more* until you're out of things to say. A man that old has no *chance* of doing anything with the knowledge, much less spreading it about all alone in the Fringe. When you're all out of things to say and the old fool still hungers for more to feed his nightly dreams... send him to me. I will do the hard part, Tibbins. I know you're a gentle soul, not forged in war and fury like I was. Ex-adventurer, right?"

Tibbins nodded. "Yes, Sir. F-rank eight."

The Acolyte's expression turned somber. He never made the cut as an adventurer. He never made it to the D-ranks, solidly stuck in the upper Fs. The fishy rank. The failure rank. Tibbins then glimpsed a different path his future could take. "Would you tell me about your cultivation secrets along with the old man, sir?"

The Head Cleric, unfortunately, was ready to crush such a hope, yet found that incentives could be applied here. "I tell you *what*, Tibbins. You're a good soul. You keep that old man interested enough to the point where he comes to ask me things, and I will overlook whatever he might tell you in return. How's that?"

It wasn't direct knowledge, and using the old man like a filter wasn't *ideal*. It did get the required motivation for the Acolyte to stop slacking so much in his care of the Elder. Though he hadn't mentioned it, the old man wore an utterly *dour* expression when he was referred to as 'Elder'. He decided it was best to keep that to himself. "Yes, sir!"

Tarrean nodded and was about to dismiss him from the tent. "Good lad. Before you go, the old man, does he have a name?"

Tibbins nodded. "Artorian, sir."

He saluted and left the tent as the Head Cleric pondered on the name in bewilderment. *Artorian*? What kind of a name was *that*? What region was that from, nay, what *country* or kingdom? A dukedom, perchance? Naming conventions and types changed depending on what corner of the world one was from, but this... was out there. He shook it off and decided he didn't care. With the Acolyte motivated to take care of his charge, it meant one less thing on his plate and more time for... *other* pursuits.

Tibbins arrived at the medical tent with some pep in his step and heard some warm laughter from inside before he ever moved the flap. Ducking his head in before pushing through fully, he saw one of the wounded soldiers nearly hacking up a lung with a helpless smile on his face, strongly hitting his knee while the old man sat there with hands folded, plainly self-satisfied.

"What happened?" Tibbins' voice was full of bewilderment.

"Oh, just a *harmless* joke," Artorian answered with pleasant mirth, his eyes lazily moving to look at Tibbins. The particular method in which the old man had replied to the Acolyte made another snorting fit assail the laughing, injured priest.

The Acolyte composed himself, or tried to, as he felt the old man's gaze. No, no that's not what it felt like. Tibbins didn't feel like he was being looked at; it felt like he was being looked *through*, as if there was an object behind him that the old man was inspecting instead. The gaze felt awfully *familiar.*

Had his charge possessed Essence, he would have thought his meridians might be under inspection, but the old man clearly wasn't using Essence. It *might* be a good idea to have a proper look at him after Irene's warning. "Right. Well, I've the go-ahead from the Head Cleric to indulge you and answer your questions concerning cultivation. I must warn you, I'm no expert. Give me a moment to look at your Center, and we'll begin."

The laughter behind Artorian sputtered to a halt as the peanut gallery noticed the ten-yard stare their technically-superior-officer was dropping into. "No, Tibbins! *Don't!*"

CHAPTER SEVENTEEN

Cleric Tibbins was confused but dismissed the warning. He was *evaluating* one old man, not something that was exactly hard to do. "It's not dangerous unless he is far stronger than I am, and I have the Head Cleric's permission. What's he going to do with cultivation knowledge with his age and condition? It'll make for a pleasant dream at best."

Still, the wounded priest was shaking his head '*no*' and crossed arms while waving it off... *begging* the Acolyte *not* to look at Artorian's Center. Cleric Tibbins paid no heed, cycling Essence to his eyes.

"Artorian, please do sit still, so I can... so I can..." Tibbins was *lost*. He could barely comprehend what he was looking at. Corruption to be *sure. So. Much. Corruption.*

Unexpectedly, it wasn't all one kind. It was an awful, *hectic*, chaotic mixture that churned and moved through the old man's system with the combinations of a raging river, volcanic diffusion, howling storm, and holy light. This corruption didn't sit still at *all,* and that made *no* sense. Corruption didn't *budge* even if you wanted it to. Heavens above, the majority of the cultivation process *relied* on *preventing* corruption because it stifled and stymied progress. That the old man had so much of it was certainly no surprise. He was old and weak enough to fall dead on the spot.

"How are you *alive*?" Tibbins freaked out slightly as he processed the view.

"I *warned* you!" the quip snapped from behind Artorian, but the wounded commentator went ignored. Tibbins held his sickened head. Watching the display of living corruption tumble about inside the old man like a field that never stopped being plowed.

Artorian crossed his arms in defiance. "Young man, that is *quite* rude. *Explain yourself.*"

"I... I just." Tibbins halted his Essence sight. He was the one that needed to sit on the medical bed.

He stole another glance at the injured priest behind the old man, who was also trying to sit more upright. "Hey don't look at me, *Acolyte.* I'm an Initiate of lower rank than you. I can use a spiral, keep it going, and use Essence on my eyes. That's *all.*"

"Okay. *So.*" Tibbins didn't like this. He held his own hands and looked at them, then back up at the old man. "Do you by chance already know what Essence, Corruption, and a Chi spiral are?"

Artorian shook his head 'no'. Tibbins held his chin. "Well, the Church has a *skewed* interpretation. I also have a strong feeling that, if I tell you *that* version, you wouldn't be too happy with it. Before I was an Acolyte, I was an adventurer for a short while. That really just means I didn't make it past the probation period. I'm an F-rank. *Right!* I need to explain *that,* as well."

"So, everything is made from Essence. Think of it as the smallest thing that everything else is put together from." Tibbins motioned all around him. He had to pause, but the Elder gave him the '*move on*' wrist motion.

"You understood that?" Tibbins quirked an inquisitive eyebrow.

"Young man, I'm *aged,* not dumb. I'd even occasionally call myself clever. Keep talking, and I will stop you when I get stuck on something. What you've told me so far, well, I already guessed. Just not with the terms you're using."

Tibbins raised his hands in defeat. "I'll repeat what my instructor at the Guild told us. Though he only told us once. Everything begins as the purest energy, the stuff the universe creates other things out of. This energy either comes *from* or flows *through*—I'm not certain which it is—the heavens and the earth. When it does, the heavens and the earth turn that energy into the universal basic elements."

The background Initiate filled in, "Rocks and stuff."

Tibbins gave him a leer and resumed, *"Essence* is what this universal energy is called before it's a particular '*stuff*'. Corruption is almost like Essence, but it's more a side effect of the purest energy being turned into universal basic elements. We think..."

Tibbins staggered for a moment, trying to think of better examples. "The word you're looking for is byproduct, my son."

"Yes, that!" Tibbins snapped his fingers at the old man with a smile. The Acolyte continued, "Everything takes in Essence so long as it lives. Doing so makes something such as a plant larger, healthier, stronger, and in general, more powerful in comparison to its counterparts. Unfortunately, corruption is also taken in along with Essence. The more corruption you embody, the more likely you are to die of something when you accrue age. For people with high earth corruption, these are generally events like heart attacks."

Artorian patiently didn't respond and queried when the Acolyte paused, "Earth? As in from the 'Heavens and the Earth'?"

The injured man behind the old man shook his head as Tibbins course-corrected. *"No, no,* the *basic* Essence types. There's six! Even I know that one. Fire, earth, water, air, celestial, and infernal. Almost all people who are clerics have celestial affinity channels. By which I mean that celestial-type

Essence is what we naturally draw in more of. Even *I* was told that affinity channels come in four official types."

"Closed, Minor, Major, and Perfect. Perfect doesn't often occur *naturally*. There's also clogged and ripped, but they're never something you want. Ripped, well. R.I.P. indeed," Tibbins sadly stated.

Before he could continue, the injured man interrupted again, "Closed and clogged are considered the same for the purposes of Essence draw. Nothing of that type gets into your system. Clogging tends to happen during certain illnesses. As odd as it may seem, *not* having Essence is a very quick way to die, especially if you need a certain type and can't draw it in. Though that's only a problem when you start doing more with it and become dependent, I'm told."

The injured man quieted after realizing that he'd hijacked the explanation. Tibbins was giving him another stern, castigating glare. "Is Mr. Broke-His-Leg *quite done*? A minor Essence channel means you draw in very little; a Major Essence channel means you draw in a sizable amount. While we're talking *passive* draw so far, it becomes a very different story when someone begins *active* cultivation."

Tibbins got a set of nods as a reply. "When it happened to me, I would say I'd describe it as being shown that I was drawing energy from a bucket full of water. Then that bucket was in a river. If I removed the bucket and just drew on the river water, much more came to me."

It wasn't too hard for them to distinguish passive from active differences if they considered the amount of water involved. "Essence forms together in complex ways. If two or more Essences come together to form something else, we call it a *higher* Essence or a *compound* Essence. It makes the more complicated stuff. Water and air make mist. Mist is a higher

Essence. Fire and earth make lava, also a higher Essence. It becomes far more complicated than that—such as anytime celestial gets involved—or more than two Essences are at play. That's not for right now."

"People who actively use the energy of the heavens and the earth are known as *cultivators*. We take the raw energy of what's around us and use it to reinforce ourselves, speeding up the process of natural growth. Instead of letting time do the work for me, I'm putting effort into accelerating the process. It can be... *painful*." Tibbins winced at the thought of when he first began. Heavens, preparing for cultivation had *hurt*.

"Every cultivator has this required Essence-refining technique—which is a fancy way of saying we figured out a trick that lets us feel, control, see, and interact with Essence. The first part of the technique—after figuring out how to do all that—is to make what's called a Chi spiral. This *spiral* is responsible for pulling in passive Essence at a much faster rate. More importantly, it helps store and refine while rejecting corruption."

The background priest shuddered, pulling a blanket around himself for comfort. "Absorbing tainted Essence is terrible for a person since any amount of corruption limits the available space a cultivator has to work with for the Essence he pulls in. Lots of corruption means you can kiss your Essence-refining progress goodbye. Usually, corruption in the body is pasty, thick, and doesn't look like it wants to move."

"I don't know what's going on with you, but *your* corruption looks like a living storm. There is a thing that cultivators can do early on called Essence cycling, and we can move the energy around to enhance the ability of an organ. Usually, this means the eyes since doing that lets us see Essence and corruption in others. Fairly easy." Tib made an unpleasant, circular motion at the old man's stomach, then paused as Artorian moved to sit on his cot.

"I don't hear a particularly big difference between '*a heaven*' and '*an earth*'," Artorian stated as he sat, having been told too much about his personal unpleasantry.

The cleric in Tibbins wanted to explode, but he kept his collected calm. "The earth is what we stand on. However, it refers to the planet we are on as a whole. The heavens are..."

He made hand motions to the sky as if presenting it to someone for the first time. "All of that, out there. The space for things beyond. Without putting a cleric spin on it."

Artorian sassily agreed, "You've *wonderful* insight. I would take *poorly* to the religious rhetoric."

Tibbins mockingly copied the sass, "Apologies, Artorian, but by the time someone is *your* age, you can tell who *is* and who is *not* religious—with *no* hope of turning that to the correct avenues."

Artorian appreciated the understanding. The young adult was correct and so moved on to the next question, "So, Essence makes stuff, and *that's it?*"

The Acolyte wavered. "Not... *quite?* This is a little more complicated."

Artorian challenged with a roll of the shoulders, popping his neck. "*Try me.*"

Tibbins decided to fight and die on his hill. He was going to give the best explanation he could possibly make. "So, when Essence becomes *a rock*, the rock then starts giving off earth Essence. Not much, but it does. In that sense—what Essence makes—it then also makes more of. I don't mean rocks make *more* rocks. I mean the basic element of earth makes rocks, and then the rocks provide the basic element of earth."

"The more *something* of a *particular Essence* you have in an area, the more plentifully available Essence will be. So being in a volcano means you are surrounded by a constant assault of fire and earth Essence. Water cultivators tend to submerge to the neck in a body of water in order to draw in their appropriate Essence." There were gentle motions of understanding. More of one means more of the other. Not difficult.

"A complication happens when higher Essences become involved. If you have both an earth *and* a celestial affinity, you can draw Essence through both of those. Unfortunately, it's less important that you *can* and more that you *have* to do so." Tibbins received some frowns but continued.

"Your body has spent its whole life depending on that combined Essence, and taking it in with *improper balance* leads to *massive* increases in corruption. So, we can't just try and draw in energy from anywhere. It *has* to match us. Fire and water might require steam, but it might also be fire-brandy alcohol or a finer gas. Combinations *complicate*. Just '*the right coupling*' isn't good enough anymore for *some people*. That only gets worse as *more parts* become involved. Three is a *nightmare*. Four..." The fringe Elder grimly exhaled. He was starting to grasp the problem.

"Since you now already know that cultivators *need* Essence to survive at a certain point, this can become a big problem. If we *spend* any, we have to replenish it. Good news! Essence takes years and *years* to deplete on its own. Reaching the higher ranks of cultivation also makes this take *longer*. The progress aspect my Guild instructor droned on and on about out of spite was that *more* affinity channels mean *faster* progress and *fewer* bottlenecks. However, it also means higher chances of gaining corruption since you have a higher chance of drawing in something that *isn't great* for you."

Artorian quipped as he did before, just to keep the jumpy Cleric on his toes, "So, Essence always becomes the *same* thing?"

The Acolyte shook his head 'no'. "Ah, so, I think there are two ways it can go? The first is that Essence will gather and over time and *randomly* make what its inherent properties would normally generate—something that *matches*. The second is that an identity is embedded into the basic energy, and that then *makes* a rock. When the pure energy of the universe dilutes to basic Essences, it gains an '*identity*', though that also corrupts the Essence. Again, we filter out this corruption using our cultivation technique—the Chi spiral—to refine it back into a state of greater purity. Does that help?"

Artorian pensively brushed his hand along his long beard. He had entirely different ideas for what he was hearing but was quickly approaching the stage where he absolutely needed bed rest. "I have some ideas on things, but I won't know for certain until I understand more. To begin, why were you all so shocked when you cycled this Essence to your eyes? I'm the only one here that doesn't know. Second, how do you gain the basic awareness of Essence?"

Tibbins rubbed the back of his arm in severe discomfort. "You have... if I had to guess, *four* major types of corruption in you, and they are wreaking *havoc*. This also means that you likely have..."

He needed to steady himself, taking a deep breath. "*Four* major, naturally occurring affinity channels."

Water spat past several beds in disbelief by the injured background priest. "*Four*? No wonder you mentioned you didn't know how he was still alive! I thought it was just going to beat you with the nausea stick."

Tibbins waved away the shouts and turned his attention to Artorian. "May I ask how old you are?"

The old man retorted, "Certainly, *almost* fifty."

Well that made sense, they supposed. "Artorian, have you been told you look *eighty*, if not *ninety*?"

"By rude clerics, yes. Only very recently, though." The old man laid himself down on the cot. "Saying it won't make me feel any younger my boy. I quickly grow weary. For doing very little today, I am quite drained."

Tibbins noted it down, including that he *dodged the question*. "You're slated for significant bed rest, given your condition and corruption base. I hope that our knowledge has given you some thoughts for pleasant dreams. Per your second question, it involves looking inwards, feeling shifts that are *not physical* move within and then grasping them with your mind and will. However, you're not *willing* the Essence to your desires; I would call it being convincing instead? There's no dialogue to be had with Essence, so it's not the easiest comparison."

The Acolyte broached a difficult topic, "Most of us also went through a procedure that... I'm *sorry*, Artorian, won't be available to you. There's a way to pull corruption *out* of a person, but it risks pulling your life out as well. You're in no condition to have even a *sliver* taken. It would just all be over, and the Guild would *flay* me for trying without direct supervision if we began something like that."

"There are ways to also be given a cultivation technique, so you just know what to do. However, that's limited to those with *significant* funds or Guild access. Even if you had the funds, we're in the Fringe. None to be bought. Not that I've *ever* seen one for sale."

A tired-looking Artorian nodded with languished effort. "Tell me of your spiral whilst I fall asleep."

Tibbins sighed but obliged, "My spiral is a thread of Chi, essentially Essence that I *shaped*. It's called a spiral because it spins and spins, separating Essence from corruption and letting ever more refined Essence remain in my Center. A Chi spiral in the body feels like it is beneath the heart, almost against the spine—near the center of the body. However, once you're able to visualize your Center and step into that space, it looks more as if you're in a big nothingness. Corruption is easy to see and difficult to work with."

Tibbins was interrupted by the injured background priest, but the man wasn't wrong, "You mean *impossible* to work with."

Artorian still kept his eyes slightly open. "Mhmm. It just... spins?"

The Acolyte ignored the Initiate and kept up the explanation, "It spins in a very *specific* way and at the best speed I can manage while keeping the technique *stable* enough for it to do what it should. All the Essence is directed into my Center, where it is *refined* and then stored in my spiral. The *most* refined Essence I let seep into my body, which can more efficiently store the energy instead."

Tibbins stole a glance, noting the old man was still awake. "The older you start cultivating, the *less* Essence your body is able to store. My spiral refines drawn-in Essence, preventing corruption from being absorbed. I do have *some* corruption the Guild couldn't get out with the Beast Core. I threw it up too early, and some got left behind. That little *bit* of corruption is responsible for keeping me *stuck* in the F-rank—or failure-rank, as it's called by many."

Tibbins stopped, the old man was frowning. "What?"

Artorian lolled his head from left to right. "*Prevented*, not *purged?* You can't push the existing corruption out using your spiral?"

Tibbins almost had a laugh, stopping himself. "No, no *spirals* can't do that. That's why it's such a constant chore to keep on top of things with refining. Now, there are different kinds of techniques, and I've heard Royals have the best ones, methods that are a hundred times more potent—if not a thousand times—compared to the little Chi spiral I have going on. Our superior—the Head Cleric—is in the middle or late D-ranks, so he has managed to turn his spiral into a *fractal*."

The old man was at risk of waking back up. Tibbins could tell by the visible reaction he'd gotten from throwing that information out. He soothingly slowed and continued, "A fractal is a more advanced and evolved version of the basic spiral. It can do everything I can do, just an unknown amount of times better in every respect."

Tibbins started to get nervous, and ah, yes, there it was. More questions. Drat. He'd hoped the soothing segway would have gotten the Elder to slumber.

"How do I do that, my boy?" The thin line of 'I don't want to deal with this' almost squeezed out of Tib's lips.

"I..." He didn't bother looking at anyone, momentarily very interested in the floor. "It's not good for me to tell you this... but there is really no point in hiding it. Making a cultivation technique takes *years* even with a master helping you, and then you'd make progress only *after* the corruption has been stripped out of you. Nobody can do anything with that sloshing mess mucking around *uncontrolled* inside of their Center."

"I have *all* the time in the world, my boy. Have some *faith*, cleric. Nothing but rest, a good lad to take care of me, some good souls for company and stories, and all the time I would want for this cultivation business." Artorian chuckled gently. The nearly asleep, mumbling man retained his smile. "I'll think of *something*. Before I close my eyes... what affinities do I have?"

Tibbins still wore his trademark thin line expression, disbelieving the very words he was about to say. "Fire, water, air, and... *celestial.*"

Yup. Still couldn't believe it. The bestial snore that erupted from the resting figure let him know the old man had checked out. Tibbins couldn't *wait* to make himself scarce. This was *awful.* He was giving an old man false hope and knowledge that was useless so his superior could gain something. This wasn't how the *Church* should operate. He kicked an apple after crossing a small stream he'd slipped in. Soaked in salty Fringe water, he stared at the fallen fruit as some cogs turned in his head.

An unnatural influence struck him. Thinking a distraction would be good, he stomped to the orchard and pushed up his sleeves. If he was going to have a bad day, he was going to have a bad day with apple pie. He'd wanted to cook for weeks, and the sudden drive spurred him forwards. If there was one thing Tibs could do, it was *cook*!

CHAPTER EIGHTEEN

Artorian would say he was having terrible dreams—except he was very much awake, and they *weren't* dreams. His perception dabbled in a deep void, boundless... yet confined.

The masses of... he was going to call it *filth*, twisted around in a sickening cascade of colored maelstroms. The hues outright *refused* to settle or get along with their counterparts. Only the brightest component seemed as if it was particularly distanced from the other three yet, in some way, fully inherent in all of them. It didn't remain that way for long as all four 'corruptions' swirled about inside what must be his '*Center*'.

Artorian had been given beyond-adequate information in order to start constructing what was likely a more accurate tale than the *loaded* words his young priest had provided him. While finding the Essence may be impossible for the moment, he also had no need to focus on it. He had something far more wild and unruly to observe. Artorian likened it to a moving stomach ache, an itch behind the sternum that couldn't be satisfied.

Whatever corruption was, it was part of him, and it made him think and feel in vastly different ways depending on which bit of it was on top. Even then, chunks of corruption vanished into holes otherwise invisible, spilling free from other directions that coincided with some of the common pains he felt travel around his organs. Discomfort was awfully *easy* to track. Having been provided a mental sketch of what to look for, Artorian was informed enough to construct the basic idea. It had taken him an hour of not-feeling—just lying and *being*—to follow the discomfort and pain.

He'd occasionally felt the empty void behind the sternum but never thought much of it until now. The wandering pain always stopped to gather below the heart and near the spine, but it diminished there so he'd previously considered it a minor boon and reprieve from suffering. He'd never have noticed that *specific* location if it hadn't been pointed out or been concerned about its significance.

The mental gymnastics needed to understand how to inwardly self-reflect was not all that complicated. Especially given he had such solid proof that others were already doing it on a far more advanced scale. Since proof of concept had long since passed, what he was doing amounted to playing catch up, or at least, that's what it would seem like he was doing to everyone else. Self-reflection was to quietly think about what you've done, why you did it, and if you liked the outcome so you could do something else next time if you didn't.

Inward-reflection was like being in the building of self-reflection and going to the basement. It involved sinking into the mind rather than sitting at the table atop which one organized their 'did stuff' papers. At first, the vast emptiness seemed endlessly deep. A void of depression and bleak pulling sensations from the beyond haunted you there. It wasn't uncommon for people to avoid it, but he had no such luxury. Within this mental vacancy, even a minor distraction resulted in a great cacophony, so strict was the sensitivity to the otherwise unnatural.

Artorian had certainly not found Essence, no. *Corruption*, on the other hand, made its presence known with all the subtlety of a drunk, opinionated significant other. Four of them in his case and all equally unwilling to compromise or back down in their thrashing outrage. Artorian didn't try to interact with the corruption; he just watched. It took maybe a few minutes to understand why his heart hurt at random or parts of him ached. The majority of the massed corruption was quite literally in that part of his body at the same time he felt the unpleasantry. That gave him some good, correlating information to work with.

Psst.

"Hey," the hushed, whispering voice of the Initiate that had constantly interrupted Tibbins peeped up, trying to remain quiet. "You awake?"

Opening a cautious eye, the academic squinted into the darkness. There was nothing to see but replied in whispered kind, "Hard to sleep after that lecture. I think you may have annoyed that Acolyte, my friend."

Even without being able to see, the motion in the dark of a comment being waved away was telltale. "I'm Kota, and he should have known better. I'm an aspiring scholar and couldn't help myself. My stint in the ecclesiarch is temporary. I'm not going to be cleared for additional duty anyway. My cultivation is stuck. Spat the corruption-siphon out too soon, so I'll never leave F-ranks. You mind a question?"

It was never a bad time for scholastic lore for Artorian. "Pull that bowstring and fire away."

Kota bundled up in the dark. "Did the basis of how the Acolyte explained Essence and corruption seem... odd? Indicative of a stark viewpoint? I'm holding this 'Guild' in scrutiny. Tibbin's explanation had been colored by a perspective that—all things being consistent—was either incomplete, inadequate, or wrong on a fundamental level."

Artorian nodded in the dark, then verbally confirmed, "Indeed. Corruption by itself seemed to be vastly misunderstood if the explanation given was the general understanding of the 'corruption stuff'. If everyone got rid of it right at the beginning and did all they could to keep it out and away from them, then efforts in understanding are not going to be too fruitful, are they?"

He had a different theory already in the works. "Based on the initial explanation, Essence is mutable, adaptable... changeable. Corruption, as described, is just a misunderstanding. Instead, would it be that which Essence was *not?* The immutable, the unchangeable. Both of these concepts have some identity already applied to them in order to give them these defining aspects."

Kota responded with what he had in mind to try and help, "If it's anything like ordinary refining, I imagined corruption as sand being shaken through several sieves with holes of decreasing sizes. Everything that falls through qualified as a particular grain that could be known and identified based on which sieve corruption could move through, while the 'stuff' originally added in the sieve was an unknown energy of a categorically higher purity. I have a water channel, and all my corruption is liquid. So, when Tib said it was supposed to be *solid...* that threw me."

Necessity demanded Artorian return to the academy one of these days; his theorems on Essence needed recording. On one hand, you had 'the stuff' that was intended to change, intended to be worked with, intended to be given form either by inaction or the action of an outside will. On the other, you had 'the stuff' that refused *all* of that. The difference appeared to be the one type of stuff knew what it was and didn't want to change, while the other didn't and changed happily. The lynchpin there must have been the presence of identity. Luckily, he knew a thing or two about that topic.

"I think it may heavily have to do with what the energy *thinks* it is. There are some requirements to assigning identity if Tibbin's example on rocks is to be believed. I'm of the current opinion corruption is merely that which could no longer change. Its properties are set, and all it wants is to settle and simply *be*, refusing all change from within or without. Anything it applied to would be forced to take their qualities rather than the other way around. I've got some proof of this."

Kota shifted to sit up in his cot. "How are you putting this together so fast? He told you a scant few hours ago. You shouldn't be able to even find your Center yet."

Some pride fueled the academic. "My boy, this just happens to be something I'm exquisitely skilled at. I compose philosophy like a seasoned bard strums a lute. The Acolyte earlier told me enough basics for me to figure it out. I spent years of my life trying to pick the universe apart. I failed, only to have new building blocks fall into my lap, the missing pieces of an existential, cosmic puzzle. This topic is one of the things I live for, and I have scoured scrolls for the most esoteric of tidbits in search of my answers. For a boy who spent the majority of his life with his head in the clouds, this is child's play. Here, I'll explain what I mean."

His pillow propped him up, and it was getting difficult to whisper. "There are several corruptions running rampant in me, and they're easy to find. They cause my pain and grief. When the redder corruption stuff was in my stomach, I feel it burn. The various shades of blue strike my sinuses, and I have a sniffly, sneezy nose. When the flighty variant is abundant near my organs, I feel those agonizing air bubbles. Those are some of the individuals. Mixed masses remain in my wrists. My fingers uncontrollably tremble as result, and *abyss,* do my bones hurt. When it passes through my head, I have a migraine. Such seems to be the observable nature of corruption."

Kota took the listed examples and found they matched things he'd heard. "Do you think the knowledge intentionally hidden, or do people simply not know due to inherent bias and rejection? Certainly, this stuff is terrible to have inside of you, and knowing about it honestly makes it worse."

Artorian stifled a grumble, as that was true. What also did not help was that currently, he had no method of influencing or altering this sloshy, wild, childish, chaotic energy. A thought struck him. Acolyte-boy had said *convincing*, not 'willing'. This was getting him nowhere at this point, and he shook himself from his looping thoughts.

Hmm.

"Probably, but let's consider something else. Why would Essence need an identity at *all*? There's nothing wrong with simply *being*. However, even if something is different, you cannot differentiate if you don't also have terms that show this."

The aspiring scholar extrapolated, "So, *language* is a necessary component?"

Artorian pondered that and swiftly reached agreement. "Let's take the route that it is. If Essence is incapable of *being* by itself, there likely would be no earth to walk on or air to breathe."

Kota shot a quick confirmation query, "'Being' as in existing independently?"

Mhm!

Artorian had long wondered why humans existed or where they come from, a common existential query. Could it simply be that Essence formed us over a long process of randomization, and once we were formed and intelligent, we began to do the rest? He considered the defining feature of a human to be its ability to self-reflect.

"Language requires creatures smart enough to make one, use one, define one. So, what then were things called or known as before the first language-users walked the dirt? Likely, such concepts didn't even exist, unless there's something other than a human with human-like ability to think, reason, and reflect. If not more-than-human."

Kota cut him off there, "That's speculation. Let's stick with what we know."

The old man grumbled a touch, but the young man had the right of it. He returned to their prior topic, "Essence is meant to induce change and means to be *malleable*. Why would a world give its creatures the toys of the universe to craft with? The cosmos is allowing identities to be shaped and reshaped until you have corruption, which is so *fully* certain of the exact thing it is that it refuses to be anything else."

He considered a child, and a light blazed into being in his thoughts. "If the universe *itself* was still learning and trying to set identities... what better way than to let an entire species of sentient good boys and girls do it for you? If humans are good at anything, it most certainly is bickering and argument. Having other minds do your consistency checking for you is very helpful in setting a stable order. Abyss, it's the entire point of peer-review when it comes to releasing scholarly articles!"

The Initiate liked that and continued in the same vein, "The immutable is likely that which the universe has decided it is content with. That which needs no further change. So, corruption is immutable or unchangeable because it is something the universe does not *want* changed further."

"Possible!" Artorian was sleepy but excited. He half-woke some of the others nearby; that had been too loud. Dropping back to a whisper, "Let's work with it as that and alter it if we run into a fact wall. Let's hold to the theory that corruption is likely set this way, due to the base structure of pre-existing creation being reliant upon it!"

Kota pulled the blanket over him, curling back up now that his thoughts had settled and the question was answered. Even if it left him with several more. "Let me think on it and come discuss it later. I need sleep."

Artorian's hands quietly wrenched together as he dropped into his Center. This was certainly *quite* the experience. Not only did he know he was awake, but he also knew the rough location of where he was in his body. All of this was using a part of his mind he'd not properly used before, which made for a new and exciting experience. If *everyone* could do this, it meant the body came pre-equipped with the ability to do this particular kind of thing; otherwise, it would not be able to do it at all. Still... it was new to *him* and enjoyable.

Artorian observed for a while longer before the edges of this view began to dim. He'd fallen asleep while in his Center, but it didn't appear to fully let him. Mentally pulling back, he returned to the perspective his eyes were used to seeing as the blurry tarp of a medical tent returned to his view. That was enough for now. The plan was simple, but it had some flaws.

Live.

Save the children.

To do that, he had to survive long enough to see that through and be powerful enough to get it done in the first place. First problem: at the current rate, he had a season to live.

Second problem: major affinity channels. He had *four* of the buggers, and it already sounded like just *two* made it quite complicated for any sort of progression. So, he had to find something that provided all four of his affinity channels with sustenance—at the same time—while rejecting already accrued immutable Essence. Not merely deterring new immutable aspects from entering but expelling what was already present.

Given what he'd seen of it so far, that wasn't happening anytime soon, was it? He listlessly laid on his cot, pondering as the injured priests snored around him. His mind wandered over to them. From his understanding of the explanation, they all cleared their Centers and were now using Essence via a technique. He suspected this was a term that saw wide use over a variety of topics that didn't have better descriptions.

Artorian did not have any such thing to work with as of yet. Just the swarming, soapy mass that fought itself like a clump of spiteful cats. Even now, he was aware of it roiling around near his liver, a newfound downside of additional awareness. As soon as he'd discovered his Center and the absolute mess within it, he'd found he could no longer ignore it. Nor could he make the flow of information cease. Center-awareness was a new sense loudly announcing the minute movements of where severe discomfort was going to strike next.

The young priests didn't appear to be having that issue, so it must be isolated to corruption. In his eyes, they too were all just children. In truth, he was just glad to have someone to talk with. Still, the youngsters had said some odd things. He'd get clarification on the terms later, but there was a mention he just couldn't get out of his mind as it meandered.

Artorian mumbled the words out loud, "How are you *alive*?"

CHAPTER NINETEEN

"Well I'd say I'm not clever, but I am hardy," a feminine voice replied from the corner, one of the young clerics who had been injured in the fray.

Apologetic breath inhaled so his words could tumble out in a hush. "Oh, I'm terribly sorry, my dear. I didn't mean to wake you. Just mumbling to myself."

There was a moment of silence, but he could hear the woman sit up and hiss, sucking air through her teeth as she pushed through the pain of her injury. He didn't need to see the cringe to feel it. "I can't rest with these lumberjacks sawing through forests in their sleep."

One of the boys snored deeply right in the middle of her mention. She didn't seem the talkative type, but people don't sit up and chime in if they didn't want some company.

"I'm Artorian. Who might you be, my dear?" His sleepy question rasped in the back of his throat.

Her voice sank. "Don't laugh."

The aged words promised with sudden clarity, "I will not."

A small peep winced in her throat, but it continued even as she slightly shrunk away. "Yvessa."

Artorian rhetorically mumbled, "Why would someone laugh at such a lovely name?"

Yvessa peeped out the reply like it was practice, complete with a fully dejected sigh, "The boys keep telling me it means 'ugly idiot' in Elven."

Artorian thought that wouldn't do at all and came up with something on the spot. "Are you certain they speak Elven, my dear? That's not what it means at all."

With a shift, he rolled away from her, the side of his cheek pressing to a not-as-soft-as-he'd-like pillow. To Artorian's lack of surprise, Yvessa's voice brimmed with interest, "D-do you know what it means?"

Her pitch gained the same interested rise that his well-beloved younglings had when learning about something they were interested in. "Oh, I'm just an old fool, my dear. I would have said that it means 'to bloom out of great drought'. If I spoke Elvish, perhaps I would also tell you that it's reserved for people able to overcome great difficulty and trial, who not only come out successful—but better than they were. To bloom, as it were. Regardless of the sapped circumstances one found themselves in."

He shrugged in his cot, lifting his hand to the air to let it drop on the axis of his wrist. "But what do I know?"

Yvessa flushed. She pushed back down under her covers, gritting her teeth to kill the sound of discomfort her injuries caused her. Her voice peeped from under the blanket. "That... that's a nice thought... Thanks."

"Do you consider yourself to be in a great drought?" he chimed out, ignoring a bear-like snore from the upper side of the medical tent.

Yvessa's dull reply sounded somber, "Can that describe my life? It sort of does. I'm always at the end of my rope somewhere. How else would I get wrangled into this mess and end up in a place where there isn't even a map? Nobody believes in me."

"*I* do." Artorian didn't indulge her self-loathing. "Also, my dear, I look forward to seeing you bloom."

She felt like she was missing something here, and scrutiny pulled her through. "You're not... a cleric. Why are you in the camp? Civilians aren't allowed to stay overnight in expedition camps."

Artorian shrugged. "Well, since I believe in you, I suppose I'm *nobody*."

Her ire gathered. She could almost feel the warmth of it fill her cheeks. The old man put effort into sitting up and turned to face her. "My dear, I believe in you because even though you're injured, you're alone, and it seems like you have no one to rely on... you're still here in the medical tent, and you're trying to live. So, something inside of you has decided that it doesn't *want* to give up. That you don't *want* to quit. That you don't *want* to die. Even if you have little to live for, you're giving yourself the chance to find something worthwhile enough to really hang your coat on."

Artorian straightened as he spoke. "It's clear you're not with the Church because you're a particularly devout believer, or you would have started reciting scripture already. You're not here for them. You're here for *you*. That you think the situation is to blame is unfortunate, but honestly, it is the wrong question to consider. The situation is irrelevant. What you do and how you choose to do it... is all that matters. Since you have chosen to pick yourself back up from the dirt and keep trying to live..."

The old man pointed at her, determined and certain. "I believe in you, and I believe you can do it. Because there is simply nothing—and I mean nothing—wrong with the idea that it's alright for you to believe in yourself just for wanting to put one foot in front of the other for one more day. So, if you're struggling, and you don't believe what your body is telling you is true. Then, my dear, I will tell you I believe in you. Because I do, and you can do it. If ever you falter in that belief, by the heavens, you come bother me. I will remind you."

His arms crossed in defiance. "Cultivation problem? Keep trying. Keep living. You can *do* it! Severe injury? Recover. Get up. Keep living. You *can* do it!"

This was the moment where it felt right to address a source of her instability. "Your name is delightful, and it is filled with wondrous meaning. Someone gives you a hard time about it? You punch them in the face, and you tell them how you feel about that. Every single time those big, dumb boys try to pry their claws into you, you just remember this one thing, young lady. What you do and how you choose to do it is all that matters."

With dramatic flair he flung his blanket around himself like a cape, which made Yvessa snort with an unknowing, little, dumbfounded smile. "I..."

She didn't have the words. Pride burst from her chest due to the encouragement. Only then did she notice her fingers had clamped into her pillow. She'd been glued to the words of support for her with the same necessity as the gift of cool water in a hot desert. "Are you sure it's okay I come bother you?"

"Anytime," mused a very confident and welcoming response. "Even in the middle of the night, where the stars are the only companions willing to let us be at peace."

Another bear-esque snore tore through the tent as one of the priests rolled over. That elicited a small giggle from both of them. They hadn't bothered to whisper their conversation, but it hadn't woken anyone further. "Thank you, Elder."

Artorian winced and felt a slimy crawl nestle up his spine. "Ut-tut-tut. Please don't call me that."

A chuckle left Yvessa, figuring he didn't like to be reminded that he was old. Then her mind sparked, and she frowned. "Why did you mumble what you did? Before, I mean. The..."

She didn't really want to say it. The old man remained firm, nodding with his eyes closed. From what she could tell, he'd accepted it, but that didn't make it any more pleasant. "Are you a cultivator, my dear?"

"F-rank four. Like most of the other new people, we've only been cultivating for a few months." She listed things off on her fingers. "In order. Beast Core, cheap Memory Stone for the basic spiral, learn how to pray and sing to draw in Essence, basic combat, and off into a squad for live training. I just didn't think it would be out here. I overheard half the superiors say the mission is 'special', others that it's a complete chore, and the last few that this whole thing is a complete waste of time and gold. I'm pretty torn about being here."

Artorian had a decent grasp of her situation and explanation. A Beast Core seemed to be a name for a tool that extracted corruption. Given the name, it likely had some unpleasant side effects... ones he could not survive. A *Memory* Stone he was very familiar with. You just press the stone to your forehead, and the knowledge contained within would become yours, as if you'd gone through the events yourself. Expensive things. He'd seen them in the old days but had never touched one.

A spiral was the Essence technique for refining, although he was still stuck on why it needed to be a spiral and found this an excellent moment to ask. "Actually, do you happen to know why it needs to be a spiral?"

Yvessa was dumbstruck. "It... refines the... Essence stuff. I thought it was just because it worked. I heard once that even if you know how to move and shape Essence, it just does nothing if it doesn't match some kind of stable pattern, or worse, it does something *unexpected*."

"Oh, you mean... Well, it actually looks like a spiral."
Sparks of clarity had struck late. She drew something in the air,
but Artorian squinted so hard that Yvessa figured he could not
see it. Having found something to do, she stumbled her way out
of the cot and hobbled over on one foot. Then drew it into the
blanket fabric. "Like this."

She mimicked the spiral that she had inside of her. It
was a small, frail little thing, but it was great to have. "It spins in
a direction, and the faster it spins, the better it is. However,
keeping that up is tiring, and I'm terrible at close control like
that. I'm good with my hands. Building houses and chopping
wood all day? No problem. You need a precision cabinet? Can
do. But so much of cultivating is being able to think of the right
thing, imagine the particular movement, and then apply it with
your head. It gives me *incredible* headaches. If I don't have a
specific set of steps outlined in front of me... I'm just stuck."

Yvessa *tsked* her tongue. "There are clever people in
the world. I'm not one of them. It took the Head Cleric a full
month of support just for me to understand how to properly hold
the spiral and keep it going as I slept. He repeated the word
'aptitude' so many times. I don't know what it means, but I know
he thinks I don't have it. It's... hard to believe in myself when
everyone gives me such a rough time. All the time."

Artorian scooted over so the young woman could sit. He
was a little surprised that she did, but then again, Tychus had
been like this too. His heart pained at the thought of the boy,
and his jaw grit together as he momentarily held his chest and
bent forwards. "Oh, the pains of being old."

Yvessa frowned and watched but wouldn't know how to
help if she wasn't told. A few moments later, Artorian was
breathing deep and waved it off. "What's holding your
cultivation back, my dear?"

Yvessa looked conflicted—as this was a Church secret—but decided that it was better to get this off her chest. "Time, I think? See, the Church has a bunch of limitations for cultivators, and we ourselves have some limitations too. I don't know if you've heard, but the majority of us are celestial-based. It's dangerous to cultivate when the Essence isn't abundant because you'll draw in more corruption than anything else. All your time will go to spinning your spiral faster to prevent it from getting in while still getting some Essence out of it. We can only cultivate during main prayer, which happens shortly before high noon."

"We all begin our chants while under the early-noon sunlight, and when we feel it brighten as our prayers receive attention, we can then actively pull Essence since there's enough of it for us to do so. A little past the point where the sun stops being at the highest point it can be in the sky, the added brightness and cultivation time ends." Her words bitterly drooped. "Even *if* we keep chanting. So, we have a very set slot of time where we can try to make any progress. Any tasks we might have must be completed beforehand, so we tend to be punished with tasks that take a lot of time. That badly bottlenecks us. Even if you're like Jin, who is the Head Cleric's favorite young priest. He always gets prime time for cultivating. Each daily chant only gathers so much Essence, which can only take us so far."

"We're limited by amount, and honestly, we need so, *so* much more. We've been told that when we reach higher ranks in the Church, we will be 'blessed' with knowledge on new chants that let us cultivate for longer and under more favorable conditions. If you exceed and get written permission, you can even get signed on to take a trip to a dungeon for one day."

"One single day in a dungeon can mean weeks of progress for a cultivator. The Essence density in them is just...

wow. You really feel the difference between being out here and in there. It's such a rush." Yvessa was breathing much heavier than Artorian was comfortable with, his hand cautiously pressing to her shoulder.

"My dear? Come back."

"Huh?" She snapped out of it. "Oh. Sorry. I was only in a dungeon for two hours, but I get *cravings* now. They pulled our corruption out, gave us the technique, and in that dungeon, I jumped from F-rank-zero all the way to F-rank four. In two *hours*. Now I'm out here, and after months, I'm still at F-rank four. I'm *close* to five, but I don't know the breakthrough details. All I know is 'have enough Essence in your Center' and you'll reach a new rank, but to me, that's a lie. There's always something new I need to do in order to actually progress. If it's not some new chant, then it's to 'make my Chi threads finer'."

She mimed in mockery, then sighed with resignation. "I do what I'm told. Dishonorable discharge from the Church is ugly. They're just rumors, but I heard that they strip you of the chants you know when you leave, if you were really bad. Especially in the Choir, which is our particular branch of the Church. Chants not only affect our growth but our overall fighting ability. I don't know if you've ever seen a Choir war host in action, but every cultivator matches the chant of every other. Each voice added to the whole increases the power and ability of each person whose voice is involved, through some kind of celestial or aural sympathy."

"Not having chants means you can't draw celestial Essence anymore, and if that's your only Affinity channel, you die slowly and painfully. Everything needs the correct Essence to live and keep living, and if it didn't have it, then it just doesn't."

Artorian was looking at Yvessa with wide, twinkling eyes. She leaned away from him with concern, her voice hesitant. "...What?"

The old man settled back where he was, a broad smile on his face. "My dear, I believe you may have just saved my life."

CHAPTER TWENTY

Tibbins waited in front of the Head Cleric's tent, ready with the report of the first week. What a week it had been. In fact, Tibbins was convinced that this was entirely the reason why he was being made to wait so long. The heavy cloth flap of the tent swung away, and Keeper Irene hurriedly passed him. The Acolyte snapped to a salute. He still firmly believed that the entire 'saluting' affair was awkward for one following the path of the priest, but as this expedition was classed under 'military', he had to abide by the rank and file rules.

"Enter." Tarrean faced away from the opening, nimble fingers closing the last few buttons on the top of his uniform. It used to be odd to see him out of the ornate armor that was ever so boasted about, but it had received a prime spot against the tent wall, fully fitted on an armor rack meant for human-like display. The mood in the tent fell before Tarrean ever turned to face the Acolyte. "Tell me you have some... *sane* news, for a change?"

Tarrean cringed as he could feel the flat lipped reply plastered on the Acolyte's face without glancing. There had been a week of this, but based on the old man's condition, it likely would only last for a few weeks more. "No, sir."

Finally, the Head Cleric turned and sat down on his comfy, new stool. He picked up the deteriorated mug with the word Elder on it, observing it as one would a polished skull. "Do you know what I saw yesterday, Tibbins?"

The Acolyte closed his eyes and drew a needed breath. "I have a suspicion of it, sir."

"Take a seat, Acolyte." Tarrean put the cup down and folded his hands.

"Yesterday, the camp was roused not to the morning routine but to the clamor of an old man running about with only his pants on, pulling fluff and feathers out from a pillow, throwing it into the air, and baying 'it worked, it worked!' Then he bent over backwards to madly cackle."

"When one of the guards returned from hunting the raiders, he approached Artorian to assist. The guard was taken by the lapels as the old man beamed the biggest smile he'd ever seen and ecstatically exclaimed, 'It fits inside. See? It fits inside! The fluff can compress. It can compress!' while wildly waving the pillow around and stuffing the feathers back into the torn cloth... with what I can only describe as manic glee."

He paused to let Tibbins sweat. "Well, yes, sir, but I'm *sure* it's under control now."

"Is it, Tibbins? *Is* it?" Tarrean spoke, voice volume rising. "Then *certainly,* you can explain what happened during prayer *today?*"

The Head Cleric's leer bored into the Acolyte, who thought it was getting rather warm. "Well, it wasn't so bad, sir. None were harmed. He merely walked up in the middle of our chant, and–"

Bampf. Tarrean filled in with a fist slam to the table. "Threw. Off. His. Robe."

"He disrobed in the middle of our congregation. Prayer was halted because everyone was choking on their words. Not even mentioning that arms-up pose he did like he was about to hug the abyss-blessed *sun!*"

Tibbins quickly tried to salvage this. "He did seem... happy about the praising, sir."

The Head Cleric just about threw his papers. "I'm sure he *was*, Acolyte! The smile was huge, and everyone for leagues saw those *awful* scars. I had to assure the congregation that I would *personally* tend to those egregious wounds. I was going to slam down brimstone scripture on that old fool's head, but for reasons beyond my abyss-confounded control, my troops 'like' the man."

Tarrean was fuming and squeezed the bridge of his nose. "They are sneaking him food. I *know* they are. I understand that. What I *don't* understand is how he ended up with three dozen of our pillows! I went to the medical tent this morning, and an entire corner next to the only window flap—which might I mention is open *against* protocol—is covered port to stern in pillows."

"Several containers of water stand nearby, and chairs from the longhouse have *mysteriously* made their way over to the medical tent. Which is now no longer the medical tent, as the majority of occupants have recovered and the herbal medicines moved. It is now the tent my troops go to on their time off!" Tarrean was strangling his arm bracer out of confounded vexation. "I see them entering with sour, downtrodden looks. I hear the laughter, and then they leave filled with merriment. I am *dying* to kick that old man out of the tent and out of my camp, but I can't do so without losing face with my entire expedition squad. What do they *do* in there?"

Tibbins did his best to keep his tone neutral as the corners of his mouth lifted. He could *not* afford to laugh. Not here. Not now. "They... tell him what's bothering them, sir."

The Head Cleric looked like he was about to have an aneurism. "They can come to me! I am their superior!" Tarrean flopped down on to his seat, needing to rub his forehead.

"You are, sir. However, you are also busy all the time, and it's well-known you dislike being disturbed. There's also a punishment for entering your tent unannounced."

"About the chairs and pillows…?" Tibbins got the 'move on' motion, and so he did. "You did say to get the man what he asked for, sir."

Tarrean squeezed the bridge of his nose again, recalling that rather late and only because his subordinate had mentioned it. "Just… give me your report, Acolyte."

Tibbins unfurled some vellum. "As of the return of the hunting party, Jiivra has provided her report."

It didn't take more than a glance at the painfully thin stack of vellums to know what the news was going to be. "While she found the tracks and the caravan belonging to it, it had been emptied and abandoned by a fishing outpost at the closest point one could reach a river. The raiders did away with the fishing crews and likely took all the boats. No raiders were captured. No goods or gold were recovered. Tracks were found, and they do include small-sized feet. We have confirmation the children from the village are alive. Since it seems unlikely they would be kept for ransom, we expect they are being kept for more… nefarious purposes. The boats went upriver."

The Head Cleric stopped him. "*Up*river?"

Tibbins nodded. "Yes, sir. We expect someone with some intelligence is part of the captured group. Jiivra found ripped apart flowers littering the bank of the river in a rather odd pattern. She described it as flowers being ripped apart and thrown on the bank, in ever-decreasing quantities. We think someone gathered flowers on the way and left them for any possible pursuers to find. Which, by itself, is odd. I don't know why some of the captives were expecting that we would come. We never had a chance to interact with them, but it's in the report."

Tarrean rubbed the side of his head. "I believe it's good for the captives to have faith. In who or what isn't important until their rescue by the Church. Their devout thanks will fall on sanctified ear every noon."

Tibbins said nothing; his superior was assured of the facts the Acolyte had stated, and he chose to continue his report, "We suffered no casualties, just more tired troops. They're all resting and performing expected duties per your wishes on the growth of the forward base. Anything useful found in nearby wreckage goes to the effort. Otherwise, a logging camp is planned to be established near the closest forest."

"We cannot find the logging site the village had, and the Elder does not know. The other old person that we found a week ago is still catatonic and neither moves nor speaks. She simply eats when directed, and we have some junior priests practicing hospice care on her. While usually the expedition group would ask for follow-up orders, the entire camp is suffering symptoms of severe exhaustion and mental fatigue."

Tarrean sighed in defeat. "Leave it *is* then, though I don't know to what or where. There's nothing to do here, nowhere to shop, no money to gain or spend, and gambling is forbidden. I will set expected tasks to the minimal work required, and everyone may have the rest of the time as leave. I know the Fringe can be taxing, away from everything they know. One week, Acolyte."

The superior exhaled the order and re-folded his hands. Seeing Tibbins was at the bottom of his list, he decided it was time to press the personal matter. "I take it our guest is uncooperative per my... request?"

Tibbins put the vellum down. "Artorian spends the majority of his time bedridden, sir. He has perhaps an hour or two per day where he can get up and move, and anytime I've seen him lately that isn't during visiting hours, he is sickened or exhausted."

The Acolyte stiffened as he relayed the next bit of news. "Any time that he does get up... well... he does strange things: putting mud and water in a cup and spending an entire hour stirring it only to pour it out and do it again; hitting the flat of his palm on still water just to watch the ripples; lying in the grass with only his pants on in various parts of the village at various times of the day and night; randomly stopping and standing there. You know he's gone mentally as he looks off in the distance. Or he visits a home and breaks down in tears as he weeps for a lost villager."

Tibbins closed his eyes and shook his head. "I assume he must have had a great amount of family here. We've caught him talking to himself on multiple occasions, and there's an actual report of him crumpled at the village lumber storage site, sobbing that he was sorry. We don't know for what or why. Nobody has the heart to ask him. He's a man being eaten by his regrets."

The Acolyte began to furl his vellum back up. "A priestess tried getting him to open up once, but he got up, had a fierce expression on his face, and just told her that, 'He was going to do it, for them,' with such strength of character that she lost her voice for a moment."

Tibbins quietly kept to himself that the priestess had then sat down with him and had been the person to break down in tears while getting grief off her chest. That it was the Initiate being consoled and supported and had, as thanks, started the pillow smuggling operation. He doubted his superior wanted any words of that. "I do have one spot of good news per your specific request, sir."

Tarrean raised an eyebrow. "Go on?"

Tibbins straightened himself, picking his words carefully, "He wants an item that is... a little too expensive to just write off. However, he mentioned he'd be willing to barter for it."

Tarrean's eyes began to hungrily glint, his posture warming up as he finally got something to work with. "Go on."

"He said it might be too much, and it might be too late, however, if possible, he wants to buy or barter for a Memory Stone containing a simple cultivation technique." Tibbins buried his face into his hands from frustration. "I've tried to talk him out of it. He's nothing *but* corruption. It roils inside of him like nausea manifested. Looking at it makes *me* physically ill. I've already told him a Beast Core would just kill him, but he doesn't relent. A cultivation technique is only going to give him hope, and then... then he's going to expire when he tries to use it. All that corruption will be forced..."

Tibbins silenced himself at the sickening thoughts. Tarrean remained all business and mentally compared costs to benefits. "Those are expensive indeed, Acolyte. Bring him in. I'll see if I can't barter something of value with the man. I see no reason to deny him life's last little pleasures or any hope he wants to gratuitously pay for. If Artorian believes that some knowledge of a cultivation spiral will make him feel better before the poor old man slumbers to his end, then, why, Tibbins... we ought to take care of him."

Tibbins felt frozen solid to his chair. He so hated this side of his slick superior. Always looking out for number one. The Acolyte gabbed just to feel better, "He seems plenty happy spending his days with many of the recruits. Initiate Yvessa and several others who were injured in the tent at the time he was there may as well be called his personal attendants. Oddly enough, those same Initiates have gotten their hands on food we didn't know was available in the village. Certain secrets are being shared with them, and they're silently reaping the benefits."

He mentioned it purely to dig something unpleasant into his superior's kidney. "I'll fetch him for you, sir. You're far more skilled at negotiation than me."

With a respectful salute, he left the Head Cleric to simmer. Tarrean spat, "Dismissed."

Tibbins exclaimed with surprise as he left the tent flap, "Oh, Artorian!"

A broad smile warmly greeted the weary Acolyte. "Tibbins, my boy! I've been looking for you."

Artorian's smile grew even further. "I have *news*."

CHAPTER TWENTY-ONE

Tarrean heard a hug-in-progress and cringed. Likely because he was still envisioning the old man half-naked; that view was going to *scar* him.

"Artorian, *great,* you found me. I was looking for you as well. The Head Cleric has need of you. Could we speak after? I have tasks that I am in a hurry to complete," Tibbins excused himself with as much smoothness as he could.

"Of *course*, young man. Take good care of yourself. You look a little pale. Get some sun; it's *wonderful* for you. I *guarantee* it!" With a pat on the back, Artorian stepped back into the tent, fully clad in the wealthy lapis lazuli robe. For an old man on the verge of death, a man that should be falling over in a few weeks, he was awfully chipper and well-kept. His snowy hair had been trimmed, and his long beard cleaned up quite well, though it remained at a healthy length.

Tarrean carefully dissected the *entirely* different-looking Artorian. The bald, old man was clean. Well washed. Nails trim and even. This man wasn't at all the crying *wreck* he'd seen a week ago. That made no sense... Artorian's condition should have been *deteriorating*; instead, it seemed to have stabilized. Tarrean noticed that his gawking had not gone unnoticed and coughed into his hand to regain composure. He seated himself in a more refined position on his fancy stool.

"I usually *declare* when people can enter my tent, Artorian. Since you're already here, please, do sit." He spoke with forced kindness and an equally forced smile. The Head Cleric may have had his pride stepped on a little, but the land-ownership vellum was burning a hole in his pocket. The matter needed attending. "Before we get to business, how are you feeling?"

Artorian shook his head left to right, eyes gently closed. "Contrary to what my appearance may be, being up and about takes more out of me than I'd care to admit. The amount of time I can be out of bed is in decline, but that's alright. I'm going to go ahead and address your silent query. Yes, I do *look* well. It's for the sketches Yvessa and some of the boys are making of me. They're caring kids, granting an old man a kindness. I expect I'll be stuck in bed for quite a long time, and having a visual reminder of when I appeared healthy will be good for everyone."

The old man mused to himself, "I won't hold you to my ramblings, Head Cleric. Shall we bicker and barter? I'm convinced you've already heard what I'd like."

Tarrean nodded and pulled some pieces of paper and vellum on to his desk. Artorian beamed a fox's smile at him. "So... how large of a pillow can you get?"

The Head Cleric dropped the inkwell at being so startled. "A what?"

Artorian carefully tilted his head to the side. He repeated his words, pretending that the short man had simply not heard him, "A pillow. What did you think I was referring to?"

Tarrean scrambled to prevent anything else from falling, adding item after item on the desk in neat little rows. "The, eh, the Memory Stone. I thought."

Artorian nodded in understanding at the mention. "Oh, *that* minor thing? I thought that would be a trifle for you. Initially, I thought it may have been difficult, but when I heard it was *Maccreus Tarrean* leading this expedition team, I chuckled at my own ignorance."

Tarrean twitched. Where had this old man picked up his full name? Still, if it gave him some leverage over the nosy old-timer, he'd take it. Some part of him also felt soothed, his pride fluffing up like an attention-seeking kitten. "Ah, well. Of course!"

He felt off-balance, yet the matter appeared to be leaning in his favor. Tarrean decided to simply go with the tide and see where this landed. He regained his composure with this line of thinking and leaned in. "I doubt a large pillow would be particularly difficult to b—"

He stopped himself, realizing that he was about to fall into a pit trap. "*How* large?"

The Head Cleric's eyes squinted at the wizened, sly, old man. "Oh, I was hoping for a... *hmm*... twelve-by-twelve?"

That was an average-sized pillow, and Tarrean didn't see what the problem was. He'd been expecting something extravagant, but the old man must have been joking about. Yes, clearly, that's what this was. This sly fox was trying to distract him from the huge cost of a Memory Stone. The cleric waved off the issue. "Just give the details to Tibbins. I'm sure a meager pillow is fine."

Artorian brightly smirked. "I shall certainly do so."

Tarrean sifted some pages, then lifted his porcelain cup, sipping at some water. "Now, about the stone. You mentioned you had something to barter with?"

The old man folded his hands over one another and nodded slightly. "Land."

The Head Cleric felt like he got kicked in the sensitives as he choked on his water. Coughing into his sleeve, he had to look away to hide his expression. His *greed.* Artorian half-stood. "Head Cleric, are you quite alright? You appear ill! You've been coughing and dropping things since I entered the tent. Please do go and get looked at."

The short man bit back fury; he was being played like a stringed instrument. "Yes. Yes, land will do for a stone."

Artorian nodded and clapped his hands together. "Oh, good! I was thinking about it and came to the conclusion that you wouldn't accept salt. I'll speak with Tibbins about having something suitable drawn up."

Tarrean waved him off dismissively. "No, that's not necessary. We can take care of all of that right now. I simply need some signatures."

Artorian appeared flummoxed and ponderously stated, "Some... *what?*"

"Signa... oh. Your name written out." The old man's ponderous expression bent into a frown as Tarrean finished speaking.

"A signature? For official *documents?* In the *Fringe?*" The old man was now giving the cleric a look as if he was insane. "Why would we *ever* use something so unreliable?"

Tarrean was suddenly having a crap day. That abyssal vellum was a *fake?* No. No, it couldn't be. That would wreck this entire plan. He leaned behind him and fished it from a bag. "I would assume so. Isn't this a signature from this village?"

He hastily laid out the land deed vellum for the village of Salt. Leaning rather close to it, Artorian read the document, lifting it and moving the vellum upwards as he read line after line until he came to the angrily clawed signature.

Switch.

It had been *Switch.* Artorian closed his eyes, hands cramping. Tremors from anger-created stress forced him to take deep breaths to steady himself. "I'm sorry, Head Cleric. This is *not* legitimate."

With the tremble only worsening, he rolled the vellum back up and put it on the table. "To think that... someone would want to sell all of *this*... all the *people*. For some... for some..."

He couldn't bear to finish the sentence, a new hatred for greed finding a place to fester and grow in his heart. To be fair, the mess of corruption still moving through his system may have had a hand in that. Tarrean visibly deflated. The entire, *heavily* planned investment had been foiled by a piece of abyss-cursed vellum. He said nothing about the old man's shaking; his own hands were very much unsteady as he sipped from his water.

"How long was your expedition going to be, Master Cleric?" Artorian slipped in with a weak half-whisper.

Tarrean mumbled procedure back, too tired and unwilling to think about the next steps to really put thought into it, "Expeditions may last up to three years and three months before a forced return or writ of exoneration is required. Unfortunately, I only retain the full force for the duration of a season before they must return. That is in the event that the immediate threat has been handled. A five-cleric cadre is all that can maintain a stationed position for the full duration."

The short man continued to deflate as he saw his dreams caving in. Artorian was the one who sat up with straight-backed composure. "Oh? How curious. A Fringe land transfer takes three full rotations of all seasons, which is about three years. It's a shame that I'll likely pass before then. Had you been here that full length of time, I would have been able to confer on to you the required name that would grant official land benefits in the Fringe. Of course, I'd sign any documents at that point if another country or some such was involved and needed their own version of proof."

The heavenly light of hope filled the Head Cleric's eyes as the old man threw him a lifeline. Then his dreams went a little sideways as he realized the other end of this bargain. "Do you believe you *could* live for three years?"

Artorian noisily hummed out a sonorous thought. *Hmm*. Ponderously running hand down his beard, Artorian listed the requirements, "With attentive care, solid bed rest, nutritious food, and pleasant stories about this cultivation stuff to keep my nightmares at bay... I believe three years is quite doable. Besides, I heard the Master Cleric was quite knowledgeable, and I would *adore* hearing some of your stories and experiences. My love for knowing things has always kept me alive. May I ask what you plan to do with the land?"

Artorian leaned forwards, pressing the matter. Tarrean, feeling crammed into quite the corner, decided to explain fully, "It's... I would *love* to say it's for a forward operating base for the Church. Unfortunately... that's not true. It's for my... son. He's a good lad but thin and slow to cultivate. He lacks any shred of ambition, and the smallest, dumbest thing makes him happy. As his *quite* driven father, I must see that I can keep my boy in a safe corner of the world—at whatever cost I must pay to have that done... even my own pride."

Artorian let free a long, relieved exhale. "Jin is a *very* good boy."

"He is, if only..." The Head Cleric nodded in agreement. A dangerous, razor-sharp look stabbed straight into the old man. "How did you know Jin was my son?"

"Before or after you confirmed it for me?" Artorian chuckled. The fox's smile came and swiftly went, along with his answer, "You're a shrewd, zealous, and guarded man, Master Cleric. You're harsh, distant, and keep a militaristic relationship with all but *two* people. For a person so devout in not showing favoritism, your boy receives an awful amount of care to always be at the forefront of cultivation during each chant and prayer. If someone would have blocked him from being able to have full attendance, they suddenly and *inexplicably* receive additional tasks."

Artorian brushed himself off and rose. He slowly turned to leave. "I'm at about the end of what I can handle for a day. So, let me say it simply, Master Cleric."

For an old man, he took an indomitable stance, rising straight with all the poise one expected of a military commander addressing a well-organized Legion. "I offer you this deal. Keep me alive for three years and indulge an old man his fancies. Then you'll have your wish. Do we have an accord?"

Tarrean felt his heart stop for just a moment as the old man rose up. For that half a twinge of a second, he was reminded of being in the same room as a Vicar, a monster of influence. His voice was confident, but it betrayed him at that moment. "We have an accord."

Artorian turned to leave, but before he opened the flap, the Head Cleric quick-fired a voiced worry, "Who was the second person?"

Stopping short, Artorian's expression and attitude turned caustic. He didn't turn to address the Head Cleric and merely spoke with controlled rage, "It would be *ideal*, Master Cleric... if the treatment of Keeper Irene was in proper standing of what she *deserved*. She works hard, and she..."

The tent flap fluttered, and Artorian left without finishing his thought... leaving Tarrean to pick up the shattered pieces of his pride.

CHAPTER TWENTY-TWO

"Good morning, old man! How are you feeling today?" Yvessa carried the steaming bowl into the 'medical tent', the flap pushed aside by her elbow. The full-raiment-wearing priestess nicked the bowl against the side of the improvised nightstand before setting it down to rest. A whining set of groans were the reply from a man-shaped lump swaddled in thick blankets on the cot.

Pillows surrounded Artorian on all sides like some elaborate funeral casket. A small gathering of fresh flowers sat in the window, the falling-apart wooden cup of his used as a stand-in for a vase. If nothing else, it held water well enough. Yvessa was glad that *she* didn't need to use such an ugly thing and took care to always leave it alone. Wriggling movements came from the swaddle as she pulled up a chair and sat it next to his bedside.

"I am going to *insist* you eat the full bowl today," she demanded. "Now that there's no prying eyes and ears, you *also* better tell me why we needed to swaddle you up, you old codger. Don't pretend to be asleep. I know you've been awake the whole time I've been here."

A single eye opened on the old man that was doing his darndest to appear asleep. The weary eye looked around and closed again. Maybe, just maybe, she'd pretend he wasn't awake yet. If he was quiet enough.

"Up with you!" Yvessa threw his covers off and snapped at the lazy, old man who never wanted to go along with anyone else's wishes. "Delighting in being stubborn again? I suppose I'll have to let you eat by *yourself* in that case."

Artorian opened both eyes with a squint. Blast. His bluff got called.

With a long and drawn out stretch of arms above his head, he rumbled incoherent grunts and pushed away the cloth keeping him swaddled. Kicking it out and away, his arms trembled while gradually easing himself upright. There wasn't a hint of sleepiness in his voice, betraying that he had been awake for quite some time after all. "A pleasant day to you as well, my dear. *Must* you yell so brutishly at an old man in the morning?"

Yvessa lowered the wooden spoon, pointing it right at his nose. "I'll show you how brutish I can be with this spoon if you don't saddle up and behave, you big troublemaker. We have to be in full dress to come attend to you now, Mister Official Charge."

Pap. She rapped the spoon on top of his head. "Ow!"

With pouty lips, Artorian rubbed the top of his head and sat up in the full and proper resting position against the wall of pillows. He had a lovely look outside as the sunlight bathed over him. "Ah, that's *much* better."

Yvessa's spoon returned to the front of Artorian's' mouth, except this time, it was filled to the brim with finely cut venison. It was even lathered in sauce—Tibbins' work, no doubt.

Another week had seamlessly gone by, and events in the camp had stabilized after the Head Cleric had gone on a noisy tirade where many things were thrown. Artorian had been referred to with numerous expletives. When the meeting was called, Tarrean attended in full regalia. With surprising clarity and poise, the Head Cleric announced a change of operational plans. *Everyone* was now excused from tasks when prayer time came, incentives for good performance were laid on the table, and a care project was announced for the old man.

Filed under hospice care practice, to smooth any issues with the accountants. The priests already knew the *real* reason and shelved the ones Tarrean provided away under political guise. Acolyte Tibbins had not thrown Artorian out when he entered the tent. Instead, he'd pretended to leaf through his pages as the old-timer listened in on the whole thing, the gossip was too juicy not to play with. Keeper Irene was *considerably* less miserable since she didn't need to pretend not to be in a relationship with Tarrean, and Jin was afforded actual time with his *father* instead of a superior ecclesiarch. You could not hide something in plain sight after everyone knew about it.

"That's quite good," Artorian managed to say between inhaled bites, quickly blowing air in and out of his open mouth to cool the meat after he'd gotten it in too hastily. It was just so *hot*, and waving a hand at his face didn't actually help.

Yvessa just blew on the spoon some before shoving the next portion into her charge's mouth. "If you can talk, then you can *explain*. Quit being such a sneak."

Artorian noisily swallowed, using a full-sized towel to dab at the edges of his mouth. "I was poking around in my corruption again."

The fiery look she stabbed into him could have put the big, bright sky orb to shame. "You *what?*"

Artorian failed to repeat himself as the rapid-fire barrage from Yvessa hit him with such velocity that he couldn't keep up or even grasp what she was saying.

"It's fine, it's *fine!*" He waved her words away as she continued to go off on him.

"No. It. Is. *Not.*"

"It is! You even helped swaddle me!"

"What does *that* have to do with anything, you fool!" Yvessa was fuming. Her anger bubbled as this infuriating, old man coolly smiled back at her. She squeezed the utensil and threateningly shook it at him.

"Not a *spoon*!" Some laughter erupted from the old man as he held both hands to his chest. "Very well, very well! Do you remember all those moons ago when I'd mentioned you saved my life?"

"You never explained *that* either." The wooden utensil didn't budge. Yvessa's entire body language screamed that she was quite fed up with being left in the dark.

Artorian settled and parroted her words, "Everything needs Essence to live. For every open affinity channel, an influx of that particular kind of Essence is required. People were all surprised to see me alive, and you helped me puzzle out why! While I am not a cultivator and have no method for preventing or purging corruption from my body or my Center, I passively take in Essence."

He waited a moment for her to consider her own words. "This, rather than make me *stronger* as it normally would, instead goes to keeping me sustained and alive. I am quite stuffed with the malaise. Therefore, if I was not *already* receiving all the right types of Essence... I would be dead. As you've likely heard, I don't simply just have one open affinity channel."

"Yes. *Four*," she groaned out the words incredulously, still not believing it. The Head Cleric would rage about it for hours if he found out. He'd been lording his double affinity channel superiority over them since day one. The caretaker's expression grew grim. "We also heard your corruption is... ugly. After one of the Initiates threw up from accidentally glancing in the direction of the medical tent with Essence sight, *everyone* outright avoids looking at your Center if at all possible."

"So, to my continued annoyance, *I* don't know what you're up to either or why under the heaven-blessed sky you're prodding at *corruption* of all things. How do you even... such filth. I just... ugh." The shuddering young lady had to hold her stomach and turn away. Nausea struck her just thinking about it.

"I've had a particularly... *eventful* life, my dear. Unfortunately, I am so jaded to trudging around face deep in all sorts of unpleasant situations that I barely even notice that aspect. I instead notice the pain, where it is, what it does. I've puzzled together some interesting facts and interactions. If you're at all able to acquire me some parchment, vellum, or something to scribble on, I would like to compile a treatise and send it up to the Skyspear Academy. I believe I owe them both for my madness in being able to handle this and recompense for the sheer vocabulary they left at my disposal."

The priestess didn't quite understand that but didn't need to. "We can get you something to write on. Now, *out* with it!"

Artorian waved the white flag and started talking, "Since I am very much still alive, it means that whatever Essence I need, I am getting. So, even if I need four specific types, which I hear is demanding, something in my daily activities has been providing it. Not only do I believe that I've figured out *what*, but I may have a bead on why... though I lack some much-needed information to puzzle everything together."

Yvessa's face was fully deadpan. "Well?"

Artorian beamed and pointed at the sky. "I believe your scripture calls it the provision of Heavens."

The woman knew that was the name of the chant to one of the prayers. "The above provides for me. I just have not puzzled together exactly *what* up there does it. However, it's the only consistent source that has been in my life."

"Old man... if you're about to convert, *I* want the credit." Yvessa pushed her finger hard into his chest. Her arms crossed, and a knee shortly followed to slide over the other as she leaned back.

Artorian burst out in a solid laugh. "Oh. *Oho*! No. No, my dear. I'm not being spiritual about this. I'm being quite *literal*."

Yvessa was lost, and it showed in her frown.

"The *stars*, my dear. It's the stars!" Artorian appeared truly content. He brimmed with confidence and enthusiasm. "It's going to be an upward struggle these next few years, but I'll make it. Even if I'm bound to this cot and can only wander out for a little bit... it's enough, and I'll make it."

Yvessa was taken aback by the pure determination that filled Artorian's posture. His body language was exuding that he fully and absolutely believed this. "Awful confident for someone the rest of us believe might fall over any day now. Please tell me you've got some reasoning for this."

"Very well!" He chimed quite the enthusiastic tone in retort to her request, "It's the *corruption*!"

Yvessa's breath intake was tense and severely displeased, her response startling some passing Initiates outside as the wooden spoon snapped in her hand. "*Ar*. Tor. *I. An*!"

CHAPTER TWENTY-THREE

"Truly, I *mean* it! It's the corruption. Allow me to explain." Beginning his breakdown of the next topic, Artorian took another bite of his meal, "I'm deteriorating because I'm playing with corruption, and to be honest... it's terrible for me. I don't require a lecture or to be told not to do so. I'm *very* much aware that I am spending my vitality on tackling the issue. It's honestly why my ability to roam dropped like a rock in a pond. Now, I will say one thing—worry not; I've not done this without some greater gain. My confidence doesn't stem from confusion, rather from requirement."

Artorian then trailed off, took a breath, and launched into full grandfather lecture mode. "When I am in my Center, corruption behaves differently. There is a notable feeling that can be discerned when I am actively engaging or observing it in comparison to when I am not. When it is not under observation, it's *just* corruption. It's annoying, it prevents cultivation, and it has a slew of terrible effects. All of this you know. As to what you *don't* know, I asked to be swaddled because I found a method to *isolate* my various corruptions!"

To Yvessa's silent lament, Artorian's enthusiasm was intoxicating. She was absolutely enraptured by Artorian's ramblings, and a spark of hope bloomed in Yvessa's chest for the man. Her wavering attention snapped back to him as Artorian continued speaking, "After isolation, I then interact with each individually! I 'touch' it, so to say. See, corruption is a poorly applied word. I prefer 'immutable' instead, as that's the main property of what it is. Corruption doesn't accept change. The identity of what it *is* has become so strong, so *certain* of itself, so *absolute* in how it perceives itself."

"Corruption, instead of being afflicted, forces *its* properties on whatever engages with it." He paused to wiggle his hands in a so-so manner. "Pretty sure about that. As Essence is fed to corruption, the corruption spreads like a disease. This means corruption is—by itself—an aspect of change. Specifically, an aspect that makes all things it comes in contact with change in order to better suit the properties of that particular type of corruption!"

"When I touched water corruption, I was immediately whisked from my Center with a great dread. All activity was suspect, and I wished to do nothing. Nothing at all. I was lethargic to a fault, and rather than just feeling it with my body, this was an outlook forced upon my mind. I did this several times after recovering, just to ensure that this was a constant and not simply my mind playing tricks on me. Sure enough, similar veins of lethargy struck me."

The old man had a few more bites of offered venison to stave off Yvessa's wrath. "I asked to be swaddled since it would confine me. I requested this pillow fortress of entrapment since I could not be sure what sort of effects the other corruptions would have on my mind, but my dear... I found out."

"Fire corruption makes me *angry*. Raging fury, wild clashes that make me abandon all rational thought. I lose myself to fury and curse all that comes to my mind. All is to be hated, and anything not aligned with single-minded focus burns away at the fringes of my thoughts."

"*Berserker*–" Yvessa obviously wanted to chime in with something more, and her eyes were flashing with the fury he had just described.

Artorian quickly cut her off, "Air corruption made me... flighty. I'm ashamed to say my testing of that particular corruption has been responsible for my displays of... *ahem*...

uncouth behavior. I simply didn't feel any social pressure and did whatever I pleased in the moment, free as a leaf roaming on the wind. Everything was activity. Things require doing, need doing. Need doing now. Quickly. Swiftly. Impatiently. Only action. My attention span shattered upon all the things my mind jumped on to, all the things that it could do. I could lay in the grass! No, I could lay in that grass over there! No, I could be in the stream. Let's *run* to it!"

Several calming breaths were needed for the old man to even out, but even so, he was smiling. "The celestial corruption, however. Oh... that... that's a *frightening* thing. I became full of myself, an unstoppable force. I utterly believed that *anything* which might challenge that truth was wrong in the worst way possible. I was imbued with haughtiness. I was above anything and anyone else, a paragon of my kind. I was the tip of the spear that led the charge into the future, the bringer of *all* that is righteous!"

"My confidence exploded into arrogance at the cost of caring for anything else. In truth, it made me understand many of the clerics I have met in my life. Your Head Cleric was a textbook example once I understood the perspective forced by the corruption. I found, with startling clarity, that corruption doesn't merely affect you *physically*. The identity of the corruption reflects on to you. Sometimes as slowly as a trickle, sometimes in a large amount. It's much worse when actively engaging with it."

"When your mind is present in that space, you are not afforded whatever natural protections you have. Now, I have no idea what infernal or earth corruption may do. However, I'm glad I was blessed to have neither of those. I am certain that if I had an earth affinity, I would have perished in my thirties... if not sooner." Artorian took a breath and furrowed his brow, explaining himself slowly.

"If my assumptions hold true and consistent, then earth would not have 'meshed' with the other corruptions inside of me. This may be useless knowledge to you, dear Yvessa, however... corruption of different kinds seems to also have differing densities. Water corruption is the most prevalent within me, and I believe it is because I receive more of that Essence than any other."

"At first, I thought that the water and fire corruptions were the main culprits for everything inside of me... how to say... *hmm*... moving around? Swirling a little, like sewage would? They are fully opposed, after all. One demands action while the other demands inaction. But I found that air corruption added to this conflict like someone cheering on barbarians in a bar fight. Then I wondered... what effect does celestial have to do with all of this?"

"In my example, is celestial perhaps the *barkeep*?" Artorian knew that he was blasting Yvessa with information that was mostly philosophy and conjecture at this point, but to her credit, she was trying to keep up. Though her expression was lackluster and her brows were furrowed, she did not interrupt. Perhaps she was treating this as a lesson straight out of academia?

"As I kept prodding at the various pustules of corruption and observing their interactions, I realized that it is not fire nor is it water starting the brouhaha." Artorian waggled his finger. "Oh no, the reality is *far* less kind."

"Celestial corruption is the *main* culprit. It infuses the others with itself, unlike the others who fail to exert their influence upon each other. What I have within me is not fire corruption; it's *celestial* fire corruption. The core identity of fire is altered to be an empowered version of itself! Not merely rage and fury but *both*! Then! *Then* tempered with an unhealthy influx of pride!"

Artorian took a deep breath, shuddering lightly. Another bite of food helped him warm up enough to keep speaking. "It evolves into *obsession*. Mania clashing against celestial-infused water-corruption, which is not just mere lethargy but indifference and disinterest made manifest. Air corruption began as flightiness and a desire for activity but became volatile fickleness. A frivolous wanton *whim* that cannot see bounds, nor care for them if it did."

Yvessa scraped the contents at the bottom of the bowl into a pile, giving Artorian a chance to breathe. He just looked so *pleased* to have someone to share his thoughts with. She made him get back to the point. "How does knowing about corruption help you? It's still eating away at you. Corruption doesn't just go *away*."

"My dear, *knowing* is half the battle." She saw his expression as she prepared the last spoonful. When her eyes met his, the spoon abruptly stopped its movement. His look was icy and cold—a look she had never seen on him before and hoped to never see again.

Yvessa stuttered out an icebreaker, "Oh... W-well. I must have been wrong then."

The old man calmed down and patted her on the hand. "Not *wrong*, my dear. We all learn. Some of us just need to learn the hard way. *Mm*. Do thank Tibbins for me. Won't you please?" He opened his mouth and ate the last spoonful.

The full-raiment priestess nodded that she would. "I have some more time before I must attend to duties and prayers. You said... you handled corruption 'individually'. How did you separate that mess?"

Artorian wiped the provided towel across his face. "I suspect much the same way your spiral must separate Essence from corruption. I spun it! Given, I do have the benefit of clashing corruptions that refuse to settle. In fact, I'm fairly certain that if one does settle, I die."

He nodded to himself, certain that he was correct. "To prevent extreme exposure to their effects, I had to believe certain aspects of me were immutable. A 'fortress wall' against the waves of influencing corruption, so to speak. It takes a lot of mental effort to continue, so it's a temporary trait that I am cultivating. Oh! Oh-ho, not *cultivating*, but... pursuing. No need to worry."

Artorian gave her another comforting pat, realizing his expression must have unsettled her. "I cannot influence my corruption directly or even begin to pressure them into anything that might alter them. This is *my* body, however, and I do have some Essence in it—or I would be dead. I thought about how a cultivator must interact with... friendlier aspects of themselves while in their Center. I came up with several ideas to try, and it cost me."

"I found that direction, shape, and design are malleable things, so long as you have even a *little* Essence to work with. I presume that your spirals work by pulling down what is good for you and pushing away the thick, muddy chunks of corruption. For this reason, a spiral does nothing for me. I have almost no Essence to pull down—only corruption. So, I thought to myself, 'Why is it required that Essence be collected in a spiral?' I came to the conclusion that for what I need, it *isn't*."

Yvessa patted him on the shoulder and stood. "It is good that you are feeling better, but I really have duties and–"

"One more moment, please! I am nearly finished. Now, I believe that I require something entirely different and thus am designing various shapes and movement inside of my Center. Finding the Essence was actually rather easy once I knew what not to pay attention to. They are the motes of light that had been swallowed up by the corruption. While the corruption refused to follow my requests, will, or desire... the motes of light that broke free happily danced and moved in whatever fashion I directed them."

Yvessa smiled and turned away, her smile turning into a sigh as Artorian continued, "Essence is oddly similar to a child in that respect. The Essence looked to me for guidance, and I think... I think that before I gave it direction, the Essence looked to my corruption for guidance! It seeks to change, to become, to adapt, and be part of a whole! It craves identity, function. So I, as the fifth—and most powerful—force inside my Center... directed a simple, absolute, unwavering desire into my Essence."

"*Spin.*"

"You had them dance?" Yvessa was breathing deeply at this point, trying to be accommodating to Artorian but also needing to get going. "That's nice. Well, be careful with–"

"The motes were convinced to follow this directive and are now doing so by themselves. Dancing... perhaps, but I would say it looked playful! The motes of light with my direct attention were at least twice as swift, and I noticed the force of its movement pushed corruption away from it."

"I reached out at that point, finding pain in the attempt, and pulled another mote of light to the first. They merged from proximity and my will. I praised them for doing so, and the reaction was incredible! The feedback the mote of light received from me fed back in on itself! I thought the spinning movement had been swift before, ha! Now it is spinning with such intensity that the mote became a thread. I touched it, and I felt a wholeness that I'm... not certain how to describe."

Yvessa leaned in and added some details to clarify Artorian's confusion, "Celestials above... you started actually making a cultivation technique. Artorian... there is no way to tell you how important it is that you keep this information to yourself. At least until you are strong enough to fight your own battles."

When she saw that Artorian was taking her seriously, she explained herself, "What you are describing, the motes of light? That was Essence, and what you describe as a 'thread' is called a Chi thread. It sounds like you discovered the first steps of creating a Chi spiral, and that's both incredible and strange. Controlling a cultivation technique and using it naturally takes years of understanding and practice with a Memory Stone. I know that you've asked for one. I also know it's not here. That means that you have an intrinsic understanding that many people would recruit or murder you for, and you are not strong enough to resist either option they will offer."

Artorian responded after a few long moments of thought, "I understand... but let me clarify for you. What I am doing is *visualization*, my dear. I do not have an understanding that others do not. I simply have better tools for understanding what I can observe."

"I see the shapes and movements I wish to happen and put those forth to the Essence. Since being in my Center is incredibly similar to being in my own mind, it was doable. I visualized myself with the shape of the idea in my hands, and I offered to hand it over to the Essence. The motes of light flocked to my promise of change, and as best I understand it, I gave them a choice to do something. They liked my idea and decided to do *that* instead of following the corruption. Then they formed a large ball, which is a sensation similar to... *hmm*... having overeaten is the best I can think of."

"How, and more importantly, *what* shape are you following? What are you making your Essence do?" Yvessa was finally invested in the conversation, and she seemed to have forgotten about everything else that she may need to be doing.

Artorian smiled at her and decided to explain rather than simply tell her his reasoning. "Keeping the Essence flat, as if on a plane of water, was exceedingly easy, but I found that any change was effort. Making ripples on my flat surface nearly made me violently sick. I had to go and hit water for hours just to see what sort of effects I should be expecting with a liquid since the reactions of 'stuff' out there in the physical world and 'Essence' in my Center appear to be consistent."

"So, what I did was make a *circle* rather than a spiral. I connected the end of the thread with its beginning and set it to spinning. The Essence then formed a loop that, while a little wild and unruly, reached enough velocity to rebuke the corruption that had been attempting to flood over the exact midpoint of my Center. Speaking of the midpoint, a question for you... is there supposed to be a hole there?" Artorian quizzed her, not sure how to phrase his question differently.

Yvessa was startled, and her reply was uncertain. She realized with a blush that she had gotten comfortable in her chair and was listening intently. "Let me look."

She closed her eyes and delved inwards. Even given she had a considerably cleaner Center than the roiling maelstrom of the man next to her, it still required significant effort to find the hole even though that she was actively looking for it. "Huh. I never saw that before. Yes, there certainly is a hole there. That's odd. I have no idea what that... *hmm*."

The old man was pleased to have the confirmation, but Yvessa didn't give him room to gloat. "You deviated from what I asked, old man. You never actually told me how you're separating your corruption."

Artorian wiggled his nose while thinking about her question; for some reason, it made him itch. "Then I shall. My Chi circle, as I suppose I'll call it, is merely a proof of concept. My actual project is ongoing and far more complicated. Instead of 'circles', think of a tube that connects to itself. Spinning it too fast makes all corruption push away from it. However, you recall I mentioned that they had differing densities? The speed at which I spin a tube determines what kind of corruption is pushed away from it and what kind can't escape once it is trapped inside. If I spin it at *just* the right speed, the inside of the tube may fill with, say, fire corruption."

"That makes no sense at all," she complained and would have done more if he hadn't raised a hand to stop her.

"Hold on, I'll get to the point eventually. No, if I spin the tube slightly faster, water-corruption fills it instead while the rest is rebuked. Unfortunately, this constant motion requires far more Essence than I currently have, and I don't even want to talk about the leaks! Keeping any part of the tube uneven breaks the entire thing. So, as I said, it's a work in progress, but... just *maybe,* I'll turn it into something magnificent."

The idea of a clearly defined goal made his expression shine, and his fingers mimed the shapes his mind was making. "I will make four tubes, each for a specific kind of corruption, and I shall trap it *all.* See, I discovered that while the *amount* is constant, the *size* is not set. Corruption can be *compressed!* More corruption than I thought possible can fit in a circular tube. It was as if two buckets of water managed to fit in one without spilling. I marvel at it."

"I *did* ruin a perfectly good pillow that day." His excitement turned somber at an unpleasant recollection. With a sigh, he pushed away from the softness-laden wall. Laying back down on the cot, he opened his robe to let more of the sunlight hit his chest as his caretaker ventured yet another question.

"So... how have you not choked on corruption? You should have long been out of Essence to work with." The young priestess was once again packing up to leave but couldn't contain her curiosity.

This, at least, Artorian could answer easily, though he knew that she may not like the answer. "Do you recall, my dear, how you mentioned that you could only cultivate at a very particular certain time of the day?"

Yvessa nodded, interested to hear where this was going. Artorian decided to simply put it out there, "My source of Essence doesn't rely on such specifics. I am cultivating by sitting in the light of the sun—the sun always shines, or the light of the stars always reaches us. The sun does give me a better influx, however, starlight works just fine. Therefore, there is a constant source of *something* that is ever-present. I am not actively cultivating—still working that out—I'm merely letting my passive absorption work with some directed will."

"I have not yet figured out how one *pulls* Essence. Yet, while I lay here, Essence slowly and steadily fills my Center. When I have a good handle on how much I need to keep alive, I will use the rest to play. So far, I have clearly been using more than I have to spare, and I shall work to remedy that."

He motioned at himself to reflect on his poor state. "The results are visible. I am bedridden. My absorption doesn't end, so long as I keep myself exposed to starlight. I'm going to try and tune myself to it like the strings of a harp. The heavens and the earth may provide Essence, but if the Essence of the earth is spoken for by countless cultivators, I will simply direct my efforts to less tapped sources. Since one would need all four of my affinity channels to not retain massive amounts of corruption from drawing from such a source, I imagined my intake would be sizable. I can't say I'm holding it well, as it merely floats freely in my Center. Yet, I was certainly not wrong."

Having eaten and spoken much, his energy was spent the same as if he'd run several laps around the village. His eyes sank to a half-lidded state, and his breaths turned shallow as the pleasantries of a full stomach pushed him to rest. That was fine with his caretaker; Yvessa had much to think about. Only monks who had nothing but dedication to the art of cultivation were generally so knowledgeable. All they did all day was cultivate and think about cultivation. The old man wasn't that different, even if another purpose seemed to drive him. He had a burning *need* to live, and Yvessa couldn't say he was doing it for his own sake.

The conversation had given her some ideas for her own cultivation, and even the small enlightenment she had gained would prove beneficial. She'd get him lots of things to write on and then read the results. Though she had warned him not to tell others about creating his own techniques, she was protected by the umbrella of the Church and was already planning to spread any useful information to a few people she liked before passing it on.

Nobody knew much about corruption, and since Artorian had mentioned the Skyspear Academy, her mind had put two and two together on how he'd figured so much out. Someone had been blessed with an education at some point in life. Not that this made any sense for what the old man was doing out here all alone in the Fringe, holding all that expensive knowledge. His mention of diverting his Essence into a circle had been unpleasant; moving Essence into new patterns *hurt!*

The time it had taken her to pull her first Chi thread alone... putting her spiral together had left Yvessa with headaches, stomach problems, and she didn't want to think about the actual feelings of pain she went through from direct manipulation. Then there was this absolute nonsense about starlight. She'd nodded and smiled her way through but hadn't truly believed what he had been saying. If he was talking about stars, why mention the sun? At least half of what he had been rambling on about was garbage, the ranting of a man on his deathbed. It would be difficult to separate out the wheat from the chaff if she did get notes from him.

Specifically, a sunlight cultivator was unheard of, a pipe dream, and she thought the old man must have been losing his train of thought and grasping at whatever hope he could find to keep going. She sighed and shook her head. She was late and had much to do; the nearby village of Lapis had agreed to a meeting.

The expedition had gotten contact with the traders in an attempt to once again get goods flowing in and out of the area. The designated trader for salt had gone missing, sort of. The cart found at the raider trail was identified as property of the prior trader, so killed in action was the actual writ on the official report. To her delight, new traders coming meant a variation of goods and a use for her silver. Finally. All in all, things were starting to look up for this on-paper-only expedition crew.

Time to give the requisite compliments to Tibbins. The special ingredient he'd added that helped induce sleep had been wonderful. Maybe the old fool would actually sleep for a change. His constant pretending was getting on her nerves! Yvessa muttered to herself as she strode back to her personal tent, "Thank you, Tibbins! A little rest for all of us, thanks to you."

CHAPTER TWENTY-FOUR

The changing of the season was the signal for great activity at the encampment. In particular, it was what people had been waiting for; the majority of the expedition force had served its due time and was to be released to go home.

A predictable and set pattern repeated itself almost daily in the camp. With proper structures and fortifications now built, the cleaned-up village resembled a remote cloister. Every high noon, everyone attended the prayer chant. This included their two hospice charges. With the threat of the raiders gone and no sign they would be returning any time soon, it was time for Tarrean to announce the cadre that would remain behind.

The selection could have been guessed, and some gambling did indeed make the rounds. Coppers and silvers exchanged hands between those who thought their line-up was correct. The rules for the new cloister had become ever laxer as Tarrean learned how to be a father first and Head Cleric second. At this point, when basic duty was done for the day, all Clerics could do as they pleased. Arbitrary tasks had simply been removed. The Acolytes and Initiates could, of course, expect the tedious tasks to return as soon as they rejoined the arms of the Choir.

To the expedition's grumbles, there hadn't been a *single* conversion in the Fringe. The Lapis village was equally as stubborn as their hands were blue. When the announcement of the cadre staying at this new cloister came, nobody was truly surprised. Gossip had become as valuable as currency, as tips on cultivation were often included in the daily gatherings.

Remaining behind was Tarrean, which people had expected ever since Tibbins let some things 'slip'. Possibly as a punishment for his gossiping, Tibbins was to remain as well. The group at large was going to miss his cooking; Initiates swore up and down that he had food Essence rather than celestial. Jin was to stay, of course. The young lad had never been so adamant about something in his life. Returning to the Choir was to leave the family he'd come to love over the last season.

Tarrean may have been a prideful, haughty man, but he had an obvious soft spot for the wellbeing of his boy. Not even he had the heart to send his son away. This also meant Irene would remain; the reason she gave was that the Fringe let her study the scriptures in peace, that there was no better place for her than a cloister. The expedition force might have even believed that reason too, had an Initiate not seen Jin asleep in her lap on the edge of the salt flats.

This sparked a whole new round of gossip, as a surprising number of recruits hadn't known she'd been in a relationship with the Head Cleric. The fifth member of the cadre had volunteered at the last moment, to the utmost grievance of all but one gambler. Yvessa would remain since someone was needed to attend to hospice care. With her cultivation stuck and stifled and the clear skill at handling what many of the other Initiates considered a chore, there were no complaints.

The surprise for the group came when Tarrean rose at the end of the daily prayer and promoted Jiivra as the new Head Cleric. Rounds of applause met the increase in station as several Initiates were lifted to Acolyte, creating a cascade of cheers each time another name was called. The Head Cleric had the paperwork all prepared, signed, and ready to hand out. When they reported back, many of them would be able to benefit from their new rank.

The rise in status was well-founded with the individual's accomplishments, requirement of cultivation standard, and more.

Such glowing accommodations would be enough to give several Acolytes the opportunity for even greater advancement in the Choir. There would be a small celebration in the evening before the tent encampment was to be broken up the following morning, leaving only the wooden cloister, defenses, and several minor structures behind.

The festivities saw the resurrection of the Salt village's bonfire pit, and after, it doubled to serve as one big cleanup pile. Before the sun dipped under the horizon, a guard called out that a merchant caravan had been spotted in the distance. The path taken by the caravan allowed the guard to determine that the merchant must have gone to Lapis, then come to their new cloister. While that in itself added to the celebration, certain deliveries were cause for concern. That very concern was what had the new Head Cleric knocking on a small door with all the mirth of an unamused lioness.

The zealous Battle Leader didn't wait for a reply. As far as she was concerned, bedridden, old men weren't supposed to answer the door even if they were awake.

"Come in," Jiivra heard a tired and half-asleep voice mutter the words and realized that her entrance had cut off whatever else the old man was going to say. His surprised look was distant, though it focused as he observed her. "Good evening, Artorian. I trust you remember me?"

The tired Elder squinted at her, face neither fully awake nor aware. His words reflected that, being pensive and uncertain. "I'm familiar with your voice, my dear. I hear it in the mornings during drills. You take care to consider the well-being of your people rather than their readiness. Jiivra, If I'm correct?"

"Head Cleric Jiivra, now," she corrected swiftly.

"Oh, *congratulations*, Head Cleric." A slow smile flashed to her, the uncertainty removed from his face. "I don't believe you've come to visit before. As I recall, you're not too fond of me. May I take it this concerns more... official issues?"

Jiivra watched the old, well-bundled, and seated Elder regain his poise before she began. She set her heavy helmet down on the small table and leaned her war spear against the wall. It gave a gentle, metal *tink* as it bumped against an iron pot on the table. Jiivra remained professional and at attention, her voice holding a surprising amount of smooth depth. "I don't dislike you *personally*, Artorian. However, I have a strong dislike of things that disturb the unity and order of the Church."

"I have had to throw my weight around to keep these slacking recruits and Acolytes in place and on their toes ever since the rules became lax. It's not good to let things skew from regulation, and I'm against such poor work ethic. As the new Head Cleric, I will train this expedition crew back into a respectable shape long before we reach the Choir. I will not arrive with some chatty, haphazard force." Jiivra stopped as the tiny, persistent smile on the old man's face unsettled her. "Something tells me you knew about my promotion."

Artorian quietly nodded. "It may have come up in conversation. I also may have recommended you for the position when the topic came up. I have a nose for talent. Won't you please sit with me, Head Cleric? I feel that we have much to discuss."

His voice was passive and a little too smooth for the zealot's liking, but she found no reason to distrust the man; in fact, she had to admit that she felt curious. A few deft, heavy steps sounded as she made her way to the pillow-covered chair next to the invalid's bed. Well, mostly invalid. She saw him every now and then as she went about her day but never for more than a few minutes. Usually, though, this codger was up to something. "Talk, I can do. In fact, I'll just get right to it. Did you by chance have Tibbins order a... pillow? I believe there was a mix up."

Artorian's smile grew thrice-fold, and Jiivra suppressed a sigh as his raucous laughter split the air in the small space. After taking a deep breath to firm up her self-control, Jiivra's voice was able to remain steady. Yet, the undertone showed a lack of patience that would have been clear even to small animals. "Twelve... by *twelve*."

She received some giggling nods in response as the old man was beset by helpless laughter, trying to catch his breath as he patted his chest. "I believe I can safely assume you meant this as some kind of prank on the Head Cleric?"

Artorian, having gotten a hold of himself, gently shook his head in the negative and explained, "I *very* distinctly made it clear that my requested item would be costly. It was brushed over, considered not to be a problem. In fact, I was ordered to just note it to Tibbins. I received no further retort. That I put down *feet* instead of inches, well..."

The sly, old man had a smile plastered on his face that simply would not budge. Tarrean's fuming outburst could already be heard near the storage site where the caravan had been allowed to pull in and where twelve men had been required to unload the puffy beast. Jiivra's words were cold, pushing on to other business. "Since that *monstrosity* is already paid for, and I am now responsible for explaining that expense to the Choir, I was hoping that we could come to an... agreeable compromise. You've put me in a very unpleasant spot, and that is even before we have the talk about this."

From her belt pouch Jiivra retrieved a very finely wrapped, small object. Upon unfurling the Memory Stone, it gave off a minor radiance. Artorian locked his eyes on to the small rock, and his hands were already squeezing each other. He very dearly wanted to reach out and cradle it—all that beautiful knowledge, answers to the holes in his reasoning that he had not managed to figure out. It was indeed going to take years to figure this all out on his own, but if he had more access to the basics... he could do more. So much more.

"I am quite interested in what you have to say, Head Cleric. Please do begin." His words had some haste in them, not wanting to tarry. A sharp nod from Jiivra was all he got before she folded the stone back up.

"As authority of the expedition force now lays in my hands, I am fully entitled to rescind offered gifts. Now, I have heard rumors of what caused Tarrean to make such a ludicrous deal with you. However, those details don't concern me. I am an instrument of the Church, and the wellbeing of my Choir must come first."

"That giant pillow is *ridiculous*, and I have no interest in carting it with me. The trader equally refuses to take it back after it was unloaded, and there's no space for it anywhere except the middle of the cloister. That's an irritation but not my main focus. No, providing you the stone is what I'd like major compensation for."

"To this effect, newly minted Acolyte Yvessa has provided me the full writ of various philosophical papers and thought on cultivation that you'd like to have delivered to the Skyspear Academy. While this is a kindness we will gladly do, I would like a personal copy as a donation to the Church. I don't need to explain to you that this is valuable material, and as an aspiring Paladin, I must seek to grow the Church. I will, of course, remove your name from all future interactions so that you are not hunted down and squeezed for all the information you can provide."

The Battle Leader paused to take a breath, planning to continue with some other ideas. She'd prepared an argument that would hopefully convince him to give up something far more valuable than some borderline useless cultivation technique. She never got the chance; Artorian instantly agreed, "I accept."

"The Church I..." Jiivra brushed aside his objection and then began her attempt to convince him. Her brain took a moment to catch up with the information she'd been provided so calmly. "You... *accept?*"

Jiivra's expression finally faltered from her previous stoic countenance, melting into surprise and cautious confusion. Her fighting sense told her this must be a trap; everything too easy was always a trap.

Artorian took over the new conversation, "No need to look so taken aback, my dear. You may have heard much about me, but I have in turn remembered who you are while you've spoken. This conversation was not what I expected. I honestly thought you would ask why I recommended you, but I will not press the issue. Yes, Head Cleric, the Church may have a copy of my findings on corruption and the little I've puzzled together to form my brand of cultivation. It would be far more beneficial for people to know more about this awful malady. After all, does the Church not provide for those who cannot easily provide for themselves? Hmm?"

Jiivra regained her stature at the glowing comment about her beliefs. "Yes, of course. Even the Choir, of which we are part, puts the wellbeing of the common folk before the hunting down evildoers. I was... under the impression that, while you may get along with certain individuals, the Church as a whole was the same as Skyspear Academy in your view."

Artorian waved his hand left to right to say it was not. "I hold firm to certain beliefs. That your group is part of the Church has never concerned me as much as anyone seems to think that it does. If it helps you reconcile your thoughts, I am not giving this information to the Church as a whole, my dear. I am giving it to you. As in my eyes, you are the true Church."

Seeing Jiivra's features light up, he smiled and continued to lecture, "You are the single most devout upholder of values that I've met, and as much as you may silently hold me in poor graces... I do not hold you poorly in mine. I see you weighed with a great burden and that you have laden yourself with a responsibility heavier than the mere tasks of being Head Cleric. I would like to speak with you about this before you go, if that is alright with you. I think that I can help. I will say this—I think you are a good person. A great leader. Someone who stands with her beliefs and her people. Now, would you say our transaction is concluded?"

"I... yes, I do." The Battle Leader felt trapped in the chair, and she hated the feeling. An anchor in her stomach kept her rooted as the old man had prodded a finger straight into her hidden worries. To have her fears exposed by an old fool made her anxious and angry. Jiivra tried to hide this in front of him, but her best efforts could not convince herself that there were details he didn't already know. The old man simply had a reputation for cutting to the heart of matters. She grit her teeth and pushed through, "Yes, business is concluded. I shall hold you to your word."

She picked up the finely wrapped lump in the cloth and put it in his cupped hands. Artorian closed his hands so tightly that they shook, and Jiivra didn't know what to think about the sparkle of childlike happiness in his heavy blue eyes. It was as if he had never before gotten a present and had just been handed something he loved. Jiivra decided to take her leave. "Pressing the Memory Stone to your forehead is all you need to do. The rest will just come naturally."

CHAPTER TWENTY-FIVE

"Will you leave after I have used the stone?" Artorian carried a somber note in his tired voice. "If that is the case, I'd love to just have a small amount of your time to talk."

The weight in Jiivra's stomach increased, surprised that he hadn't used the Memory Stone immediately. She hadn't particularly wanted to stay, but better to just... get it over with. "I was going to, yes, but if you'd like to have a small chat first, I suppose... that would be acceptable."

Given the room was silent and Artorian didn't start the conversation, Jiivra simply opened up like so many others had done. The small hovel felt safe; it was tiny and well-constructed, but more than anything, it was filled with comfort. A small fire burned in the corner of the fireplace, and the square construction of the house made the room feel boxed in enough to make all the little, personal touches feel pleasant.

The old man had drawings, handwritten notes from Initiates, and several objects just stashed all around the room that seemed more like a container for memories than the stone that sat in his lap. The place had nothing but chairs and pillows, a single bed and table, and a large corner where someone could sit and measure out all that was needed for the day.

It felt awkward to share, but this was fine. It was fine. She carried a burden, and it spilled freely when given the opportunity. "I was supposed to lead my own expedition team before this, but a few... tests went awry. During one such test, my hands began to shake, and I could not focus. What everyone wanted me to do, needed me to do... it just became too much, and it plagued my thoughts like an endlessly ringing bell. The pressure of the test made me collapse in front of a full congregation, and I took that... poorly. I don't have the luxury to fail! I need to succeed! When I reached D-rank one and I qualified to take the test... it all rushed back and..."

"Artorian, I am supposed to become a *leader* of the order—a frontline force and beacon of the Choir. I sought endless opportunities to overcome my fears and cope, but in truth, while I have the title now, it only sickens me. I feel an unbearable weight fill me. Uncertainty creeps into my head, and it screams at me that I will not succeed. I was told, endlessly, that this is my fate. A Head Cleric is just not who I am. I can fight with the best of them, but leading? Being in charge, determining the fate of the people that rely on me? It's this fearful thing that haunts me with every s-*step*."

Jiivra wrenched her hands together as the words and worries gushed out like water from a broken dam. More of the same message kept spilling from her—with a few repetitions—as the woman started to heavily stutter and lose focus. Artorian patted her hands to break her out the spiral that she had fallen into. "Allow a few words from this old fool, my dear. A truth that is small, like a coddled flame."

The old man released her hands. After years of bottling up her fears and anxieties, the invitation of support felt amazing. Jiivra regarded Artorian and, for a moment, was a small girl again. His calm, grandfatherly countenance set her at ease, the crackle of the fire making the back of her neck tingle. Jiivra's anxious mind craved whatever nugget of hope he might offer that would help her fulfill the duties she so dreaded. She felt trapped by her assigned obligations.

"Fate this, fate that," he rumbled the words out, slightly upset with them. "A secret for you is that, in truth, there is *no such* thing as fate, just as there is no such thing as *talent*. When someone else wants you to take on a role, it is frequently masked by mentions of 'fate'. Oh, she's *fated* to be this. Oh, she's *fated* to be that."

He waved that prospect away. "No! You are not stuck being what someone else wants you to be! That's not their choice to make. A sense of identity, who you are, is decided entirely by you. You can choose to be who you want to be. Fate is a cheap comfort and nothing more. It is the lie someone holds on to when they don't know what to do with themselves, and we know that is not true for you."

Artorian stopped speaking and leaned away, reaching for a small, bound book he'd been gifted. Opening it, he showed her that the entire interior was blank. He flipped the cover to the first page, laid a quill next to it, and popped open an inkwell that joined the other tools on the little table.

"Write," he said this word with certainty, confident about the message he'd given her. "Write your hopes, your dreams, your wants. Ignore what everyone else has told you. Close your thoughts to such whispers and listen only to the words that come purely from you."

Jiivra was hesitant and didn't particularly feel comfortable with this command. Still, she felt so off-balance that she took the quill, dipped it, and without saying a word, slipped into the mode that made her follow orders. Orders were easy. Orders were convenient. She thought of her dreams when she was in the convent, what she had declared with her prideful mouth. Endlessly getting in trouble and laughing off the repercussions before the rank and file structure became her life and the call to become a Paladin consumed her. The first page was filled before she looked up to notice it.

Artorian had remained quiet the entire time. He'd not interrupted or even moved. With her realization that she'd written so much, the old man slowly started easing the cover closed. Without resistance, he took the quill from her hesitant grip. Loud, sharp scratches ripped into the cover as he carved colored letters rather than merely scribe them. When he was done and returned the book, she took it and read what he'd etched. Emotions bubbled inside of her, and the weight in her stomach fluctuated.

The front of the book now read 'Jiivra's Fate'.

Her brow furrowed, and she questioned the old man with a look. Artorian remained calm, merely smiling at her. "Your fate, my dear. Fate as chosen by the only person that has say over it. You. Keep that pocketbook; it's yours. Together, you'll journey far."

Jiivra didn't have words as she watched the old man prepare to move to his next task. He unfurled the cloth and pressed the Memory Stone to his forehead. It didn't seem too exciting from her perspective, but she remembered what it had been like for her. When Jiivra saw his face, she sighed and had to roll her eyes.

The aged academic was having a delightful time of it. Answers that had eluded him rushed forth in the form of someone else's memories. The information started with the creation process of a basic spiral and was completed with the feel and methodology for actively cultivating. All crucial information that Artorian did not previously have. The basic functions, now that he grasped them, were all so simple. When the rock came down, his other hand went up.

Slap!

His open palm whacked against his eyes and forehead as a soft laugh eschewed from his throat. "That was *it*? That's *all*? Actively cultivating is the willful effort to *pull* while you're present in your Center and visualizing drawing from that which is around you? I'm truly a blind, old fool."

Artorian used a towel to wipe his face, preventing himself from getting teary at all the wonderful things he'd just learned. Answers to issues he had not even considered to be a question... he found solutions for. He was burning to set them into motion. "There is such *risk* to cultivating! I wasn't aware that you needed to sacrifice awareness of the world around you to such a degree while you focus your efforts inwards."

Jiivra didn't share his epiphany nor his joyful manner. This was all basic information she'd had for years. Instead, she was torn at the oddly thoughtful gift she'd just been given. Not just considerations that the word 'fate' shrouded the wishes of others but that her own desires had become solidly codified in book format. Something Jiivra had never thought of before; words were stronger when written.

They felt real rather than ephemeral. Jiivra still felt off-balance but less from the weight that had eaten at her for years. For the first time, she had an alternative literally in her hands. She still believed she would walk the path of the Paladin, however, the reason as to why was beginning to change. Jiivra was going to be a Paladin because she wanted to be, not because some high-strung Vicars had told her she needed to be one.

The difference in how it sounded was minor, but the difference in how she felt about it was profound. Her shoulders jerked when she realized Artorian was carefully observing her instead of being enamored with his own thoughts. "May I ask a cultivation question?"

Jiivra was more than happy to leave the prior topic behind and jumped on the new one with the same speed that she mounted her Diretusk Boar. "Certainly."

She didn't see a reason not to go along with this talk. There were things she wanted to attend to, but the twinkly-eyed scholar and his varied interests constantly made her curiosity flare up. Artorian thanked her and launched right in, "What can you do with Essence other than just keep it within you and refine it for your well-being?"

Jiivra's face flattened; that was a far-reaching topic he'd set up. "Difficult question. The basics are generally core cultivation, followed by Essence sight. Which, by the way, is done by cycling Essence to your eyes. There is basic healing, which celestial Essence excels at... *hmm*. Incantations, which are powerful, single-use, large-scale effects, but you lose all of the Essence you invested into them. Basic enhancement, which is what I'm currently working on... though my technique isn't without flaw. Then techniques, which... cover a lot of things."

Ergh. Fumbling her words, she found that she really couldn't continue that line of questions further without something more specific to discuss. "There are a few more options, but those will be of no use to you unless you're capable of the ones I just spoke on. To reach D-rank one, I needed to turn my Chi spiral into a Chi fractal. It's an enhanced level of the current cultivation technique you just learned. Almost everyone starts with a spiral and goes up from there. Only Royals have access to other methods, and they are kept secret."

Artorian shared Jiivra's expression; both were visibly confused. "I don't know the differences between ranks. Is there a reason I never hear E-rank? I've heard F and D while talking with the other Initiates."

Jiivra sank back in her chair ever so minutely. She'd explain that at least, his first easy question. "F-rank is where your average adult human begins even if they do not cultivate. E-rank is a... special rank. It means 'Echo'. Someone in the 'Echo' ranks has had someone else's cultivation technique 'echoed' into them, allowing them a quicker rise through the ranks. This is usually because a gifted technique is better than what someone can cobble together themselves."

"Anyone of D-rank or higher can do this, but the process is incredibly costly and dangerous, as it requires a direct connection to another person's Center. Such techniques have many dangers. If something goes wrong, it ends poorly for both participants. I, as example, could Echo my fractal on to someone else. However, the Essence it would require would leave me so dry and drained, that I am nearly guaranteed to die."

The Battle Leader was giving a lecture and started to ease back into a place she was comfortable with. Teaching others was something that she liked. "After D, come the C-ranks. These people are truly powerhouses. The general comparison is that a D-rank could take on ten F-ranks in a fight, and one C-rank could take ten D-ranks. A C-rank cultivator can be recognized fairly easily. Usually, their bodies have been imbued with Essence, and they generally have a very powerful Aura—so much so that non-cultivators can be suppressed just being near them. I have only met a handful but standing next to one always felt like I was standing next to pure danger."

"To become a Paladin, I am required to achieve C-rank one. I'm told to take my time, as entering the C-ranks will take whatever cultivation technique I have and make it 'solid'. What was meant by that I'm not sure. After the C-ranks, there are Mages. These are the B and A-ranks and are so complicated and secretive that I know next to nothing about them... except to never make someone in that rank mad."

Jiivra ended the quick rundown, but it seemed Artorian didn't have any issues with her explanation, a joy to her after needing to deal with recruits all the time. Artorian's soft words prodded at another sensitive topic. "Could we go over techniques in more detail?"

The new Head Cleric didn't want to go through the entire gamut of explanations, but now that she'd gotten herself into it, she tried to cobble something together. "It's a term for an Essence effect that has a... foundation? It doesn't crumble right away like an incantation does, and the cost varies depending on how good that 'foundation' is? I know of a few superiors who can use their Essence in the form of an attack, and that's also called a technique. That's... *still* not it. It's *hard* to explain."

Tapping her lips, she disregarded Choir-lore and explained it the way she thought of it. Practical applications were easier to explain and implement than their lofty ideal counterparts. "A technique is a specific method and manner in which very precise amounts of Essence are moved in order to achieve some kind of effect. As an example, when I move one 'unit' of celestial Essence to a muscle in my arm, I gain temporary strength and speed before my muscle burns through that Essence, expending the unit of Essence."

"Unlike cycling Essence to your eyes, which keeps the Essence in you without great loss, a technique is a stable method for expending Essence in trade for temporary power. Flashier and larger effect techniques require greater amounts of Essence, with additional costs for everything else you want it to do. Don't let anyone ever tell you they're 'free' or 'you always get the Essence back'. That's only if you're compatible with the technique and can perform it perfectly. Which, as you can guess, is almost never the case."

Jiivra's voice betrayed some irritation at past failures, but she didn't elaborate and instead marched on, "I can heal someone by concentrating my celestial Essence on their wounds, and that is draining. However, I could *also* do that from a distance. The problem is every bit of space my Essence has to cross to reach that person vastly increases the Essence cost to the point that it is prohibitive and thus never done. You run the risk of draining yourself dry from attempting a technique you're not suited for or that is vastly too flashy."

"To most people, the useful thing about proper techniques is that they allow you to burn off miniscule amounts of corruption with each use. The effects of the techniques undergo drastic changes when corruption is added. Why that is the case is something we didn't really know, but with this writing you've provided, I have a few thoughts. A technique always starts from your Center, where you keep all of your Essence. I take mine from the Essence stored in my meridians, and I hear stronger cultivators can apply a technique from their Aura. I don't know how that works, but my guess is since an Aura is always around you at any given time, you can move Essence swiftly."

"For myself, I begin at my Center, take the appropriate 'units' of Essence, and order it to the place I need them to be. When the celestial Essence is in my arm, I push the energy in and think of striking harder with my spear. My arm then consumes the Essence, and for that one strike, my power is significantly enhanced. More units of Essence means a better result, but there's a limit."

"Pump too much Essence, and my arm flares with pain. I get the natural effect of celestial Essence instead of the effect I wanted, but the celestial Essence heals the damage I've done to myself. If I can't focus on what I want the technique to do, it all falls apart. The real nasty kicker is when someone tries it with an Essence that isn't celestial." Her expression turned gruesome as she held her upper arms while shaking her head to get the image out. Failing body-empowerment was a terrible way to die.

"It's all very visual and mental, horribly difficult to do. I keep to the quantifiable and just focus on appropriate units. As a reference, I would say my arm can take one-hundred units. A unit of Essence is different for everyone, but I've found my method to yield good results. I'm not very imaginative, but I'm excellent with numbers. If you want to see someone truly skilled at precision Essence use, consult Keeper Irene. She was a beast before she accepted the position as Keeper. Irene measures her Essence capacities by the individual muscle."

Artorian was still making mental notes as Jiivra stopped and looked at the window; she really needed to go. "Don't let me keep you, my dear. You've been a delight."

He sunk back into the cot and prepared for more rest. "The pillow can go wherever there's room for it. As to your new journal, why don't I send you letters? We can keep in touch, and you can tell me how your dreams are coming along. In the meanwhile, I can sneak you any little bit of insight I gain while I lay here pondering."

The Battle Leader stood, pocketbook still clasped in her hand. Jiivra couldn't deny that his offer wasn't enticing, so she just asked the worry that was on her mind. "You don't mind that I'm likely to share your findings with the Church?"

Artorian reached out, eyes half-lidded. He'd had a long day—for him. "I don't mind sharing the little I find with *you* at all."

The old man appeared to slow significantly, and his hand slipped and fell from her glove. Jiivra caught it and gently placed it back on his resting chest. It seemed that was all the old fool was able to handle today. She treasured the idea that as far as Artorian was concerned, she already was the beacon she wished to be.

A Paladin.

Jiivra parted her new volume and ripped a page from the back, describing how to send letters to a priest in the Choir.

She placed the folded page under his water cup and pulled the blanket over him. What a strange, little man. Jiivra kept her hand on the blanket longer than she needed to and didn't even notice her own smile as it grew in the flicker of the firelight.

"Stay alive, long beard. I want you to read this book when it's full." The cleric closed her eyes and focused inwards, pulling on her celestial Essence to bring it forth. She brought it up through her arm and concentrated energy into her palm, a soft glow seeping through. Essence moved through the cloth as if it wasn't there and bled into Artorian's chest. His breathing wheezed a little easier as the clean energy was absorbed by hungry cells, and the aged heartbeat came ever-so-slightly more steadily.

She heaved the recovered helmet back on to her head and felt the familiar weight of her spear in her hand. New confidence found her; it was time to be a leader.

CHAPTER TWENTY-SIX

After the expedition team had left, life in the cloister fell into a very predictable daily routine. The clerics who remained behind, while devout in their faith, settled into a more family-oriented pattern. Prayer was still daily, chants were recited and taught, but the work focus shifted over to food production and long-term stability. With so few present, the available workforce was limited to mostly Jin, Tibbins, and Tarrean.

Irene made everything operate smoothly, though Yvessa filled in when she wasn't tending to Switch and Artorian. Switch was still unable to speak or interact with the world around her, but Artorian was doing well under their tender ministrations. The apiary had been re-established, the apple grove was healthy, but the salt flats had been abandoned in favor of small fields that grew basic crops.

Cultivators were *vastly* more capable than an ordinary person, and progress requiring physical labor was *incredibly* easy for them. On certain days, they even had time to harvest some salt from the flats; though they all had to be careful to lock down their passive cultivation. They couldn't afford to take *any* Essence from the Scar, even if it might be tempting to tap into that huge resource.

The new trader, Olgier the Northman, came once a month with additional meal options that were bartered for with salt. Luckily for Tarrean, their bedridden, old fox knew all of the values and weights for proper and *fair* bartering. The trader—to his teeth-gnashing displeasure—was unable to swindle or get overly favorable transactions. Still, he was there every month without fail.

As an additional bonus, when the huge, red-haired Olgier swung by, he was usually given a few parcels to deliver. One mail parcel always went to a Head Cleric in the Choir. While another was sent far, far forwards to some Academy in the mountains. Olgier didn't particularly *like* to play mailman, but an extra bag of salt went a long way toward making him forgive the hassle. Rutsel—his town of origin—was well-known for its hunting grounds, and salt was needed for preservation.

To Artorian, the quiet days where he merely laid down and basked in sunlight were *quite* busy, though not that many people knew it. His Lazuli robe hung neatly on his old bow, having remained there after Artorian noticed he got better results when more of him was... *exposed*. He wore some warm, winter pants and kept his pillows snug all about him to retain warmth. As a minor bonus, the pillow wall blocked just the *tiniest* bit of extra wind. For the majority of the day, sunlight poured through the open window and washed over the old man.

The earliest part of the day, where the sun just wasn't *quite* in the right place to stream through the opening, was an excellent time to wrestle his way out of bed. He would mosey over to the stream to wash himself and take care of necessities. Artorian adamantly *refused* to let Yvessa bathe him, even if his clumsy stumbling meant that there were times he desperately needed her help to actually *arrive* at the stream. Though everyone else only saw the tired, old man rest, eat, and talk to himself, Artorian was fully absorbed and attentive to the activity in his Center for the duration of nearly every day.

It made time absolutely *fly* by, and even the interruptions where he was nudged for a meal were swiftly forgotten so he could bolt back into his new favorite play-zone like an impatient toddler. He wasn't actually muttering to *himself* during the day; he'd found it was easier to be vocal and bicker with his Essence to keep himself focused. It helped smooth progression, and the breakthroughs he had were *phenomenal*, even if they came with a cost. Still, after gaining the knowledge from the Memory Stone, things were looking up.

His control of Essence wasn't fantastic; it required great practice and patience to get things right. He tended to run out of patience and would pause only to throw ideas at the wall. One of the few times he bothered to snap out of his fantasy was when someone needed a word or when a flash of brilliance struck him that had to *immediately* find its way on to paper. His desk contained a messy pile of notes compiled on cloudy days where cultivation was going to be inadequate.

Artorian's contributions to the Academy were in the order he figured things out, rather than a cohesive step-by-step build. Hopefully, those sharp minds sitting on their tall rocks would parse the documents in the correct order. As the sun rose into the correct position, Artorian settled in his bed again for the day. However, he found Yvessa firmly seated in the bedside chair with her arms crossed.

"Yes, my dear?" he quizzed with the expectation of something being amiss.

"What are you up to, old man? You've been... *suspicious*. I can ignore all that mumbling to yourself, but I cycled Essence to my eyes yesterday to have a look at you. Frankly, I have no idea *what* I'm seeing. Your Center was a disgusting mess—it still *is*—but now it's this," she made a floppy, circled hand motion of uncertainty, not knowing how to explain herself, "mess of colored rings? I can tell it's corruption, but nothing I know of tells me it could *possibly* behave like that. Did you *actually* make tubes of Essence? That's *horrifying*! To sustain that... the sheer amount of Essence it must suck down is more than I manage to actively cultivate in a whole day!"

Her gaze sharpened. "*Explain.*"

Artorian rolled his eyes. He could *pretend* to be all innocent and know nothing, but he was more than aware that she read his mail. Yvessa was capable of looking at his Essence flows anytime, so trying to be stealthy while making progress was not happening either. "Shall I explain from the *beginning*, then?"

Yvessa leered at him with demanding expectations. "Of *course,* from the start!"

"Fifty years ago, I was born. From there– *Ow*! Rude! Not the beginning then... So, Essence. As discovered, there are two draw methods: passively taking it in or *actively* taking it in. If I consider a drop of Essence to be a drop of water, then my *Center* is a bucket, and my *body* is a well. Both can only hold so much. Corruption comes along with Essence, and for every *one* drop of Essence, you have roughly *two* drops of corruption."

Artorian paused to make sure she was following. "A normal person likely isn't bothered by this intake until they're about my age, at which point the body starts to break down. Really, it's just corruption being a nuisance. Once you get to the entry-stage of cultivating, one's ability to actively draw Essence in speeds up the process of dying if you are not careful. So, preventing corruption intake becomes *paramount*. The technique *you* have allows you to separate the drop of Essence from the whole and *mostly* reject the corruption from entering your bucket. I noticed you all have a little celestial glow that shows the main bias in your Essences, so your technique is *not* flawless."

"For every ten to twelve hands of time, I would say you passively gain what *I* consider a single unit of Essence. It's not an exact measurement, but there's an average I can deduce after having watched you all so long. For ease of understanding, twelve hands are an hour, as one hand is five minutes. Even if you would gain a unit in ten hands, I'll call it twelve so you can follow this next section." Yvessa nodded to show that she was following, and the resting man went on.

"This part will differ slightly for everyone. The reason why I round it out is for convenience. See, I heard something *interesting* from Jiivra. Adding too much Essence into muscles causes 'backfire'. Also, *never* add corruption to your body if you can help it. Sweet *mercy*, what a day that was. I lost *weeks* of progress cleaning that up." Artorian sighed and rubbed his forehead, taking a good drink of water while his caretaker smirked.

"When you actively cultivate, the rate at which you draw in natural energy increases threefold. Three and a *bit*. That's the basic spiral, which is rather good even with its limitations. Tarrean draws in three times as much as *that*, so his technique is a vast improvement over the basic one. He somehow broke up his spiral into two additional spirals. Reminded me of a diagram from my Academy days. It seemed to be the beginning of a fractal? The shape was a... triskelion? Yes, that."

Yvessa laid a hand on Artorian to pause his words, her smirk now a frown. "You can cycle Essence to your eyes and study someone's cultivation base? *How*? Who taught you that?"

Artorian scoffed but dodged explaining that secret for now, "Not exactly *difficult* once you figure the basics of Essence out. Now, back to the lesson! For every drop of Essence *you* gain when actively cultivating, Tarrean gains *three*. Just to give you an idea of how useful it would be to enter the D-ranks. Now, that is only counting a *single* affinity channel. So long as nothing is interfering, you get one drop per affinity channel of every affinity so long as you are somewhere they can be gathered."

Her voice cut his off lecture, "Interfering?"

Artorian derailed for a moment before finding his thoughts once more. "Oh, yes. Say that you, for some reason, could not cultivate nor passively pull Essence. You would be stuck with the Essence you had in you to sustain yourself. I'm sure you'd be fine for *years*, but it is possible to be cut off from replenishment, and that would be an awful fate indeed. Say that you had a water affinity. If you went somewhere, say a desert that held absolutely no water. You'd wither not just from the environment but internally as well."

"You have *one* affinity channel. Passively, you pull in one drop. Tarrean has two affinity channels. Passively, he gains two drops. I have *four*." He could see her fingers drumming on her arm—more lecture was needed. "When I actively cultivate, I do not get three times the intake. I only get two. I am *not* using the spiral from the Memory Stone; it didn't suit what I needed and would most likely have just killed me."

Yvessa cycled Essence to her eyes, determined to have a good look at his Center and whatever idiocy he was concocting. To her surprise, she could see details that normally eluded her, like a veil had been moved out of the way and she was looking at something she was holding in her hand. "Just. Just walk me through... this."

A veil of sorts did indeed protect the internal secrets of powerful cultivators. Normal folk were free game, having no protections, and some of the Initiates only had a wavering tarp. When Artorian had checked, he found that Tarrean and Irene possessed vast, *thick* veils. Yet, those protections diminished as people slept. Equally, they also strengthened when Irene had noticed she was being observed. He didn't know *how* she'd known, but the veil had thickened in the span of a thought.

His assumption was that she'd purposefully not desired her inner workings to be seen. That had made him wonder—

could that mean the opposite would hold true as well? Her clear gaze gave him hope that his test was succeeding. "How many rings do you count?"

Yvessa counted on her fingers. "Five, six... nine?"

Artorian clapped softly with one hand on the palm of the other, pleased that she was able to see so deeply. Checkmark one success off on the list. *Wanting* your method to be seen was sufficient for his entry-level abilities. "*Correct*, I'm currently at nine."

Her distressed voice snapped at him, "*Currently! More* of these things are going to be added?"

Artorian settled back into his pillows, quite pleased with himself. "Oh, *yes*. Allow me to give you a tour of Boday de` Artorian! They're only circles when you're looking at them straight down, as you are. In truth, they're as you guessed— Essence tubes formed as circles. I've spent a *grand* amount of time spinning my Essence in all manners of woven varieties. I have found that not only does the *corruption* separate, but *Essence* does as well. Every circle going outwards from the Center holds a denser type of energy. From inner to outer, the separations are as follows: the purest Essence I'm able to get refined to that quality–"

He was interrupted *right* away. Yvessa surprised him with her observation, but it only made him proud. "Is that inner circle going the complete *opposite* way of all the others?"

"Indeed! That is the only circle I have *pulling* inwards, while the rest *push* outwards. The interactions of the spin are a little complex. I'm not merely going around in a circle, but inside to out as well, and there's some additional direction that makes all but the innermost circle spin from its center outwards."

He got back on track; he *loved* the cleverness of this next part and hoped his caretaker would as well. "So, the innermost circle is the purest Essence. Then in order: celestial, air, fire, and water Essence, followed by circles of corruption in the same order. Water is always the densest, and it pushes away the furthest. Yet, even the *thickest* of water Essence will always be *less* dense than the lightest celestial corruption! I am spending all this Essence on the circles because it is paramount that I keep everything moving. If anything settles, that's it—I'm dead."

"My survival thus far, while painful, was dependent on my body receiving large amounts of Essence to keep it functioning. While the corruption was fighting amongst itself, as they each attempted to force their identities on the others in an ugly mix, separating them has allowed some insight into their interactions."

He needed another drink of water from speaking so much, and he was excited to keep teaching. "So, as Essence and corruption flow into me in their raw states, like is pulled to like. The greater the speed at which I have things moving, the less difficult it is to refine something and the more it ejects unsuited components to the next circle. I found some tricks to keep the density filters without sacrificing speed, though I'm going to need to disassemble more baskets to get a grasp of it."

"When some celestial Essence enters my inner circle, it gets refined. The purified Essence moves inwards, and the separated corruption shunts outwards, where it is entrapped and slowly refines further to release additional Essence. The corruption is launched out of circles it doesn't belong in, then bounces further and further until it gets trapped in 'its' tube."

"Again, when the celestial Essence refines to a greater purity, it loses density and sinks back to my inner circle. It's like this for all the Essence types I have. I refine them all individually, yet at the same time. The purest Essence is what I use to sustain the circle-tubes that hold everything together. It's a poor technique... in that it's *horrendously* wasteful."

"On a happier note, I am slowly making adjustments to the design, hopefully into something more permanent and stable. It takes extra Essence to 'basket weave', but efficiency rises. I save an extra little bit of Essence from then on. Progress is incremental, but by the *celestial,* I'm getting the hang of it!"

"What is particularly entertaining is when some water corruption enters the weaved tube that holds the fire corruption. It's as if there's a brawl! A fiery warrior jumps from his seat, ruthlessly barrels forth, and slams his fist into the water corruption's face to send it launching back out of a rowdy tavern. They do not at *all* play nice, and any interactions are violent." Artorian was beaming sagely, still amused at the memories of the complicated interplays in his Center.

Yvessa nudged him in the arm. "Sounds like you're not as bored as you seem, Mr. Sleeps-All-Day. I think you're trying to hide letting slip that you're going to add even more circles. How would that help?"

Artorian had his hands back up defensively. "Well, right now, I am on the verge of... *ahem*... exploding into large, meaty chunks."

CHAPTER TWENTY-SEVEN

"Artorian! You explain yourself right *now*!" Yvessa refilled the water cup and handed it over, glaring at him as she waited for an explanation.

"*Make* me! ...Just teasing, please don't." He flashed her a playful smile, though she didn't relent in the slightest. As her face puffed up, he quickly got back to it.

"As I was saying, I can squeeze and condense Essence down so until it fits in the tube. Even then, I can only condense so much into the rings before I reach a critical mass and... hmm, *pop*. I am already at the point where my circles are expanding in size, which leaves the spot closer to the middle of my Center a little vacant. So, I will be adding additional circles for further and further refinement and containment. There will come a point where I run out of room, but I've a plan for that!"

She was clearly displeased with him as he told her this. "You are just allowing corruption to *accumulate*? What's wrong with you? That's a massive disaster waiting to happen."

Artorian's waving hands were instantly back on the defensive. "No, *no*! I have two methods to my madness! One, confining the corruption not only neatly stores it in my circles but prevents it from roaming about inside of me and doing harm. Since the types I have are rambunctious, corruption is instead pulled out of my *body* and stored in my Center."

"Two, the compound Essence I absorb purifies me as I actively cultivate. As I take in new Essence, the starlight that strikes my Center also burns off some of the corruption I'm keeping trapped in my Center. I'm not sure what to call that kind of lost corruption, but the light just shears it away, and it flows out of me. So long as the starlight blazes and my circles rotate, I am losing more corruption than I gain on a daily basis."

Having the wind taken out of her sails, Yvessa just shifted in her seat. Rather ladylike even, but it came with the distinct emphasis that she wanted to backhand him. With a hard stare, she moved on to the next accusation, "*Rotate* doesn't sound the same as *spin*. I think that you are playing with forces that no one understands, that you are going to make a mistake, and that there will be no one there that can help you. There is a *reason* we all use the same or similar cultivation technique."

Artorian was at a loss; for once, he didn't know how to explain himself. He started with the cultivation motions. "It goes up, and... around, and they all sort of move like a ball spinning in a ball, which is also in a ball..."

"Just... just watch. Easier to show you." He stopped speaking, losing the thread of his own explanation. His mind dove to his Center. Yvessa cycled Essence to her eyes and watched, hoping to be able to save him if he started to accidentally kill himself. Artorian's Center began to glow as he shifted into active cultivation. Concentrating, he let the suction of his Center grow beyond the confines of his being.

Rather than omnidirectionally pull from the land around him—as was typical for cultivators—he aimed to only take from the direction of the sun above him. The influx of Essence changed to an upwards cone, and Yvessa saw the Essence flood into him faster. From a cone, it focused again, reshaping to a pillar angled towards the sun. Yvessa had to hold on to her seat when she felt the *thrum* of energy moving around her. Her hair frizzed, and little pops of static snapped over her garb.

When the raw energy of the heavens crashed into the old man, his Center *exploded* with resplendent starlight. The innermost ring began to rotate on a new *axis* rather than merely spin in place on a flat plane. The circle-tube itself still spun in a variety of directions to control and contain the Essence flows, but now, the entire assembly of rings moved as a whole.

She started to understand his earlier explanation after seeing it. When each ring spun and rotated fast enough, it had the appearance of a ball. Each ball fit inside of another ball *exactly* large enough to hold it. The celestial Essence ring started getting up to speed after the *purified* Essence one. Then the air ring followed suit, then fire. After a long minute, all the rings were spinning, and raw Essence *and* corruption were filtering between them at an *astounding* rate. It was a conflux of denser things moving to the outer edges, while the lighter energies moved further and further inwards.

The bright blaze collected itself in his Center, visibly bleaching and searing off scraps of colored corruption in the outermost layers. Yvessa likened it to a fence which had the paint stripped away over a great many years but in fast forward as the compound starlight Essence streamed in at a pace beyond her comprehension. The sheer amount of Essence he was taking in outstripped her personal cultivation by *leagues*—even if her spiral was better than the circle at protecting her from corruption in the first place.

Yvessa's attention snapped to an out-of-place bubble of Essence developing in his Center. It didn't follow the patterns of everything else going on, and she watched it move out of his Center entirely and travel to the back of the old man's shoulder. It was clear that Artorian was *intentionally* moving that little bubble since the nesting spheres continued without pause.

In a dark spot on his back, deep down in the smallest parts of his body, that bubble drew out corruption and scooped it up. Dark masses collected in the wobbly orb, one group of thick energy after another. Even some blood and tissue when he wasn't careful enough; the process wasn't flawless. The gathered corruption had been causing him pain there. With it gone, he would no longer feel it, or at least, it would hurt *less*.

Yvessa couldn't believe what she was seeing. He was *cleaning* his body just by shaping and moving Essence? By the celestial... he was expelling impurities! She tried to think about the situation logically. Sure, this was great for his well-being and might even let him steal a few years back, but overall, the damage was *done*! Or... was it?

The bubble filled with corruption, but the large patch was also shrinking. Looking closer, a lined network of Essence was being used as fuel to sustain the shape of the scoop. It took Yvessa several minutes of deep observation to see that Artorian was pulling Essence from the celestial ring and refilling the cells with it after he stripped out the corruption. Body repair with celestial Essence? No *wonder* his progress was slow; he was literally patching himself up from the inside out!

Yvessa closed her eyes, retrieving the Essence from her eyes to her Center. Her fingers pressed to her stressed temples. "You made a cultivation technique, found a way to remove corruption from your body, and managed to find an Essence source that satisfies all four of your affinity channels at once. *All* this... in the span of a few seasons?"

Artorian heard her, given that he had been expecting her to speak eventually. He began slowing and stopping the process of his active cultivation. It took a full minute before she had her response, and his voice intoned a profound tiredness. Each step of properly starting, maintaining, and stopping his method took effort.

"Not *quite*, my dear. I made the *concept*, and now, I'm building it after finding methods that work. I have some nasty anecdotes of failures and accidents I'd rather not speak about.

The reason I know where to look for certain corruptions that have filled my body, for example, my entire left shoulder is my own fault. I lost control of my corruption tubes due to a bad Essence weave and flooded myself with corruption wherever the leak happened. I was so panicked that I shoved my purest Essence out of me. I would rather have my progress *abandoned* than it get devoured by all that corruption."

Yvessa had one of those looks again, and Artorian twiddled his thumbs. He was about to get a not-informative lecture, and he knew it. "Yes?"

"Then why do I think that not only did you *not* lose your Essence, but the corruption didn't get it *either*?" She spoke slowly with deliberate words. Artorian looked like he was about to try to weasel his way out of speaking like a petulant teen, but she snapped her fingers at his face to force him to focus. "I'm on to you. *Tell* me."

The old man hadn't wanted to touch on this yet. "I may have *accidentally* discovered how Essence is stored in an Aura. I didn't lose a single drop of Essence; I just found a... new storage space. In truth, I've been using it to hide what cultivation level I might be at from all of you. I don't know how the system works when I'm not playing by the normal rules, and I will likely never have a fractal."

"An Aura is incredibly useful as a storage shed, and every aspect I've told you about so far still has leaps and bounds of potential for individual improvement. Since I know you're going to ask, I'll give you the list again: your Center is a bucket, your body is a well, and your Aura is a village. When I prodded before, I couldn't begin to understand all that beautiful space. How could I not make it where I store all the good stuff while my Center is a canvas of struggles?"

"I'm a child exploring the forest, gleeful to discover what I'll find next. I have such ideas for techniques, but I won't spend a drop of effort on them until my bases are covered. With my current progress, two years is about where I see myself properly being able to walk again."

He trailed off, and Yvessa pushed his drinking cup into his hands, reminding him to hydrate. "Oh, thank you, my dear."

She nodded and scooted her chair closer, scraping it across the floor. "Listen... Artorian."

Her voice was soft. Yvessa didn't want him to make himself suffer like this; all that internal Essence moving must have hurt. She also found, very suddenly, that she didn't want to stop him. "Just don't go overboard or get to a point where you can't call for help. Now that I've seen what you're doing, I know exactly how wasteful it is. This is *not* something an F-rank should be doing—if you can even be considered in that rank at all. This is upper-D kind of stuff at the *minimum*, and I don't know of a single person not in C-rank that figured out how to use their Aura."

"Eventually, you're going to find something by accident that isn't healthy for you. Not to mention the problems you'll run into from a technique that nobody else uses or can support you with. A way to clear out corruption? Even if it is slow? The progress you're making has *me* incredibly jealous, and I don't know how I'm going to explain this to the others."

Artorian tensed. "I don't suppose I could convince you... *not* to share this? I don't mind knowing you all read my notes. However, I don't like the idea of my personal growth being shared. I can't imagine that... Tarrean, for instance, would be pleased with me."

Yvessa shook her head as a firm no. "I don't believe he would, no, but this is something I feel needs to be shared, Artorian."

Artorian shifted uncomfortably, considering less than savory alternatives. His voice was pensive but low. "What if I were to give you some cultivation? Boost your rank? A small bribe between friends?"

Yvessa felt electricity course down her spine and jumped from her seat in shock. "Long Beard, don't you *dare* lie to me about a possibility like that. I have been struggling with growing my spiral, and that is a *horrible* slap to my face now that I know just how quickly you gain... you gain..."

She was shaking, her breath unsteady. Yvessa had her hands balled so tightly her knuckles were white. Artorian regarded the borderline enraged cleric and shook his head because he wasn't playing with her. "Not a lie. A trick I learned from Jiivra that would allow me to directly push my Essence into your system. Perhaps not your Center but certainly the system. Before she left, she tried to heal me and pushed Essence into my chest. I was still awake, not that she could tell."

"If I take the time to tap purely from my celestial source, I believe I could do it. We'd have to hold hands, where one of our hands pulls Essence while the other pushes. I'm reasonably confident of the safety. I really don't want you to tell them, and if it costs me my time and effort to bribe you to look the other way... well... I am willing to pay that cost. Are you?"

Without further ado, he held both of his hands out to her and sat up with a grunt. Yvessa was clearly a person torn. On one hand, speaking out was the right thing to do, the proper thing. On the other, a gain of Essence was unbelievably beneficial. Unlike her, who could only cultivate a few hours per day, Artorian could afford to cultivate nearly non-stop. If he wasn't actually asleep or doing some other activity, he was gorging in the influx of Essence like an endless feast. Not only did he pull in mountains of the stuff, but he had the type she needed neatly sectioned off and already corruption scrubbed.

She had no idea just how much Essence he was hiding in his Aura or even how to read one. Since he had so forwardly offered, the sacrifice he was making wasn't irrecoverable. But if she took his hands, she would be hiding important information from her order; she would be complicit in losing what could end up being an amazing option for her order. But she would gain something amazing for herself. "Abyss it."

Yvessa took his hands and drew a firm breath to steady herself. She could already feel the push of energy building against the skin of her left hand. It was deterred from moving as Artorian only formed half of a conduit, and so the energy just waited. With a hesitant acceptance, the young priestess began cycling her Essence through her body as if she was starting active cultivation. She pushed her Essence out from her right hand and had the horrible fright that she was about to lose it for good.

Then she felt the connection knot together like two loose ropes being tied, their hands acting as the bonds as she willingly completed the conduit. With a short gasp, she instinctively pulled from her left. Heaving, her stomach exploded with tingles as a sensation of numbness coursed through both her arms. The right felt drained while the left was overburdened, but the Essence... oh, the *Essence*.

Instead of the slow, melodious pull to her Center that she gained during daily cultivation, this was a torrential river. Yvessa directed the energy to siphon straight into her spiral, allowing her body to store it in her cells. Doing this, she realized why it was so valuable for Artorian to externally cultivate with his Aura. He couldn't store a lot of energy in his aged cells. His body was still nearly completely tainted, which must be why he was cleaning it up.

Artorian funneled from the celestial energy circle but was pushing it with outer energy that Yvessa could feel crackle and pulse as it danced along her fingers. F-rank seven. F-rank eight. The ebb and flow of cultivation level spiked as her cells saturated in what seemed to be minutes but was instead hours of real time. F-rank *nine*.

"Stop, *stop*! I feel like I'm going to burst!" The flow of energy halted slowly, the knot of their hands tightening and forming a blockage. She ceased giving him refined bits of Essence to keep up the bond and stopped drawing in rivers of it via her other hand. She was bordering the upper limit of her current rank, and her spiral roiled in a whirlpool of activity, further refining the energy. Unable to keep up with the previously unseen volume, her spiral just did what it could.

With a final crackle, Artorian released some Essence to close off the connection, forcibly sealing the openings on Yvessa's hands as well. He collapsed on to his bed, out of breath, drained, and exhausted. The old man was sweating, and his hands, wrists, and arms were bright red from swelling and internal injury; conversely, Yvessa's hands were spotless—the clear difference between a clean, young body that held Essence and an aged, tainted one.

"Oh, that *rather* hurts." The diminished old man's voice was weak, yet Yvessa reeled with power. She was drunk off the rapid rise but forced her head into reality when she gathered just how taxing it had been for Artorian.

"Well. *Gasp*. Why don't. * Gasp *. Why don't we wrap those up after treatment, with all this extra time I have from *not* making a report?" She spoke the words but realized they went unheard; the old man was out cold.

Yvessa broke into the D-ranks a month later.

CHAPTER TWENTY-EIGHT

Two *years* had passed since Yvessa entered the D-ranks. This morning was notable for only one reason—Irene had unbalanced the daily routine by making a massive cacophony at the gate. She was *furious*, and it roused absolutely everyone from whatever they had been doing.

A messenger had come to declare a new expeditionary force once again chasing raiders was moving their way in. The scout was there early to bring the matter to the attention of the cloister since the area was officially bound to the Church. The expedition force would be occupying it as temporary lodgings and would use the centralized outpost as a headquarters while they performed their duty. Irene was irate not because this disrupted the comfortable days they had come to know but because that *swine* known as Keeper *Kendra* was part of the incoming force.

This was that day everyone learned that Keepers *famously* do not get along and hold bitter rivalries due to their interpretations of the scriptures. Interpretations meant different opinions. Unless there was an Arbiter on the matters being discussed, the discussion was more along the lines of screaming. Keepers became aggressive and violent to one another, never feeling the need to hold back in order to come out on top.

Artorian was woken that day by the crude sound of a guard tower crumbling to the ground as shattered splinters. He poked his head from the window, only to take in the absolute smackdown raging between two livid Keepers. Both of them found the energy to scream obscenities—as well as break half the cloister—without regard for what the other appeared to be uttering.

The argument was something about... the correct amount of *bread* one took during prayer? Artorian couldn't tell, too distracted by the shrapnel slicing through his open window. Kendra was *infuriated*, and she picked up a wooden beam from the ground like it weighed little more than a broom, sweeping the courtyard with the support pole. The beam was kicked away by Irene, forcing the tip to slam into the hardened ground. This provided more than enough stability for her to leap on the beam and dart a few steps along its surface to roundhouse kick the other Keeper.

Kick may have been too gentle a description, as Irene spun her body before unleashing the Essence-fueled blow. Kendra didn't have the time to pry her fingers free as her world went blank. The woman crumpled into a pile after being launched into the damaged cloister. Cracked scaffolding noisily collapsed on top of her.

* *Thud**!

"I said. *Half.* A. Loaf! *No* exceptions!" Irene vengefully *punted* the unconscious Kendra out from under the ruined logs and sent her barreling into the surrounding expedition force members. Before a raging Irene had a chance to continue the attack, the freshly arrived group rushed their Keeper off to get medical aid. Glancing back to ensure there was no pursuit, they saw the sizable new hole in the outer wall—a hole made during what had likely been the *gentlest* of arguments to come.

Tarrean arrived in full armor and cleric regalia to break up the commotion but only managed to disperse the onlookers when his shouts were joined by Nefellum, the Head Cleric of the expedition force. They firmly shook wrists on meeting and plowed through welcoming rituals with elaborate hand-sigils. Artorian stopped paying attention once the action passed, feeling no further need to spy. The gossip mill wouldn't be turning for a while, but it would be sure to catch him up in due time.

This new expedition force looked to be all business, and Artorian recognized no one when he cycled Essence to his eyes to get a better look. Having forgotten what cycling pure Essence did to your vision during the day, the colors lathered in richness and the sunlight stabbed right into his eyes. "*Argh!*"

The shiny sky orb was *always* there with the sneak attack, just waiting for you not to pay attention! Artorian stopped cycling and smoothly eased his way out of bed, doing some test motions. He went through basic stretches, bothered to dress properly, and picked up a gnarled walking stick that hung next to the table. The commotion in the cloister already made it sound like regulations and organizational plans were in full effect. He could hear a large man snap at Initiates to pick up the pace, followed by the distinct **fumble-bump** of someone hitting the dirt. Artorian made a mental cue to expect more yelling, and sure enough, it was almost instant.

The drill instructor's voice was a hardy baritone. "Get *up*, Initiate! If I have to pick you up from the dust *one* more time, then by the celestial... I swear I will find the worst job in this cloister and dedicate you to it for a week!"

The wet **fwack** of a strong hand striking a rear spurred the risen Initiate to start jogging laps around the cloister's outer perimeter. Poor boy looked like he was going to collapse any second. Artorian's shout was far friendlier than the one the drill sergeant had let out. "You can *do* it, m'boy! Don't let up!"

One could tell from a distance that the cleric in charge of the Initiates was a simple man with simple tastes and simple methods. The drill instructor's dark head shone like a cue ball, perfectly bald and smooth. His ashen skin made it clear the man was from a warm climate. Right now, his arms were crossed, and displeasure was aimed at the old man shambling along in the Church's holy cloister. "*Sir.* I must please ask you to leave the premises. This is holy domain. Members not part of the Church are *not* to tarry here."

Artorian put some pleased pep in his stride. It had been *ages* since he'd gotten to be sly, and the opportunity was given to him on a platter! "Oh, goodness *me*! No, my good man. I very much live here and have for quite a few years longer than your cloister has been up. I suppose you should consider me the current landowner until the reigning Head Cleric is granted the title."

The drill sergeant's eyes went wide. Oh, *abyss...* did he just insult the landowner? He knew well that he could be magically persuaded to leave the lands by force of Mana if he was told to do so. Whether the old man knew it—or *not*—was not a risk he was willing to make. "My apologies, sir. I did not know. Please, do be careful in your travels. My Initiates are blinder than moles, and I do not wish for their incompetence to cause you harm."

Artorian slowed his shamble, his hand pressing to the small of his back dramatically. After all, why *not* play the cards you were given? He took his time and strolled right up to the instructor, holding out his hand in greeting. "The name is Artorian. Well met, my good man."

The instructor shook wrists with the assumed landowner. "Marud, Choir second-in-command Battle Leader. It is both my pleasure and a *surprise* to meet a member not of the Church in the domain. May your health stay firm through the sands of time."

Such a *strong* shake! Artorian shook his wrist for effect if only to unsettle the large man. Why were all the people in the Church so *tall*? He dismissed the thought; after all, he *was* slightly hunched over. "I do appreciate it. Teaching the kids to run?"

Artorian watched one slop by with the dexterity of a drunk rabbit exclusively using its hind legs to push onward.

"*Indeed,*" Marud stated with displeasure, keeping a watchful eye on his slacking recruits. "Move your *feet,* Initiate! Even this villager here could outpace you!"

Marud's eyes went wide as he got a sassy reply from the exhausted man. "No, he. * *Wheeze**. Abyss-well. * *Wheeze**. Couldn't!"

Before Marud could scold the recruit, Artorian had stabbed his walking stick into the dirt and was disrobing, hanging the lapis lazuli cloth on top of the firmly planted stick. With a twist, it pushed deeper into the ground than an old man should have any capability to do. His words were full of *fight.* "Young man, I am going to shuffle my way over, and I will be hot on your heels. When I catch you, I am going to give you a scolding on the benefits of being *kind* to your Elders!"

With a truly awful gait, the old man waggled rather than walked forwards, wearing only pants and shoes. His scars and shriveled appearance unsettled even the seasoned Marud. However, the instructor could see there was health hidden in the man. Sure, he might *look* old, have terrible posture, and a beard so long you could make rope out of it... yet he also had what Marud recognized as war-scars. In Marud's culture, one didn't gain honor-marks by resting on one's laurels.

His drill-instructor attention caught that Artorian had a vibrancy to his skin. There was a brightness in his eyes and a forward momentum to his step that said he didn't hurt one bit when he was getting a move on. He was just *awfully* slow. The old man *clearly* could not run. His legs were thin and spindly, and there was so little muscle on the aged wreck that Marud didn't want to put any effort into thinking about how the old codger even remained upright.

What was he, *eighty*? Still, the old landowner was a *delight.* The instructor now had extra fuel to light under his recruits' rumps. If they could not pass the aged grandfather, then he could hold that against them in future training and long-term practice. Marud's thick fingers rubbed his forehead at the thought 'long-term'. *Bleh.* They were going to be stuck here for at least a full season. His dark eyes watched the old fool fail to keep up with his exhausted recruit—much less catch him—but Artorian didn't quit.

Four hands worth of time later, a disheveled, sweaty, heaving, and out of breath old man was pressing a hand against the small of his back before he hobbled his way to the point he had started. Once there, his hands fell to press on his knees, catching his breath as his iron gaze caught Marud's amused little smirk. "Again. *Gasp*. Tomorrow."

Artorian coughed out the words with an energetic wave of the hand, grabbed his walking stick, then draped his robe over his shoulders before staggering off. "I am going to catch those unbaked little loaves and put them in the oven!"

Marud suppressed a snort at the old man's ire and persistence. He was fine with this, as it was just a few more measuring sticks to goad the recruits. "Sure, old-timer, come back tomorrow."

"Ah... *ahaha*! I did it. I *did* it!" Marud's face snapped back to the Elder, who sounded absolutely *elated.* His fist was shaking in the air. Even though Artorian was wobbly, he was clearly pleased about some sort of accomplishment. What? Had it been a few years since he'd even made it around the perimeter?

"Hah." The drill instructor didn't see the Elder again until the next morning came. When the second in command rolled up with a powerful stride, ready to discern which recruits to chastise, he was surprised to actually find Artorian mingling with the crowd of Initiates. In fact, he was joining in their stretches.

"No, a little more down, m'boy. You want to push your leg down as far as it will go while you keep your opposing knee bent. Feel the muscle stretch in the taut leg. That little tremble? That's what you're looking for. Remember to stretch *after* training as well; it's awful being sore."

Marud let the instruction slide, and his voice boomed through the mottled line of tents. Half-asleep Initiates scampered, partially dressed, from their resting spots and made their way to the front gate in a hurry. When they were all present, Marud firmly gave them a short speech on preparedness. Only one person had vanished.

"Now where did the old man get off to?" He called out for Artorian, looking around for the old man.

One of the recruits pointed around the bend of the wall. "He started already, sir. Said he was going to get a workout in and catch us before he washed today."

The instructor threw his hand in the direction of the corner. "Well, get *going* then! The old man is beating you all in performance! Move, move, *move!*"

The stampede of feet began in a hurry. That day, they all passed the old man at least *thrice* before he'd made it back to the front gate. As before, Artorian needed to stop at that point.

Marud couldn't hold back his enjoyment nor his commentary. His gleaming white smile countered his natural darker profile. It was rather delightful to see, artful even. "*Ah-ha-*

hah! What are you *doing*, landowner? You plan on being here every day to catch my Initiates?"

"Indeed, I will, my boy!" Artorian replied with confidence as he straightened up and did more stretches. "I can't catch *raiders* if I can't even keep up with *your* lads!"

"Sir. *Please.* You joke too hard. *You...* catch raiders?" Marud broke down in hearty, thick laughter. His disbelief mounted with his humor. "I would not let a gentleman such as you leave the safety of the cloister! That is what the Church is for—we protect those who cannot protect themselves."

The smile on Artorian's face matched Marud's but for a different reason. "Well then, I'll just have to outpace *all* your Initiates, won't I! *Let* me? Pah! I'll get so fast that you won't be able to *stop* me!"

Artorian pressed his fists to his hips and posed with conviction. It only made Marud double over once more, failing to control himself. "*Oh.* Oh, you are too much! Please. Come. *Outpace* my recruits. I wish to see this."

"And. You. *Will!*" With a stern nod, Artorian was off, swaggering off to the stream. He spoke with the stubborn, self-assured tone of the old man that he was.

Artorian was back the next morning, the next, and the next. What *did* surprise the seasoned instructor was that not only was the old man *succeeding* in such strenuous daily activity, but he was *improving*. His crippled shamble had developed into a smooth jog. His knees no longer bent at odd angles, either. Every day, some incremental change or progress could be seen in the aged man's posture, breathing pace, or muscle strength. After just one week, what Marud before believed to be a cripple was now doing *two* successful laps around the cloister. By the second week, he did *three*. By the fourth, he *caught* the slowest Initiate.

Marud had a *field* day that morning. "You let him *catch* you? What happened to being a proud member of the Choir, *recruit*? Are you holding out on *me*? On your *team*? He caught you! He. *Caught*. You!"

The recruit was in dismal spirits after that. That evening, however, the young man heard a tapping on his tent. "Excuse me, is this Initiate Que'els' tent?"

Que pushed the flap open, and his dark features fell even further upon seeing who was waiting for him. Confusion replaced the expression as a skinned rabbit was pushed into his hands. "Eat some extra meat, my boy, and don't tell the big one I gave it to you. I'm thinking that your growth is slowed because you're not getting enough meat to eat. Some extra rations in you can only help."

Before the Initiate could thank the Elder for the gift, he was gone. Artorian was learning how to move *annoyingly* fast for such an old man. In fact, the next morning, the old man outpaced *everyone*. Marud held his face in his hand as he watched the farce of a training exercise. The long beard could only handle seven laps, but he finished them before his recruits did—and their current limit was *also* seven.

When Artorian walked to the stream like an unbending ironwood tree that day, he secretly relished the verbal beating the Initiate squad was suffering through. He was mid-wash when the booming baritone *finally* ended. Even then it stopped only because the clamor had attracted Marud's superior, who demanded an explanation.

Their bickering forced all the Initiates to pay shamefaced attention to their feet and keep their heads down. The Head Cleric of the expedition was *roasting* Marud on the performance of the Initiates as Artorian strolled up with all the swagger of a star athlete. "Excuse me, my boys, why all the noise?"

Artorian would have said more, but an armored finger pointed a bare inch from the tip of his nose. "Is *this* him? Is this the fool that made all my recruits look so *shameful?*"

Marud kept his mouth shut tight, but his body language betrayed the answer. "Explain to me. *Explain* to me! How my top-class Initiates were left in the dust by... *you*. These men and women are the cream of the crop! Their potential is *astounding*, and now, I heard the aged landowner outran them? *All* of them?"

The... huh... *short* Head Cleric was almost foaming at the mouth, and Artorian would have been very interested in making a quip... if he wasn't so puzzled by the pattern of behavior he'd observed in cleric leadership. Maybe it was chance? He shook off the thought and looked at the recruits. "*Greetings,* Head Cleric. I must admit your armor is quite the impressive symbol of your order."

The Head Cleric wiped the back of his hand over his mouth and straightened up. *Yes*, yes it was excellent equipment. At least the landowner recognized *quality*. Artorian continued, this time not quite as flattering, "As for your Initiates. I'm not entirely certain why this is a surprise? They're *barely* eating! If they got some chow in them, I would never have been able to outpace them! I'm not sure what you've all agreed upon between the other superiors in the Church, but you are more than welcome to till some land and grow some crops for additional food. The work may be too demanding for the recruits since only the *strong* should labor like that. Still... you're welcome to do it."

The expedition Head Cleric adjusted his gauntlet-strap and replied with a textbook answer, "Rationed meals are exactly portioned and even for every single Initiate. There *is* no issue with their intake."

Artorian just shook his head, reminiscent of a disappointed father. "Would you have your troops drink more water in the desert or bundle up with an additional layer in the cold mountains?"

The Head Cleric crossed his arms as if the answer was obvious. "Well, of course I would. The environment demands it."

Artorian nodded sagely, glad the man understood. "Then you *understand*, good sir, that this is the *Fringe*. Individuals require more intake than is ordinary when they are in this region. While I don't know why this is the case, it is *true*. If you have been giving the Initiates regulation meals, which was my assumption, then they are *without a doubt...* malnourished."

He clarified when he saw the Head Cleric didn't seem to understand him. "Underfed, Head Cleric. I won't ask you to believe me, but if you give them a few days with additional rations, I'm betting you'd see *significant* improvement."

The primary Battle Leader grumbled but faced his vice-commander. "Marud, give them double rations for a week. No harm in checking the truth of this matter."

As the superiors walked away together to discuss adapted meal plans, Artorian stepped past them and gave some of the tired recruits a pat on the back of their shoulders, humming along with a whispered, "You're *welcome*."

He had just gotten them all more food for the week! *Everyone* loved more chow. More than anything, Artorian smiled about his progress. He could walk again and *properly*. Excellent progress. He just about jumped into the air but held off. One thing at a time, old boy.

One thing at a time.

CHAPTER TWENTY-NINE

The first big hunt the expedition returned from had proven unfruitful. This fact soured moods and raised irritation among the whole cloister. They'd been certain it was going to be a victory, but the raiders had abandoned their activity midway. A small blessing, as the village a day's ride away remained untouched as a result. However, the Choir expedition had spent resources and didn't have a single decisive victory to report to the Keepers.

Speaking to the Keepers remained a conversation Nefellum didn't want to have. The two were still beating the ever-loving abyss out of each other every few days. At least they had moved on from bread. A bowstring's *twang* split the air as the tired force tromped back into the cloister's camp. A few heads turned, and they saw Artorian had set up a makeshift target. He was holding a cobbled-together bow that looked poised to snap from the pitiful construction alone.

Sure enough, his next draw cracked the curved wooden branch right at the handle. He held the bottom half and watched the top dangle by the now-loose string. With a complaint too quiet for anyone to hear, he tossed it in a pile of two more snapped bows. Their quality was equally poor, and the expedition put the oddity out of mind, aside from a chuckle.

They recouped over the next few days and put together a new plan. As the days passed, the expedition members found the old man standing in a variety of places, staring at walls or off into space. They laughed at seeing him squint at a bucket of water, which he seemingly splashed into his own face at random. Beyond sputtering, Artorian didn't budge at that, simply taking a few steps forward or a few steps back while half drenched.

The behavior was odd, but nobody wanted to ask. Just another old person doing strange, 'old people' things. After a few smirking stories spread about some of the demented things the codger had pulled in the middle of prayer several seasons ago, the expedition Acolytes decided to just give Artorian a wide berth. The Initiates followed suit with this behavior, but unlike their direct superiors, they kept their mouth shut on snide commentary.

Nobody who managed to secure extra rations for your entire troupe was going to get that treatment. They were all distinctly happier with more comfort food in this middle-of-nowhere cloister. Who knows, maybe the old man would end up doing something similar again? Freebies were a valued commodity in such an isolated no-chance-to-spend-your-silver place.

The Choir superiors approved of the change to farming the land, if only that it forced their Initiates and Acolytes to pay more attention to learning their chants and to focus attention on their cultivation. The extra field to till doubled as group coordination practice and offered a use for their unspent physical energy.

Yvessa was excluded from the majority of those tasks and was not up for playing the devious old skeleton's games. With an *ahem*, she tapped him on the shoulder and felt the corners of her mouth creep upwards as the startled old man jumped a few feet.

"*Whow!*" He fumbled for the bucket and quickly dumped the rest of it into his face, soaking his long beard, bare chest, and baggy cloth pants. He squeezed a hand down his face to press the water off and blinked, then without squinting had a good look at Yvessa. "Oh, *hello,* my dear. You look lovely!"

The Acolyte had never been complimented on her appearance by Artorian before, and that set off warning bells in her mind. Her arms folded across her chest, and she slapped aside the attempt to distract her. "Uh-huh. What ridiculous scheme are you up to now?"

Artorian looked offended, his hand pressing to his heart as he leaned back. "My dear, why would I be up to *anything*? I'm *harmless*."

He attempted to play it off with a forced, sweet little smile, but Yvessa wasn't buying it. "My fractal-cultivation *butt* you're harmless. You're pacing and have creeped out nearly the entire camp. They think you're *senile!*"

Artorian straightened after a shrug, hunching right back over as he squeezed the water from his beard. "I don't see how that's a bad thing. It gives me some space, nobody comes to ask questions, and I can nose my way around at leisure. I can ask all the strange questions I want, and since I wander off when they answer... well, hee-hee, they've learned that it makes me go away! It's a momentary inconvenience for them, and I shan't pretend I don't hear the jokes at my expense, but I am unbothered."

Yvessa took a daunting step towards him. He was deflecting again! "What. Are. You. Up. To?"

Artorian's shifty look to the side made the stern woman clamp a hand on his shoulder. This reminded him that the Acolyte saw through his wit, so he decided to just let her figure it out. He'd give her a few small clues to see what he could get away with.

"Have a careful look at... my eyes." Yvessa didn't relish the idea of peering deeply into the old man's eyes, but she ever-so-gently leaned down and had a look.

"Bright blue, look spirited, lightly glazed, so a healthy coating that prevents the eyes from going dry. They're excellent... I don't see the problem." She let go of him, expecting an actual explanation now that she was playing along.

Artorian just gave her another clue, "I too no *longer* see the problem."

That was an odd thing to say, and Yvessa leaned back in and had another look. "I still don't get it. They're just eyes which—in my opinion—look like they ought to do all the things eyes do."

She decided that she must be missing something, so she cycled Essence to her eyes. "Oh. Oh! You *cleaned* your...! No. Wait. Are these... *new?* As in *completely...*"

Artorian smiled and gave an ever-so-minor nod. Yvessa paced around him like a curious animal, using Essence sight to inspect from differing angles. "How did you...? Did you go blind and rebuild your eyes with pure Essence? How did you figure out how to do this? I was only told about meridians last week, and this isn't even remotely similar."

Artorian puzzled her words out and looked to the sky for a moment in befuddlement. "Meridians... do you by chance just mean vital inner organs? The six Yin and six Yang? Helps Essence move through the small, inner holes that are on the edge of your Center, then loops? Correct?"

He waved off her raw bewilderment. Yvessa rattled off her knowledge so as to not feel like she'd been left in the dust. "I was told meridians are energy channels that transport life energy throughout the body. Life energy is also known as Chi—or Essence—depending on what part of the world you're in. They're very important for one's affinity channels, being the pathways along the meridians that Essence flows through. Having multiple affinities will open more pathways, allowing more Essence to flow in at one time."

The old man winced and filled in how he found out in his own terms. "I had corruption flowing through those channels. I am very much aware they exist, how they work, and where they go. Pain is a memorable teacher, as your Initiate's instructor seems to understand. Now, I have a vague idea of the increase in longevity the reinforcing of meridians—or vital inner organs—may grant. However, it comes with a cost I currently cannot pay."

He held his hand up to halt her inevitable retort. "Yes. I rebuilt my eyes completely. If it wasn't clear before, my eyesight had been significantly damaged. Cleaning my eyes of corruption and dumping said corruption into my Center for storage was insufficient. At best, it restored my eyes to the best quality they could be in the state that they were. Which is to say piss poor."

A snort came from Yvessa at his sudden language, and he'd said it with emphasis and a sharp up and down movement of his head to drive the context home. She held her questions and let him go on. "So, little by little, I painstakingly siphoned individual cells rather than repairing them. I fueled this by a combination of refined and celestial Essence, with the intent to replace what was lost. When the cell formed, it did so in the best pattern it could be rather than simply 'repairing' the damaged segment. Mind you, the process is slow and took quite some doing in order to keep the identity of the Essence steady while it set. I am becoming quite adept at the basics of shaping, moving, and convincing unformed Essence to be something other than what it wants to be."

Yvessa held up her hand to pose a question; she had a few now. Artorian nodded to his student, falling right back in teaching mode. "Why are you pacing around if your eyes are fine, and what do you mean by 'basic functions' and changing those?"

"Ah." Artorian grasped the question and began walking in the direction of his dwelling. "Come with me so we're not just standing here. The sun has moved, and it's about to put me in the shade."

Yvessa was immediately suspicious and glanced at the old man's Center with Essence sight, having figured out the trick to see through the thin veil of protection a Center otherwise had. The person targeted needed to be unaware of what you were doing or otherwise willing to let you see. Not wanting your Center to be visible thickened the protection, but unless someone was putting active effort into keeping their Center hidden, it was child's play to see through low-ranked cultivator Center-veils. "Third question, how many... *circles*... is that? I can't get a proper count."

Artorian tilted his chin up and slapped his beard left and right to force it to dry faster. "I've lost count. I simply keep adding smaller circles for additional refinement when I have the Essence to do so. I've had to *completely* redo the weave on all the tubes after I found a much better method. Taking numerous woven baskets apart has its benefits, and that alone was worth the jokes at my expense. Every ring increases my ability to refine Essence. I wouldn't put a number on it, but you're likely seeing what's currently going on."

Yvessa moved her fingers in complete circles to follow the track. "All of them are turning like a ball, but you're *not* actively cultivating. Oh! I figured this one out. There's so much Essence moving around between all the circles that the push of all the light is enough to force the whole system to move on its own! Your passive cultivation now must be almost as good as your active cultivation *was*."

Her tone held just a touch of jealousy, and the priestess mimicked Tibbin's classic flat-lipped expression. "Impressive."

CHAPTER THIRTY

A light blush colored Artorian's cheeks as he proudly swaggered into the sunlight. "My active cultivation currently has less to do with my ability to refine and more with how much I'm *able* to draw from starlight. Passively, I take in quite a bit more than before—excellent observation! I'm *quite* proud of your progress, my dear."

The smoothness of Yvessa's cheeks did a poor job of hiding the additional pink that colored her sun-bronzed skin when Artorian's compliment made her flush. He remembered seasons ago when she was deathly pale but didn't mention that; instead, he returned to her questions, "Essence has things it does by itself. Let's take the one that will be useful to you. Celestial Essence heals... except that it *doesn't*. From my observation, it instead removes impurities and imperfections from where it is added. While I'm certain that it would have *restored* my eyesight entirely, I lack the amount needed to create that effect."

"Dumping more units of Essence into an issue allows you to reach the intended effect even if you do nothing else to help it along. Removing sickness *is* a function of celestial Essence. However, it achieves that state because the healer is heavily intending for the Essence to lend its natural qualities to the focus of a similar but alternate purpose. 'Remove this infection,' the healer says."

Artorian was making broad hand motions for effect. "Instead of removing damaged imperfections from the system, you've the clear intent in mind that the infection is an imperfection. So, rather than *heal* an injury, it spends its energy on purging the infection. It's a minute difference, but the celestial

Essence will now *only* attack the infection, hunt it down, and disassemble it—as it would any other imperfection."

"You can't easily convince an Essence type to do something it is opposed to doing naturally; however, you can skew it to the left and right. This is why the majority of clerics use celestial rather than purified Essence for direct muscle empowerment and enhancement. In the event of an accident, celestial patches you up automatically. I've watched no less than several dozens of bouts between the Keepers, and that brings me to now."

Yvessa was patient and just made the circular *go on* hand motion as they paced in a circle around the inner cloister. Artorian, old codger that he was, needed no further encouragement. "By cycling refined energy to your eyes, you see with increased clarity. Everything becomes this horribly rich and lathered landscape, and even Essence flows become visible. I have simply found that I can pierce the veil of higher-ranked cultivators at the cost of not seeing the flows of Essence in the area. By focusing on one effect instead of a general effect, I ignore the veiling fog. Thus, even though Tarrean is a higher ranked cultivator than I am, I see his triskelion clearly."

Yvessa had known this already based on his previous statement, but it was good to know how. "Alright, I'm following so far."

The long-bearded teacher kept striding along. "So, as we've noted, more units of Essence invested to a body part equates to a more profound effect. A body part has an upper limit of what it can handle. Everyone also only uses refined Essence for their eyes from what I can deduce, out of concern for possible damage to the vital organs."

Shuddering, he paused to speak with emotional emphasis. "An entirely reasonable conclusion. Even slightly unrefined Essence can wreak havoc on your body. Investing fire Essence into my hands without it being sufficiently refined gives me a horrible rash that itches for hours. Don't recommend it."

Artorian collected himself with a patient exhale. "Essence has stages of refinement. Refined Essence that still carries hints of its prior Essence is safe enough. All my additional circles have their purpose and 'grade' of refinement quality. I am consistently impressed by just how much purer Essence can get. Now, your question—adding other types of Essence to your eyes causes distinct and significant changes to not just what you see but how you see."

"Celestial gives you an idea of imperfections. Things out of place and notes of something lacking, which hints at what is supposed to be there. Tearing a leaf from a plant and then observing the plant gives a clear but fading imprint of some kind of pattern. More Essence invested means that they become more obvious."

"Air Essence makes me able to slightly see the movements of wind as if they were gently fogged. The flows and movements freely alter and dance as nymphs during play." He made an exaggeration, never having seen a nymph. The Acolyte was enraptured with his words and didn't interfere in this particularly valuable lesson. "Fire Essence lets you get a grip of the innate heat in things and—in some odd way—the cold. When I look at a person, I can see where the heat they are generating is."

Artorian coughed into his hand, momentarily uncomfortable. "Not always a sight you want to see."

Yvessa quirked a brow but didn't stop the old man from carrying on. She had been a healer too long to fall prey to embarrassment about other people's bodies. "Water Essence should be obvious; it lets you discern the movements found in liquids—the pumping of blood in someone's body or the churning motion of the stream. Most everything else in my vision melts away and is replaced by brightly colored hues in black, grays, and whites. The more something moves, the brighter it is. It's *incredibly* jarring. These Essences can be mixed, and when you do, everything you see changes again. This weirdness is why I'm stepping back and forth lately."

"A certain amount of Essence can only extend your sight so far, and the amount of Essence you spend also determines how well you ignore objects in the way of what you're looking at. Cloth is a breeze, wood is difficult, stone is borderline impossible, and anything metal is hopeless. No matter how close I get, I just can't get my line of sight restrictions to overcome metal matter. Perhaps if I had earth Essence? Regardless, fire and water. You'd think they'd have a big fight in your eyes?"

Yvessa nodded in affirmation to Artorian's question because that idea seemed reasonable. "Turns out, not so much! You see the heat and the liquid movements at the same time, and for a reason I simply can't understand yet, you clearly see a person's muscles."

Yvessa was clearly confused, but Artorian was right there with her—*equally* lost. "Slapping celestial on top of that creates one wonky visual adventure. You don't just see the full movements in the body; you can deduce where the body is likely to be based on the pattern it holds. If someone was walking towards me and I had all three of those cycling... I am convinced that I would know when they were going to stop before they did."

"Activity in the muscle is proportional to the amount of energy given to it, so if I see someone's arm lightly glow, I have a decent chance to guess where they would be moving. I feel that this has incredible combat applications, but unfortunately,

I'm too slow to capitalize on such information." He paused as Yvessa started shaking her head back and forth.

"That could do *wonders* for the military! Though... the Essence it takes..." She clearly dismissed the idea. "Never mind."

"I had the same thought when I was starting to test these; trust me when I say that I understand where you're coming from." Artorian counted on his fingers and nodded, having remembered where he left off. "Now, I know that it might be the thought that adding air Essence would also allow me to see their breathing pattern, adding to this huge pile of information. You'd be right, but the overload on the senses is horrible. Thus, the bucket of water."

"I splash myself because the attempts dried my eyes out so badly that if I didn't fully and immediately hydrate them, I'd regret it again. My previous eyes would not have been able to cycle anything other than refined Essence. After cleaning, my eyes may have been able to handle two, but these newly made eyes can handle all four. I am firmly of the opinion that I skipped a step somewhere. I get splitting headaches now from cycling too long. The information my eyes take in is different than what the rest of my mind can handle."

He had to stop, rubbing his closed eyes with his palms. "Still, it's nothing in comparison to what I see when I apply precise Essence combinations. I have seen a world of violets that shows me designs otherwise invisible. A world clad in nothing but reds that I barely know the words to describe. It's more pronounced than mere fire Essence; it's deeper than mere heat— a below red. My vision blurs to gradations of red and blues. Hotter is redder. Cooler is bluer. The violets are beyond just color."

"There is a... *luminescence* to the world. All this from differing units of Essence being added and kept in a specific balance. It's rather costly, as you still need to add exact amounts of Essence for a better effect." Artorian stopped mid-stride, the pensive beard stroke returning. "Is Essence *additive*? I have the suspicious thought that it may be."

Artorian then realized he was hungry and could also go for something to quench his thirst. He missed the taste and texture of fish and sighed it out loud, "I want *fish*."

Yvessa stopped as he did, having no idea why Artorian suddenly changed the subject to such a degree. A thousand-yard stare into the distance, only to question Essence, then segue straight to fish? That's where Yvessa knew she'd lost the ancient-looking man. "Alright, old-timer. You've satisfied my curiosity. Go home. I'll bring you something to eat."

Artorian perked up, thoughts consumed with the promise of a good meal. "Oh, that would be *lovely*. Thank you, my dear!"

He looked around for something, stance puzzled and out of sorts. "Errr. I do believe I've lost my bucket."

Yvessa rubbed her forehead, slapped her hand on his shoulder, and marched him home. "Come on, skeleton man. You're skin and bones. Mealtime."

Her hand squeezed, and she realized she was wrong. Artorian *wasn't* skin and bones like he had been, and only by touching him had she realized it. She just *remembered* him that way, an old wreck of wrinkles and impoverished movements. His ribs used to be defined and visible, but now, they were no longer. He looked... *well*. While still a little on the weak side, his frame had bulked up nearly to the point of a young man. There was even some gray coming in at the base of his snowy beard-hair, and his face was considerably smoother. His walking cadence was not the labored step of a ninety-year-old; visually, he now appeared a respectable... *sixty*.

"Have you been replacing more than just your eyes?"

Artorian shook his head 'no'. "Dear *heavens*, no. That process was *atrocious*. I've just cleaned myself up and fixed up problems with celestial Essence. It made me feel better than using refined Essence, which just temporarily improved what my body was already doing. Celestial actually patched me up. I have years to go until I get to a nice and healthy state, and I am going to have trouble with what you call meridians."

The Acolyte's hand on the old man's shoulder caused him to relax. "Oh, why is that?"

As this was something she was struggling with at the moment, she hungered to know more. Having been told in secret that her lifespan would vastly increase—a desperately needed trait for a cultivator—she had sizable interest. Finding the thread of conversation again, Artorian rambled on while looking around on his way home.

"Vital organs are called *vital* for a reason. When I had corruption running through those channels, I also became aware of all the densely gathered impurities present in those organs. Take my heart as an example; I can gently scoop it clean of corruption, but that doesn't account for parts of my heart that have become steeped in it over the years. If I push Essence into the meridian channel that goes to my heart... I am... I *believe* the impure aspects would be forcibly ejected. In other words, I would have a heart attack just by attempting."

"The cleaned portions of my heart have become so bound by Essence that it relies on Essence to continue its primary function rather than what typically regulates it. That is, Essence keeps it steadily beating, keeps me alive. If I fail when opening that particular meridian, the heart attack would force me into such discord... I would lose my trained concentration on my Center. The entire system would collapse in on itself, and just like that—*pop*.”

“No more Artorian.” He folded his hands behind his back and locked sharp blue eyes with the young priestess. “You won’t have this worry, as your cultivation technique doesn’t have the chance to fracture like mine does. Your only concern is having enough Essence in your system to let it flow through you and allow the binding of your heart to happen. If I had to measure by the corruption in me before, it would take more Essence than you currently have in total to bind all your meridians at once.”

“So, if you are at all able, find how to stop after only a single or small number of meridians have been affected. I need to speak to someone who knows the right words for this, but the idea remains the same. I’m merely using simpler terms. I believe there’s a difference between what I did to my eyes and what I expect binding meridians does. Somewhere I skipped a step, and I’m paying a price for it. If I could do to my vitals—or body—what I did to my eyes... that would balance things out.” Artorian took a deep breath. “However, if I try that now, it’s just a death sentence.”

“The amount of Essence it requires is *vastly* above the maximum amount my organs can hold. If meridians are a middle step that allows one to skirt around this, that would be delightful indeed. I need more data.” He grumbled to himself under his breath. Yvessa opened the door to his abode in the cloister, ushering him in. Without needing to be prompted, Artorian slid on to his bed and pulled close his writing implements. He needed to jot all of this down while it was fresh. He failed to notice Yvessa had left and returned with a full meal until there was a strong nudge in his shoulder and a spoon full of stew in his face.

"Oh. *Stew!*"

Yvessa snorted. "Artorian, for a man with so many options for sight, you're awfully blind."

The old man rubbed his left eye as he scarfed down the offered spoonfuls of well-flavored food. He was so busy eating that he didn't register her jab. "This sauce is always so *flavorful.* I do enjoy it. Not to complain, but wasn't there talk of fish?"

Yvessa calmly nodded with a flat expression while she got him to eat the full bowl. She took his quill and paper sheets as his hands stopped moving, using a wet corner of the nearby towel to clean his mouth off. She hoisted him properly into a sleeping position on the bed and then tucked the dozing, old man in. If she was going to do anything today, it was making sure this wily academic got proper sleep.

Even if she had to use Tibbins' 'special sauce' to do it. Tibbins had been growing quite the herb garden and was the cloister's unofficial-but-official cook. He had found his passion in the craft and barely did anything else he didn't need to if it meant getting more time for his herbs, kitchen, and culinary experiments. Patting the snoozing Artorian on the head, Yvessa noticed he wasn't wheezing anymore when he slept. Good.

"You keep getting better, old man. Just keep getting better." She quietly closed the door behind her and left the snoring body behind. When the door clicked against the frame, Artorian slowly opened an eye and reached under one of his myriad pillows to pull free a small satchel. Chewing on some leafy greenery contained within, he swallowed the bitter antidote to the sleeping draught.

Pleasantly patting his tummy, he settled down into his bed with a wry little smile. As if he didn't know what crushed Valerian root tasted like when it was used as a food additive. He'd sleep when he was abyss-well ready! Artorian picked up his neatly stacked pages from the desk. Dipping the quill, he once again began merrily scratching and scribing.

Today had been a good day. Tomorrow... oh, he had *such* plans for tomorrow.

CHAPTER THIRTY-ONE

Artorian woke late, covered in an abundant pile of messy papers that spanned the area of his immediate reach. Odd. He'd missed *hours* of cultivation time, and the cloister camp was full of activity. He must have gotten whacked by that powdered root even after taking the antidote. That the mess was still present told him Yvessa had *not* been by this morning.

An *excellent* opportunity to hide the scene of his crime and stack his papers with professional neatness! He hadn't been an academy scribe for *nothing* back in the day, and he was pleased to see that his script was delicate and impeccable. A little flowery, but who cared so long as it was legible? Artorian snatched the robe off the wall and called it good. The academic felt grimy without his morning wash but decided he would postpone it until he had some clues about the current kerfuffle.

It took the span of leaving his front door to see wounded priests being carried into the medical section of the cloister. What in the *abyss* had he missed? Sleeping drugs, how he *hated* them! Wading through the busy mess of injured people being carted back, he didn't even get the chance to ask basic questions. His eyes widened at the sight of a captured raider being wrestled down. Even bound, the man was a wild animal. The raider howled like a mad, terrified beast.

Essence powered punches to the face *failed* to shut the man up... until his head was bashed against a rock to force unconsciousness. What did these monsters *endure* to be able to shrug off blows like that?

"Raiders? *Again*?" Artorian spun in place and held firm to this particular clue. Asking any of the superiors would put him in the way and may delay needed efforts. No, he had *better* sources to ask. Breaking into a run that immediately took a toll on his breathing, the blue-robed old man zipped past tents, bursting into the medical section.

The noisy medical tent had a few priests in it already. Based on the number of cots being dragged in... he had a good hunch there would be more wounded incoming. The Acolyte in charge of restoring the Initiates to good health didn't have time for him, fully focused on closing an ugly arrow wound that oozed with some slick, crystal clear venom. The Acolyte was sweating, having to wipe the wetness from his forehead with his previously white sleeve. The edges were drenched and bloodied from triage, and he was doing his best to tend to the uncooperative wound.

The weariness of the thick-bearded man was clear, and the tide of wounded continued to pour in. Artorian advanced and cycled celestial-Essence sight in a hurry, providing his irises a minor golden outline. He learned that the Acolyte was trying to find a balance between purging the venom and healing damaged tissue. Artorian was swift in his words and actions, pressing hands around the wound and ignoring the irritation of the Acolyte.

"I'll cover basic restoration. You have proficiency in this matter, focus on the venom." The grumpy Acolyte wriggled his thick mustache but could see that the old man was funneling celestial Essence into the wounds, slowly allowing them to close. With half of his problem accounted for, the Acolyte focused his efforts on this pain-in-the-ass venom.

By the time both of them had cleared and stabilized the Initiate, *four* more had been laid in cots. The young ones looked equally haggard, many of them pale and resisting the slow call of death as paralysis spread through their vitals. As soon as this one was stable, Artorian hurriedly followed the healer to the next man to save. Artorian had his bloodied hands pressed to the wound as the injuries bled without clotting.

With the healer checking for venom, Artorian was silently allowed to continue providing basic restoration, matching the healer's pace and stride. Not a word was spoken between them as they moved from patient to patient efficiently until they finally reached the eighth person. Two more healers ran into the tent, bloodied and dressed in the regalia of the expedition group. The mud and grass still sticking to their clothes was a clear giveaway that they too had freshly returned from the battle.

Relieved at their arrival, the heavy-mustachioed healer collapsed from Essence exhaustion. Sweat stained his clothing, and the ragged breathing betrayed just how much he'd overexerted himself to get this far. Artorian was beading sweat as well but had his wits about him. With the practiced clarity of a battalion commander, he forced the new healers into position. "Venom removal is priority! Two-man teams on an envenomed Initiate—dedicate one healer to venom and the other to restoration!"

He'd made this call based on the priority order he'd seen the healer apply. Artorian didn't question the healer's choice of pattern, so he adopted the trend from the person that did this for a living. Initiates with small injuries were in pain, but they were going to live. Larger injuries needed attention, but they had longer than the ones with envenomed arrows pin cushioning them. That *killed.*

Artorian stepped right into it to pick up the slack and was glad to have one of the new healers whisk to the opposing side of the Initiate he was keeping alive. Venom treatment was picked up by the expedition healers, having been given a primer on what to do before arriving.

An Acolyte that was healthy enough to get back up carried the collapsed Head Healer out of the way, laid the stocky man down, then sped off to fetch additional healers so they could save more Initiates. From the complaints and clamor, captured raiders were apparently being tied down one tent over; they would just have to wait until the clerics had been tended to.

Artorian was *burning* on the inside. His fire corruption was *screaming* with glee inside of the entrapping ring. Captured raiders meant possible answers, and if he wasn't focusing his attention on patching up the Initiates... he would have happily taken the role of an *Inquisitor*. It had been over two years, and there were things he *needed* to know. Something. *Anything* concerning the current status or whereabouts of his sproutlings. His impatience to patch himself up to standard had netted him a few setbacks, and he had needed to come to terms with the truth.

Artorian was not going to be able to do anything for his little ones if he was unable to survive. He was going to have to fight once again, and if the current status of these Initiates was anything to go by... he was considerably outmatched and outnumbered. A palm tap on his shoulder broke his train of thought. The Head Healer was behind him, now glancing at the Initiate Artorian still had his hands on.

The gruff voice carried a dwarven cadence. This healer didn't sound like he'd grown up in a human household. "Oi! Don' be draining yourself like I did now. Rest if you need teh, or we'll just be adding another injured body to the growin' pile. I'm Hadurin *Fellstone*, Head Healer of this motley expedition crew."

A strong handshake was shared between the two men. Fellstone had quite the experience under his belt. From the width of his belt, that was a *lot* of experience. "Artorian. A pleasure, my good sir."

Hadurin slapped him on the back and pointed at another lad that needed help. "I've heard of ye. Heal a soul while we chat. I didn't think you'd be of any use, given ya have a personal hospice caretaker an all. Now, look a' *this*. All capable of caretaking others. Wish I'd have known *earlier*, would have put ya to work!"

Fellstone released as hearty of a laugh as he could manage with his Essence drained. "Ah abyss, I'm dry as an empty bottle. An' look here, not a drop in sight. *Bleh.*"

Artorian chuckled at the words as he tended to a youngster that had serious wounds but didn't require venom tending. Hadurin had fallen still and was watching with interest. "Ya know yer way around wounds *far* too well teh just be a wee old lad. That robe isn't doin' ya any favors neither. Sore thumbs stick out less than yer blue butt."

Artorian smiled and chuckled louder. This man had a *great* sense of humor in him, and the grandfatherly figure was rather fond of the directness. He told the dwarf-raised-man what to do, "Look at my Center."

Fellstone folded his arms and used a tiny bit of Essence to have a look. The flabbergasted mixture of horror and surprise on his face was more gratifying than the sweetest dessert. "By the cracked bones of the dreaded deeps."

The Head Healer quieted himself after catching himself say that a *bit* too loudly. "Yer in the D-ranks, but you've got no *fractal*. Not a single one of yer meridians is open? Somehow, you've got yer Aura storin' Essence like a C-ranker... though it's not the least bit built or infused. I would have said yer body is a wreck, but if I didn' know better... I'd say you either infused your eyes or figured out how to do somethin' even better. I've never even seen a *C-ranker* with eyes *tha'* infused. It's like they're *made* of the stuff."

"I don't even *want* to know what that spinny thing is where yer spiral should be. Reminds me of a gyroscope my Pa had me play with as a wee lad. Awful bright in the middle of it though. I can only catch glimpses when none of the circles are in the way. Quit *moving*, ya wee bastards!"

Artorian's laughter forced his hands to jerk, almost doing some damage to the Initiate with a badly pushed energy flow. He verbally deflected the healer's words as he looked down at his own chest, "*Keep* moving, don't listen to *him*. You're pretty and useful."

Fellstone was the one to have a chuckle this time. "Oh, now that's a treat. Ya talk to yers, too? Behaves *better* when you do that, don' it?"

Artorian was pleased to have found someone else who talked to their cultivation system and felt the thought that he might be crazy for doing so fade. "Indeed, I do. It makes everything behave *much* better. I have theories as to why, but nothing I can share just yet. You said quite a few things just now that I have questions about. However, would you happen to know how I could open my meridians without falling over dead? Even *I* know my heart can't take it."

Fellstone had a merchant's grin on his face. "Oh, *sure* I do. Depends on what yer willin' teh trade me for it, Mr. Four-Open-Affinity-Channels and somehow still walkin'."

Artorian knew that had been coming. It seemed there was really no such thing as a free lunch. He had to simply be satisfied that at least Hadurin hadn't asked why he wasn't dead. He was so *tired* of hearing that. The Head Healer could tell that the old man was taking him seriously. The stare into the distance look showed that Artorian was thinking through his options.

"I believe all I'm able to offer you is my time. I have no goods worth mentioning, and you have knowledge of cultivation past my own understanding. My only bargaining salt is your earlier mention that you'd have me work for you. Let's not play. I'm aware you can't draft me nor *force* me to do work. If I offer... well, that becomes a different matter, does it not? Let's talk."

Hadurin was amazed that the old man was so sharp. He'd been expecting a fragile, old dog who could provide some extra healing, but no! Artorian was full of goodies, and all he needed to trade was knowledge? Information that this sly fox could potentially get elsewhere?

"Aye. I want all teh time that ye can manage to stay standin' for teh duration. As long as the expedition is here, since I can't make ya come with me after. If ya can do that, I'll help ye out with yer meridian problem."

Artorian held up a hand with all his fingers spread wide. "I can give you a hand's worth of hours each day, but any more and my health will suffer. I am bedridden on paper, and when my caretaker finds out what I'm up to... well... she is going to drag me by the ear to my cot and force me to sleep."

Hadurin extended his rock-hewn hand. "Aye, that's a fair trade. I get yer skilled labor when I need it, and ye get yerself a few extra years to enjoy livin'. Not gonna pretend I didn't notice teh sty of corruption ya got there."

The old men clasped wrists, firmly shaking on a deal well-struck.

Chapter Thirty-Two

"Let's patch up your sons and daughters. After, I'll go and see if any of the raiders you brought in are talkative. They may not talk to someone in a cleric's regalia, but... they may speak to me."

"Aye, got as much luck gettin' anything out of that lot as I do findin' a drink in teh cloister. I'll be getting teh reports together from this lot." Fellstone liked this plan, mostly because his new temporary recruit was right. He paused to carefully watch Initiate healers pile into the tent and get to work on the priests with major and minor injuries. He had to get involved a few times to set priorities, but otherwise, the work was assigned in a hurry.

"From what I gather so far, this group of raiders is a splinter faction. Lots of infightin' in teh clans. Got bold and pushed a surprise raid on Lapis. Bastards didn't know there was an expedition force next door. They got trounced, we captured a few. Preferably, we need 'em alive for questioning, but seeing as you won't be patching up many more people... I'll leave it up to yer discretion so long as ya can get a good tale out of 'em or can make one squeal. Come talk to me about yer meridians when you're nice and full up on Essence. You'll be needin' a *caravan* load of it even with me keeping ya alive as you get it flowin'."

A strong pat hit Artorian in the upper arm as the Head Healer released him from the area. Both of them nodded as they went to their respective tasks. Hadurin nudged an Essence drained healer and caught his breath. "Lad, ya overheard me. Tell the guards one tent over that Blue Robe over there can talk to the captives. Also, it might get a *touch*... screamy. Roll with it."

With a pat to the back, the experienced but drained healer was on his legs. He managed to make his way over to Artorian, and both of them walked the short distance to the guarded captives' tent. After the healer explained the situation, Artorian was allowed in, and the flap was closed behind him.

Several of the raiders were awake and full of fury. Most of them were gagged. Artorian slid his hands behind his back. He wondered how to introduce himself but found it best to lie and go with an option they might recognize. "Good evening. I am the Elder of the village of Salt. I'm here to take care of you."

The raiders grunted, not buying the story. They communicated in sets of muffled sounds and angry whines through their gags. Artorian just stood there and felt himself dip into the sea of fury splashing around his heart. His voice existed in a flat plane of emotion tempered with control... but filled with rage. "I'm only going to ask this once. I don't particularly care *who* answers. If you answer *one* of my questions, you live. Please be aware... I only have *two* questions. One. Where are abducted children taken when they have been snatched from a village. Two. Why the attack on Lapis?"

The questions didn't continue, but no answers came. The old man walked to the closest raider, and seemingly without feeling or remorse, broke his neck with a *snap*. It silenced the others, who had previously been laughing at him through their gags. Cold terror suddenly replaced mirth. A muffled reply from the second raider whose head Artorian casually and gently embraced, "Mno... *Mno!*"

Snap!

Silence and the slow pitter-patter of footfalls from the old man were the only things audible in the tent as the second raider was ended.

"Mno! *Ait!* Unno. *Iunno!*" The third raider went icy with panic, struggling against his bonds as his head was gently held. Tears *almost* had the time to develop before a *snap* ended that possibility. A panicked raider near the middle of the room wasn't going to die like this.

"Uoolf affle! Ufkove Affle! Idf awe achen cho ufkove affle!"

Rather than break the fourth raider's neck, the pitter-patter closed the distance to the talkative boy, and his gag was removed. "Once more. With *clarity.*"

Artorian's voice was flat, cold, and leveled a sense of finality. The panicked breath this surprisingly young raider took shuddered, and he barely got the words out, "Duskgrove *Castle.*"

The other raiders thrashed against their bonds at the traitor, or at least, the brainwashed majority did. Two weren't budging, very aware that with only two questions available, only two of them were going to have a chance to live if the rules were ironclad.

"We take kids on orders. The big boss likes them young, says they're *pliable.* Whole lot of seasons back, big boss slaughtered a whole castle after posin' as hired mercs. Place is called Duskgrove Castle. Reaper faction o' the raider clans flies a high flag. It's where we'z told to take the lil' unes. Please dun' kill me. I was just followan' orders. I was just... followan'. If I din't..." His words broke down to chuckled tears, unable to continue. If any of his fellows got out, *they'd* end him. If the rules that had been set were a lie... then he was about to die anyway.

Artorian gave the broken raider a pat on the cheek. There was hope for this one. "You live, youngster."

He paced to the flap, tapped on it, and poked his head out. Swiftly, the guards were inside, and the entire cot the raider was bound to was carried from the tent. Talkative raiders were useful; no need to waste them if they thought they were going to get out. That decision was up to the clerics now. With absolute, *inhuman* calm, Artorian paced back to the thrashing fourth raider he'd ignored prior to the lad answering a question.

Snap!

The muffled speech of one of the quiet ones who hadn't thrashed earlier picked up on the far edge of the cot line. "*Oear ab*!"

The old man saw fit to remove the gag. The also very young raider quickly stated, "Power Grab! It was a power grab! Why kill my friends? They *couldn't* say anything! They have gags on!"

Artorian normally *appreciated* questions. This was *not* that time. His grip moved around the raider's head. "Tut. It's rather simple. When it comes to things I care about, I'm *remorseless* in my pursuit of them. To me, you're not just simple, little raiders trying to feed yourselves. To me, this is *war*. You see, any society that I consider worth going to war with must have social aspects that so *violently* conflict with my nature... my view of the world... that your 'suppression' is inadequate."

"I don't hold the view of war being a 'minor disagreement'. This is not 'he took my sock'. It is the willful understanding that the beings I have designated as enemies are so *anathema* to what I believe in that it warrants their utter destruction. In the event something ought to be destroyed, it, therefore, ought to be destroyed in its *entirety*."

The raider died with the tone of a sharp spinal *crack*.

"You've all seen fit to knowingly make everyone else's lives miserable... for the simple benefit of yourselves. People may change, but patterns *really* don't. The amount of effort it takes a person to change is sizable and also requires the *desire* to do so.

Merely saying you've changed is irrelevant. It must show in your behavior, your actions, for years to come. Frankly... I don't *have* the luxury of time. My response now is that I see your intent to destroy all I love and hold dear. You have no desire for diplomacy, or you would have attempted it. I see no way for you to thrive in life alongside me without me risking *everything*. Therefore..."

Snap!

He strolled to the next raider. "*Therefore*, with much sadness in my heart, I declare that you—and all who take part in the eradication of that which I cherish—must be eradicated in turn. I don't despise you for your choice. I merely tell you that this response is the outcome I am *willing* to live with. This is my peace, as I now send you to yours. I condemn you."

Snap!

The bonds of the raider that hadn't thrashed began to fray. Releasing the head of yet another dead raider, Artorian turned and cycled some Essence. "Oh, how curious. A *cultivator*?"

The raider buckled against the restraints, getting both his upper arms free at the same time. Maliciousness burst in the raider's eyes, but it simmered to a pale chill as both his hands were grasped firmly by the old man. Artorian was holding the straining hands with his own, still having a look deep inside the man. "That's *quite* some progress you've made! If you get *any* more freedom, I believe you'd have the upper hand. You know... today, I am *not* a good man."

The raider bit through his gag and spat out the scrap of cloth. "I'm going to tear you apart, or I am not Alphas!"

"Hush now. I'm knowingly and willingly doing some *awful* things. I must thank you for the opportunity you've provided me. In truth, I've been *dying* to know how this interaction worked."

Essence built against the raider's right hand, and a void pulled at his left. Being stuck on the cot, the raider saw an opportunity for free Essence. He tried to siphon from whatever technique the old fool might be building.

Alphas the raider had the best Chi control of any of the secret cultivators in his raiding clan. He was a proud F-rank nine. Overpowering an old man was going to be no effort at all, and now he'd even be able to steal some free Essence from the pathetic old man's skill. A vicious smirk snapped into place as he pulled at the Essence the old man was pushing. Power poured into him with the force of an ocean, and he willingly accepted the conduit link. He started laughing as he was immediately pushed to... F-rank... *ten*? That didn't *exist*!

Then he felt dreadfully *sick*. If there had been an F-rank eleven, he thought he would have been forced into it. Instead, he was physically ripping and about to burst from the inside as too much power flooded in. The raider's muscle pulled so tightly on his bones that they tore along his arms and legs.

An F-rank body simply couldn't hold that much, and the imbalance was *shredding* him. Looking for any sort of outlet, he pushed his Essence on to the waiting, pulling void and completed the connection fully. Excess Essence drained off as his eyes and ears suffered profuse bleeding, already long past risk of severe internal damage from Essence overdose.

Then... *then* came the part he had not been ready for. He both felt and saw the completion of the energy flow in who he was connected to, and the literal sun that exploded with resplendence overloaded his numbed senses. This wasn't a pathetic old man at all! He'd been tricked!

In a panic, the smile vanished from Alphas' face. He forcibly tried to sever the connection, but it was to no avail. Alphas felt nauseous as a full rank of cultivation was *ripped* out from his Center with all the gentleness of a log being struck with lightning. A second rank of cultivation quickly followed, dropping him to F-rank eight. Something *worse* was afoot. Alphas realized that what the right-hand connection was pushing into him wasn't *Essence* anymore.

It was... heavy. Dense. *Bad.* It felt like Essence at first. Once the bubble broke inside of his system from the pull, he learned otherwise. The ripping twist of force drained his Essence out of his left-handed connection, while a sick, *vomitous* stream of corruption bombarded his Center from the right.

Being hit straight on by siege weaponry would have hurt less than the agony which quickly built. Endless streams stifled, drowned, burned, and whirled inside of Alphas as he dropped to· F-rank three. His Center space was aggressively being replaced by torrential maelstroms of corruption that didn't get along, destroying the man from the inside out. Channels that needed *Essence* to sustain themselves were clogged by the corruption, and with a pained final sputter... *Hurk*!

Alphas felt his very spiral being rent from his Center as it fully filled with a bloating force that was going to drive him insane. Only when the last of his Essence had been pulled from his left hand did the connection break, preventing any of the corruption from cycling back into the old man's system. Alphas *convulsed* on the cot. He shook, trembled, and turned a violet red as his eyes spotted bloodshot and thick foam slid from the sides of his mouth.

A few moments later, Alphas was dead. The noises had cowed the remaining raiders. A few of them wet themselves from the absolute horror they'd just heard from the strongest among them. Artorian quietly took stock of the result, having watched the full process in as much detail as he could. His voice had the pitch of an epiphany.

"Ah. I *understand* now. This is what a small fraction of my corruption does to someone else? I too would wonder how I'm not dead. I suppose I can stop getting annoyed when I am asked."

CHAPTER THIRTY-THREE

Hadurin let out the *heaviest* sigh once he sat himself down in the confined cloister meeting room. His satchels rattled, and some vials clinked about in a leather pouch. He wasn't one to wait on protocol and pressed forwards on the table from wrist to elbow. "Did ya *have* teh kill 'em *all*, Artorian?"

A grumble went around the table as Head Clerics Tarrean and Nefellum compared notes, still far too busy for this annoying little spot of news. The Keepers were sitting opposed to each other, faces indifferently filled with an air of 'I'm not talking to you'.

Marud and Hadurin also sat on opposite sides of the table, but unlike the other four, they had turned their seats and their attention so they could listen to whatever nonsense the old man had pulled this time. Yvessa and Tibbins leaned against the back wall with their arms crossed, silently whispering bets to each other on the outcome of the not-quite-roundtable talk.

Ordinarily, this would be called a debriefing, but Artorian didn't get the benefit of such procedure since he had technically been operating under the instructions of the Head Healer, whose buns were now over hot coals. What interested the old man was the Head Healer's name listed on the vellum in front of Hadurin. It made his mind work as the cogs of recollection turned. How... *interesting*. Hadurin was lying about his last name? He'd have pressed the topic if he didn't feel dead tired right now.

Hadurin *Fellhammer* didn't care about that, his voice gruff as usual. "Wasn't a very good thing to do."

Artorian slumped back in his seat, hands folded in his lap, his eyes locked on to an empty spot of the table with half-lidded effort. "*Wasn't* it, my friend?"

The table made a dusty thump as Hadurin dropped his fist on it. Everyone simply held on to their particular stack of papers without so much as an additional glance. They knew what the dwarf-raised human was like.

"No! T'was not! We got *one* chatty one! When we came in to check on the rest, it was a broken neck party that everyone was invited to!"

"I suppose it's true that I didn't *need* to kill them. I *could* have simply prevented them from harming anyone ever again." Artorian pressed his thumbs together. Fellhammer threw his hands up at the oblique statement. "Then I thought about it some more... and realized I was being delusional. I couldn't have stopped a thing."

Hadurin felt his general mood alter from admonishment to confusion. It showed in his tone as his arms dropped. "Wha...?"

Artorian released his hands from one another and held up his thumb, counting with his fingers. "Good and evil are words that get thrown around a lot. Yet, when it comes up... someone tends to twist the meanings and rules so it will fit the outcome they'd like. Something can be both good *or* evil with a simple change of perspective. A persuasive enough person can convince you of such. That's my warning to *you*, my friend. So, rather than argue with you on your beliefs, I'm going to lay out what I was thinking. Then you give me your opinion. Fair?"

Fellhammer squeezed his lips together and crossed his arms in defiance, but the grumble that left him was one of assent.

"I believe there's a difference between *willful* evil, *uncaring* evil, and evil that came about because you had no other choice. A lesser evil, if you will. Now, I'm not going to bother getting into if it's a 'bad thing' to kill someone. I know the Church wants to keep their image intact, but those Initiates were awful bloody, and the raiders captured were maybe a *fraction* of the ones who died in the field."

A few people in the room didn't know what the word fraction meant, but they just followed along best they could. "I gave a clear directive to all of the raiders. Something *simple*. I set a requirement, and I set an outcome that let them avoid it."

Hadurin crassly interrupted him, "You were breakin' *necks*."

Artorian tiredly exhaled. "Crude and unkind, yes. Also, *effective*. It got the point across in a *snap*."

Tibbins and Yvessa groaned, and a small pouch from the both of them was tossed to Marud, who caught them with a glimmering smile. Artorian ignored the gamblers and continued, "The report from the Keepers told us more about what the survivor spilled and confirmed that children are specifically taken at a young age. The reason of it being 'easy to make them think a certain way' is what bothered me. Once someone has a worldview and way of doing things, it can be impossible to break from that pattern. So, I hold that most people either can't or, if they could, *don't*. I've heard plenty a sob-story from a young woman on how they wished their partner would stop certain behaviors, was told he did, and then... clearly didn't. Raiders are no different."

Artorian took a drink of water, as he had their uncomfortable attention. "The survivor, the boy. He was the last category, doing evil because he had no other *choice*. You could tell from his voice, his willingness to cooperate, to let me know that he was in that mess against his will. Doing what you're *told* isn't good *enough*!"

He paused to collect himself, and several people swallowed hard. "I have the years, the experience, to tell the difference between tears and acting. He isn't a bad lad, just had everything working against him. Given a chance, his pattern can change. Even a small section of the report from the Keeper is enough proof for me to believe he wants to, *badly*. *That's* the kind of drive that allows a person to become someone new."

The old man paused, but there were no questions. "*Uncaring* evil is the same as apathy. These people simply don't *care*. There's *no* reasoning with them, as nothing you say could possibly have an impact on the actions they've chosen to take. If they're a raider, that's it. You will get nothing out of them, and you can't turn them around. The same is true in anyone. If you don't care, you won't do."

"*Willful* evil is in people who are easier to blame. They are *excellent* scapegoats, as you can tag the wanted poster on them. They enjoy making the lives of others miserable and put *effort* into it. To the *abyss* with those people. A trip to the gallows for every last *one* of them! I don't care what position, social status, or power they might hold!"

Artorian raised his hand and snapped his fingers twice to make a point. "I ended people who would do nothing other than commit acts which would eventually harm or kill people, as they committed willful or uncaring evil. Does it make me an evil person to put my foot forwards and sweep the broom to clean the dirt off my floor? Is it justified, or does that not matter? People make laws about don't do this and don't do that. In the *Fringe*... that boils down to social understandings with one another. *Nothing* is written in that fashion; we just know the rules we've agreed to follow with one another. Writing it down is needed when you have to lord it over someone to *enforce* your rule."

"To my firm distaste, it is the people at the top who tend to then make *additional* rules to protect themselves or their interests, rules their subjects can't *prevent* them from creating and enforcing. The Fringe is clear on what to do with someone unwilling to be of a benefit to the community as a whole. They are named *Poison*."

Hadurin grumbled, "I can already take a strong guess as to what happens to 'em."

Yvessa was given a small pouch by Tibbins, who was sour-faced having to let some of his prized herbs go. Artorian shrugged. "My point is that I understand that rules have their place, and it's *better* to do good. However, I'm too old to base my decisions on rules that are questionable at best. So, I've firmly decided to only act on the decisions where I believe I will not regret the outcome. I make the choices I am willing to live with. Even if the outcome isn't what I thought it was going to be—my choices, *my* actions, my life—lived out the only way it matters."

The Head Clerics had stopped their page ruffling, now paying attention. Marud knocked his knuckles a few times on the table for attention, his baritone cutting in. "That's one strong personality hidden in that fragile shell of yours. I'm going to cut this short because the situation isn't as bad as it looks. The report says that Hadurin listed 'At your discretion'."

The large vice-commander tapped a pointed finger at the document in question. "The information we needed, we have. By all accounts, your personal views are not being called into question. The task you were requested to do was fulfilled. Your viewpoint gives context on why we have a tent full of dead raiders that needs sanctifying before we throw them on the bonfire, but I'm not interested in the philosophical debate here."

Marud then changed his face to a scowl directed at Fellhammer. "If you had been here on *time* to hear the full report, you would have known that. The guard came to tell us you were pacing in your tent muttering to yourself about how the old man got you in trouble. We have the information. So. *What* trouble?"

Marud's sharp look warmed up to his trademark smile. Celestial were his teeth white. Hadurin felt a weight drop from his shoulders. The Head Healer slumped deeper into his seat than even Artorian. The healer rubbed his face and took a sharp breath, getting a hold of himself.

"Right then! I'll catch up later. Where are we?" Joining the meeting, he reached out his stubby fingers, and Irene leaned over to hand him a freshly scribed copy of the agenda and notes for the day. Fellhammer frowned as he looked at the next item. "The old lady is awake? There was another one?"

An unscrupulous look swept across Artorian's face. He sat back upright in his chair to pay attention.

"*Please* tell meh it's not another one like ye. What's *this* one got in her Center. *Squares*? All the squares come together to make circles or something?" The Head Clerics looked at one another in confusion. Squares? That was the moment Hadurin realized that these superiors didn't *know*. They didn't *know* Artorian was cultivating, or they would have gotten the joke about the circles. Everyone else, except for the expedition Keeper and the Head Clerics, had a thin smile on their lips. Just like that, everyone knew who else was in on it... and the silent pact to keep it hidden from the others was reinforced—if only to see how long they could.

Lots of secret betting pools were riding on it, after all. Artorian waved off that item as a footnote. "I'll take care of her. I know what she's like. Can she walk?"

Yvessa cleared her throat, and eyes turned to look at her expectantly. "She's a... how to put this... a screamer. If she's not passed out, she's breaking down and blurting out nonsense, but there are a lot of words in there that sound like 'raiders' or something to do with raiders. A familiar face may help settle her. Yes, she's able to be on her feet."

Her voice turned lemon-sour. "I preferred when she was catatonic. Her main reaction to anything is to grab something and beat me with it. *Endlessly.*"

A chuckle went around the room, but Yvessa remained stoic and unamused. Her face was covered in some marks that could now easily be recognized as stick-shaped bruises rather than training injuries. Tibbins looked her over, and Yvessa didn't spare him a glance to acknowledge it even as the cook began speaking, "So... *how* did she get a stick?"

With the eyes of the Head Clerics on her, she couldn't afford not to respond. Yvessa bit her lip with irritation. "I thought that it would be easier for her to calm down and have a walk if she had a walking stick. So, I got her one. I didn't know she was going to turn into a beast straight from the abyss! That woman is *crazy*! The wanton yelling that I'm a 'worthless child' isn't improving my mood either. If she was like this before her mental shock, I believe I would have followed Keeper Irene's example of conflict resolution."

Irene's pleasure was palpable as she got a mention. The Keeper's eyes flashed to meet Keeper Kendra's, whose butt she whooped on a nearly bi-weekly basis. The beatdowns had become so one-sided that betting had completely ended. Artorian rose from his chair without the usual **humpf**, his hand making a motion to Yvessa. She happily pushed off the wall and sunk an arm under his shoulder to help him up. Had to keep the image up in front of the Head Clerics.

"I am proving a distraction to this meeting and will excuse myself to go deal with that inconvenient old toad. Yvessa, could you be a dear and help me do a proper bow so I may excuse myself?"

Tarrean just waved his hand left to right with wild and impatient dismissal. "No need, Artorian. You're pardoned."

"With all the various connotations that brings."

CHAPTER THIRTY-FOUR

Yvessa 'assisted' the hunched Artorian with his dramatic show. He had even pressed a hand to the small of his back on the way out. Certain Church members at the table bit back laughter. Once outside, Artorian gave Yvessa a conspiratorial pat on her hand. "I'll be alright to go alone, my dear. If she sees you again, she might start swinging."

Yvessa's face fouled like she'd smelled a fresh carcass. The caretaker didn't say anything; instead, she just turned around so he couldn't see her violent cringe as the muscles in her neck went taut. Artorian just kept on moving. His caretaker had the right of it. He heard the tent flap open and flop to a close as she returned inside. The thought of Switch and what that greedy bat had done still plagued him.

He was trapped in his mind until his fingers brushed against the rough wooden door of one of the exterior cloister buildings. One he had avoided for over two years out of sheer, blatant discomfort that he wouldn't tell a soul about. This matter was *personal*. The door creaked open, and Artorian stepped in to find a bare room filled with only the most basic essentials. Switch woke up as a chair was moved, announcing that someone had sat down.

She croaked, "*Get out.*"

When the chair didn't make the sound of pressure being relieved from it, she bothered putting in the effort to turn her face... only to feel like she died of shock as dread beat through what was left of her heart. Artorian swallowed, attempting to get his words out, his face mired in a deep, contemplative frown. He looked at the floor with his hands pressed together. He *still* couldn't bear to look at her as he repressed the roiling emotions. "Why did you do it, Switchy?"

The woman crawled away from the specter. "What. No! You're not *real!* You can't be real. You should be..."

Artorian felt his anger boil over as he jumped to his feet, grasped the chair by its back, and threw it against the wall. The thoughtless motion was performed with enough power to shatter it on impact like she'd done to a cup all those years ago. "*Dead?*"

It had all occurred in the span of a moment. Switch cowered in the far corner of her bed, back pressed to the wall as her lower jaw shook and her teeth chattered. "E-elder, *please.*"

The malice had died in her tone, fear replacing it. Artorian found himself incapable of feeling pity. Considering it a moment, he didn't know if he was *capable* of pity anymore. Instead, all he felt was a calm sea frothing with endless anger. "I don't go by *that* title anymore. There are *no* remaining Elders of the village Salt. I use it for convenience or for some clever gain. Otherwise, that word merely *chafes.*"

"One can't be an *Elder* when there is nothing to be an Elder *of.* The village is *gone.* All *gone,* Switch. Burned to dust seasons ago, along with most all its people. Our *people.* Our community. *None* got away, and my only grace is that some were *taken* instead of slain. Even that small reprieve turns my stomach. No, Switch. I'm *not* dead. I have to stay alive. I won't die until I've fulfilled my one, last *promise.*"

"W-what promise?" Switch slurred out the words, just trying not to wet herself at this impossible titan in front of her. He felt so much larger than life. An unseen Aura oppressed her by sheer proximity, and she didn't understand how or why. The crone felt crushed. It was difficult to breathe.

The Aura that oppressed her increased in pressure as Artorian spoke. It wasn't that she *couldn't* breathe but rather that something was making it nearly impossible to do so. Artorian didn't realize he was causing the effect and just spoke with a voice filled with sadness, "I told them I'd be there for them. Those children are my world."

The effect relented and released, the mental image Artorian had been upholding crumbling at the thought of their gleeful faces. He couldn't hold on to hate when love tackled him from behind with such a comforting hug.

"Then... then why are you here?" Switch stammered.

A sigh came from the old man as he looked at the open palms of his hands. He spoke slowly and with deliberate intent, "Unfinished *business*. See... at first, I wanted to ask... no. *Demand* answers to a thousand questions. As the seasons flew by, that fell to hundreds. Then maybe ten. Eventually, I was content with just... one. Now... now, I need *none*."

"I no longer care *why* you did it. I have a decent idea after finding the vellum you so disgustingly scratched your name on. I no longer care *why* you sanctioned the slaughter of everyone we held dear. I only care that you *did*. I'm not here to admonish you, Switch. I am here for something that will satisfy a hypocritical, terrible, old man."

Their eyes met, and he finished his rant. "I'm here for *justice*."

To Switch's confused relief, Artorian turned and began to walk away but stopped short at the door. "Pick up your walking stick, you old toad. We're going on a walk."

The door opened, and the old man stepped through, his shadow visible through the opening while waiting on the other side of the threshold. It took several minutes for Switch to collect herself or even consider moving her legs out of the bed.

Night terrors had plagued her for what must have been seasons. Her mind had been trapped in the endless loop of mind-breaking, day-long nightmares that she found no way out of. No amount of repetition made the grueling agony dampen or hit her any softer, leaving her either unable or unwilling to interact with what was real.

The thick, old lady had thinned significantly, and she only really noticed when her feet finally hit the ground. The walking stick was taken from the table, and she leaned on it to support the majority of her almost nonexistent weight. The first rays of sunshine blinded her vision, but the sight that met her was nothing like what she remembered.

The hills and green plains were all the same—a similar landscape with a different fate. Nothing was left to show the village had once been here. Almost nothing. A new apiary was in place, the stone mill still stood, and the flats still reflected sunlight off of its thin sheet of water in the distance. She kept her hand in front of her face and saw Artorian had moved a good ten feet away, waiting on her to catch up. She wanted to talk, to say something meaningful.

Something that would make this all better. Her thoughts found nothing. So, they walked and walked. It was just to the stream where people washed, but the journey was draining. She was *furious* that the old man wasn't the least bit tired. He actually looked *healthier* than she remembered. Far healthier.

He was waiting at the stream, his back turned to it as he looked up at the cloister in the space they'd crossed. It was simple but pretty, the way the buildings were organized. Even a simple few buildings were pleasing when they were placed in a harmonious formation. Supposedly, it helped with a cleric's cultivation, to lengthen the amount of time they could cultivate their blessing from the heavens. He didn't quite believe it, and he wondered how someone had come up with that idea. Was it architecture or faith that had come up with this layout?

Artorian looked down and noted Switch was still taking her sweet time staggering her skeletal frame over. Artorian stole another look a short while later, and Switch was almost at his side. She was so full of flaws, Artorian shook his head and found that he was losing himself to thoughts again since Switch was taking the extra time of his silence to catch her breath.

"Why... *wheeze*... why the stream?" Switch's question was answered by a finger firmly pointed at the cloister.

"Look," he ordered.

So, she turned and looked. The scene was the picture book representation of a religious compound, filled with plenty of buildings that all seemed rather small, save for the main cloister construction closest to the center. "It's just a *church* now."

Artorian shook his head at her words. A solid, dissatisfied *no*. "You're looking, but you didn't *see*."

This was immediately frustrating to the old bat, and if she wasn't leaning so heavily on her walking stick, she would have swung it at him. "See *what*? It's buildings, walls, a big church, not a person in sight."

"That's right." Artorian nodded. The unexplained agreement made Switch's teeth clench, and she *just* about found the energy to chew him out. "Not a person in *sight* indeed. So, you looked, but did you *see*?"

A terrible thought struck the old toad. Balance nearly lost, she couldn't feel the grip on her walking aid. She turned to firmly look again, hoping to see a person. A single someone. Anyone. Anyone at *all* who might be looking this way. She found no one. "Oh... oh... no... *witnesses*."

Artorian again quietly nodded. Switch swallowed. It dawned on her what he'd meant by justice and hypocrisy. She was going to die. "I take it you'll tell them I didn't make it."

The walking stick clattered to the ground and rolled down the dike. It plopped wetly into the stream, and the piece of wood floated off and away. She was afraid and yet... felt relief. She wouldn't need to suffer anymore. There would be no lengthy question and answer segments that slowly unveiled how she'd betrayed and murdered her entire community. The punishment that could come upon her from that felt worse than her current fate. Rather the abyss she knew than the one she didn't. She fell silent.

"You stepped into the stream, lost your footing, and were dragged away. One of the hollows in the deeper sections pulled you under, and you were gone," the slow, tired, old voice filled in. "The only kindness I'm willing to give you is one you did not provide to the people we were responsible for."

Switch felt out of it, like she wasn't quite present in her own body. The will to live fled from her. Still, she caught his meaning as she closed her eyes. The haunting metal flavor still filled her mind, her taste, and overpowered any other seasoning. If the Elder was going to look for his Fringe children, she *needed* to relay the horror she'd caused.

"She took them. One by one. She made me watch as her gilded knife opened them up like pigs for slaughter. She bled them, ended them, and only *silenced* them when they could no longer make the screams she demanded." Switch shuddered and brought her hands to her face as she stood still, tears of regret fell down her wrinkled, bony, scrunched-up face. Her words broke apart, as did her breathing. Artorian stepped behind her to place hands on her shoulders, and she found strength.

"The woman you're looking for is called *Hakan*. She leads a raider and mercenary group named the Reapers. Her humor was as unbearable as her laughter. It's easy to recognize her. She wears more blades than actual clothing and speaks with the smoothness of a healer performing bloodletting as he calms you."

"I can't recall her face. Only the laughter and the smile. Every single one of her men fears her. She slashes their faces at any hint that they might have been disobedient, but I remember the girls were all untouched. She gives them leadership positions and makes them do her cutting for her while she watches and directs. Don't let the way she stands fool you; she's *fast*. Uncannily fast."

"*Boro* was the middleman. All the traders are in on it. *All* of them. There isn't a single merchant who operates in the Fringe who doesn't have to pass through raider territory, and I imagine it's only gotten worse. Their numbers were more than I could count, but most of them were young and not at all smart. A select few tell the rest of that horde what to do. Most of those boys could barely think for themselves." She staggered and nearly fell. Artorian kept her upright with strength she didn't understand. She took a deep breath, the crisp, warm air beaten away by the ever-present, soft Fringe breeze.

The sky was blue, and barely a puff of cloud hung in the vast sky. She'd grown up here, lived here; it was only fitting she'd die here. She knew nothing else to get off her chest that might give any semblance of recompense. Switch stood there moments longer, looking at the sky.

She didn't even feel the hands that sent her into the stream. Only the sensation of falling was noticeable, then water rushed to surround her.

CHAPTER THIRTY-FIVE

Artorian wasn't doing so well. He'd been quiet and had holed up in his abode for *days*. Yvessa came to check on him, and a few of the Initiates dropped by his window. He gave some weak handshakes, but even the Initiates could tell that something had taken the wind out of the man when the old lady had the accident.

The otherwise daily addition of his presence to the Initiates' training left a sore spot, as there was just that much less... mirth. The Head Healer had come to do a check-up on long beard as well but found nothing physically wrong and had to assess that the drain was mental.

Artorian was excused from needing to start his support-healing duties right away, and the Head Cleric had a hunch that maybe killing all those raiders hadn't done him any favors. All in the same day no less. Well, it *had* been two days, but none of the healers nor Artorian had gotten any rest that night. Over the next few days, all the old man did was cultivate. His efforts were focused on patching himself up. Something to keep busy, to keep *occupied*, as he let the mixed emotions of Switch's passing wash over him. Pull, Refine, Move, Refine, Move, Refine. Repeat.

He had no hope of counting how many circles he currently had in his Center. At any point where it *remotely* felt like he was reaching some sort of refinement limit, he added more circles. All the good refined Essence still held a hint of starlight to it, regardless of how pure he seemed to get it. *Everyone* had a tinge of coloration in their Centers that differed in minor ways, usually based on the Essences they refined from.

Then again, almost everyone else was using the main cultivation technique that went around. There had to be *more* than he could glean from the basic information he had. So again, from the top. A cultivation technique encompassed the knowledge of how to consciously 'pull' Essence from the heavenly and earthen sources, how to control the Essence, how to 'allow' it to flow through the body, and how to circulate it to your 'Center' without damaging yourself. This included how to do so without gaining too much corruption.

All these separate aspects lent themselves to the practice of how to build a Chi spiral, so Essence gained was not Essence *wasted*. Those who gained the knowledge from a Memory Stone also got a clue on how to look into their own Center. 'Clean' energy was better, and when Essence was poorly processed, it retained some features of its source. That showed up as some kind of color based on a person's affinities.

Combined Essences had different properties than singular Essences, and that let him make sense as to why instead of a single color, his Center diffused a shining resplendence. Once you had a spiral going, the next step *seemed* to be opening the governing and conception meridian sets.

A total of twelve vital organs separated as six Yin and six Yang. Acupuncture charts had somehow figured that out, though they listed the governing and conception meridians as independent from the twelve vital organs. He'd figure out later which practice was correct. Artorian checked his notes from his early days when corruption ran rampant, running down the list to refresh himself. He licked his thumb and turned the page.

"Alright, so. The Yin heart meridian—it receives flow upwards and then turns and flows downwards to the Yang small intestine meridian. The Yin lung meridian—upwards, then downwards to the Yang large intestine meridian. The Yin pericardium meridian—up, down to the Yang triple warmer meridian."

Artorian shuffled to the next page. Now the reverse ones. "The Yang stomach meridian—receives flow *downwards*, then turns and flows *upwards* to the Yin spleen meridian. The Yang bladder meridian—down, then turns up to the Yin kidney meridian. The Yang gallbladder meridian—down, then *up* to the Yin liver meridian."

He put the pages of notes side by side and then ruffled through a collection of healer's scribbles he had compiled from the Acolytes. This listed what all those words meant, what body part it was, *where* it was, and what it did. The notes from acupuncture on the governing and conception organ—if there even was one—were confusing. It supposedly served as the source for connecting the kidney, heart, brain, and... uterus? He didn't have that... He was *pretty* sure.

Artorian had learned too much about anatomy this last season. His head hurt. The document described the flow as 'branches' that veered off and connected everything together. Did it mean the *spine*, by chance? Artorian furled up the documents and bound them neatly for stacking. He had enough of *that*. He picked up his notes on progression. "Opening your meridians is dangerous with any corruption in you. It is like opening the front gate of a castle in the middle of a flood. In relation to water corruption, everyone would drown. Fair enough."

"A clean system is necessary, and once a vital organ is opened, it likely uses Essence for a majority of its support rather than what you eat. Getting the Essence to them properly... hmm." He hadn't figured that one out. His previous idea to flood the channels with Essence had been a bad one. After you have your meridians taken care of, your body ought to be able to hold more Essence than ordinary, your health improves, and your resiliency increases slightly, or at least, it *should*.

Once the meridians were open, a lack of Essence would kill you. It was a one-way road. Stopping your Essence cycle after such a point was suicide, but surely, nobody would want to do that after they'd gotten this far? He waved off the thought and worried about consequences. Opening a meridian was going to forcibly cleanse it of all the things negatively affecting it, which is why his heart meridian was such a concern. With help, only *less* so.

If the Head Healer could keep him alive, then Artorian could focus on opening meridians and keeping his circles going. If he had to keep himself alive on top of controlling the process, his attention would be too split and had a significant chance of sending his entire system into a cascading crash. Sure, most of his Center ran on its own without his direct guidance *now*, but the weave on the corruption he was holding needed daily care. He'd gotten rid of a hefty chunk by pushing it into that raider, but the very act had been *horrible*.

Artorian would rather not do that again if he could help it. "Once all your meridians are good, normally, you'd turn your Chi spiral into a 'fractal'. A fractal is leaps and bounds better than the ordinary spiral by a factor of at least threefold. How can *I* use this information?"

Irene had given him a headache, as she had hundreds of fractalized spirals when he'd looked. His math was good but not *that* good. Still, it had added additional leverage to the idea that Essence was additive. Much as his own rings added improved gain as he kept tacking them on, fractalization had much the same effect. The latter was better for Essence-influx, but it was a tradeoff he was willing to take... even *if* you'd need a gargantuan amount of Essence to keep improving.

Given his discovery that you could remake yourself, Artorian figured that the next steps would ordinarily be to enhance or infuse your body and your organs. This would make them even more Essence dependent, but you'd gain natural resilience to a higher degree. Then there was the matter of *Aura*.

It had been let slip that his wasn't built or developed. So, *more* than just a convenient storage area? He supposed it made him an *external* rather than *internal* cultivator. A problem for later. Currently, he depended on it to survive, as it stored all his 'good' Essence due to his body being... unreceptive. He could try to store it in his cells but, abyss, did it *hurt*. There must be a solid reason older people didn't normally become cultivators, and this was definitely a sizable part of it.

You could simply *not* rely on your body anymore. After Aura... he didn't know. Although, there was a chance building up his body and internals would mean that he could finally begin storing Essence in it. That was a good while away.

Then there was the mystery of that infinitesimally small hole at the very innermost foci of his Center. He'd found it by accident when he was still working with Essence motes. A few of them just... disappeared. When he looked for the exact spot, he found that when Essence was passed over it, motes just *vanished*. He'd not had the courage to explore that just yet and was going to wait until he finished what he'd been learning about.

Artorian laboriously slid from his bed, bringing the work to the cabinet bench to neatly stack them. Somewhere along the line, you learned tricks that made you better at something temporarily, such as cycling Essence to your eyes. He'd found you could do it to more than just your *eyes*, having cycled it to his *brain* as often as he could handle.

Particularly on days like this, where a little extra all-around clarity went a long way. So long as it didn't leave your body and the effort was slow and sustained rather than released in a burst, the Essence could be recollected to one's Center. Big bursts of Essence were great for sudden increases in performance, but you *lose* the Essence because of it. Much like the incantations his caretaker had spoken of.

Sustained flows of Essences just made everything work more *optimally*. He tried it with his nose once but had regretted passing by the latrine for *days*. His ears made him hear things that had been equally regrettable. Mostly because once the organ was enhanced, it did *everything* better while refined Essence was cycled to it. Overhearing conversation was significantly easier but so was the ambient background noise. Tuning out certain sounds was going to need a new method of practice. Taste and touch worked similarly. It took a portion of your Essence away to uphold, but he got it back, so he didn't complain.

Actual combat techniques were things he hadn't worked on after some initial attempts. All progress was focused on getting him up and running. Fancy toys could wait. Any tricks he might cobble together would permanently relieve him of Essence, and that was too much to ask for right now. He spent Essence on the ever more demanding task of core operations, his circles, and his Center. Every little improvement to the weave needed to be fully capitalized on, and every ring required careful creation.

The basis for everything ate *months* of his life to work on, and that was with the bonus of being able to ceaselessly cultivate. Active cultivation was better, but he was location-locked for the full duration. Hunger and basic needs still fought for his time, and no amount of willpower ignored the pressing need to go relieve oneself. He kept significant pots of potable water nearby and relied on the steady influx of food from Yvessa to carry on. If he needed to arrange for meals himself, hours of his day would have been spent handling it.

Active cultivation wasn't possible when distracted or otherwise engaged. Not for lack of *trying*, mind you. The best he'd been able to accomplish was letting the influx of sun and starlight do the heavy lifting for him. Sunlight was significantly easier to work with, likely due to the intensity. Starlight had some incredibly strange properties to it that he simply had not been able to pin down. Of course, until recently, he hadn't even *seen* what he was trying to pin down.

Artorian was fond of the discovery and recounted it on his fingers. "Twelve parts water, one part air, three parts fire, and eight parts celestial Essence."

Wham!

Having cycled that exact combination of Essence, his vision lit up with light rays. He could see *light*! What it went through, what it didn't. How it interacted with things, people, and objects. How it reflected and refracted. A world of observation invisible to all. The best part of this kind of sight wasn't that he saw objects. It was that he *didn't*. Only light was visible, and everything else remained a black emptiness of where 'stuff' was.

If there was light, he had full vision so long as he cleared the line-of-sight restriction. Another addition in the same mixture of units altered the effect. Twice the correct Essence meant twice the range of vision and twice the penetrative power. He stopped cycling his sight and rubbed his eyes. The changeover from his old eyes to these Essence-constructed ones had *massively* increased the maximum amount of Essence they could hold before a backfire. It was somewhere around four times the amount of what normal, uninjured eyes should have been able to do.

He'd been over by eight units *once*. Never again. Blindness and eye-pain for a full night, *while* he was healing and mending them, was not worth it. Then again, overload on all the senses did that, and if you couldn't heal it, the loss had a big chance to be permanent. That included Essence-built eyes, as the overload distorted the identity of what the organ was supposed to do. He'd rebuilt them slightly better the second time, but it was still something he'd rather avoid ever doing again.

The cost to do so had caused his Aura-stored Essence to drop by a loss measured in months. Still, he should have known better when he stacked his eyes with light-sight sixteen times. *Seventeen* is what had been the problem. The memory of the pain alone was enough to make him lose complete focus on what he had been doing.

Artorian violently recoiled and got back to work. He had children to save.

CHAPTER THIRTY-SIX

Artorian slapped himself on the cheeks, took a deep breath, and decided he needed some fresh air. Maybe he would go wild and have a *conversation*. The cloister had returned to the rhythm everyone was accustomed to. The drills, tired Initiates, chanting prayer, and material being dragged about filled the area once more. Tarrean had gotten the idea to lay cobblestone pathways, and that was a noisy endeavor. Acolytes and Initiates alike tended fields, saw to the growing orchard, carried bags of salt, and complained of bees.

The Keepers kept track of it all, and the superiors directed the efforts to keep things running smoothly, and none of these activities were things Artorian could take part in. So, having gotten his hands on a gnarled walking stick, his nose led him to the small abode near the apiary. Scents and smells prickled the senses, pleasantly bubbling from a large pot that released a delicious aroma. "Tibbins, my boy, are you here?"

The old man pushed the door open to find not only a wide-eyed Tibbins but also Hadurin Fellhammer with wooden spoons halfway into their mouths. Their bright eyes were parted like they'd just been caught red-handed stealing treats before appropriate mealtimes. Since the Fringe Elder had been right about needing a heftier food intake, rations were strict, in place for a reason, and they all knew it. This made food all the more precious, and thieves were punished *harshly*.

That Tibbins was an excellent chef didn't alter the punishment or the orders themselves. The silence grew awkward as the three men unblinkingly stared at one another. Artorian curled his lips into a smile and started tapping his walking stick on the floorboards as he took some cautious steps forward.

"Tibbins? *Come* now, my boy! Say something! You know I can't *see* very well. Are you going to let a *blind* old man just wander about?"

He dramatically glanced about to random parts of the ceiling for effect. Tibbins and Hadurin quickly cleaned up and stowed their spoons away at his good-natured understanding.

"Down here, you old codger." The Acolyte-turned-cook tapped his free hand on the paneling next to where the pot was bubbling, a large rod held to stir it.

"Ah, err, yes, greetin's, Artorian. How are ye feelin'?" Hadurin settled on to a stool next to a well-organized rack of herbs.

"Hadurin! You're here as well! Always good to have company. I'm getting better. Honestly, I thought I'd sneak in to see Tibbins and save Yvessa the trouble of bringing me my portion today. Chat a little. What brought you *here*?"

Hadurin picked up on the questioning notes that were emphasized when certain words were said particularly slowly. "Oh, well... I'm just helpin' Tib here with some... err... herbs!"

Hastily, the Head Healer snapped some greenery behind him and pushed it into a stone half-cup. The sounds of pestle grinding against mortar churned as the herbs were crushed in haste.

"How nice, Head Healer. Would you mind if I ate here?" Artorian sat himself down on the only proper chair, arm heavily leaning on the table as he set walking stick down upon his lap.

"O' course not! I'm sure Tibbins has some for ya." Tibbins didn't need the nudge in the ribs the healer gave him; he was already spooning out a meal's worth into the usual bowl.

"Here you go." The chef set the steaming cuisine down on the table and handed Artorian a smaller spoon.

"Thank you, my boy. How have you both been?" Artorian looked up when the reply wasn't immediate, starting to waywardly stir with his spoon. Both were staring at him, clearly wanting *him* to answer that question first. "Oh, don't look so *concerned*. I'll be well enough with some time. I'm even considering picking up a hobby."

"Archery perhaps. I lost my bow in the fire... oh, years ago." His expression turned somber at the recollection. "I tried making replacements, but they snapped so badly that they contributed to firewood."

Tibbins felt bad for the old-timer but shrugged it off. "It's just a bow, and don't *stir* like that. Scoop in from below with the flat of the spoon. You're just moving the top layer about and not actually cooling your food any faster. Now, the bow. I'm sure requisitions have a spare or two lying around. They *always* have spares."

Hadurin nodded to that statement. "Dey sure do. Standard practice is to have a little more than ya need with an expedition force, specifically for unforeseen circumstances. Ya never *truly* know what you're goin' ta need."

The stocky man stopped grinding herbs and crossed his arms, nodding sagely. He gave his vial-filled satchel a pat, and the glass clinked on the inside. "The apothecary wing of the Choir even saddled us with excess weak-grade healing potions. Just for small injuries mind ye, but it's a whole crate full! Heck, I picked myself up a satchel just to hold 'em and have some on me at all times."

"How *helpful*," Artorian flatly intoned, hiding the gears turning behind his twinkling expression. "Will I be needing to use those if more injured arrive, as before?"

The Head Healer's expression slipped from sage to grim. He wasn't fond of seeing Initiates flood his tent with horrible injuries. "Aye. The faster we can get those souls back up on their feet, the better it is fer everyone. I'll show ya how application works when needin' to use it as a topical. Otherwise, just pour it down a throat. Doesn' work as well, but gets the job done."

Artorian blew on a spoonful of food and tried it. His cheeks flushed to a darker pink, and a jovial *mmm* left him. His eyes closed to really *delve* into the flavor. Tibbins felt satisfaction at the happy old man with a good bowl of food in hand and verbally went through the bow list. "Requisitions likely won't just hand over a composite or a takedown bow. Longbows are a copper a dozen, but I don't think they'd be spotted dead with one. Clerics have a reputation to uphold. A recurve bow, perhaps—unless they have a ceremonial bow that otherwise just gathers dust."

"No ceremonial bow. If I accidentally harm it, Irene will use you as a pebble, then count how many times she can skip you across the surface of the salt lake." Artorian scraped the wooden spoon against the bottom of the bowl, gently interrupting. Tibbins compressed into himself and didn't enjoy the spastic, cold shiver curling down his arms and spine. "Recurve would be delightful. I could borrow one with a draw weight not normally used. Say one that's a little too high."

Fellhammer raised an eyebrow and regarded the old man with a question, "No explanation needed? Ya just knew what that type of bow is?"

Artorian swallowed his spoonful nonchalantly. "It's not the first time I've indulged in the hobby. I'm decently versed in tiny spear hurling."

He put the spoon down in the empty bowl, having been delighted with the scrumptious meal. "Since you're feeling *chatty*. Meridians? Just what do I *need*? I can already cycle

Essence and temporarily make certain bits work better, so I'm not sure if I follow the difference."

Fellhammer's displeasure grew in an instant. "Old man... are you telling me that you've been cycling Essence without having a single meridian open? You're not supposed to cycle until you've got at *least* one! The Essence don't come back fully if you don't have something stable to connect it to."

"Abyss be blazed.... what did ya *do*!" The Head Healer then immediately realized this had not been a problem for Artorian. Cycling Essence to his eyes, Hadurin investigated the old man's Center. "Yep. All meridians still closed. Nothin' to tether a cycle to."

Artorian smiled. He relished in the little outbursts anytime the topic came up. He looked inwards, pensively stroking his beard without thought. "There most certainly *is*, my friend. All you need in order to cycle is to have a set return point with a firm enough Essence weave. So, *any* of my rings will do. Now, I can only bind a single cycle to a specific ring or set of rings, locking off those sources for anything else I may have needed them for. I will admit it's not very efficient, but it *does* work."

"I don't see the problem. Looks like it works fine, just that a meridian would be much better," Tibbins joined in. His cooking was fine to let simmer, and he didn't want to keep being left out. The cook was exploring around Artorian's cycle with Essence-filled eyes, fascinated by just how *different* it all was.

"I'm honestly having difficulty telling what rank you are." Tibbins had some newfound pep in his voice, and Fellhammer joined him.

"Aye! Yer entire method blurs the clear lines of separation we've come to expect. Can't say you've broken through into the C-ranks with how yer core is set up. It *ain't* solid. So, I'd set ya in a solid D but anywhere from one to five!"

Artorian pulled his attention out of his Center so he could answer. "My incremental improvements lead to faster breakthroughs and weaker bottlenecks. I've no need to break my spiral into a fractal, as I follow the theme of the progress by adding additional rings. From what I've seen, the vortex of a spiral is just repeated in a fractal. Two spirals just mean twice the refinement. A fractal could likely be any *number* of vortex spirals, but the method of gain remains the same."

He paused and grumbled, "I must admit it's incredibly space efficient. I'm still working on discovering optimal distance between rings myself. Two rings just *can't* occupy the same space or intersect. Both will break when they impact each other, and that's quite the mess. However, we're getting off track. *Meridians?*"

Fellhammer snapped back to his explanation, mesmerized by the spinning artwork on display in the old man's Center. "Oh, ya just spindle yer Essence. Think of something like a rope or a line. Ya poke the tip into the holes on the outer edges of your Center. It's harder than threading a needle, but after ya *do*, the Essence thread will get pulled. So be prepared to visualize a *bunch* because it's going to unspool straight from yer spiral. It's going to feel like you're being drained of Essence via it bein' *ripped* out of ya, but really, it's just condensin' and makin' new paths all about yer insides. It's all still *there*; it's just spread out."

"That means ya aren't actually losing any Essence; it's jus' put to *permanent* use. I warn my Acolytes that they're likely to drop some ranks in cultivation and to expect pain. Essence is forcing a new, energy-only cardiovascular system to exist in yer body after all. This is why in the Choir the first meridian we open is the heart. It's the most dangerous, and we don't want to lose a person when they've gotten that far. From the heart, ye can go most anywhere else. But for Essence, it connects to the–"

"Small intestine," Artorian interrupted him.

The Head Healer lost track of his explanation from the mention and turned in his stool. He had been expecting some questions, not total understanding *beyond* what was told. "...Aye. How did ya figure that one out?"

The kindly old man just laid one of his hands over the other. "All those pathways used to be filled with highly volatile corruption. I've got a grasp of them but just didn't know how to connect them with Essence. Flooding the system didn't seem like the way to go, but I hadn't figured out how to move Essence out of my Center without it being lost or spent. Cycling Essence by itself is costly. I was using a weave like what I'm doing for my circles to accomplish the effect but being told you can just thread the Essence and feed it in is very helpful. I'm honestly surprised it's that simple. I take it the process is *exceptionally* painful, or you wouldn't have bothered to mention it?"

The Head Healer dropped the need for explanation, concerned about the patient instead. "Aye, every single time. Tibbins can tell ya."

Both older men turned to look at the cook, who was already violently nodding. "There isn't a cooking accident that has hurt me more than the pain I experienced when opening my heart meridian, and I have neither the Essence nor the tolerance for the next. Not only is controlling the flow crucial, but it took me a year to have enough stored Essence just to not run dry during the attempt. Now, I always need a set amount in my system, or my heart will outright stop. It may be easier for the next one, but then I'll need to keep hold of more 'safety' Essence, and I'm just... not ready for the pain."

Artorian and Hadurin nodded in understanding, and Artorian held his chin in thought. "So not something an abundance of Essence is sufficient to fix, as the pain will overwhelm you. I expect that's not the only downside."

Hadurin groaned at that next part with a miserable sigh. "A~a~aye. Ya expel all teh impurities that teh meridian previously held as it opened. I get a cleaning crew ready when I've got enough people that need *serious* punishment."

Artorian leaned back in the chair, pensive. "Would being in a stream at the time of opening help? Swifter cleanup?"

The Head Healer shrugged. "Ah s'pose it'd mitigate teh need for a cleanup crew."

Pleased, Artorian snatched his walking stick, rose, and did a minor stretch. "Very well, then. I'm off to the stream to open my heart meridian!"

The clerics snapped their heads to look at him in unison. "Right *now?*"

"*Right now,*" Artorian confirmed their fear and was already striding to the door. Tibbins could not leave his station since he had meals to cook, so he threw a pleading look at the healer who was already scrambling to his feet and following a very determined Artorian to the stream.

CHAPTER THIRTY-SEVEN

Hadurin chased after Artorian in a panic. "Ah *can't* recommend ya do this! Slow *down*, ya stubborn bugger and think clearly about this! Ya only *got* one chance."

Artorian slid off his blue robe mid-walk, folding it up while remaining dressed in the proper gi beneath it. "*You're* here, my friend. One witness is plenty!"

Hadurin Fellhammer had seen some *audacity* over his many years of tending to fools, but this old man was *really* working to reach the top of that list! Already understanding he wasn't about to change Artorian's mind, Hadurin threw his hands up and cursed in Dwarven. Both rolled up their pant legs to the knees and waded into the stream. Hadurin remained standing, but Artorian plopped down right in the middle of it, getting into lotus pose as the Head Healer kneeled behind him.

"Yer crazy, but I can't let ya just keel over here. I'll be stabilizing yer heart. Don't abyss-blasted *fight* me when I'm influencing yer system. It's to keep ya alive, ya stubborn git."

Artorian laughed at the mention. "Ha! It will be quite alright. I'm going to get quiet and Essence-coat the outer edge of my Center, then begin threading my meridians. This should be a novel experience!"

Hadurin leaned to the left to speak over the eccentric's shoulder and honestly didn't understand what the old man was talking about. "Yer gonna *what?*"

"Just *watch*," Artorian retorted, releasing Essence from a refined circle and sending it barreling outwards at significant speed. The motes were suddenly significantly slowed back down by a barrier. A zone of differentiation between Center and regular body *did* exist, it seemed. This small area filled with refined Essence like glitter ensnared in gel.

The glittering light made the holes in his Center easy to 'see' and a formed thread spun and lined up with a clearly visible path. It was clear that Artorian had been hard at work getting everything prepared for this. Hadurin sighed with relief; if he had prepared so heavily and practiced, then this wasn't a hairbrained attempt to end it all.

The thread left Artorian's Center, followed the meridian, and traveled directly toward his heart. He exhaled *hard* as the Essence impacted with the force of a hammer. For a few moments, his eyes boggled and his body clenched. He grabbed at his chest as a full-blown heart attack tried to begin.

"I've got you. Fight through the pain!" Hadurin ordered, using his own Essence to keep the heartbeat steady. The old man had a strong heart for someone of his age, but opening a meridian was no joke. The thread looped around Artorian's heart in a tight weave, tighter, *tighter*... until the organ had the thread moving through every part: tissue, artery, and capillary. The weave remained intact as the thread veered off to continue along its meridian.

The pain subsided in its wake, and his heart ceased needing the healer's direct attention. Hadurin *thought* the process was going to end there, but he cursed and pushed his hands against the old man's lower back. "You ragged, pebbles-for-brains, old *fart*!"

The thread had continued, flowing *downward*, and it hit his lower intestine. It *did* hit with less force than the heart, only creating a weave in a small area before splitting to move up to his lungs. The high energy-and-velocity Essence thread impacted both areas roughly enough that Artorian doubled over with wet coughs. Breath left him, along with a *significant* amount of blood. He never noticed, as his focus was purely on chasing down and trying to catch the overzealous—and out of *control*—thread.

The weave around his heart and lungs repeated itself, and Artorian went pale and blue. He couldn't breathe until the pattern completed, and it seemed to be slowing down. *Terrible* timing! Though this did allow him to catch it, and he *forced* it to do an additional loop in reverse. Artorian was convinced that this was the same feeling as being dragged along by a startled horse running from a snake.

The thread rejoined his Center from a separate opening than it had exited, as expected. Rather than smash into the circles of his Center, the end of the thread *shattered* and spiderwebbed connections among the free-floating, purified Essence in the limbo-zone of his glittery Center. Artorian opened his eyes and heaved before fully collapsing, blood spilling out of his mouth. The stream engulfed him for just a moment before the Head Healer managed a proper grip on him.

"I've got ya, ya mad fool! What did Tib '*just*' say about holding the flow back?" No internal damage needed patching up, but he was still whacking Artorian's back to loosen the gunk his body was now forcing out. Thick, wheezing breaths were interrupted by agonizing coughing fits, and they sounded nearly as awful as they felt. It took a solid few minutes of repeating the breathing and slapping cycle before he began to chuckle.

"Well then. That was–"

Hadurin interrupted him this time, "A *terrible* idea? A great way teh scare yer healer half to death? *Aye.* Yer heart would've just *stopped* had I not been here to make it keep beatin'!"

Flustered and red with anger, the grumbly healer checked his patient over. "Looks like heart, lungs, and lower intestines. What even *was* that thread ya made? It was dense... but looked like it was gonna fracture at any moment. I've never seen that space between the inside an' outside of a Center be so clearly defined either. I can even *see* the rest o' yer meridian channels."

Artorian nodded, needing to breathe deeply. He slowly spoke, "I wasn't sure how to stop the thread. Once I let it go, oh... did it *go*. On the way back to my Center, I needed to convince it that it was something other than a thread and altered its identity."

He could feel Hadurin *drill* him for information with just a look. "Admittedly, I was a touch scared—which naturally made me think of spiders. I'm also scared of those. So, rather than thread, my mind went to 'web'. I don't believe I got it all the way, but before the thread could make a mess of my entire cultivation system, it shattered and split, 'webbing' out to encompass all the glitter points. The broken thread used free, refined Essence as guideposts for where to tether. Now, I don't know what this webbed circle around my cultivation is going to *do*, but currently, it's what is actually connected to my meridians."

Hadurin helped him up to his feet and grumped, "Likely for the best. I dunno how your technique would have reacted to a direct meridian connection. I can handle that fine, but as usual, you've surprised us."

Standing on his feet again, Artorian felt wobbly while the healer steadied him. His gi was drenched, but he was alive. That's a trade he'd make any day. Still, the old man was confused. "For such a big, painful, life-altering effect... I feel surprisingly good?"

He'd been expecting to *still* be in severe pain. Hadurin grinned and shook his hands to get the water, grease, and blood off. "You'll get used to yer meridians bein' open. In short, any benefit you got out of 'em before is going to improve. Your stamina is going to see a nice boost. I was expecting more taint as well, so you must have cleaned yerself up a little better than ya thought."

Hadurin grimaced and looked at Artorian. "You still need to clean yerself and burn that gi. Listen, I'm wantin' a full, *written* explanation on how ya did that. As yer healer, I *insist* ya get two full days of bed rest followed by at least three *weeks* of recovery before ya attempt another meridian. Most people wait a *year* or so, but I feel like ya aren't gonna do tha', are ya? I want ya in the medical tent five hours a *day* as soon as yer rest has concluded. We'll need to check you over for side effects, and I can't keep lettin' ya *weasel* yer way out of teh deal."

"Yes, *cough*, yes. I'll be there. Is light exercise fine?" Swinging an arm around Fellhammer's neck, Artorian finally got steady.

The Head Healer thought about slapping the man silly, and an annoyed gruffness rumbled in his words. "Define *light*."

"Morning jog and some archery?" Artorian smiled out the tired response as Hadurin was already dragging him back to the bank.

"Ya just *love* gettin' that big nose o' yers in trouble, don'tcha."

In response to the healer's quip, Artorian tapped the side of his admittedly large nose. "It does it by itself, I swear."

Fellhamer snorted a *phah* and picked the dry robes up to carry. "Aye, that little bit is fine, but I'm siccin' Yvessa on ya the second ya leave my care. Wash."

The glum groan that left the hanging old man made the entire stream event worth it for the healer. Artorian flopped into the water, kicking and splashing. He grabbed sand and started scouring his black-oil-coated skin, then did his hair. Frankly, he looked like a toddler having a tantrum, which only made Hadurin happier. The sheer pleasure of siccing a caretaker on Artorian—one who delighted in forcing Artorian to rest and sleep—made Hadurin enjoy a cackle.

"Oh, look! Speak of the abyss!"

"*Artoria~a~an*!" Yvessa's furious voice cut across the field as she stomped her way to the pair. She was *livid* and not hiding an iota of it. Artorian had not only snuck off without *telling* anyone but had likely hoped for a bonus serving of food by sneaking to Tibbins! She was *fuming*, and the motherly expression only made Fellhammer break down in raucous laughter as the dejected groaning of the man cleaning himself intensified.

"Hah! Ha-ha, that's what ya get for sneakin' about. *Hello*! Yvessa! Over here! He's naked and doin' odd things again!"

Artorian pleadingly glanced at the Head Healer for mercy, but there was none to be had. His groan petered out into a whimpered puddle. He wasn't going to hear the end of this after Yvessa found out he'd not only snuck off... but opened *meridians*. Hadurin *lived* for this sort of torment. He was relishing every moment as Yvessa chewed Artorian out the *entire* walk home.

There were always fringe benefits to being Head Healer.

CHAPTER THIRTY-EIGHT

A full week later, the beatdown Artorian received from Yvessa was *still* making the rounds in camp. To make things even juicier, Tibbins had been assigned duty when Artorian had arrived for a checkup at the medical tent after his assigned bed rest days expired... only to discover Artorian had opened his large intestine meridian in the meanwhile.

The Head Healer had hunted the old man down as long beard darted and ducked between tents. Artorian was laughing. "You're *laughing*? You keep tryin' ta kill yourself when no one is looking? I'm gonna finish the job! Get *over* here, you dusty tumbleweed!"

It was *quite* the day for the Initiates when they were awoken up for duty via an old man careening through the window flap of the tent. He was squealing with amusement as Hadurin's endless streams of Dwarven insults followed him, always only a step or two behind.

The levity cut short when a loud **gong** resounded in the middle of camp, and the still-laughing, old man fell on his butt after running straight into Tarrean's *very* ornate armor—with Tarrean very much *in* it. Having to explain to the Head Cleric that Artorian was having such a happy, energetic day was because his *meridians had started to open* was an adventure in facial expressions.

Tarrean's face was stuffed with evolving disbelief, concern, and hints of tormented jealousy. More and more of his face became obscured behind his hands as the explanation went on. When he heard the news that Artorian had *four* major affinity channels, his forehead was pressed to the table, and he outright asked for a drink.

When Hadurin finally got around to Artorian's checkup, the entire upper echelon of the cloister was present and observing. They had to *see* it to believe it, and even *then* they didn't understand half of what they were looking at. When the checkup was done, Marud was in *tears* from laughter. Tarrean had his head against the main support pole of the medical tent out of sheer, rampant depression.

Irene crackled with the tenderness of living lightning and stormed off to demand written accounts from Tibbins and Yvessa. Meanwhile, Hadurin was trying to suppress giggles at the visual dichotomy of Artorian's peaceful resting expression... which clashed with the despair that hung over both Head Clerics.

The expedition leader was haranguing Tarrean about *why* this man hadn't been drafted yet, and gossip once again found life as secret after secret tumbled into the open like dominoes. When everyone left and it was just Artorian and Hadurin in the tent, the Head Healer slumped over to a padded cot and lit up a rolled-up bundle of herbs to puff. Practiced releases of shaped smoke blew from his nose and mouth as his leg lifted to lay on his opposing thigh. "Are ya *pleased* with yourself, old man? I know ya did it on purpose."

The previously 'snoozing' Artorian opened an eye, then sat upright like he'd never been asleep at all. Which, of course, he hadn't. "It was getting too *quiet*. A little life goes a long way, don't you think? I can't *tell* you how tempted I was to try and open a meridian while they were all watching. *Ow!*"

A pillow struck the side of his face, originating from the Head Healer. It smacked Artorian right back down on to the cot with an *oof* He grabbed and settled it behind his back with the others and peacefully sunk down. "Oh, another pillow. Wonderful!"

Hadurin shook his head, needing a strong inhalation of his makeshift cigar. "Ye'r a piece of work, Artorian. Ya don't adhere to anyone else's speed. Ya *realize,* of course, they're goin' teh be watching ya closely from now on?"

To Hadurin's hidden enjoyment, the long-bearded man was once again a bundle of smiles. "My friend, I'm *counting* on it.

The Head Healer rubbed his temples and took an extra-long drag of his cigar. "Alright, codger, I'm interested. What are ya plannin'? All these small things you've done over the time I've known ya all add up to some *big* hullabaloo. Ye've got the same look the Vicars do when they're puttin' somethin' together."

He blew a big smoke ring right at the ceiling. "One old soldier to another. Sell me on it."

A sigh of relief left Artorian, who had gone from energetic and laying in comfort to drained and tired in the span of a heartbeat. "Releasing cycled Essence always takes it out of me."

Hadurin knew the feeling well. "Aye. I imagine you're quite tired when you're not usin' it for a boost. Ye may have some good cultivation, but yer still *old.* Meridians are gonna help, but it's not like yer twenty and spry. Someone with less cultivation and better training can cut ya off like a bad joke. Now, *out* with it. Yvessa warned me ya like to *dawdle.*"

Artorian sat up, faced his new friend, and laced his fingers together on his lap. "The raiders took my children, on that day the first expedition arrived. I believe they're *alive*, and I'm going to get them out of that terrible life if it's the last thing I do."

Hadurin's brows rose. *That* was a bigger punch to the gut than he'd expected. Artorian continued, "I have been reckless, done my best to be patient, and have spent these last... nearly three *years* working on my cultivation for any kind of *edge* that would let me get them back. I'm not one to ask for help, but I do *trade* for it. In a few months, the season will end, and the expedition will go back to the Choir. The trader comes once a month."

The healer didn't understand why that last mention was important and made a hand motion that matched his befuddled expression. Artorian explained with a snarling retort, "The trader is *complicit* with the raiders. I have it on good word from... the other Elder of this village, before she passed. I simply haven't informed the cloister."

This pissed Hadurin off more than a little, but contrary to his personality, he held his tongue. There was going to be *more*. He knew there would be, and Artorian didn't disappoint. "The third visit from the trader, from this point, is about at the time when the expedition group needs to disembark. If I tell the trader the expedition party will be *gone* that day... a party of raiders is *guaranteed* to follow in an attempt to flatten this place and take it for every coin it's worth. It will take me but a small mention to bait that hook."

"The raiders I'm after have holed up in Duskgrove. I know the castle. It's a wreck but a well-armed wreck. On that third trader visit, I will be leaving the cloister and going with him. I know he won't be able to resist the opportunity to cleave my head and claim this robe, so he won't decline my company. Rather than follow the trading route back out of the Fringe, he'll detour past Phantomdusk Forest in order to get to a place he can hide the evidence. That gets me to where I need to be."

Hadurin cobbled the information together, inspiration tingling as understanding struck him. He puffed from his herbs and tapped it to remove ashes. "I see. Would be an *awful day* for the raider group if they assaulted a position that *wasn't* actually abandoned, and it would be *equally* handy if a good bowman were to annoy a castle that ran on a skeleton crew rather than a full one. Yer running was the basic training ya needed, and archery is yer problem solver."

"You've got teh Essence intake to build meridians, and unlike most people, pain isn't a deterrent so much as it is something you've accepted you're going to deal with. Ya don't actually care about yer life, and you're *spending* it with abyss-cursed abandon to finish a war the raiders don't even know they started."

Artorian relaxed back down from his strong position. It was a delight to sit with another sharp-minded, old soul. "You're a clever man, my friend."

Hadurin shrugged and puffed. "Just old, and it's not my first war. I'm not gonna try to stop a righteous cause like this, so I'm on board. What do you need from me?"

"A good bow, enough arrows for it to matter, and *quiet* checkups as I barrel through opening my meridians." Artorian raised his hand and counted the necessities on his fingers, then winced at the memory. "It hurts like being chewed up by a beast, but I'm not *actually* losing Essence from the process, so I have plenty. I'm opening *all* of them before two months have passed."

Hadurin's face hardened stoically, understanding the aged soldier's march to his chosen end. Artorian swallowed and continued, "Potions if you can spare them, rations packed in a sack since I expect my personal siege to last a good while. Some basic sparring? I know better than to hope I'll stay lucky enough to remain at range. For the remainder, I'll rest and cultivate. I *might* be able to send my children back here, but I suspect I could be too spent to return."

Hadurin harrumphed. "Sword?"

Artorian just shook his head 'no'. "Won't do me any good. I can't handle the weight, and I don't have the time to oil up my rusty skills. Hand-to-hand and bow are the best I'll be able to do, and then only because I know I can drop the bow to run if I need to. I'm going to be using some rather... *idiotic* tactics."

The Head Healer just took a cigar drag and spoke along with a cloud of smoke, "Such as?"

"I plan on assailing the castle... from inside the Phantomdusk Forest."

CHAPTER THIRTY-NINE

"That's askin' to die! Nothin' passes through teh forest. Everyone and everything just *dies*!" Fellhammer coughed and hacked on his breath, beating his own chest to get that bad swallow out. "Hunters, search parties, raiders, and clerics alike fall to the phantoms of teh grove. We've got *deeply* written history and orders to avoid steppin' *foot* in! Death is as guaranteed as the Ebon Plague."

Artorian sighed and squeezed the bridge of his nose. "It's the only place with enough height to get above the walls even with an arced shot. I can practice the shots here, and I may have a way to detect where raiders are inside of the castle, but it's a moot point if I can't actually take enough of them down to cause the needed panic."

The Head Healer was particularly interested in that last word and put aside the absolute insanity of the plan. He wasn't about to stop a man who was already knowingly walking into a situation where he *was* going to die. "A few arrows don't cause a panic, my friend."

Artorian eased himself out of the cot and stood, brushing his robe off. "It will not, but this may. Extinguish the flames, would you?"

The Head Healer picked the torches off the wall and doused them in a bucket of water. The last one out made the tent enter a pitched darkness. That didn't last very long, as Artorian started counting, and a burning, red glow built where his eyes were.

"Ten." Right away, Hadurin could tell Artorian's irises were bright red and glowing.

"Fifteen." It became more than just a glow; a crimson tint emitted from Artorian's eyes so strongly that it was downright unsettling.

"Twenty." The tint flared so brightly his eyes may as well have been flames.

"Twenty-five." *There* it was. The crimson flames now looked like searing orange and white eyes, burning and surrounded by an unsettling red gloom. The view completely obscured the old man's features, his eyes unnaturally large and threatening in the dark. Hadurin felt as he was back on the fields with the undead, except that these unnatural eyes held a far deeper dread.

"Alright, *alright.* Stop that. You're giving me the shakes, and I'm not sure if I want to run or strike ye." The glow died back down significantly faster than it came, and the cleric re-lit the torches. "What *was* that?"

Artorian rubbed his eyes and sat back down on the cot. "Not *quite* refined Essence cycled to the eyes, given an identity to increase the visual effect and potency rather than push added sight. With specific units of corruption in particular measurements, I see something I've come to call *infrared.* It came with the benefit that I could make some truly scary eyes, and in the dark, it's all you can see. Now, imagine that while those eyes are looking at you in the distance, every now and then, one of your comrades just... *dies.*"

The cleric nodded, both pleased and impressed. "*That'll* start a nasty rumor, and they won't be keen to send people out to explore. If I didn't know better, I'd call that being attacked by a phantom of teh forest. Yer going to need a *real* good bow."

Artorian scoffed at such obvious truth. "I take it you're on board?"

Hadurin gave him the flattest, most severe look he'd ever levered on the crazy man. "An old soldier just told me that he's going to stroll into the abyss itself, punch demons, and all so that he can rescue people that he loves. With the clerics here, you can afford to push past the point of safety—you are even willing to die, so long as your mission succeeds. I am *firmly* of the belief that I know the look of a man who thinks like that. Celestial knows I've buried many men over my career. Making light of the serious, being jovial about the end, and underneath it all, you're dead *tired*."

It was Artorian who was full of surprise. He didn't think someone could read him so well. "What a *book* I must be to you to be read so easily."

The Head Healer scowled and extinguished the end of his herb cigar. "A book I've read the ending of too *many* times. Come back *alive*, ya fool. There are people here that *thrive* because you're around. You can't throw yourself into the jaws of death that easily. We're going to open your meridians, ready you up, and set up the best counter-ambush the Fringe has seen in a hundred years."

He slapped a hand to Artorian's shoulder. "I have Irene for a check-up later. Get out of here and rest. I've got a Keeper to cobble a plan together with."

A rare occasion in his life, Artorian did what he was told. He clasped wrists and counted it as a cordial goodbye. Artorian heard the healer mutter, 'Stubborn idiot,' as he left, but it lacked negativity; he didn't think on it any further. Yvessa was waiting for him at his abode with a *nasty* expression on her face.

She said nothing as he approached, just sharply pointed at the door. Silently, he entered the building, and she followed him in. He quietly shuffled in and hung his robe. Being properly dressed today, he then undid his gi and hung that up as well, leaving him with a simple shirt underneath. He settled into his pillow-laden, slice-of-heaven bed and relaxed under the starlight. That checkup had taken *ages* thanks to the audience.

Yvessa eased into her usual seat and seriously controlled herself before speaking, "So Tibbins fainted."

The matter of fact statement made Artorian simply nod.

"That meant I had to give Irene the entire report by myself. *By. My. Self.*" She took a deep breath, calming herself with a controlled nasal exhale.

"I am going to be on you like salt on the plains. *Every. Single. Day.* For the next few weeks, until Keeper Irene has a properly compiled report on the daily activities of a *hidden cultivator* who, on paper, is listed as *bedridden* for three *years.* I have seen unwritten reports that *already* have that line on them. I had to explain, in *detail,* the ridiculous, *impossible* chaos that follows in your wake, and I had to start from *our* expedition. Tarrean, on top of now handling severe depression, also can't escape the endless nagging of not one... but *two* Keepers."

"Do you have *any* idea how draining it is to even have a *single* Keeper chasing you down? They're working so long into the nights that they've taken to falling asleep on that massive pillow kept in the middle of the cloister structure. You know the one. Your practical *joke.*" Yvessa was venting, fuming as the conversation switched between irritation and badly needing to get things off her chest.

"Can I say that I'm glad it is getting some use?" Artorian quipped. When Yvessa was all out of things to say about *that* joke, she was out of breath. Through all of this, she had braided and unbraided his beard *twice* out of frustration.

"Why aren't you *talking* anymore? You usually can't wait to get a clever word in on someone."

"Would you believe I learned my lesson?" Artorian voice held a hint of mirth, but he sobered quickly. "Can I just remark... you held your own against Irene through all of that?"

Yvessa frowned and threw her hands up. "*Yeah?*"

The grandfather kindly smiled and, with much satisfaction, praised her, "I'm so very proud of you."

Yvessa was stunned, mouth slightly agape. She didn't know how to feel. "You just can't help but catch people off-guard, can you?"

The frustration thawed from her face as Artorian sat up to embrace his caretaker. He spoke as she crammed her stressed face into his shoulder. "I remember a shy, little girl who was trying her best to keep her confidence together. Look at you *now*, standing up against a *Keeper*! I told you, you could do it! After all, *I* believe in you."

He let go when she pushed away and took his time re-adjusting to his bed. "Ow!"

Yvessa had punched him in the shoulder without a word. She pouted and glared at him. "You keep treating everyone like they're your children. I'm *not* a child."

Artorian closed his eyes. "That doesn't make you not *family*, my dear. It is the role of a grandfather to stir the pot, and I am happy to be a grandfather to all who find themselves in need of one. I am the warm coat in a cold winter, a listening ear for a heavy heart, and a funny voice with a big nose for a small child who can't help but cry."

He sighed and pressed fingers over his forehead. "Hadurin, my friend, I'm afraid you were *right*."

Yvessa had a quick look around but didn't see the Head Healer. The old man must have been talking to himself. "He isn't here, Artorian. Are you... seeing him right now?"

"I certainly have my work cut out for me. Oh, I'm going to be so tired, but I'll be back. I'll have to make it back." Fingers snapped in front of his face as his caretaker tried to pull him back to reality.

"You're *slipping*. What are you getting into now to make life hard for me?"

A small chuckle left Artorian. "Scheduling! Mornings, train with Initiates. At noon, eat. Then at high noon, cultivate. Assist in the medical wing all late afternoon, then eat again. End the schedule by alternating between days of basic sparring and archery from a bit before sunset to evening curfew. Sleep. When the merchant comes, I need a chat."

"Oh, *no*. I don't believe that *one* bit. You on an actual *schedule*? As if."

Yvessa was *immediately* suspicious. She pulled his blankets over him and tucked in the puffy sides. "I am going to be here at sun-up with my paper and board in hand, and we're going to record *all* the things you're up to. I'm not letting you wiggle out of doing actual work! Go to sleep, grandpa."

Artorian couldn't help but feel *delight*, and his expression reflected the feeling. She'd never called him by that title before! Hadurin had most *definitely* been right... his suicide mission needed to turn into *just* a mission.

He couldn't knowingly end the happiness even one person had due to his presence. He was going to have to put *actual work* in so he could survive. He fell asleep before realizing it, and Yvessa didn't leave until she was *sure* he was out.

Tomorrow was *sure* to be interesting.

CHAPTER FORTY

Yvessa spent the next few months bashing her face into what had become a sizable clipboard. That *infuriating* Elder was actually sticking to his schedule with a *painful* amount of accuracy, and her days were so predictable that they'd become *horribly* boring.

She could abyss-near tell the time based on when the old man was doing something. She was there every morning when he woke, holding his breakfast bowl in hand. He ate and was followed to the front gate where he joined Initiates in the training morning run. Ten laps around the entire cloister later, and it was time to wash in the stream. Artorian then ate again and spent hours in bed where it looked like he was resting. That was merely the lie visible on the surface.

Yvessa was getting *very* good at cycling Essence sight to keep track of what her favorite eccentric was doing, and in truth, it made her feel terrible about her own daily cultivation speed. Even with her *fractal,* she wasn't drawing in nearly the amount his strange sun-Center was. Every addition to the array of circles just kept on *increasing* the amount he drew in.

He was taking in but a *fraction* of what was available to him. It blew her mind that he was taking in only a *tiny* amount compared to what he *could* if he didn't care about refining. Therein lay the issue for him; it was the *refining* that took time. Unlike her fractal, which pulled purity and repelled corruption, Artorian's rings relied on centrifugal force to move energy of a certain 'density' to a higher or lower layer.

That interaction mostly just broke her brain as the number of rings—and thus layers—wasn't one she could count. It didn't help that almost every *week* another meridian was opened. That would then alter the *entire* process of his inner workings, which made things just a *tiny,* little bit more efficient. Still, unlike her passive fractal, Artorian expended a significant amount of Essence to keep his operation *running.* He needed to cultivate every day *without fail* even if just to purify his body and Center.

Becoming a cultivator when old had *significant* drawbacks, and he was going to need decades and *decades* to do what a Beast Core could have done in a few minutes if his body could have handled it... but that option was gone. As an upside to his technique, breakthroughs were *much* easier. It came with the cost that figuring out his ranking was a hazy headache at best, but that was a minor annoyance in comparison to the luminous benefits.

Sure, the sunlight Center was slow in its own way, but once the downsides were accounted for—downsides counted in *decades*—he'd outstrip a fully formed fractal by leagues so long as he took no critical injuries. Actually, *making* it to that age was no longer just a passing dream but a possible *reality.* The caretaker was forced to take a daily break in order to cultivate herself but always found that the old man hadn't budged when she returned.

From Artorian, Yvessa gained *stacks* of notes on medical procedure, organ placements, appropriate treatments, differing methods of potion application, sickness markers, and a full *treatise* on crystal venom. She carried enough documents on her person that some of the Initiates had taken to ask her for details on certain procedures since she had the notes readily available. When Artorian was present in the medical tent, she was his shadow.

Except for the *one* day a week when there was a class trip of every single healer to the stream. Acolytes and Initiates alike were present to take notes on the tribulations and effects of the opening of a meridian at an advanced age. On days where things didn't go as planned, he experienced the effects of opening *more* than one meridian.

Any day where one of the senses of the old man were affected, they found it was going to be a gruesome endeavor. *Severe* scrubbing was required to get the gunk off him when the more severely affected meridians opened. His skin *alone* had forced such a severe reaction that the Initiates had outright *fled*, then avoided being downwind while a face-masked Acolyte team took a full hour to scrub him clean.

On the plus side, his physical injuries now looked like cuts instead of sandpaper wounds. *Considerably* less gruesome overall. After a full medical examination back in the tent with another compact round of lectures and note-taking, Artorian was excused. He picked up a recurve bow from requisitions, complete with a full complement of arrows.

That was normal and just fine. What *wasn't* so great was how Artorian focused more on striking his targets through high-arched trick shots rather than direct collision. While he didn't skimp on basic footing and form, he took *far* too long to fire a single arrow. To the bow users among them, it felt like he was nearly *mocking* their training.

Artorian let the side of his robe down so it wasn't in the way of the string. Holding the weapon firm during aiming, he gently let it swing as an arrow flew free. His feet were positioned in a stable 'L' shape, legs slightly bent at the knee as he pulled. The bow clearly had a draw strength too high for a non-cultivator.

The *twang* that reverberated each time an arrow loosed made it vanish from the bow entirely. A telltale *thock* became a common impact sound as the arrow hit somewhere on the target. It wasn't often in the middle, where the target was situated, but after mere weeks, he was scoring hit after hit. When asked, he mentioned that he'd done bow-stuff once or twice before.

With this sly fox... they didn't quite know if he'd been hunting for two decades or had never picked a bow up before that day. Still, it was a strange thing to watch. The old man held his shots until suddenly he *didn't*.

Thock!

Another successful strike to a target that *should* have wildly blown off course, but no amount of wind ever seemed to deter his arrows. A few of the seasoned archers had come asking how he'd pulled that off, but the answers had been... cryptic. "The wind is your friend, if only you take care to see in which direction it wants to play."

He even offered to show them, but the archers could not seem to understand what he did. The interesting part came in later weeks when Initiates started carrying moving targets. They'd agreed only because he'd requested the training be in the dark, and the chance of an arrow hitting a target was slim to none. That had proven to be a horrific lie. The *thock*! of arrows striking the wooden target scared the abyss out of the recruits. It *also* loosened certain coin purses as old-man archery was a prime subject for gambling.

On days where there was no archery, Artorian joined in on hand-to-hand training. What should have been self-defense was instead an *onslaught*. Keeper Irene had decided that on those days, she needed to relieve some stress. Great anticipation spread through the camp like wildfire anytime the call went out. "Artorian is fighting Irene!"

The first fight they'd ever had set the pace, the betting rate, and the guaranteed high-attendance rate as several of the Initiates went full-fanboy.

"I am *done* with you. I have *had it.*" Irene power-walked on to the field and threw her papers to the ground. That was the first sign that told everyone something was *amiss*, and it momentarily hushed them as it stole attention. The second sign was that she erupted into a Choir combat-chant and charged right at the gi-clad old man without so much as a warning.

A roaring outburst boomed from the excited Acolytes, followed by a collective gasp from the Initiates as they were about to see a slow, old man get decked in the face hard enough to send him flying farther than Keeper Kendra. To their amazement, Artorian held aloft a single finger. With a small, circling inner arc, he pushed on Irene's wrist as she flew by. His left foot shifted backward; his right shoulder pivoted to fill the space she'd previously been occupying. Her punch missed *wide*, her balance was gone, and Irene barreled right into the mud with all the velocity she'd built up.

Artorian just blinked, quizzically observing his finger while stroking his beard. "*Peculiar*. Is *that* how this works?"

Fury embodied shoved upward with a wet *thud*. Covered in mud, the irate Keeper didn't *care* if that was a fluke. The surprise humiliation filled her with blind, irrational rage. She pounced on him with all the ferocity of a Morovian Liger, which just so happened to be the name for her particular combat-style. "*Artorian!*"

It was a back and forth that was difficult to follow until the old man slipped and failed a block or deflection, unable to get in a single offensive strike on her while Irene continued pounding him like a hung slab of meat. "*You. Messed. Up. My. Filing. System!*"

He took quite the pummeling, and the clamor of many acolytes hesitantly died down while they watched the one-sided beatdown. At the end of the bout, the old man didn't need his robe in order to look blue. He was wheezing, on his back, and in a layer of plowed mud. He'd been the plow.

Irene wasn't satisfied with a single day of sparring. *Oh no*. This Elder had caused her *significant* administrational grief. She'd taken *exception* to that and would not let it go easily.

CHAPTER FORTY-ONE

Every other day, Irene fielded her combat expertise like clockwork. The winner was always easy to discern. Irene was without equal during practice, yet there were definite moments where she did *not* have the upper hand. The happenings were sporadic and sudden, but certain attacks Irene launched at Artorian found that an unexpectedly perfect counter awaited them.

Not only did she fail to strike the intended target, the blow was redirected back on her. This threw her off balance, dropping her to the muddy ground that *Artorian* usually found himself in. The first time the old man had done it on purpose, he'd raised both fists to the sky and excitedly burst out a, "*Wooo-hooo!*"

His momentary elation led to a mistake. He paraded the short-lived victory to the lauding cheers and cries of observing Choir members. When his gaze met his caretaker's, on the other hand... Artorian noted she was looking *past* him rather than *at* him. "Oh, dear."

He could tell she mouthed the words '*get him*' just before his stomach and face dropped. The shadow of a tigress loomed over him before he took an all-too-familiar skidding trip across the mudscape with a noisy *fhwa-pwap*!

Sure, there were clerics on standby for patch-up duty, but Keepers hit *hard*. This was trial-by-fire as far as getting the rust off from fighting-skills was concerned. On more than one occasion, a booming crash and stilled body hushed the crowd. Clearly, they thought he was finally struck hard enough that he'd kicked the bucket. Then a thin arm moved, and a persevering thumbs up showed to the sky. The crowd was always instantly cleared of their concern, and they'd release another boisterous cheer. Which, of course, only served to agitate Irene further.

With increasing regularity, Irene's more deadly strikes were deflected or ignored entirely. Then a counterattack hammered into her frame. These cacophony-causing counters made their fans go *wild!* It also had them duck for cover against the inevitable mud-wave that came after it. A few weeks in, a makeshift wooden wall had been erected around the mud pit. Makeshift due to it getting wrecked almost daily. It prevented a good amount of mess but getting *some* mud on you had become part of the experience.

Fan clubs had secretly begun to develop. People who showed up in some cheap variant of blue backed the old man, while people who showed up in full regalia backed the Keeper. When asked what sort of style he was using, Artorian didn't understand their question. "Style?"

A fan-Initiate scribed things down with enthusiasm. "Yeah! Are you using Sabertooth Claw Strikes Angry Bird, Heaven's Palm, or Splitting Mountain? We're debating in our tents where your fighting type might be from. Popular theory is that it has Phoenix Kingdom influences. A few of us were fans of coliseum events before joining the Choir. We've got quite a collection of fighters and their moves. Irene's fan club found out she uses a style based on a ferocious creature from her homeland, Morovia."

The old man considered the query but still wasn't following. He didn't quite know where or what this 'Coliseum' was. He'd been out of the world-news loop for... a long time. "I didn't get this from anywhere, my dear. I'm just building it as I go. All I'm really doing is preventing Irene from getting a solid hit on me, so I suppose you could just call it 'No'?"

That got a laugh from the fans, but when they wrote it down as '*No Style*', it thwarted their desires as that meant something entirely different. To their aggravation, after having a glance at the writ, the long beard had a good laugh and refused to call it anything else. A few of these clever fan-Acolytes had puzzled out he'd been doing something with Essence sight in order to give himself an edge. It was the only way they could explain some of the odd mid-fight mannerisms.

During bouts, Artorian had to wipe his eyes after he managed to fully deflect a hit from Irene. He would call out numbers to Yvessa that made absolutely *zero* sense to anyone else. "Twenty-two IR is *insufficient!* Note that for me, would you?"

During one match where he was sternly decked in the schnozz—in addition to crying out in pain—Artorian rose with a bloody nose from the mud and kicked at it. Mad that 'Air is entirely useless,' whatever *that* may have been about. Another gem was a complete pause in the middle of a fight where he just pushed his hands over his eyes and doubled over. "All that blood is driving me bonkers! It doesn't tell me anything *useful!* *Argh*!"

The Initiates wrote it off as the old man being just a *teensy* bit senile, while the Acolytes chalked it to some kind of distraction or delay tactic. Artorian kept private notes—ones that he'd only jot down when Yvessa wasn't present to spy. In truth, he'd been using evening practice to feel out combinations of Essence sight. Not *everything* worked, and some things that *did* work were utterly useless. Being able to see air currents did nothing useful during hand-to-hand combat, unlike during archery.

Awareness of the cycle of liquid in a system was no good, and infrared and ultraviolet only gave him *horrible* headaches if it wasn't already night. Light-vision was a *trip*, and while it was good for determining if something occupied a space or not, it was *terrible* in a fight when your opponent was a pitch-black lump.

The only truly *useful* sight was the costly one—muscle sight—which allowed him to predict the motions that would be coming at him. The mixture of celestial, fire, and water taxed his eyes, actually *drained* Essence even if he cycled it, and gave him a *killer* headache. All for *minimal* returns.

Stacking roughly five sets of the correct kind of Essence allowed him to deduce a zero-point-one-second prediction based on muscle, Essence movements in the opponent's system, some golden glow outlines he didn't understand, and where the body was going to be forced to go because of it. At *best*, he could stack it fifteen times for a zero-point-three-second prediction, and he'd gotten lucky with it the first time—when Irene made that first lunge on him in the field.

He'd *clearly* seen a golden outline of her entire frame about to collide fist first with his face. Artorian had reflexively pushed Essence up along his arm, wrist, hand, and finger as a temporary boost. When his finger impacted the side of her wrist, he'd been able to push the golden outline away as reality caught up to it. Then he simply stepped out of the way as Irene flew past him. The cost had forced him to turn it off immediately, but the results had been *spectacular*.

Being beaten by Irene was certainly *painful* and left quite the patchwork of bruises. However, having a skilled combatant as your opponent had its upsides—learning was faster and more in-depth. The fact that she didn't pull her punches was a deterrent for the Initiates but a boon to the aged Artorian who needed a crash course in survival. *Not* being hit was ideal, but ideal was usually far from reality. He had greater success denying Irene an attack than he did landing one on his own.

Her masterful control of Essence was a true mosaic of muscle-infusing at specific times and with precision-measured amounts. Enough to beat him... but not break him.

Artorian was forced to be on the defensive, and that needed to change. Finally, it came to him. It was the way arrows launched that had given him the idea, and the lessons from how he managed to counter Irene reinforced the thought. If you could at all deduce what an opponent might do, they had a disadvantage against you. An arrow took that window of opportunity away as it accelerated and struck a target before one had a chance to react. So... why not *become* the arrow?

It was a chilly day when Artorian stepped on the training field again. Several healer Acolytes came prepared with the usual array of minor potions, and he was administered one before ever getting started. Both he and Irene did a full set of warm-up stretches as the empty space around the field filled up with clerics.

"Want anything *special* today, old man? You been wanting new teeth? I bet we could get your hair to be pretty if I ripped that scraggly beard off and we regrew the hair from new follicles!" Irene taunted from the other side of the field as Artorian was doing in-place jumps on solid ground.

He stopped and took a stance in reply. Irene took this as a challenge, just as she always did when he signaled he was ready. Her advance was calculated and confident, a tigress's smile on her face. She was going to *maul* him today.

Artorian focused and began applying his theory. He pulled Essence from his Center and spooled it through his spine, reinforcing it. More went into his legs, gathering around the bone to prevent shattering and funneling into the muscle for raw output. As much as he could stomach was filtered to his ankle for flexibility, while a significant amount was rammed into the front of his foot and toes. When running, the amount of force you could put down determined just how fast your forward push would be. He'd discovered he could *amplify* that force and really shoot forwards if he kept a constant cycle of energy.

That's not what was happening today. Smoothly cycling was being set aside. This was a *burst*. A quick, sudden, and explosive **boom** cracked the air around them. A spherical indent formed in the mud. Essence was pushed along his right arm to form a channel as the movement began, surrounding the bone and reinforcing the wrist... just in case. He opened the Essence channel on his right palm...

The sheer force of the send-off split the muddied ground into a tiny canyon from where he'd stood a moment ago. The steaming mud was forced away, and his vision became completely unreliable as the world devolved into a sharp set of lines from the extreme, *burning* increase in speed. Only Essence sight was providing his brain information quickly enough to operate on.

The attack was a straight-shot launch, Artorian's body brushing against the air and irritating it severely, causing extra-flammable parts of him to burn. His on-fire body-made-projectile reappeared when he planted the pivot foot. He buzzed back into focus in front of a wide-eyed Irene whose surprised expression was matched only by the haste with which she erected Essence defenses.

Sight returned as the sheer kinetic might of all that velocity twisted and spun up from his leg, carried through the spine, funneled through his reinforced arm, and hammered into her chest through his open palm. A noise similar to a thunderclap matched the point of impact. The devastating blow struck her sternum directly. All the velocity and kinetic energy he'd built up... *transferred*.

The technique had been exhausting, incomplete, and *terribly* flawed. Still, Irene had a sudden lesson in flight as she was launched forty-two feet into the air at an upward angle. She *easily* cleared the height of the far wall on the farm end of the cloister. With a sopping **whap**, Irene rolled dozens of feet through wet grass as she landed. Artorian collapsed from the effort, not even realizing he was on fire. Snapping out of their stunned and rooted positions, clerics ran over to throw buckets of water over his burning frame. Fans hopped the fence on all sides, and entire *platoons* of Acolytes sprinted to the side of both combatants.

A half-unconscious Artorian had found a handful of drawbacks and problems with the technique *immediately*. He was bleeding from his nose, eyes, ears, and... more private and chafed areas. Even with reinforcement, it had hurt him *tremendously*. He was administered several healing potions and prompt celestial care. When he was lucid enough to give the usual shaky thumbs-up, the surrounding crowd erupted in a cheer! They didn't grasp the extent of the damage; regardless of how self-destructive that may have been, it had looked *awesome*!

When Irene was recovered from the fields, she too was immediately escorted to the medical block. Hadurin had his work cut out for him. The strike hadn't just broken her sternum, it had *pulverized* it. He could and *would* mend it with time, but he gave Artorian a few harmless whacks on his concussed head while firmly telling him to *never* do that again. Several of the old man's tendons had *significant* tears in them, he had bone fractures, and a *slew* of other minor internal and external injuries that accelerating oneself to *stupid* speeds caused.

Luckily for Irene, her chest could be reconstructed with the combined help of nearly every healer at the cloister and a good number of potions. Still, she felt the damage when she woke, and the leftover bruise was a thing of beauty. It *ached* like the call of the abyss, and she groaned, "*What*," she coughed, and oh, *celestial* did it hurt, "*was that?*"

Artorian was awake and recovering in the cot next to her. He was in equally not-great shape. He was pleased as *punch* to have the opportunity to lay this one on her, tossing her words back at her.

"Something *special.*"

CHAPTER FORTY-TWO

Olgier, the red-haired trader from Rutsel, was having a *fantastic* season! Those *boors* at Lapis didn't know the value of their product had risen sky-high. He'd just bought and sold at the same stock price he always did. He'd made a *killing*! With *rocks*!

To build profits even higher, that salty village Elder at the cloister had just given him some information worth its weight in *gold*. Olgier's money-loving voice oozed mercantilism as his hairy hand pressed to Artorian's shoulder. "*Really?* An anti-venom against the stuff raiders have been using? That is *truly* a celestial blessing."

His gap-toothed smile gleamed at some passing Initiates who picked through the bundled wares on his cart. Using the local vernacular was *always* of benefit. Artorian had a grumpy expression smeared across his face. Small, little grumbles emanated from the old man.

"They very much did, and not a copper of it is going to the village. Not a *copper!*" He huffed again with a finger waggle for effect and leaned into Olgier's side. "It's time to *go,* I tell you. A few days before your next visit, the expedition force is *leaving*."

Olgier felt a rush at the little prizes just falling into his lap. Was it a holiday? The trader felt rushes of skewed pleasure at the physical outburst of the venting old man. "*Leaving?* Surely not. Taking their findings to their Choir, you mean."

"*No. They're. Not!*" Long Beard's gnarled walking stick swung through the air a few times, demonstrating apparent frustration. "They're leaving it here to be finished, and they'll be back only when it's done. Something about 'bureaucracy and paperwork' requiring them to only leave a token force behind, since the majority of the expedition must return."

Artorian leaned back in closer to whisper in Olgier's ear, "Next time you visit, could you drop me off at Rutsel? I can have all my important things packed in no more than a handful of sacks. I'd pay for the trip, of course."

Olgier gave a supportive pat to the old man's shoulder, nearly knocking a very wobbly Artorian off his feet. Silly him! He didn't know his own strength some days. "Of course, *of course.*"

Schemes were already flying about his brain. He could *say* he was taking the old man to Rutsel, *but...* if he took just a *minor* detour... that would put them in 'business partner' territory.

Nobody would miss an old man. Plus, his life's most valuable gatherings were going to be right in his hooded cart? Not to mention that untarnishable Lapis robe which hung over the Elder's other clothing? An absolute *steal.*

Artorian let out a relieved sigh and pulled some packets from his side. "These are the *last* letters. I've written in them that I likely won't be sending monthly mail anymore, as I'll be traveling. Hopefully, it should prevent the Choir and the Academy from getting worried. This first parcel ought to be delivered to Paladin Jiivra at the Choir. I'm sure she's made it by now. The other still goes to the Skyspear Academy and isn't addressed to anyone in particular. I'm certain they've got a library section for my writings now."

Olgier again patted the old man to assure him that wasn't going to be a problem. After all, who looked such a gift in the mouth? Free stuff and all the cover-up work was being done *for* him? So long as those parcels were delivered, this was going to be the easiest grab and go ever! Next month would be *quite* profitable, even with the cut he had to give to his 'associates' for safe passage.

A handshake and some minor trades later, Olgier was on his way out of the cloister. His fat thumb popped open a fancy water skin. The clear water was crisp and cool as he downed it with a satisfied *aah*. Reins in hand, he snapped them taut to make both his horses move on. He didn't bother turning to Rutsel, instead taking the earlier turn that put him on the path to Duskgrove.

The Phantomdusk Forest was vast, dense, and a *true* terror. The exterior tree line pressed together with thick, *toothy* foliage. The border trees weren't the kind you'd normally see in the Fringe, and the extra depth of dark green in their leaves and brown bark made them stand out even in the distance. Colossal, *brutish* creatures reportedly moved around inside, and you could simply never see them. Mad whispers and sketchy reports comprised the majority of stories.

At best, *phantasms* had been confirmed, the supernatural forces leering at you from the depths of canopied darkness. The thought was unsettling, and the sight was brown pants worthy. The only saving grace was that even if you *saw* a glimpse, nothing *left* the Phantomdusk. You had to *enter* to make any of the denizens pay attention to you, and for that reason, it was respected and feared as an inescapable end. You could stand right outside the edge and be perfectly safe, but one toe over that line and the forest itself would turn to dice and devour you with its roots.

Following the cleared path, two big hills rolled up and down before you saw the 'castle'. The forest split near those hills, forming a natural crevice where the woods didn't connect. Cobblestone led to a wide-open grove where Baron von Dusk had—centuries ago—decided to plunk a small castle as a show of status and vanity. Just to show he *could*. Coffers of gold went to buying the surrounding lands *just* so the Mapmakers' Guild was forced to rename the forest to something of his liking, and the lavish design clearly showed in the castle's construction. All that *really* meant was that while it looked nice in *form*, it did a *terrible* job of *function*.

With only a single tower, thin walls, and ostentatious courtyards, the structure was meant to be a place of flirtatious flaunting and capricious courtesans. History had proven otherwise since its position on the edge of the Fringe had turned it into a prime strategic location. The reputation of the forest allowed the castle to be easily defendable. It *encouraged* armies to sneak through the forest, ignoring the rumors in order to assault the position from a considerably less defended wall. None of those soldiers ever made it back out. Their howls and cries were all that remained, moments before the unwelcome trespassers had been silenced.

Olgier recounted that it had been quiet lately, but anything with '*Phantom*' in the name was well known as a place where people easily went missing and terrible events happened with ease. On the second hill, Olgier squinted to see some static figures. The shapes were haphazard and about as far from professional as you could get, but the telltale markers of the 'Toll Guard' were clear enough for the disgruntled trader to make out.

They rose from their lazy positions and unwanted duty, their intimidating body language shown along with rusted blades. The Northern accent was thick in Olgier's voice. He didn't want to play their games today. "Put that away, you *mules*. Fetch your leader women. Olgier is here to pay his toll. Also, I have information to sell Hakan. Pricy, *valuable* information."

Olgier wasn't the least bit against using intimidation tactics against people trying that on *him*. Name dropping important people made even these dumb muscle boys shrivel. They hurriedly spit words between themselves and played some sort of game with their hands. The loser groaned in defeat, not wanting to go but running off to the castle regardless.

Brigan and Ulno clapped hands together. They didn't need to risk getting their face cut by fetching a leader. When Olgier got closer, they recognized each other and Ulno shared some words. "Oh. It *you*. Why no say? *Come!*"

Brigan made a wild come-along motion, and the hill guards strolled along with the hooded cart while Olgier slipped right into a chatty merchant role. The rectangular tower on the castle was right in front of him when he went down the hill. The flat façade hung large flags but only to hide the holes in the construction from siege damage over the years. Currently, the flags were crude and drab with scythes painted in dull browns.

Large portcullises were seen in the connecting left and right walls, but the left was a crumpled wreck that had half a battering ram rotting away in it. The right gate wasn't in much better shape. Technically, the portcullis was closed, but the metal had been sawed out in places to let traffic pass through. Several patches of stonewall had hammered wood panels filling up holes to cover weaknesses. The structure itself still stood fine, but the whole bastion had seen *centuries* of better days.

Olgier drove his cart into the main courtyard, which served to show off the rest of the lavish layout. It led to two smaller courtyards where wildflowers bloomed, the first main structure nested between them. From the third balcony above the ground, a stern woman was leering down at the main courtyard. The empty lot swiftly filled with brutish looking men who counted respect based on the number of facial scars they had. Olgier was dismounting as a young lady with her hair braided in a single line stomped up to him.

"Ah, my lady Lunella! How wonderful it is to–"

Slap! He was cut off as she stepped all over his words. "How *dare* you call for the Mistress of the Domain!"

The back of Lunella's armored hand backhanded Olgier across the opposing cheek while Hakan relished in the sadism from above. "My *lady*! I have import–

Slap!

"You have tolls to pay and tithes to offer, and if... *if* they have value, then the mistress *may* see fit to grace you with her kindness." She squinted her emerald eyes at him. "Are you talking to me while *above* me, *male*?"

Olgier knew better than to fight back or quip and hurriedly bowed deeply before the simple act of paying a toll got ugly. The men around him didn't come to his aid; this wasn't worth a cut to the face.

"Oh, just *bring* him to me." When Hakan removed her presence from the window, the grouping of men created a funnel and path for the lady and trader to traverse.

The man from Rutsel knew better than to get in front of her; that was cause to lose body parts. The heated parlor of the castle foyer was *terribly* lavish. Regal carpet was scrubbed by several raiders, rugs mounted the walls and coated the floor. Rich, magenta cathedral candles remained lit, and hooded torches lined the bare spots on the walls. In some design flaw, there were no windows on the ground floor. Serene footsteps made their way down a staircase as Olgier was ushered to take a seat.

The nicest chair at the table was pulled out by Lunella, and she stood to the side of it, remaining unseated. Hakan, while dressed in her standard attire under the noble's coat, had puffy fur wrapped about the neck. She took the seat and sent a smirk to Lunella, who bowed and pushed the chair in. Her voice was as edge-tempered as ever. "Drinks."

A bustle of activity occurred at Hakan's order. Several raiders swiftly ran out to take buckets of water from those who had the forethought to gather some from the well outside. Actual glasses were filled with clear fluid. Rather than be put on the table, they were offered to the leather-clad Lunella. She carefully tasted each glass, and only when pleased placed them before Hakan and Olgier.

After, she took an empty spot near the wall, being handed a common wooden cup by a familiar-looking young male with the same emerald eyes. Only a single cut ran across the left side of his face, from forehead to the left of the eye, ending down the cheek. Wuxius didn't drink from his cup until after Lunella took a sip, acting as personal aid.

Olgier didn't dare parlay until Hakan had the first word. "*I* don't get requested unless it's *really* juicy information, merchant. My patience is the same distance as my smallest blade. *Speak.*"

With a minor bow, Olgier went right into it, "The cloister where the village Salt used to be? It has developed a cure against the venom you use for your arrows, but... the force currently stationed there will leave a few days before my next visit."

Hakan already had a knife out, rolling it between her fingers. Her dissatisfied voice rang out, "*And?*"

Olgier smiled. "They're *not* taking the cure with them."

The twirl of the knife stopped as Olgier's honeyed words reached interested ears. "Oh? Well, now... *that* won't do. *Everyone* is leaving?"

Olgier made a wiggle-waggle motion with his hand. "A token force is being left behind—from the sound of it, mostly healers if they're going to continue work on the antivenom."

Hakan pressed her fingers together, stirring her water with the knife-edge of the blade. "Your source?"

Olgier shrugged. "The old Elder of the Salt village. He's not up for sticking around. He's taking all his valuables, including one *beauty* of a lapis robe, and requested a ride to Rutsel. A shame he won't make it the whole way."

The sound of a dropped cup reached Hakan's ears. Stupefied, Lunella open-mouth gaped at the trader. She caught herself as Hakan took the effort to look behind her. All the raider leader saw was Lunella one-handedly strangle-dragging Wuxius by the neck, pulling him into the darkened passage while grumbling a, "*You little–*"

Hakan was pleased. One of her favorite apprentices had come a *long* way in treating her lesser with the proper force. She paid no further heed and turned back to the trader. Lunella's grip had been strong, but it was all show. Once around no less than two corners from the foyer, she released her hand and collapsed into Wuxi's arms, who was ready to support her. Luna's hand pressed over her own lips to muffle her unstoppable sobs.

Wuxius just held her tight, hidden from view. He too felt a deep emotional shake, but he needed to be there for Lunella right now. Luna was heaving, her fingers digging into his chest from the news. "He's alive. He's *alive*! Elder is *alive*."

Wux nodded and silently rubbed the back of her head, not caring if he pressed down on her leadership braid. His voice had gained significant depth over the years. "See? I told you it was going to be alright."

"I told you leaving flowers was a good idea." She hiccupped the words and was soothed by the tight embrace and brushing attention. They always had to do this in secret. When people were looking, she could hold her face and act intimidating, but otherwise, she didn't have it together in the *least*. Luna was falling apart behind the scenes and would have done so *publicly* if she didn't have Wux to keep her propped up, to keep her playing along with the lie they needed to survive.

She pulled the iron gloves from her hands and lifted them to touch and feel the warmth of Wux's face. Her fingers were icy, but he said nothing and let her get warm. She brushed her thumb over the scar and immediately felt the guilt.

"It's okay, and yes, you did. It was a great idea," Wux whispered support and brushed the back of her hair, just letting Lunella cope. "You're doing great, Luna. Just a little more and we'll be out of here. We just need to be ready for whatever insane, little scheme that old man is making. We've got a month. That's *plenty* to make some preparations. We can–"

Wux didn't have a chance to keep talking; Lunella kissed him to shut him up. His world whisked away into hazy butterflies. He forgot what he was talking about until Lunella had her fill, sunk into his chest, and her voice reached him, "We're going to destabilize the region, cause utter havoc between the men, and give our Elder as easy of a time as possible. Let's get back in there."

Wux took a firm step back and squeezed his muscles taut and shut his eyes. A loud *slap* resounded through the dark passageway. Wux's sharp breath let her know a nice, big red mark was sure to show. Having the visual that she'd beaten him, they resumed their positions in the foyer where Hakan was playing with knives and Olgier talked shop.

Hakan was speaking, "Profitable is the *right* word. A minor token force isn't enough for a large raiding crew. Robbing them blind is what we do, and survivors from the Choir are... undesirable. I am not fond of a cure to my precious crystal cobra venom. When I've put a plan together, it's raiding time. I need you *not* to be there so we can avoid unnecessary collateral damage."

With a waggle of her knife, she dismissed the trader. Olgier rose, performed a bow, and left the foyer flanked by Lunella and a very red-faced assistant. They handled the collection of the toll, going by Hakan's orders of what appropriate recompense was going to be. Overall, Olgier left Duskgrove with more profit than he'd arrived with. A rare occasion, but then it wasn't often you could hand Hakan a target on a silver plate.

He was going to *splurge* in Rutsel when he arrived!

CHAPTER FORTY-THREE

A month later, Olgier pulled his hooded cart into the near-abandoned cloister. The orderly rows of tents had been broken down, maybe a single cleric manned the tower, and nary a soul was visible within the walls. He reined in his horse and looked around for confirmation. Sure enough, it seemed the expedition force was gone.

Some smoke still rose from several places behind the main church building, but it was minor. A shuffling step got his attention, and what must have been a living pillow shambled his way.

"Err... well met?" Olgier was hesitant, as all he could see were brown sacks and fluff.

"Good morrow, my boy!" came the muffled response from beneath it all. "Could you help me get my things on? I can't *quite* see where I'm going."

Ah, it was the Elder. Pillows. Sure. Fair enough. The Northman hopped off his cart and lifted sack after sack, shoving them into the back of the cart. He was surprised the old man hadn't been crushed beneath the weight, but sure enough, Artorian was beaming with relief as he was freed. "Ah. Fresh air."

Olgier enjoyed a laugh at the Elder's antics. "You look well, old man! Quite healthy!"

Artorian handed over a few more sacks now that he had help. "Oh, indeed. I had several injuries for a while, but nothing some consistent cleric power couldn't take care of. Whoo. Air resistance is a *drag*, let me tell you."

Olgier didn't understand that last bit, so he simply hoisted the next sack as the Elder prattled on. "I'm afraid you've missed the host, m'boy. They all left *days* ago. It's just me and some stragglers now. I'm all set to go, no parcels this time. Did the others make it?"

Olgier held out a hand, helping Artorian clamber on the transport with a grunt. "They certainly did. I had their arrival *ensured.* How has the last month been?"

The old man pulled some pillows from one of the sacks and set them on the front of the cart before sitting down. "Eventful. I signed some paperwork for the Head Cleric here, giving him the land that he thinks he now owns." Artorian gave a conspiratorial wink to the trader, who had another good laugh. "In truth, there's no such thing as *land ownership* in the Fringe! Can't be done. Contracts are invalid since they can't be secured, and conveying him a title didn't actually do anything either since my heart wasn't in it. He can be the Cloister Elder all he wants if it makes him feel better."

Olgier couldn't stop cackling, his hand coming down on his knee with firm slaps. "Did you *trick* them, old man? How can you even tell who is in charge of the region?"

"The obvious way," Artorian regarded him, pushing his thumb under the edge of his robe to hold it out while lying through his teeth. A toothy smile followed from the merchant, and both of them shared a laugh as they settled to get going. "Aside from pulling one over on clerics, it's been much of the same. I require a lot of rest. Time in the sunlight is prized, and to be honest, I had a slew of recurring injuries that needed to heal up. I've got a good handle on it now, along with some clever new tricks of mitigating their causes."

Olgier got the cart going and envied the pillows the old man was sitting on. Why had he never thought of that? It was a great idea. Ah well, he'd have them soon enough. Speaking of...

"I need to make a small detour before I can head to Rutsel. Is that fine?"

Artorian waved it off. "Whatever you have to do."

The old man scoffed and flipped a small knife out from the inside of his inner robe. Content with the sharpness, he began grooming with it. The end edge of his long beard was frazzled and needed tending, and he had hours upon hours to kill. Olgier let the old man have his distraction.

Nearly two days of rough terrain and hills later, evening fell flat once again. The cart operator pulled away from the dirt path, which made the old man look about with curiosity as Olgier spoke quietly, "Keep your head down. *Raiders.*"

Artorian didn't fuss; he simply hurried into the back of the cart, ruffling through one of his sacks. It wasn't too quiet, but Olgier had no worries. He thought the geezer was trying to hide. He calmly watched the sizable war party pass. They saw one another, but both parties knew the plan and thus ignored each other. He gave them a signal, and the look full of malicious joy turned even *his* murder-hardened stomach. The raiders moved on, and Olgier did as well after they'd passed. He'd need to conjure a good excuse as to why he didn't go hide in the cart as well.

"Looks like they... didn't see us?" his voice rumbled into the back of the hooded cart. Not hearing a response, he looked to see what the old man was up to. The last thing he *ever* suspected was a point-blank *twang*!

The sharp end of the arrow erupted from the back of Olgier's head, and his body slumped, tumbling right off the cart. Artorian stepped back into the limelight with a strung recurve bow in hand. Without a word, he drew a second arrow. *Twang*!

The hunched man kept a solid eye on the fallen traitor, now with two arrows in his noggin to confirm the kill. He was admittedly distracted by the end of the raider horde but wasn't overly concerned. That wasn't his problem to tackle; his personal war had just advanced. The full might of the Choir's expedition was waiting for the approaching raiding party in a well-planned ambush.

It was amazing how empty you could make the cloister *look* by temporarily moving people to the salt flats. When the cart departed, Tibbins was playing guard and had signaled a well-placed scout. While Olgier had been distracted with the ramblings of an old man on the ride away from the cloister, the expedition force erupted forth to reinforce the bastion.

Choir scouts had confirmed beforehand that the raiders had prepared to move out and laid full sets of contingency plans. The raiders thought they were just going to walk all over a few cultivators with sheer numbers, and they certainly fielded a sizable crew in order to do so.

HAKAN

Hakan herself wasn't present for the cleanup job but had still allotted a hefty amount of men. You couldn't underestimate even a *weak* cultivator, and the Church wasn't known as a pushover. However, enough arrows in a man still did the job. So, she just needed to send enough men to guarantee success. So *what* if a few fell in glorious sacrifice?

At worst, there was going to be a short siege. Equipment had been sent along just in case there were some problems with that cloister wall, but Hakan firmly believed that might made right... especially when she had all the might. She'd find out how it went in a few days when her raiders returned laden with loot and trinkets. Hakan hadn't the *luxury* to go with her raiders.

She certainly *wanted* to wet her blades on some cleric necks, but her camp had been in disarray over the past few weeks. She had been unable to pin down the *source* of the chaos, but every day, there had been yet *another* small issue that made her normally cohesive troops snappy. They had even dared to almost *fight* with one another. Tensions were high, and she had to be personally present to keep order at home. She even sent her apprentices off to sort through the less important problems.

While that *did* help, it simply didn't stifle the flow of discord that developed. In truth, she had decided to send such a massive force just to get them all out of the house and relieve some tension. At most, a few dozen raiders remained behind, along with her favorites who she didn't feel like sacrificing. Mostly, that meant her girls, and she'd allowed them each to choose an assistant or two.

To her relief, Lunella was as reliable as ever. Hakan didn't approve of her consort choices, but there was a comfort in choosing servants from the village you hailed from. She had to admit that the familiarity had saved Lunella's chosen servant a lot of pain. With a strong inhale of winter air at the balcony, she made her way back to her private quarters. Of course, she had the most excessive and opulent room in the entire castle, fit for a Baron's mistress. It was even better when you'd killed the Baron and claimed the place for yourself.

Her mirth was interrupted a few hours later. Panicked noise distracted her in the middle of what should have been a relaxing night. No, surely, her servants would deal with it. She told herself that no less than *four* times as the sound continued until a bothersome knock finally killed her delusion. "You *must* be joking with me."

Hakan's snap was dry and hungry, "*What?*"

Lunella pushed open the door, her expression drab but serious. "We have a problem."

Hakan rolled her head in frustration before she had a drink. "I *gathered*. What kind?"

Lunella swallowed, her grip on the doorknob tight. "A vengeful phantom is killing our men."

Hakan spat her drink across the room and got to her feet. "Explain."

By the time Hakan rushed to the foyer, a considerable number of her troops who dared venture outside or man the walls had joined in on the death dance. Some cowered and were holding themselves on the floor; more were huddled in the corner cradling their heads or knees. The few who had an arrow whiz past their ear and kept a hold of their life hadn't thought twice, bolting for the safety of the keep.

"Quna. *Quna!* Get here *now.*" Hakan pushed her way into the huddled masses and absolutely seethed that she needed to *wade* through her own raiders. Quna, another woman in the pack that had a few more years on her than the rest, quickly responded to the call.

"Here!"

Hakan turned on her heel and dodged her way through the cowering, useless *men*. Her voice was full of dry displeasure. "*Explain.*"

Quna saluted and pulled the slumped man next to her upright, not at *all* caring about the bleeding ear he was pressing some cloth against. "Tell the Mistress what you saw."

Her order was short, and the stammering raider didn't have any choice but to bow to their wishes. "Arrows! From the *forest.* They barely ever miss, and if you don't run, the second one *always* gets you! Marcovius got lucky; the arrow stuck into his chest armor. The arrow didn't penetrate. He saw... the *thing!*"

Quna let the raider sink back to his knees, then took two firm steps and helped up the second man with considerably greater tenderness. Marcovius was a thin boy with big bones. He didn't at all fit the clothes or loose leather armor he was clad in, but his glazed expression showed that he didn't at all notice his surroundings. A few gentle taps to the cheek brought some focus back to his dilated eyes. "Mar? *Mar.* The *Mistress* is here. You need to tell her what you saw. You *need* to."

Marcovius tightly held on to Quna, his grip trembling now not only from what he had seen but also direct contact with Hakan. He *liked* his face. "Phantom. Red eye thicker and brighter than blood. Vengeance, rage, and fury. It hunted us from the forest. One glance, and it sees your death. It felt the *same—*exactly the *same* as when I was sent to the gallows by that judge. They *told* me death would hunt me. Now it's happening!"

Quna very gently shook the boy who used to be a noble's servant. "You're going to be okay, Mar. Take a seat. Just take a seat."

The boy's pupils went dull, but he followed her order and sat on his butt with all the awareness of a potato. Hakan didn't like what she was hearing; she didn't buy it. "So, there's a *single archer* pulling tricks out in the forest?"

She realized how strange that was when she said it. Still, for an attack to so suddenly hit them? In so short a time after her main force was dispatched? *Suspicious.* "How many *living* men do we still have on patrol?"

Quna didn't want to give the answer and swallowed her discomfort as she had no choice. "*None.*"

A *growl* of irritation left Hakan before a blade appeared between her fingers from seemingly thin air. The sudden sprawl of people jumping over one another to get out of the way of her immediate strike zone was a sight to behold. "What position are the attacks coming from?"

Quna was ready for this one and threw out the response. "High hill past the broken portcullis and wall. I've tried directing men to sneak to the other side for a look, but they haven't reported back. I have to assume they didn't make it."

Hakan outright bit the tip of her gilded blade. *Annoying.* "Gather the men; arm them with bows. We're going to fill every position on the keep and walls, then erupt and fire upon the position with the lights all at the same time."

A few worried glances were exchanged between raiders at their newly given orders. Hakan was already rolling her eyes and snapped them to Quna. "What *now?*"

Again, Quna's reply was on the ball, "The armory is on the second floor. The path to the armory is open to where we're being shot from."

Hakan kicked at a raider who was cowering under a table. "So duck *below* it, fools!"

Quna didn't have many more answers ready, so she marched her way to the stairs. "You all heard The Mistress. Get on with it."

Left without choice, they moved.

CHAPTER FORTY-FOUR

Hours before, when the sun was still dipping downwards in the sky, Artorian rolled a body under a large shrub. Sustenance for the plant, when the traitor eventually decomposed. The bearded, old warrior wiped his hands off and mounted the now unowned cart. With a strong **fwap** of the reins, the horses trudged along as if nothing had happened.

Artorian's replenished quiver rested right behind him, having recovered the still functional arrows before moving on with the journey. It was a pleasant day—a little colder than usual, a couple of actual clouds, and only the barest misty breeze. He knew where he was going, even without looking at a map. When the first hill came into view, he didn't make the animals pull their way over it. Instead, he veered the cart off to the side a few hundred paces and let the horses go.

They didn't run off like he'd expected; the unexpected liberty made them trot to a bushy patch of moist grass. He wondered why but wasn't going to force them. Hoisting several sacks, Artorian marched his way up the first hill on foot. He hummed an old tune under his breath and stuck close to the brambled woods without directly entering. Once atop the first hill, he had a decently good view of the second one. Placing his hand above his eyes to block some sun, he spotted a single raider keeping watch.

"That's *it?*" He was nearly certain there would have been at least three. The force sent out had been sizable, but leaving only *one* lookout was just bad strategy. "Well, can't say it isn't helpful."

The supply sacks gently hit the grassy ground with glassy clinks. Pulling one open to get the weaponry out, he nicked two arrows from a stored quiver and re-strung the recurve bow. He tested the string, getting an instrumental tone in return. "*Right,* then. War, part one."

Cycling Essence to his eyes to see the waving air current, his vision shifted to a moving artwork of ebbs and flows. The wavy lines crashed into still space and nudged it into moving. Just beautiful. The string was pulled taut, and Artorian waited for a nice calm patch as he lined up the shot. It was far too slow for any sort of military fire routine, but upon finding a nice pathway of calm for his arrow... he arced and released the arrow with a *twang*!

Ulno never knew what hit him. The arrow descended through his skull and part way down his neck, and the raider dropped like a potato sack. Obviously, an alarm was never raised. Starting to hum the old tune once more, Artorian undid his string and stowed his weapon, leisurely strolling up to the second hill to hide the body under the bushy edge of the forest.

A free snack for the wildlife. Now came the crux of the matter. He could not descend the second hill, or he'd be spotted even with the fading light. So, here was the gamble. Left, or right? Artorian rubbed his chin and thought about it. Did that really *need* to be a gamble? He cycled the Essence combination for infrared to his eyes and looked to the right, where he'd dumped the raider.

"Oh, busy, *busy.*" The heat signatures of several large animals moved about. If he had to guess, a small pack of jaguar? Odd for them to be so close to the border of the forest. The group moved away and vanished deeper into the thicket, so that was a definite plus. The proximity to the edge likely also meant that entire wing was their territory.

In other words—not the best option. Artorian turned around and had a good look to his left—a significant lack of animals but a whole host of considerably smaller and bothersome ones. He couldn't identify the roving packs of little *things*, but the creature maybe forty to fifty paces from him was definitely a skunk. His nose clenched at the thought.

So, claws to the right, horrible smells and nuisances to the left. No *real* choice there; left it was. Undoing the Essence-sight, he rubbed his eyes as they normalized. It was getting too dark to see anything, so he was going to have to choose an Essence view to find a place that could qualify as camp. He had a lot of set-up to do and very little time to do it. He might not be heading into the section of the forest with large cats, but worse things certainly roamed.

As an example, abyss-blasted *snakes*. He *knew* they were around; that poison the raiders used had to come from *somewhere*. Infrared might not pick up cold animals. Ultraviolet wasn't going to do him any good, and it gave him a *brutal* headache. The realm past ultraviolet was a *big* no-no. Watching skeletons roam was *not* his idea of a good time. Light-sight was going to put anything solid in the dark, but if something was dangerous and not moving... he was just going to suffer by walking into it.

Air wasn't going to help him at all. Wait... why was he overcomplicating this? Artorian cycled refined Essence to his eyes and saw his surroundings jump into clarity. "Yes, that will do nicely."

It wasn't as good as daylight, but by the heavens did it get the job done! With a heavy step, he pushed his way through the thorny brush and nestled himself in the Phantomdusk Forest. Another unit of cycled Essence was immediately added as the light level dropped from the dense foliage. An inconvenience but still notable that the difference was so clear. During the middle of the day, it would still look like late evening here.

Perhaps that was where the name 'Phantom*dusk*' came from originally?

The ground *clicked* rather than *crunched* below his wooden sandals. That wasn't something he'd been expecting, so he glanced down. All he saw were tree roots in the majority of the space grass didn't cover. The tree density was only awful right at the edge and eased off into broad passages. *Another* odd thing was that certain branches had a bit of an... internal glow to them? How peculiar.

He deemed it best to avoid stepping on those shining roots, as it was a very thin string of *Essence* that wriggled along the root. It reminded him of a trap string that would spring if disturbed. So was the forest a cultivator, or did it have cultivators *in* it? Either way, that explained a few things. Seventy more paces and he was climbing the hill that curved around where he knew the castle was.

Torches lining the stone wall were few, but they painted blazing targets on a smattering of raiders. Once on top of the hill, he had a majestic view of the forest. Forest that spanned a *far* greater distance than he had imagined it did. "Oh. Well, right then."

He put the weight down and *really* took in the view. Stars were visible through an opening in the canopy. While it was a little chilly, it certainly wasn't *uncomfortable*. Under the foliage, there was only the barest hint of wind. He had the passing suspicion that these trees weren't fond of air currents but didn't know why.

The old man swapped out enhanced sight for infrared and had a check up on the situation. Nothing with a significant heat signature in the close vicinity, save for the castle denizens. He noticed the foliage didn't in the *slightest* block his Essence sight. How odd... *beneficial* but odd.

He decided then and there that *this* was where he was going to set up temporary camp. After an hour of unpacking, he'd nested some pillows near a tree and neatly arrayed supplies in the order he thought he might need them. Quivers had been planted on a firing line that he was going to stand behind so he could snatch and shoot when necessary. The twin moons hung clear and visible in the sky.

"A good evenin' for a hunt," Artorian assured himself, uncorking a glass vial of honey and letting it run over some hardened bread. A few crunchy bites later, the old man licked his fingers clean. Honey was sticky, but *heavens* did he have a weakness for sweet things. He tossed the vial at his camp. He'd clean it up later.

A few brisk steps brought him to the planned firing position. A flat cliff followed by a slant in the hill offered a nice big hole in the foliage ahead. The old man did his basic stretches before getting started. He picked up his bow and kicked off the fear tactics by cycling an overabundance of infrared Essence to his eyes. He skewed the identity of the energy, intending it to invoke the more visual side effect components.

Blazing crimson eyes blossomed on his face. While he couldn't see the effect without a mirror, he was certain that any observers peering his way certainly would!

Fhwizz. The first arrow flew.

A raider on the wall found himself gurgling. He dropped to his knees as a brand new neck ornament protruded all the way through his throat and a major artery. Blood gushed freely, and gravity did its work as the man fell.

Fhwizz. *Fhwizz*. *Fhwizz*. Several more deadly, sharp whistles struck.

Bodies dropped, and the panic began.

Artorian fostered patience. When only the occasional head peeked around the wall to catch a glimpse of where he was, the heat signature gave it away long before they'd fully craned their face around. A taut pull of the bowstring and a clockwork *fwhok* later, there was one less raider.

"*Twenty*-two," he counted, adding to his tally for every heat signature that dropped away. It had been a surprisingly leisurely hunt. He doubted it would stay that way; so, with a full forty-arrow quiver expended, Artorian called it a night.

His eyes hurt, and this had been a very successful round of terror spreading. Packing up his other quivers, he brought them back to the makeshift camp and found something peculiar. A small, fluffy, little creature was using the tiniest tongue he had ever seen to lick at the inside of his discarded honey vial. "How *endearing*. Fond of sugar, little one?"

The small, fluffy thing darted for cover but didn't go particularly far. It crawled up a tree and settled on a branch above. Artorian released a tiny chuckle and rested on his pillows at the base of the same tree. Pulling a sizable gray blanket from one of the sacks, he threw it over himself and called it a night. He was tired and made the gamble that no raiders were going to be sent into the forest to come check on the threat.

Wild animals? Different story, but he had no true recourse here. His refined sight saw the tiny creature glide down and *plop* back to the vial, which it took in tiny paws, trying to lick more honey from the inside. It was *precious*! Artorian had never kept any pets, but the drive to care for things called to him strongly. Since the small critter wasn't deterred, he sunk his hand through his supplies sack and pulled out a *full* vial of honey.

Leaning forward, he scared the tiny thing off again just by approaching. That was fine; once again, it hadn't gone far. The opened vial was placed next to the empty one, and he pulled back to sink against the tree. Lacing his hands, he watched the hungry, little glider waddle and bounce back to where it had been to cautiously indulge. "Haven't seen something quite like you before, little one."

Pulling the blanket up, he pressed into as comfortable of a position as he could on the padded roots, sleepily listening to the clinking of the two glass vials. Commotion at the castle grabbed his attention. With effort, he cycled infrared sight and saw an ant's nest unfurl from several openings he'd previously been unaware of.

How *helpful*. He wasn't cycling very intensely, so there was no visible component that gave away where he currently was. His attention returned to the little critter trying to cram its entire head into the vial.

"You like sugar, and you're a glider. I'll call you a *sugar glider*. Careful, sugar glider, things may get a little messy here."

CHAPTER FORTY-FIVE

Cozy, camouflaged, and under cover, Artorian studied his adversaries. There was an ant's nest of activity in the hall of the second floor and a good number of people curving around from the opposite side of the courtyard and outer wall. Not bad, but that *did* give away all the avenues of approach he'd expect them to use in the future. The blurry, red figures didn't particularly seem to know where to go, and the great majority had their arms outstretched in front of them.

Bows? *Bows*. He was hopeful they lacked arrows, but he'd given them at least forty to work with. Retrieving ammo from downed comrades would at least cause some additional morale damage. He'd give them the night and all of tomorrow to fret. The prepared hunter planned to cultivate nearly the entire upcoming day.

Once the night hit once more, the hunt would continue. Nestling the gray blanket fully over his body and face, he calmed his nerves by drinking some water; then he sank into much-needed sleep. Laying a one-man siege took the energy *right* out of you!

Unlike Artorian, the people in Duskgrove Castle weren't getting a *wink* of rest. Between the stress, fear, and lack of something to target when they finally collected the courage to burst forth and strike... they had all but deflated. Not only did they not find a target, they couldn't afford to go looking. Shooting something at the forest from range was one thing. Stepping foot inside?

All they would find was misery. Even after some vicious lashings and threats, there wasn't a raider in the keep ready to risk that kind of certain death. Beatings were favorable in comparison to exiting the confines of the *mostly* safe walls. Roughly a *third* of Hakan's people lay dead outside her keep. Numerous bodies had been retrieved and shoved on to a burn pile when there had been a lull in the assault. At minimum, they were going to wait for the sun to be up to light the fire, as no raider wanted to chance being an easily spotted, *well-lit* target.

While the night may have been quiet, it was *truly* taxing. Just leaving the keep was done in sizable groups, and patrols either went fully armed or not at all. All remaining shields found their way into wanting hands, which was admittedly few after the war party had been kitted with near all of those precious protections. When day finally broke, the raiders were tired, sullen, and bleary-eyed. They were kept awake by an unhealthy mixture of alcohol and the fear of what might be waiting for them the next time they set foot outside.

A door wasn't opened without having shield cover. If you *didn't* have one, you fetched someone who *did*. Defending this castle was not something the raiders had done before, and that reality drove Hakan up the *wall*. Her apprentices did what they could, but she wasn't about to order any of her *girls* to go out and patrol.

The silence of the day was equally welcoming and dreadful, and many hushed whispers started more than one rumor that *nightfall* was to be dreaded. A fight even broke out on whether to have more torches lining the walls or none at all. The apprentices could not stifle the demoralizing air and conflict that rolled through the keep.

To Hakan's relieved delight, at least *one* of her underlings was useful. Lunella had brought her a plan that would solve both problems in one solid swoop. By having all the raiders be armed and positioned outside the keep at all times, they could quickly react as a group to the mystery threat. Since the crimson light marked such a clear target, the raiders would know what to aim for.

A few arrows *might* miss, but at least one or two in a full barrage wouldn't. This would be plenty to end the threat and raise morale. There was an excess of room in the courtyard, the tower, and on the walls for the raiders to set up. After the rough idea of the plan was spread around, Hakan's command spurred it to action.

When Artorian woke up in the late morning, he had quite the surprise waiting for him—or rather, *on* him. There was movement on his blanket as the claws pierced through the thick sheet. From the feel of it, numerous minute critters were skittering about on top of him.

Plink. *Plink*.

The noisy clinking of glass made the old man stir. The shifting sent waves of scattered fluffballs scurrying from his bundled, resting frame. Rubbing his face with the inside of the blanket, he woke with a *nnffff* and a crick in his back. Artorian peeked over the blanket at a parade of mouse-sized sugar gliders swarming through his rations sack. "You little *rascals*!"

They scattered. His waking words were accusatory and pointed but soft and spoken with surprised affection. Nudging the heavy blanket further down, the critters all darted away further and clambered up nearby trees. So, they're climbers, too? *Precious...* but... "You stay out of my food!"

With a labored stretch, he tugged in the ration-sack and inspected the damage. That's odd...? Most of the food was still packaged and untouched, though they'd tried tearing their way into his cloth-wrapped fruits from the look of it. He had not seen much fruit on his trek so far. Squinting, he had a good look at some of the sugar gliders while he unpacked a small bundle of raspberries.

There was something wriggling in their tiny paws that they ate. Worms? Yes, it certainly seemed as such. Both of the vials he had left out the night before were completely empty and scattered several feet away from where he'd originally placed them. Looks like honey was popular.

Fhwump. Popping the cork on a third vial, he set it out a good distance away from him, sprinkling some raspberries on the root next to it. He had plenty, and he didn't mind *sharing*. Getting *looted* was a different matter.

Cautiously, the gliders went to inspect as Artorian pulled out his own breakfast. Watching them, he tore away at somewhat crumbly, dry bread stacked with layers and layers of salted mixed meats. The resting Elder pulled the stopper from a canteen and downed half of all the water from it in a single draw. The relief of refreshment rushed over his body. "*Ahh.* That's the stuff."

He finished his sandwich, watching as a whole horde of gliders tousled and pushed to get their faces at the honey tube. Once they'd nibbled at a raspberry, the snooty rascals straight up absconded with them. The fruit made a mushy mess of their adorable faces as they dove into the berries like candy.

Oh, how he *missed* candy. The nostalgia was shaken off before it had a chance to root. Some bark fragments fell on him, followed by the soft *thud* of a glider. The impact caused a noisy *crunch*. The little thing twitched, whining as it relied on its right side to pull itself to safety. It was *hurt*?

Oof! Artorian tensed and blinked with surprise from the creature's sudden drop. He remembered what pity felt like and didn't like it one bit. "Oh no, now *that* won't do at all."

He reached over, grabbing one of the weak healing potions from a clipped-open satchel. The little glider lay unmoving, the little animal drawing labored, heavy breaths. Its tiny body shuddered from fright; Artorian was a big, *scary* thing, and it hurt all over.

The old man was focused, going into full healer mode. Applying more than a few drops of potion to the berry he'd been holding, he set the fruit down. Then he nudged it under the glider's chin. He didn't do anything more until that tiny tongue lapped at the sweet berry. The pulsating, little stomach slowed its panicked heaving. Breaths came just a little bit easier. With the tiny, precious fluff a *little* more complacent, the side of his thumb tenderly brushed across its twitching head and ear. He didn't know how to soothe this animal, but tenderness hadn't failed him yet. He considered more in-depth methods of restoring the fluff ball.

For a moment, part of him deemed it a waste to patch the soft animal, but that singular voice swiftly had the snot beaten out of it by all the other parts who ganged up as an overzealous, motherly mob. Shifting Essence sights, he had a look at the creature to get a rough idea of breathing pattern, circulation, muscle movement, bone positions, and what was out of place. Major bones in both the front and hind legs of the left side had shattered. From pre-present splinters, it appeared these bones had been fractured before. This little one must have been in pain and for much longer than merely today.

Brushing the flat of his hand across the soft fluff's back with tender care, he filtered celestial Essence into the glider. His hand ever-so-*barely* brightened, and the fluffling hazily went limp as it drifted asleep... unaware of what would have otherwise been painful internal changes.

Artorian heard small *pops* as Essence was guided to break, set, then mend the bones while keeping the muscles pushed away. After the bones were whole, he relatched the musculature on before moving to lesser injuries. The careful ministrations and delicate Essence control made him sweat, and the pull slipped from his control as refined Essence was added to the mixture.

Whoops. He was going to lose some Essence... The thought was discarded; he came to terms with it. He wasn't going to let the little thing suffer, and he wasn't going to put it out of its misery. This sugar glider was minuscule in size compared to its counterparts. Little baby would likely have had a long, healthy life, despite being a runt. Still, the bones of this little one were brittle. *Too* brittle... A thought occurred, a *dangerous* one. One he truly, *truly* should not try.

"Maybe... maybe just a *little?*" Artorian mumbled to himself.

Hesitantly pulling some celestial corruption from his trapping circle, he bundled it in a minor weave to continue the containment. Sweat beaded on his face from concentration. It took patience and *precision* to maneuver the trapped corruption through the channel of his hand and into the no-longer-wriggling glider.

It was just pleasantly dreaming, mouth and arms moving as if munching and stuffing its face as little shivers of warmth rolled over and through its limited senses. Once the bubble of corruption had moved to what Artorian considered the Center of the creature, he took a solid breath and wiped his face. Keeping the main orb centered, he pulled smaller globes of corruption all along the baby's bones. The bones sucked the corruption down, and Artorian didn't have the focus to retrieve the weave, so he let go and let the glider have it.

Artorian was playing with an untested theory here and tried hard not to let his desire to heal the fluff dip over into academic curiosity. He failed. The natural immutable aspect to resist change was what he wanted here. Having that kind of energy reinforcing bones was a minor but positive permanent change. He needed to be certain 'corruption' was merely a poorly used term. Celestial also didn't hurt like restoring with another Essence type did. 'Corruption' could not have its meaning skewed or identity bent, so he decided to work with only one type for the entire creature. *Hours* went by before he was done, needing to wipe off his forehead several more times in the process.

In only a few seconds, a full canteen and a half had been drained, and now, Artorian felt rather spent. Somewhere midway through the care, he'd bared his top half, allowing passive cultivation to hit him as the sun was crawling higher into the sky. "There we... *go*."

When the snoozing pipsqueak woke, it was up and running immediately. He hoped there'd be no unfortunate side effects, and the health of the glider had visibly improved. This did *wonders* for his mood, as he was going to be doing *terrible* things soon. Hungry, he leaned over and unwrapped an apple, cutting off the slimmest of slivers to give them to the energetic sugar glider.

"Do you like *apple*? I *hope* you like apple. I've many of them." With the speed the sliver vanished into the crunching, little snout, he'd take that as a positive. Seeing as how their companion had not been harmed, other sugar gliders had taken to crawling all over him and his blanket. They were coming to touch noses with their previously injured family member. Artorian moved his hands out of the way as the glider family nuzzled up to the runt and nudged, licked, and held the fallen fluffling. It was heartwarming. "I *love* these fluffs!"

He spent the next half hour snacking and carving slivers off his apples, feeding it to an ever-growing pile of gliders who grew ever less shy. He soon had them crawling up his beard, shoulders, and blanket. A few even nested underneath where it was warm, and others still were making his dropped robe wiggle as they walked through it. "Hmm. Big family."

Artorian had a good-natured chuckle, happily discovering he could pet a few of them. This was nice, but the old warrior sighed as he took a stern Essence-cycled glance at the keep. Shielding his eyes from the sun, he took in the impressive numbers.

"Are they *all* just out and about? *Why* would they..."

His heart nearly leaped from his chest as his blood pressure spiked. *There*... against the wall near an open door... her back pressed to it—even clad in different attire and carrying a few years of age that had really done well for her—stood a recognizable *Lunella*. In fact, she was *incredibly* recognizable. You could see that position from absolutely anywhere.

"*Ooh*. Clever, Lunella, *clever!*" He punched the air with his free hand and rejoiced in the wit she was exhibiting without a single soul catching on. Several gliders discovered what being launched was like during his sky-punching exuberance. "You wanted me to know you were alive and fine! Oh, *thank* you!"

His breath hitched, eyes wet from emotion. Good *heavens* did he feel proud. He didn't even realize he was nodding in approval until *Wux* joined her! His skin felt *electric* from sheer joy. "Excellent! *Oh*. Is that a *scar?* Oh my, it is."

Still, it gave him some character, and hopefully, he could keep it at just one. Well... based on their proximity to one another, the boy's knee was a valid target for an arrow. He hoped they hadn't had any issues, but then again... it was likely that a romance was just budding. They *did* look somewhat awkward. Still, *he* certainly wasn't going to tease them for finding comfort in such a terrible situation.

"Good show, my boy. Good show." Now. Was it just the *two* of them? They'd been the oldest, and it was possible their younger Salt friends were kept elsewhere. "One obsession at a time, old man. Count your opponents."

Something was... *off.* For some odd reason, a large chunk—if not the entirety—of the enemy force had exposed itself. He counted... fifty-seven. That *many*? That was an incredible number to remain behind. Just *how* large had that war party been?

The clerics would certainly have their work cut out for them; perhaps that bought him a day. The raiders he could see certainly appeared haggard... Had they slept? Didn't look like it. That was *excellent* since Artorian wasn't going to strike during the day; sunlight was too valuable to waste.

The sugar gliders around him appeared content. He ate a second sandwich and downed more water. The crumbs were plentiful, so the gliders made a game out of hunting the scraps down to eat. Artorian settled himself cozily back down and slipped into active cultivation. His Center exploded with light as energy crashed into it, the slow, passive spins tightening to crisp, controlled rotations. One ring helped move another, and soon, the entire Center mimicked a bright star.

With his intake settled, he got straight to refining. The purity of the light visibly *lanced* away minuscule amounts of gathered corruption. The corruption disintegrated at a fast enough rate to chip away at the stored excess as well. His Essence poured, and the ground around him gave a *thrum* as the overabundant energy radiated off his Aura. While minute, shadows in the vicinity retreated, and the local area warmed. He didn't notice that the sugar gliders bundled up against his sides... He was also unaware of the free-floating Essence that built in density around him.

He provided comfort, and the gliders cozily lounged, basking in the Essence-rich dome. A while later, a few of them began to steal apple after apple from his pack, having figured out how to undo cloth folding.

The ground didn't have any further reaction, and there was nearly no additional fluctuation in his surroundings as his pull went *tall* rather than wide. He didn't bother pulling from the earth, avoiding it like a bad toothache. It only gave him corruption. Instead, his focus shifted to drawing purely from the heavens. Artorian's surroundings thrived without his notice as his pull of Essence that couldn't be absorbed spilled over.

The sugar gliders didn't mind the extra comfort, and after such a big and easy meal, they all settled to nap on and around the long-bearded, friendly thing. He remained in that position until evening, when the sun dipped the last of its light back over the horizon. When Artorian came to—finally pulled from inward focus—he found that his beard had gained weight. Specifically, the weight of a particularly large and healthy-looking glider that had made itself cozy. The old man didn't recognize this one.

It had stark white fur that matched his snowy beard instead of the subtle, varying dark grays of its companions. It was missing the thin black strip that ran down the spine of the others as well. The long, floofy tail was the same, just thicker and puffier. They were *all* sweeties as far as he was concerned, so as the bleached puff was healthy, he let the larger-than-average critter nest without concern.

Artorian slowly unearthed himself from the entrenched fluff-bunker. The number of furballs that leaped off of him was larger than he'd expected, but that was fine. He began his required stretches, and the gliders saw fit to use him as a living playset while he moved about. He left his shirt, under robe, and

Lapis robe at his campsite to let the fuzzy, little sweethearts crawl around in it. It took some doing to string his bow with the little distractions, but that didn't deter him from setting up his firing line.

"Let's see now..." he muttered to himself as he cycled refined Essence, the darkness lifting to a far more visible view.

"Good number of obstacles. That's a *lot* of raiders still outside. I wonder if they got a sunburn?" he mused as he counted again. Fifty-five. Stable enough when compared to his prior count this morning. He was going to give himself a world of hurt if he bolstered infrared again. Then again, with the additional torches and *smorgasbord* of targets, what he was currently using was enough. Setting his feet into the stable L-shaped position, he drew an arrow, aimed for a man at the top of the tower, and released.

Fwiii!

CHAPTER FORTY-SIX

Tumulo had been in a heated debate with his friend, who had resorted to quietly grunting as the southerner just kept on talking and *talking*. So, it didn't come as a big surprise when his non-responsive conversation partner slumped into the corner with a sharp... snore?

Falling asleep in the middle of the conversation? That was a new *level* of rude. Moving the torch closer to nudge and wake the other up, the lookout's eyes went wide in dread as he saw the arrow. Tumulo took a breath to scream the alarm, but a second *whizz* silenced the otherwise endlessly chatty raider.

After the seventh raider was counted under Artorian's breath, questions started to be raised about the strange noises. Movement picked up in the keep, and when a replacement raider came to swap out the guards on top of the tower, he found that both were punctured. Someone had been sniping them, starting at the highest position and working their way down. Peering across the edge, the raider could see where people in lower positions were slumped. Panic jumped into his throat, his sudden attention letting him hear an incoming *fwiii*.

He reflexively ducked for cover, unwilling to take the risk that it might be something other than death. The arrow meant to slit his throat plinked off stone and his breath found words, "*Alarm*! Under attack!"

Additional torches were lit and raised to help pinpoint the position they were being murdered from. Unfortunately for them, without the obvious giveaway of the crimson light, they shot blindly into the forest, hoping they would hit something.

Artorian calmly pulled yet another arrow from the quiver on the ground, set his aim, and let loose. Raiders fell like chalk targets in a shooting gallery. They shambled with tired, lumbering, hesitant steps in straight lines. Not a single zigzag among them. They were too tired, stressed, and frazzled to consider tactics more complicated than 'toss arrows into the woods'.

Crash! The sound of a door being kicked down caught everyone's attention as Hakan punted it open. Her voice was shrill and full of threat. "Get into the forest! Get *into* the forest and kill that piece of lard making sport out of your brothers!"

There was going to be more to her speech, but a screaming arrow pierced the air, going straight for her throat. Artorian cursed under his breath as he was witness to unbelievable reaction time. Hakan snatched the arrow out of midair! Her head was tilted to the left, avoiding the sharp end that was currently where her eye would have been. He wasn't going to be able to snipe this beast, hmm? Well, nothing was stopping him from trying a few more times. Only *one* had to succeed, after all.

Given that she matched Switch's description, this must be Hakan. The raider leader was absolutely *covered* in blades. If there was room on her where another could fit, the old man didn't see it. Picking a new arrow, he sent it through the jugular of a dawdling raider who didn't know whether to obey or just aimlessly keep firing.

Unfortunately for the weathered sniper, that had been the last straw. The raiders with heavy axes finally disregarded the threat of the wood. They charged into the thicket wall and began chopping their way through. To the *abyss* with whatever horrors the forest held! There was an archer picking them off, and now Hakan was going to make mincemeat out of them if they retreated.

In her own words, "Cutting will continue until morale improves." The raiders shuddered at the thought and began making their way through the wall of thorns. Artorian's firing line was abandoned as he saw the charge. Hastily, he snatched the last full quiver on the line and hoisted it as he hustled back to the makeshift camp. A few dozen raiders were too much!

"I'm sorry, little ones, I need the protection."

Sugar gliders went flying from his robes as a disorganized swarm as he snatched up his clothing and shook them wildly to get the infestation of fluffs out. Throwing his shirt on, he wrapped the inner gi over his shoulders and slid his arms in, hurriedly binding the front with the appropriate cloth belt before throwing the Lapis robe over himself. Sure, it was visible, but more layers meant more protection that needed to be stabbed through. He downed a full waterskin in one go, tossing it back into the sack he was abandoning.

In a rush, he scanned over his supplies. "What do I need? What do I *need*? Ah!"

The sack with the potion-filled bandolier made its way around the inner gray gi. The sturdy cloth prevented the bandolier from cutting into his skin, so he tightened it a good amount to prevent the potions from jostling. He was about to need them. Latching the quiver on to his back, he bolted for the part of the wood where he'd first entered between the hills. After only a few steps, however, he skidded to an ungraceful halt. "Oh, *ho~o~old* on. Mustn't forget."

Refined Essence entered his eyes, and the energy lines serving as trip wires among the root system became visible. An extra second was taken to carefully step over those as he got back to hustling in the direction of the pass. He steadied his breathing as if on the morning jog, ducked low to avoid breaking branches, and stepped past the hole where the skunk lived.

Shoulder-checking the opening, he released a hiss as some thorns got him. Artorian tumbled on to grass once again as momentum carried him through. He'd outright forgotten grass was so abyss-blasted *slippery*. One day in the woods and he forgot about how things outside of it worked? That's odd. He wasn't *usually* so forgetful. Well, no time like the present to relearn.

Point of order, he had raiders on his tail. While they didn't have his current position, his miniature camp wasn't exactly hidden; they'd find that in no time. The right side of the woods was still claw-and-fang territory, so he wasn't about to rush in there. For a moment, he wondered if raiders had entered that section, then heard the yelped screams coming from the appropriate direction. Looked like *yes*. They must be trying to flank him in the woods. "Haw!"

He needed to be where the raiders were not. That meant—he sighed, coming to terms with the truth—*inside* the keep.

He didn't have the luxury of time to find an alternative, so he picked up his hustle. Climbing the second hill was still done cautiously, and he flattened himself atop it when he arrived at the crescent. His eyes darted across the landscape; barely a raider remained behind. He didn't have eyes on his children, so they must have been inside. Then again... he also didn't have eyes on Hakan. A bad feeling told him that monster was *also* inside.

* *Thwip**!

Pain seared his shoulder, and he gripped it tightly with an, "*Argh*!"

Artorian's face scrunched, and through wet eyes, he saw the protruding arrow. Swiftly, he ripped it free and checked the tip. No clear coating. No venom on this one. He rolled away from the direction of the attack and slipped a weak potion free, drinking it down before ditching the vial. A second arrow missed him, then a third went wide. Pushing from a roll into a stabilizing knee, he rose up, drew an arrow, and found the target immediately. It was hard *not* to as the impatient, distracted raider was charging straight up the hill at him.

Fhwizz.

"Hurk!" The pained gurgle preceded a twitchy slump on to the wet grass. Still moving, the raider tried to get back up but was met with a second arrow launched point-blank into the back of his skull before he could scream the alarm. The raider's world went dark as footsteps hurried past him, headed to the right portcullis of the keep.

Artorian felt his heart race. He was thrilled as only an old soldier could be, completely engulfed in the pressure like he was back on the campaign trail. At the gate, two raiders who had just left the keep spotted him, drew blades, and rushed the unknown intruder with wild, screaming abandon. Luckily, their screams blended into the cacophony of screams around the area, and the raider in front was swiftly silenced via an arrow to the noggin.

The remaining rusher had more luck, sinking his blade into the strap of the bandolier on the bearded Elder's side. The blade pierced! Showing his teeth in a dark grin, he believed the shallow cut was a kill, and the raider celebrated early, pushing to drive the knife deeper. At least, he *would* have had his spine not snapped from an inhuman impact. The lanky brute's body warped in on itself as a point-stop palm strike struck him low and from the side. The impact hadn't been powerful, but it had crushed the non-cultivator's insides into twisted pulp, and several vertebrae cracked loudly as spinal discs shattered.

That was all Artorian needed to truly grasp the difference between a cultivator and a non-cultivator. He could *indeed* handle ten men like this at a time.

Shwip!

A point-blank arrow to the skull put the raider out of his misery. Artorian wasn't having any of that 'rise up to come at me again later' nonsense. Rushing to the wooden door, he slid to a stop and lifted his bow as the door began opening again. Nocking an arrow, he drew the string taut.

"Elder?" Wuxius's face was surprised, disbelieving that the old man was truly, *actually* here in person. Wux sprung himself forwards and squeezed the Elder, who eased his bow down and wrapped his own arms around his child. Artorian felt utterly destroyed, his resilience shattered; his murderous focus was gone in an *instant*. He was getting to hold his grandson again! Artorian's chest clenched and his eyes threatened to water. The fact that he had no blood relation to this lad meant nothing. He had *chosen* to be family.

"My *dear* boy." Artorian let free an *hrk* as Wux squeezed him too hard, and the old man had to firmly tap him on the back to make the youngster let go. "*Cough*. I've come to... *cough*... get you all. Just as I *promised* I would. I'm *so* sorry it took this long."

Wuxius released his Elder and snapped to the business at hand, a trait he'd been forced to learn and master over these many seasons. "Lunella is still inside. The others were taken elsewhere years ago. We don't know where... just that it's some other raider camp."

Artorian gave a sharp nod and pulled the boy along into the building, speaking quickly, "I'll find them, just as I found you. Where is Lunella? Let's get you both out of here. Salt village will be safe enough by the time you get there; it's a cleric's cloister now. When you arrive, ask for Tarrean."

Wux nodded but saw something move in the hall and pulled the Elder back. Artorian tripped into position behind a wall like a falling child. Hurried footsteps shot past. Wux stood firm and raised his hand in greeting, but the sound of two raiders grunting at him was his only reply. Wux was relieved that his distraction was enough to make them look away from the Elder he was hiding but discovered immediately afterward that his Elder was *not* reacting as he thought he would.

Instead, Artorian dropped one of the raiders who had been walking away with an arrow.

Wux froze in place. When the other raider turned to see what had happened, he *too* slumped, landing face-to-stone with a new arrow hat. Wux just turned around and gave the old man a look, but his Elder wasn't willing to tarry. "Where is *Lunella*? I want to be in and out."

Wux didn't have a good reply; he could only glance down the dark hall those raiders had just come from. "With... *her.*"

The difficult expression marring Wux's face told Artorian everything he needed to know. "Go in there and distract her. I need that woman to *not* be looking at the door."

A confident nod from Wuxius was all the reply he got, but between two men seasoned by hardships, that was all the reply needed. Wuxius didn't need light to see in the dark passageways, being used to them. He didn't give thought to how the old man was not only keeping up with him but surprising each raider in their way with a close-range *fwiii* to the face.

The youngster from the Salt village quickly learned that his Elder liked to aim for the head or the throat and nowhere else. It made him shudder, but he ignored it easily enough since he was already having trouble reconciling his kindly, gentle-hearted, old Elder with this sniping shadow assassin. He could have *sworn* there was a light hiding behind the Elder's eyes but didn't have the time to bring it up as they reached a heavy wooden door.

"It's this one," Wux spoke under his breath as if he was about to enter a mausoleum. His bow-wielding Elder pressed to the wall so he wouldn't be spotted when the door opened. Wuxius knocked. An infuriated gnashing came from the other side.

"*Enter*," Hakan called out in a shrill tone, consulting three of her apprentices at once, Lunella among them. Wux's secret love raised a brow at the entirely-out-of-character behavior; he *never* came without being called. The assistant hastily stepped in, leaving half the door open.

"Apologies, I had an urgent message."

Hakan didn't have time for his words and rolled her hand for him to get a move on. Her free hand covered her eyes as her head sank low. It was always distraction after *distraction* with these wretches! A drawn knife swung through the air.

Shlink!

Wux's knife divided a feminine throat, forcing a gargled protest that gathered *all* of the raider leader's attention. She dropped her hand, eyes wide in surprise as the low-class *male* offed one of her prized apprentices. Hakan was *so* stricken... she couldn't *believe* what she was seeing! She would have *butchered* him, but a slimy itching on her spine screamed danger.

Fwhizz!

Hakan's hand snapped up, and the tip of the arrow managed to cut her cheek as she caught it. Her lips curled into a cruel smile as she discovered the ploy. "I was *hoping* I would have the chance to hunt the hunter."

Lunella and Wux didn't hesitate, moving as Lunella drew her dagger. Ubana, the final apprentice in the row, prepared to pull her weapon as well. A traitorous *male* and a mysterious hunter needed *cutting*! Together with her fellow apprentice and master she could... *Shling*!

She could... A gurgle of blood left Ubana as it spilled from a sizable gash in the side of her throat. Her fanged dagger fell to the ground as she clutched her neck in utter panic, collapsing from the fatal wound Lunella had dealt her. Hakan's attention was momentarily divided. Her heart *thumped* with rage and disbelief at the betrayal she witnessed firsthand.

Fwhizz!

Hakan didn't catch this one, simply knocking it away. Still, she winced, raising her hand to see the leather on her glove cut open. *Really*? What was the ridiculous draw strength of that bow? She had to jump back, acrobatically circus-twisting so she was covered by a vanity dresser. One hunter was bad enough, but one hunter and two armed *traitors*?

She snarled and spat at the ground. "Lunella, you little *cretin*! You *dare* betray me like this with your pet in range?"

Wux turned red from anger. He *despised* when anyone insulted Lunella and doubly so when it came from Hakan. He spat back, full of heart-pumping adrenaline, "To the *abyss* with you, wretch!"

Fwhizz!

Artorian stepped into the well-lit room. Lunella pressed her hands to her mouth and was brought to tears as her Lapis-clad Elder strode forth and loosed arrow after arrow at the cabinet Hakan was using for cover. A sharp *hiss* let them all know that the shafts had penetrated.

The snarl of a wild animal sounded as Hakan countered. The three Salt compatriots didn't expect her speed as the raid leader bounded to the far wall and used it as a springboard to launch herself at the primary threat. Surprised but expecting some suicidal attack that would bring a blade to his neck, Artorian let himself drop to the ground, forcing the leaping Hakan to fly right over him.

Her blade cut only air, but for a moment the eyes of opposing ideologies met. Hakan didn't know who this old man was, but she knew without a *doubt* that she hated every. Single. *Fiber* of his being. She was going to lash and claw, rip and tear, cut and *bleed* him until the husk that remained was unrecognizable.

Dropping the bow, Artorian was quickly on his feet. Rather than engage in a one versus three melee, Hakan decided to bolt when seeing the armed traitor's approach. She chose to not engage at such a disadvantage and took off at a full sprint down the hall Wux and Artorian had come through. The old man *could* give chase, but he didn't.

He had his priorities in order.

CHAPTER FORTY-SEVEN

Artorian's arms opened to receive his children as soon as they had a reprieve. This was all the invitation Lunella needed to smash her face into her favorite grandfather's chest. Bawling like the abandoned babe she was, the lack of threat made her need for support and family *skyrocket*. It was impossible for her to decipher her emotions; she could only describe it as being found again.

"My *dear* granddaughter..." Artorian held Lunella tight, not hesitating to pull Wux in with them. The silly lad had just been aimlessly holding his own arm, lost in the chaos of the moment after his plan had somehow *worked*. He was clever, but coming up with plans on the spot was *Lunella's* gift, not his. His gift was seeing plans through.

Artorian held his children close, his breath breaking into staggers from the warm tears at regaining not one but *two* of his hearts. The hug was long and drawn out. His mind told him that tactically, that was an *idiot* thing to do. Physically, he didn't care. His children needed this, and he did too. It had been *years*, and taking a few seconds to rekindle their hope into blazing bonfires was worth any additional hardship he was about to face while extracting them. When Lunella let go, so did Wux. Artorian quickly pried open the buckle of his bandolier.

"I have gifts for you. Here, take these potions. You'll need them more than me." He forced the weight on to Wux, but the boy didn't mind. Lunella took three potions from the already opened pouch and stuffed them defiantly back into Artorian's pocket.

"Take those," she ordered him with stern directness. "No sacrificing yourself."

Artorian beamed a misty-eyed smile and settled a supportive hand on her shoulder. "I shall not. I have the rest of our family to save when I find them. Also, it's about time you had this."

Without any fanfare, he took the Lapis robe off his shoulders and draped it around Lunella. She didn't know what to say, and when she tried to speak, the words refused to leave her throat.

Her Elder addressed her directly, now with both hands on her shoulders, "Years ago, I told Wuxius that he was responsible for taking care of you all. He did his best and took care of you. I'm proud of you for that, my boy." He gave his grandson a pride-filled nod; both of them were trying to keep their lower jaws steady. Artorian's bright blue eyes settled back on Lunella, whose expression was full of concern... and a sparkle of hope.

"Lunella, my dear. You are the next Elder of the Salt village, and I name you as such, even if there's currently a Church cloister on the land. I can tell when I see the deft hand of leadership at play. Rely on people. Wuxius will be there for you. Grandfather has a promise to fulfill."

He took a deep breath, and his heart was in this next part. His voice was filled with power, and authority reverberated through the air of the Fringe as he gave the words *meaning*. "I hereby grant you my dominion in the Fringe, *Elder* Lunella."

***

Far in the distance of the Fringe—in a small cavern under a village that used to gather salt—something underground rumbled to life. Vibrations transmitted through an interspatial web *thrummed* as the energetic brush of an oath being transferred caused enough of a disturbance to make waking worthwhile.

Mana pulsed and built as chaotic light gathered power, a mandible-clicking orb gaining awareness, filling the small space to the brim in a reality-warping, space-shattering instant of spreading influence. Two places across divided distances connected, aligning to allow for an exertion as the cascading waves of power *transferred* from the orb's current position to where it needed to be.

Crystalline energy stretched and flexed like a waking muscle, reaching out to fill a previously flattened space, just as a bird would stretch every individual tethered feather as the entity re-established itself. An unseen, spherical bubble surged forth, rapidly expanding its area of influence. As there were no Mages in the area, this event went unnoticed.

Teleportation Mana sucked down ambient energy with enough pull to drain away even the clouds, clearing a dome of unmarred blue in the sky in a perfect cylinder above the Core's location. The landscape took a deep breath as the Core of the Scar occupied this space once more. The water on the flats shuddered as if something heavy had fallen in the distance, and like creeping dread, the edges of the Scar's tendrils stretched once more.

***

Lunella kept her hand on her mouth as she was bestowed the title and nodded through thick tears. She *needed* to hug him again. "Thank you."

Artorian held her and gave her comforting pats on the back. "Let's get you both home now. Follow the main road out, and veer left after the second hill. I left a merchant's cart and two horses behind. With luck, the horses will still be there. Do you remember who to ask for once you reach the cloister?"

Wuxius nodded and filled in, "Tarrean."

The old man nodded sharply. "That's right. Head Cleric *Tarrean*. Don't rush in the approach. They're likely currently fending off that raider party you sent. Don't worry, they'll be fine. They're all cultivators. Keep that robe on *tight*, Lunella. They recognize it well. Heh."

He brushed it over her shoulders to fix the fit. "Yell out these names Yvessa, Tibbins, Tarrean, or Hadurin if you start being fired upon. Avoid dying at *all* costs."

He leered at them both and quizzed the duo, "What's the single most *important* thing?"

They hugged him, and Wux replied, "Stay alive. Just stay alive."

Artorian nodded and embraced them again, so *proud*. He released his sproutlings and picked up the bow, reslinging the quiver that had fallen when he'd taken the Lapis robe off. "You know the way. Ahead of me, you two. This time *without* disappearing into smoke?"

The duo nodded in sober recollection and took off down the corridor with their armed Elder in tow. His footsteps were so quiet that Lunella had to look behind her to make sure he was actually following. To her relief, he was right there, expression as stern as a battlefield ghost.

"Next door to the left gets us out," Wux whispered, taking a sharp turn to shoulder check the door and fling it open.

"Go, go, *go!*" When the apprentice and assistant whisked out of the door, a gilded dagger piercing Artorian's side informed him that he wasn't going to be able to follow.

"*Argh!*" he cried out, wincing as the blade pulled him back into the foyer. "Go, just *go!*"

He yelled the imperative at his grandchildren who hesitantly looked behind them. Wuxius was about to turn around and rush back in, but Lunella jerked his arm. Everything up to this point had been to get them out, and turning back might corner them behind a fence of reinforcements. Wuxius looked back and forth between the woman he loved and the Elder who vanished into the darkness. His hands balled up, his leg trembled, and he *wanted* to rush to the old man's aid. A second, harsher tug from Lunella made him see the worried expression marring her face. The decision was heart-wrenching. He grit his teeth, and Lunella won out. The duo ran off together while their Elder bought them the time, holding off the terror incarnate that was Hakan.

Artorian had swung his bow wildly in an arc as he'd been pulled back into the dark building by the knife and had no choice but to turn with it to avoid being outright *gutted*. The slender, powerful, and agile woman curved with all the finesse of a snake as she twisted her body in an 'S' shape to dislodge her dagger, dodge the wildly swung bow, and cut the string all in one seamless set of movements.

The **clak** of severed string snapping against his fingers made the old warrior wince. Without a thought, he tossed the stick at her to buy a precious second, but the vile predator was upon him. His free hand slid into his pocket and thumb-forced the cork off a potion. He downed it with a hard swallow only to throw the emptied vial in the raider's direction when his arm came back down. Hakan laughed at him—an amused cackle as she slid out of the way. The unimportant bit of glass shattered behind her as she moved with all the delicate swerve of sentient water.

The assassin knew she had the upper hand, and half a glance at this ancient relic told her that *he* knew it too. The venom on her knife had all but confirmed her victory with the sneaky strike she'd snuck in at the door. The gilded blade could afford to toy with her food before she hunted some traitors down. She *relished* in the opportunity of making a gory example out of them.

Artorian wasn't in great shape; he fell back along the wall to keep distance while the predator eyed him up. She'd had plenty of chances to leap at him again, and those extra seconds were prized moments for him. His Essence was in a full swing of activity as his real focus was on pouring venom-hunting celestial Essence through his right hand which held the wound.

Venom expulsion was priority number one, or this was going to be a *short* bout. He'd gotten a good amount of practice handling the venom; so, while the deep cut was certainly *painful*, it had already ceased to be fatal. The minor potion was doing the patchwork and closing the wound while he was cleaning up. Keeping his hand over the wound prevented Hakan from spotting that it slowly healed, and if it left a scar... well, that would mean he had survived.

The clear fluid stuck to the inside of his gi, which he'd hoped was just a *bit* more cut-resistant than this. Thoughts for another time. He took stock of the situation and quickly deduced that she had him outmatched in all aspects of this fray... save one.

He was a cultivator, and she was not.

Unfortunately, Hakan was a creature whose profession, passion, and self-assigned purpose were to slaughter and kill. Her skill with the blades was practiced and well-honed. Her body was young, trained, and in *amazing* condition. She had the muscle, the confidence, and the equipment all going for her. While she didn't wear armor, all those metal blades covering her were an excellent deterrent. A direct strike without a weapon was going to cut his own hand up, possibly doing more harm than any he'd inflict on her.

No, the survival plan was going to be biting a cost he'd hoped to avoid—a colossal waste of Essence. It was time to do or die. He sharply exhaled through his nose at her, eyes remaining locked as they slowly circled in the lavish room. Artorian knew she was just playing with him; he was a toy already wounded and about to fall. She just wanted to see his suffering.

Her face was full of malicious delight. The ear-to-ear smile indicated she would savor and relish the impending kill. Still, she could strike at any moment, and he needed to buy time. With some refined drama, he frowned and coughed *extra* loud and pretended to stagger, as if the venom was doing its work. His voice was hampered, and he hid the intake of a breath under it as he got to work spending a *ludicrous* amount of Essence.

"Two," Artorian muttered wetly. Hakan's eyebrow perked up as her game suddenly included killing him in a fashion that matched his own words. Two stabs? Two lungs ripped out of him? Oh, choices, *choices!*

"You only kept two of the children from my Salt village. What, were the other three too good for you?" His expression was reddening, his appearance that of a frustrated, angry, dying, old man.

What Hakan could *not* see was a swiftly diminishing Aura as his Center chugged refined Essence faster than a Dwarf in a drinking contest. Artorian was taking entire cultivation circles apart in a hurry to have enough **oomph** in his body. Refined Essence flooded his system, and with all the charismatic leadership of a seasoned commander, he directed it to his heart meridian to surge into his bloodstream. There was no way he'd have the concentration to cycle his Essence to his whole body at once, and he needed a comprehensive boost to *everything* just to keep up with her. So, that's *exactly* what he was going to do—let his body do the work for him.

It most certainly wasn't without risk, as he would be slowly filling up the maximum capacity any muscle of his body could take. This was an awful, crude, *idiotic,* on-the-spot technique that had zero finesse. He was throwing refined Essence straight at the problem because his expertise was required elsewhere. If he couldn't keep up with her, this was going to be a one-sided slaughter. To his dismay, he needed time for the torrent of Essence to actually cycle through his system.

Hakan didn't understand why, but she could *feel* the presence of the man in front of her shrink as the pressure of his Aura lessened. It was a pressure she hadn't even noticed before it started failing. So, he was dying? Swiftly as well, it seemed... too bad. She was having quite the frustrating day, and playing with her meal was exactly what she needed to relieve stress.

"The runts? As if I would keep the toys that didn't have potential. I'm running a *Queendom*, not a *daycare*, you worthless old fool. I need servants to make sure my future troops grow up to properly serve me."

The twirl of her knives glimmered in her vengeful smile. "However, if you're so *fond* of them... I'll find them again and slowly cut them to pieces in memory of your lovely contribution today. Rooting out traitors so close to my person and relieving me of incompetent apprentices was *very* helpful. I'll ensure their suffering is *deep*... and well-explained."

She would have devolved into a set of bitter laughter had the old man not looked like he was getting more vibrant by the second. Without another word, she charged right at the unarmed problem. Her instincts screamed that something was *wrong*. Her slash wasn't wild. It was a pointed, directed, and lethal swipe that was going to sunder his jugular and carve out a significant portion of his throat.

Her footsteps were light, and the carpet beneath her boots shifted from the force of her launch. Her blade was so cold and swift that the tip of the knife made a telltale, metallic, cutting *zing*.

He was dead. She was *certain* he was dead... He *should* have been dead.

CHAPTER FORTY-EIGHT

Thrum. Artorian watched the raider charge. A golden ring surrounded the outer edge of his bright, cyan-shining irises. The circular movement of his empowered arm was reminiscent of the smooth roundness of a rising moon. His cloth-covered arm suddenly occupied the location her strike *should* have landed.

Hakan's killing blow was *beautifully* deflected. She was struck with *more* than enough power to make the blade miss his neck entirely, his palm guiding the gilded blade off its destined path. Defying an expected pattern, the rest of his body filled the empty space with the grace of ritual tea pouring into a cup.

She'd expected a dodge, a sidestep, or him to move *away* in reaction to a lethal blow. Instead, the entire right side of Hakan's face became aware of agonizing, broken, pained stretching. It was the herald of a shattered cheek and jaw. That *infuriating* fool had twisted on the back of his foot, spun with his shoulder inwards, and bashed his *elbow* into the side of her *pristine* face! Somehow, the old man had hit with enough force to make her vision blur, mind go starry, and break several bones.

Scrack! The sound caught up to the feel.

With rage suffusing her blood, Hakan felt her now-deformed jaw quiver as the muscles no longer connected correctly. The bone that kept everything neatly in place was either no longer there or shattered beyond recognition. A crushing headache—a sickening concussion—struck her senses, and Hakan had to back off, an unplanned shuffle to assess the damage and dodge a follow-up punch by a hair. That strike whirled through the air with such strength that it made a whirring *vwup* on passing.

"*Imhossihle!*" she shrieked her unwillingness to accept that she'd been hit. All she had available to her were broken, agonizing sounds. The pain kept splitting through her entire face. *How?* One moment, she'd been lined up for another of her patented, *flawless* kills... and the next, her strike had been *deflected*. Her opponent had spun the same arm into the side of her skull with an elbow strike, then stepped in, spinning the other way with the intent to crush the other side of her skull.

Ridiculous! No *elbow* strike could do this kind of harm to her. Hakan began to seethe, and the dominoes fell as she swam through the effects of her concussion. This relic was a *cultivator!* She threw her gilded, venom coated dagger at him with uncanny accuracy, forcing a sidestep from the old man. Her woozy senses informed her that he'd seen the attack coming. That had been the point of the throw; it bought the raider time to down her own potion. This potion was of *far* higher quality than the one the old man had sipped.

As compensation for his earlier slight, she dropped her arm and launched the bottle at him. *Clash*.

Hearing the glass shatter, she watched as he deftly moved out of the way with agility and flexibility an old man should not *possess!* The pain in her face ended abruptly, and the visual of her face knitting back together under the skin was stomach turning. "Muchh etter. Back to torturing the truth out of you."

Hakan's words bubbled, and she drooled as she spoke. Still, she went from needing interpretation to abject clarity as she finished her words. The old man winced and closed an eye to rub it. A weakness!

Another blade found its way into her hand so swiftly that Artorian couldn't puzzle where it came from; he also didn't have the *time* to. Being temporarily evenly matched brought a different factor into the combat equation. Hakan's blade didn't *miss*, but it didn't reach its intended target either. Blood splurged once more from her mouth.

Crack.

The old man's back-kick very *much* found its target. The bottom of his sandal exploded *into* her ribs upon impact. His stabilizing foot that had been steady on the wooden floor twisted, and the floor itself erupted into splinters with an unhappy screech.

The difference between standing and *not* standing on the lavish carpet had made all the difference for his support, and the rotational power whirled up his frame with a well-positioned pivot. The sandal was cut deeply by Hakan's knife-armor protections, but his tabi stopped the blade-clad leather from reaching his skin, preventing those deadly knives from actually slicing into his foot. A victory for socks!

Hakan's ribs followed the cruel fate that the side of her face had tasted a few moments ago. The shockwave immediately returned her nausea to her as her breath belched out. Her heart was forced to miss a very *harrowing* beat. Not only had her ribs shattered along the entire surface area his rectangular tabi struck, but it was particularly damaging where the *heel* had impacted. Her cry of pain came out as a blubbered gurgle, and for the second time in one day, she was forced to back off and cut the air between them with an expendable knife.

Artorian had no choice but to dodge, needing to pull back from the stance without being sliced. That motion had to be followed up with a sequential dodge when a second potion bottle crashed on the wall behind him. An arduous set of blood spittle coughs later, Hakan was once again in top shape. Her words were back to her usual shrill of hatred. "You're going to die *slowly*, you cur."

She was *done* playing. She drew larger blades from her hips as the internal damage patched itself up. Hakan was no stranger to potions nor the addictive qualities of the stronger ones. Who would have guessed that her secret, little pleasure was currently saving her hide? Boro's special 'bigger on the inside pouch' was a marvel for storing the stronger variants she savored.

Artorian took an Irene-copied martial stance and a very firm breath. The golden light surrounding his irises faded, and Hakan *knew* he didn't have access to his special trick anymore, even if she didn't know how it worked. He wouldn't be the *first* low-class cultivator she'd carved like swine!

The pair circled until Artorian was in what Hakan considered a poor position—having a fat support beam against his back. He'd be *forced* to dodge left or right since going backward wasn't an option. To her disgust, she saw him partially disrobe as he unfurled his cloth belt and wrapped it around his right hand and wrist. He was going to block her knife with his main arm? That meant he was going for a counter after she swung to kill.

"No more games, old man. I'm not having fun anymore." The cut would be a feint, and she'd return that kick right to his gut. She could spin kick too and better than this lucky, long-bearded wreck. The carpet mushed up behind the toe of her boot as she launched herself, her smile failing to hide the malicious intent of her little plan.

Artorian wasn't doing well. The strain on his eyes had pushed him past the limit he could force, and his Aura was quickly faltering as he fueled his entire being with refined Essence. His body was utterly *devouring* the nutritious power. Nearly every muscle and tendon were *slurping* the meal to perform at the level he needed it to, and his aged body simply wasn't fit for continuous usage like this.

His bones reinforced themselves to take the additional strain his muscles were putting out, and his senses sharpened to keep up. The additional mental clarity was letting him keep on top of things, but just those few strikes had dropped his entire remaining Essence reserve by a full *third*. He didn't have the option to stall, to drag this out. This awful creature had been hiding some *powerful* potions, and he'd launched his new attack *twice*.

The cost of all the little techniques needed to perform his attack was *awful*, especially when he *correctly* used it. 'Correctly' using it meant that using the attack that didn't harm *him*. For the *proper* strike, he needed a high enough Essence investment in his eyes to see at the speed he moved while bursting; his normal vision couldn't keep up.

Celestial Essence was needed to patch him up since he was accumulating stress fracture damage. A coating of water Essence needed to be lathered ever-so-barely over his skin to deny the heat damage that built up from the acceleration. He didn't understand why he got so hot that his skin *burned* when he moved at such intense speed, but he didn't have the time to ponder right now.

Imperfect tools were all he had, and his best one was now expended with hardly anything to show from it. His eyes could handle the use of more Essence, but the predictive sight took a *special* kind of toll manifested in the form of a nose-bleeding *migraine*.

His eyes might be able to take more, but his head *couldn't*. The dim lighting in the foyer helped, but that was a moot point when faced with this still-very-much living murderbird. His eyes narrowed as a bright idea formed, and he carefully positioned himself so his back was close to one of the support pillars of the room. He couldn't go blow for blow or afford to get caught in a flurry of punches; as much as he *wanted* to pummel this monster, her armor would shred him.

Artorian's expression hardened as Hakan stepped in and attacked. The carpet didn't have the required stability of his technique, but a sturdy, *thick* support beam sure did. His cut sandal fell from his foot as he planted it firm against the beam, setting his Essence in a controlled motion.

With a booming *ka-snap*, the beam exploded into splinters where his toes had been, covering the back wall in a shrapnel cloud that eviscerated two raiders who had been hustling over as backup. The old man temporarily *vanished*... or so it would seem to eyes that weren't used to keeping up with *obscenely* fast-moving objects.

This was nothing like keeping up with an arrow. Hakan couldn't alter her trajectory as the tens-of-times faster Artorian moved. It was a pure, direct shot that moved on a flawlessly straight path. The explosion of the beam had not been the desire of the technique, merely the side effect of the sheer amount of power he'd propelled himself with.

Not a *part* of him.

All of him.

All of Artorian's weight accelerated to the absolute maximum that it could handle without ripping apart, which it had happened *plenty* during sparring. Hakan's second step had not even completed when the furious, *focused* eyes flickered back into existence in front of her. She could *feel* the *hum* of power pass from his lower half, up his spine and back, across the arm, and into his flattened, belt-covered palm... which struck her square in the chest, immediately beneath the sternum.

Boom was all Hakan heard before her hearing faded to absolute silence.

Artorian always had endless questions. One of them was being answered right now—what happens when you strike a non-cultivator with a full rail-palm?

The answer was... *memorable*. Hakan spilled—or rather *burst*—blood from anywhere that could expel it along with any air she had within her.

Scrackle!

Inner organs were crushed, and several loud breaks highlighted her brutalized spine. With a twist of Artorian's wrist, she corkscrewed into the air and slammed against the far wall in the foyer. The *juicy* impact was followed by an aftershock as the blow *thundered* through the room. Her travel time couldn't be counted in seconds... that would have taken too long.

Whap. After completely destroying the art piece on the wall, Hakan collapsed to the ground in a bloody mess beneath it. Artorian staggered backward and heaved in a necessary breath. *Abyss*... he was *out*. He ceased pushing additional refined Essence into his heart meridian—half because his body could not hold more without backlash, and half because he was teetering.

His Aura wasn't just *diminished*; it was *empty*—completely, unpleasantly, *painfully* empty. He'd not realized just how vulnerable not having an Aura made him feel. Still, the battle was over. That was the *end* of it. With shaky knees, he sunk to the ground, beading sweat and heaving heavily as his sparse remaining Essence patched his body up.

His heart sank as he jerked his head out of the way. A *third* large bottle flew past where his face had been.

This was *ridiculous*! How many of those potions did she *have*? How *strong* were they? Hakan was giggling as she got up, her movements as jerky as a marionette. Her eyes were so bloodshot that no white remained, and actual tears of crimson lined their way down her cheeks. She couldn't stop giggling, outright could *not* stop as the side effects of potion addiction kicked in.

Euphoria. Forced, unbridled, *unforgiving* euphoria.

Artorian forced himself upright as the power in him ebbed. The reviving Hakan sputtered out a phrase that she must have thought was one of hilarity. "Ah... a*ha*... a*hahah*a! I've... got a lesson. For you to take to... *heart*. Victim!"

New blades were pulled from her thighs as Artorian watched as all the damage he'd done to her regenerated in record time. Everything except for her eyes. Blood sloshed out of the corners, and whatever the potion was doing... those kept bleeding.

Artorian staggered back, pressing his hand against the broken column for support. The maniacal giggle-laughter only got louder, and Hakan sliced her blades over each other. *Zwing*.

Common sense and reason were leaving her for... some kind of murderous joy. Hakan *moaned* as she saw her staggering, end-of-his-rope prey take another cautious step back. *Nobody* challenged Hakan. Nobody *threatened* Hakan. She was the Incarnate Blade! The laughing executioner. The new *Queen*.

She would carve her way through any and all obstacles to assure that position, and sacrificing this pawn was just the next step. Giggles still gurgling through her blood-drenched stupor, she copied the foolish man and blindly bounded straight ahead. A perfectly straight attack? No, you over-aged mole, *this* is a straight attack!

"Hurkkkll!" Hakan frowned as mystery pain bloomed from her chest. Her movements slowed... stopped. Thick gouts of red liquid left her in a hurry as she looked down, stuck at an unwanted standstill she had not intended.

The thick, *sharp*, splintered beam angled from the ceiling... pushed through her now-impaled chest. Artorian had put one hand over the other and forced the beam to crack forwards. Wood fragments pierced the huntress right through her heart.

Her vacant, uncomprehending gaze met his, and only then did she see the fierce and remorseless soul hiding inside of the man. In her mind's eye, she saw two little souls running far, far away... and he was standing guard over them. Her stupor broke when he spoke with a dark rumble, "I shall, *indeed*, take your lesson to heart. You've shown you're not very fond of learning, so I took the more *direct* route to yours."

Hatred welled in Hakan's expression. The old man dared to *sass* her in this moment? He sounded *playful!* She needed another potion. Another... empty. Her digits found the hidden satchel pouch that rested above her rear but found no further chances within it. "Agha..."

Panic drooled from her mouth, and she would have spat at him if possible. Her rival had twisted on his heel around the now-bent beam to get behind her. She was going to have *revenge* for this! She was going to *recover* and hunt him until–!

With her chest pierced, body shattered, and a direct blow to the base of her head that made movement impossible, Hakan died with her eyes wide open, mouth still spewing profanities until she couldn't speak.

It was unclear if the blood loss, injury, or inability to breathe was what finally did her in. Artorian didn't have the luxury to stay and find out. He unceremoniously dropped the woman who had caused him years of grief. Ripping the potion satchel from her waist, he checked for additional major potions but found none. What he did find was that his entire arm could vanish into this strange satchel. That was a good enough reason to keep it. The sound of a door slamming open a floor above him spurred an immediate retreat toward the open door.

It was time to go.

EPILOGUE

He'd gotten so close. *So* close.

At the last minute, his heart had made him slip up and choose his passion over his logic. Weakly, he trembled to reach out and picked up the crushed, motionless, fluffy, white sugar glider. It was still breathing, but this time, he had no hope of helping it.

"Oh... my sweet little child. I'm *so* sorry." Artorian blinked as the events of the last few minutes played through his mind.

Only a few minutes had passed since then. He recalled that an arrow had sliced along his thigh the moment he passed through the open door. They were *waiting* for him. Such an unexpected attack made him slip and fall in the wet grass. His second clog flung into the air as he tumbled. Taking a potion from his pocket, he downed it. The raider sprinting at him didn't *quite* have their leader's reflexes; the tossed glass vial bashed right into his eye.

"Ack!" The distracted and dazed raider dropped his bow to hold his face, his prey already up and moving, running off in a zigzag pattern up the hill.

"Found him! *Over here*! He's going up the hill!" The raider, to Artorian's unlucky stars, was *loud.* Multiple arrows whizzed past him once he gained the attention of other raiders, but he didn't let up on the run at top speed. Once over the crescent of the hill, arrows continued flying, but he had already veered off at his enter-the-forest spot. Running to the first hill was just going to give the raiders a clear target when they got atop the second one. An arrow passing his temple made that point *exceedingly* clear as he flung himself through the thorny passage.

He fell into the dim darkness of the forest, and his hands chafed over hard roots. *Abyss*, he'd forgotten it was so *dark* in here! Another refinement ring was absorbed just to *have* the Essence to cycle into his tired eyes. Artorian heard the burly men break through the same thorny spot behind him but kept going even as the migraine made itself known.

His lungs burned, his legs pumped, and his arms swung. By his *beard*, he was going to make it out of this alive! That promise to himself was called into question as an arrow pierced his calf, dropping him face-first on to the root-covered ground. The *baff* of his head hitting sounded worse than it actually hurt.

Pulling the arrow out, he cried out a pained *nngaaah* and dropped it, stifling the sound by drinking his last potion. Pushing up to hobble forwards, he rolled over the Essence trip wire rather than messily fall on to it, avoiding the trigger. Artorian got up just in time to wobble around a tree that took the next few arrows for him. He could not tell just how many raiders were hot on his tail, but as always, the running continued. He pushed from the tree and ran deeper into the woods along the path he *sort* of knew.

Dumb idea? *Absolutely!* Better alternative? *Non-existent!*

He needed the trees for cover. This was being hunted, and he could hear arrow after arrow *whizzing* past. Screams behind him were cut short as a volley of roots rose and sliced raiders into chunks. Looked like they had triggered the Essence trap. From the awful coughs, someone had *also* angered the skunk.

A little more and he should see... the camp!

"*Oh, abyss*," Artorian muttered mid-breath. A raider was *waiting* in it. The strongman was holding an axe the size of *him!* Artorian was going to jump out of the way, but then saw something that he was *unwilling* to live with. There, near the roots, crushed beneath the axe-man's feet... were several stomped sugar gliders.

Artorian's stride didn't stop; his anger overrode his senses. With a *giyah*, he charged the axe-man while unfurling the cloth belt on his arm. The raider thought this was *wonderful* and swung his axe to bisect the easy target. *Thnick*. "Hrm?"

The raider felt his axe get stuck in the tree branch above. He'd swung too high, then followed it up with the fatal mistake of letting one of his arms drop to deal with the charging non-threat. It was more than enough for the old warrior to wrap the taut, sweat-soaked belt about the murderer's neck—which was promptly squeezed shut. Artorian crossed the cloth along the big man's spine and hung from his back while pulling on both ends to *tighten* the makeshift noose.

The strongman's face quickly turned purple, and the massive brute swung around to no avail, crushing the old man between his back and a tree, throwing himself back since he had little else to fight with.

Thud. To the raider's displeasure, it *didn't* force the old warrior to release his hold, but it wasn't going to matter. Another crushing slam, and there wouldn't *be* an old man! Who cared that he was getting a gentle neck massage? The blueberry raider fully let go of his axe and reached up to clamp on to Artorian's wrists.

"I gots a surprise for you, fellah!" the man choked out. *Crunch*. The tree shook as the brute threw his whole back into it, but this was insufficient to stop the chokehold that was now *actually* starting to affect him.

Ffhwizz. *Chonk*. An arrow hit flesh, and it signaled the limit of what a very tired Elder was able to bear. His arms were twisted and spent, his back hurt terribly, and at least a few of his ribs were cracked. When the brute hit the root floor, he couldn't hold his grip. He let go. "Oo~o~oh... *abyss*."

He'd gotten so close. *So* close.

At the last minute, his heart had made him slip up and choose his passion over his logic. Weakly, he trembled to reach out and picked up the crushed, motionless, fluffy, white sugar glider. It was still breathing, but this time, he had no hope of helping it.

"Oh... my sweet little child. I'm *so* sorry." The last few minutes had finished replaying through his mind.

The glider wasn't happy about being held, but there was no escape to be had. It came to a rest against the Elder's chest. More arrows whizzed by... but not from the direction he had come running. They launched with a *frightening* *zip* past the tree he was slumped against. He didn't have the strength to do anything except rub his thumb over the little fluff's head to soothe and comfort it. At further cost of his own progress, he broke down cultivation rings and poured the Essence into the still creature. "Rest, sweetling. *Rest.*"

He couldn't bear to let it go. Artorian also couldn't feel his legs very well. The shakes had returned—the same shakes he'd felt when he'd had no Essence and bundles of corruption in his Center. Worried, he took a moment through the volleys of arrow fire to look inwards. Sure enough, several of his ring-weaves had cracks, and their contents were leaking. He unfurled another refinement-ring and got right to patching those problems up.

That much, at least, he *could* do. Artorian hated to unfurl a near-empty tank, but he needed the reclaimed Essence to *live*. His meridians required a certain amount of juice to be present in his system, and the cultivation technique wasn't allowed to *rupture*. In a hurry, he patched it.

He came back to himself as he heard the draw of several bowstrings in front of him. Tired, injured, and out of hope, Artorian looked up. "Ah. Looks like I'll be joining you, my little, white fluff."

Blazing, forest-green flames took the position eyes should have held. All the beings present had *beautifully* ornate bows aimed at him. Each of the weapons seemed *grown*, as if directly from a branch. Not a single cut or unnatural notch was visible. The figures themselves were strangely obscured, forms blending with the forest as if they were part of the landscape. Aside from the blazing flame—which reminded him of the trick that he'd done with his Essence sight—frightening masks and exposed weapons were all that could be seen.

Ah. Here were the *real* phantoms of the forest. Artorian closed his eyes, prepared for the end. So, he didn't believe his ears. The phantoms spoke in harmony, in unison. The language was forced but contained a flawless pitch. Their in-unison accent was airy as the wind, which seemed to blow specifically to carry their every word.

"The Eldest Mahogany *demands* your presence, Starlight Spirit."

AFTERWORD

We hope you enjoyed Axiom! Since reviews are the lifeblood of
indie publishing, we'd love it if you could leave a positive review
on Amazon! Please use this link to go to the Artorian's Archives:
Axiom Amazon product page to leave your review:
geni.us/Axiom.

As always, thank you for your support! You are the reason we're
able to bring these stories to life.

ABOUT DENNIS VANDERKERKEN

Hello! I'm Dennis, but feel free to call me Floof!
(Culprit of nickname: The ever-unmanageable fluff on my head.)

I'm from Belgium, but have lived in the USA since 2001. English
is my fourth language, and that makes things very interesting
when I am putting words together into books. Particularly; the
mistakes, the flubs, and the descriptions for when I forget a truly
obvious word.

Connect with Dennis:
Patreon.com/FloofWorks

About Dakota Krout

I live in a 'pretty much Canada' Minnesota city with my wife and daughter. I started writing The Divine Dungeon series because I enjoy reading and wanted to create a world all my own. To my surprise and great pleasure, I found like-minded people who enjoy the contents of my mind. Publishing my stories has been an incredible blessing thus far, and I hope to keep you entertained for years to come!

Connect with Dakota:
Patreon.com/DakotaKrout
Facebook.com/TheDivineDungeon
Twitter.com/DakotaKrout

ABOUT MOUNTAINDALE PRESS

Dakota and Danielle Krout, a husband and wife team, strive to create as well as publish excellent fantasy and science fiction novels. Self-publishing *The Divine Dungeon: Dungeon Born* in 2016 transformed their careers from Dakota's military and programming background and Danielle's Ph.D. in pharmacology to President and CEO, respectively, of a small press. Their goal is to share their success with other authors and provide captivating fiction to readers with the purpose of solidifying Mountaindale Press as the place 'Where Fantasy Transforms Reality.'

Connect with Mountaindale Press:
MountaindalePress.com
Facebook.com/MountaindalePress
Krout@MountaindalePress.com

MOUNTAINDALE PRESS TITLES

GAMELIT AND LITRPG

The Divine Dungeon Series
The Completionist Chronicles Series
By: DAKOTA KROUT

A Touch of Power Series
By: JAY BOYCE

Red Mage: Advent
By: XANDER BOYCE

Ether Collapse Series
By: RYAN DEBRUYN

Wolfman Warlock: Bibliomancer
By: JAMES HUNTER AND DAKOTA KROUT

Axe Druid Series
By: CHRISTOPHER JOHNS

Skeleton in Space Series
By: ANDRIES LOUWS

Chronicles of Ethan Series
By: JOHN L. MONK

Pixel Dust Series
By: DAVID PETRIE

APPENDIX

Abyss – A place you don't want to be, and a very common curse word.

Adventurers' Guild – A group from every non-hostile race that actively seeks treasure and cultivates to become stronger. They act as a mercenary group for Kingdoms that come under attack from monsters and other non-kingdom forces.

Affinity – A person's affinity denotes what element they need to cultivate Essence from. If they have multiple affinities, they need to cultivate all of those elements at the same time.

Affinity Channel – The pathway along the meridians that Essence flows through. Having multiple major affinities will open more pathways, allowing more Essence to flow into a person's center at one time.

Affinity Channel Type – Clogged, Ripped, Closed, Minor, Major, and Perfect.

> Clogged: Draws in no essence, because the channel is blocked with corruption.

> Ripped: Draws in an unknown amount of essence, but in a method that is unpredictable and lethal.

> Closed: Draws in no essence, because the channel is either unopened, or forcibly closed..

Minor: Draws in very little essence.

Major: Draws in a sizable amount of essence.

Perfect: Draws in a significant amount of essence. This affinity channel type cannot occur naturally. It is very dangerous to strive for as the path to this type leads to ripped channels.

Artorian – The main character of the series. If you weren't expecting shenanigans, grab some popcorn. It only gets more intense from here on.

Assassin – A stealthy killer who tries to make kills without being detected by his victim.

Aura – The flows of Essence generated by living creatures which surround them and hold their pattern.

Beast Core – A small gem that contains the Essence of Beasts. Also used to strip new cultivators of their corruption.

Boro – A trader in exotics, this man allied himself with the raider faction. He assists in swindling deals, and robbing villages blind after flooding them with gold that they will not keep.

Celestial – The Essence of Heaven, the embodiment of life and *considered* the ultimate good.

Center – The very center of a person's soul. This is the area Essence accumulates (in creatures that do not have a Core) before it binds to the Life Force.

Chants – Affect a choir-cleric's growth, and overall fighting ability. A Choir war host in action matches the chant of every other. Each voice added to the whole increases the power and ability of each person whose voice is involved, through celestial and aural sympathy.

Church – 'The' Church, to be specific. Also known as the Ecclesiarchy, is one of the few stable major powers active in the world. It has several branches, each operating under different specifications.

> The Choir – The Face of the church, they carry the torch and spread the call far and wide. Operates as exploratory force and functions on heart and mind campaigns. The Choir's special function is to use harmonizing sound to buff and empower every member included in the group-effect.

> Paladin Order – The Fast-Attack branch, these mounted warriors function as cavalry would. The mounted creatures in question vary greatly, and most members employ a high-ranked beast for these purposes.

> Phalanx Sentinels – The Siege or Hold branch, the Sentinels are a heavy-armor branch that specialize entirely on securing locations. They are well known to be notoriously slow, and just as notoriously impossible to uproot from a position.

> Inquisitors – The Information gathering branch. This branch remains secretive.

Church Ranks – There are multiple Ecclesiarchy ranks, stacking in importance mostly based on cultivation progress.

Initiate – A fresh entry to the church faction, the lowest rank. Generally given to someone still in training.

Scribe – An initiate who failed to become a D-ranked cultivator, is was trusted enough by the faction to remain.

Acolyte – Achieved by becoming a D-ranked cultivator. The second lowest rank in the church faction.

Battle Leader – A trusted acolyte who shows promise in the fields of leadership and battle.

Head Cleric – A high D-ranking cultivator, or a person who has been a Battle Leader long enough for their achievements to grant them their personal unit. Head Clerics are trusted to go on missions, excursions, and expeditions that differ based on the specific church faction.

Keeper – Ranked equal to a Head Cleric. People who specifically keep administrative records, and interpret ancient texts. Keepers famously do not get along, and hold bitter rivalries due to said interpretations of the scriptures. Keepers tend to be Head Clerics who failed to enter the C-ranks.

Arbiter – Achieved upon becoming a C-rank cultivator. An Arbiter is a settler of disputes of all kinds, whose authority is overshadowed only by those of higher rank. Otherwise, their say is final.

Friar – An B-ranked Cultivator in the church faction. Friars are glorified problem solvers.

Father – An A-ranked Cultivator in the church faction. A Father may be of a high rank, but has fallen out of favor with the upper echelons of church command.

Vicar – An A-ranked Cultivator in the church faction. The de-facto rulers, movers, and shakers, of the church faction.

Saint – An S-ranked Cultivator in the church faction. They do as they please.

Choppy – The prime woodcutter in the Salt Village.

Chi spiral – A person's Chi spiral is a vast amount of intricately knotted Essence. The more complex and complete the pattern woven into it, the more Essence it can hold and the finer the Essence would be refined.

Cleric – A Cultivator of Celestial Essence, a cleric tends to be support for a group, rarely fighting directly. Their main purpose in the lower rankings is to heal and comfort others.

Compound Essence – Essence that has formed together in complex ways. If two or more Essences come together to form something else, it is called a compound Essence or Higher Essence.

Corruption – Corruption is the remnant of the matter that pure Essence was formed into. It taints Essence but allows beings to absorb it through open affinity channels. This taint has been argued about for centuries; is it the source of life or a nasty side effect?

Currency values:

> Copper: one hundred copper coins are worth a silver coin
> Silver: one hundred silver coins are worth a Gold coin
> Gold: one hundred Gold coins are worth a Platinum coin
> Platinum: the highest coin currency in the Human Kingdoms

Cultivate – Cultivating is the process of refining Essence by removing corruption then cycling the purified Essence into the center of the soul.

Cultivation technique – A name for the specific method in which cultivators draw in and refine the energies of the Heavens and Earth.

Cultivator – A cultivator is a silly person who thinks messing with forces they don't understand will somehow make life better for them.

Duskgrove Castle – A Location within the Phantomdusk Forest. It is the primary hideout for the main Antagonist.

D. Kota – An initiate in the choir, who has grand aspirations of becoming a scholar.

Dwarves – Stocky humanoids that like to work with stone, metal, and alcohol. Good miners.

Elves – A race of willowy humanoids with pointy ears. There are five main types:

> High Elves: The largest nation of Elvenkind, they spend most of their time as merchants, artists, or thinkers. Rich beyond any need to actually work, their King is an S-ranked expert, and their cities shine with light and wealth. They like to think of themselves as 'above' other Elves, thus 'High' Elves.

> Wood Elves: Wood Elves live more simply than High Elves, but have greater connection to the earth and the elements. They are ruled by a counsel of S-ranked elders and rarely leave their woods. Though seen less often, they have great power. They grow and collect food and animal products for themselves and other Elven nations.

> Wild: Wild Elves are the outcasts of their societies, basically feral, they scorn society, civilization, and the rules of others. They have the worst reputation of any of the races of Elves, practicing dark arts and infernal summoning. They have no homeland, living only where they can get away with their dark deeds.

Dark: The Drow are known as Dark Elves. No one knows where they live, only where they can go to get in contact with them. Dark Elves also have a dark reputation as Assassins and mercenaries for the other races. The worst of their lot are 'Moon Elves', the best-known Assassins of any race. These are the Elves that Dale made a deal with for land and protection.

Sea: The Sea Elves live on boats their entire lives. They facilitate trade between all the races of Elves and man, trying not to take sides in conflicts. They work for themselves and are considered rather mysterious.

Essence – Essence is the fundamental energy of the universe, the pure power of heavens and earth that is used by the basic elements to become all forms of matter. There are six major types are names: Fire, Water, Earth, Air, Celestial, Infernal.

Essence cycling – A trick to move energy around, to enhance the ability of an organ.

Hadurin Fellstone – Head Healer of this motley expedition crew.

Hadurin Fellhammer – Grand Inquisitor operating in the choir, acting the guise of a slightly modified last name. Somehow, that's enough to fool everyone.

Hakan – A gilded blade, she is the main antagonist of Axiom. Her personality is as unpleasant as her fashion sense.

Fighter – A generic archetype of a being that uses melee weapons to fight.

Fringe – The Fringe region is located in the western region of Pangea. It has been scrapped from maps and scraped from history, by order of the Ecclesiarchy.

Gilded blade – A weapon, status title, occupation, and profession all in one. A Gilded blade is a weapon of the raider faction. They are brutally efficient at a single thing, and terrible at everything else.

Infernal – The Essence of death and demonic beings, *considered* to be always evil.

Inscription – A *permanent* pattern made of Essence that creates an effect on the universe. Try not to get the pattern wrong as it could have... unintended consequences. This is another name for an incomplete or unknown Rune.

Irene – A Keeper in the Choir. There is more to her than meets the eye, and is far more powerful than she initially appears to be. Do not argue with her about scripture.

Jiivra – A battle leader in the choir, she aspires to be a Paladin.

Jin – The hidden child or Tarrean and Irene, and a cultivator in the choir.

Lapis – A mineral-mining town in the vicinity of the Salt Flats. They refine the color Lapis into varying shades of Blue, and are a prime exporter. Lapis Is located in the Fringe.

Maccreus Tarrean – Head Cleric of a choir expeditionary force. His pride is his most distinguishing feature, next to that ostentatious affront known as his armor.

Mages' Guild – A secretive sub-sect of the Adventurers' Guild only Mage level cultivators are allowed to join.

Mana – A higher stage of Essence only able to be cultivated by those who have broken into at least the B-rankings and found the true name of something in the universe.

Mana Signature – A name for a signature that can be neither forged nor replicated, and is used in binding oaths.

Marud – Choir second-in-command Battle Leader, of the second expeditionary force to the Fringe.

Meridians – Meridians are energy channels that transport life energy (Chi/Essence) throughout the body.

Memory Core – Also known as a Memory Stone, depending on the base materials used in their production. Pressing the stone to your forehead lets a person store or gain the knowledge contained within. As if you'd gone through the events yourself. Generally never sold.

Mob – A shortened version of "dungeon monster".

Morovia – A world region located in the south-eastern section of the central Pangea band.

Necromancer – An Infernal Essence cultivator who can raise and control the dead and demons. A title for a cultivator who specializes in re-animating that which has died.

Nefellum – Head Cleric of the second expedition force into the Fringe.

Noble rankings:

> King/Queen – Ruler of their country. (Addressed as 'Your Majesty')

> Crown Prince/Princess – Next in line to the throne, has the same political power as a Grand Duke. (Addressed as 'Your Royal Highness')

> Prince/Princess – Child of the King/Queen, has the same political power as a Duke. (Addressed as 'Your Highness')

> Grand Duke – Ruler of a grand duchy and is senior to a Duke. (Addressed as 'Your Grace')

> Duke – Is senior to a Marquis or Marquess. (Addressed as 'Your Grace')

> Marquis/Marquess – Is senior to an Earl and has at least three Earls in their domain. (Addressed as 'Honorable')

> Earl – Is senior to a Baron. Each Earl has three barons under their power. (Addressed as 'My Lord/Lady')

Baron – Senior to knights, they control a minimum of ten knights and therefore their land. (Addressed as 'My Lord/Lady')

Knights – Sub rulers of plots of land and peasants. (Addressed as 'Sir')

Olgier – A trader from Rutsel, whose greed greatly exceeds his guile.

Phantomdusk Forest – A world region that borders The Fringe. It is comprised of vast, continent-sprawled greenery that covers multiple biomes. Any forest region connecting to this main mass is considered part of the whole, entering it has a high mortality rate.

Ranger – Typically an adventurer archetype that is able to attack from long range, usually with a bow.

Ranking System – The ranking system is a way to classify how powerful a creature has become through fighting and cultivation.

G – At the lowest ranking is mostly non-organic matter such as rocks and ash. Mid-G contains small plants such as moss and mushrooms while the upper ranks form most of the other flora in the world.

F – The F-ranks are where beings are becoming actually sentient, able to gather their own food and make short-term plans. The mid-F ranks are where most humans reach before adulthood without cultivating. This is known as the fishy or "failure" rank.

E – The E-rank is known as the "echo" rank and is used to prepare a body for intense cultivation.

D – This is the rank where a cultivator starts to become actually dangerous. A D-ranked individual can usually fight off ten F-ranked beings without issue. They are characterized by a "fractal" in their Chi spiral.

C – The highest-ranked Essence cultivators, those in the C-rank usually have opened all of their meridians. A C-ranked cultivator can usually fight off ten D-ranked and one hundred F-ranked beings without being overwhelmed.

B – This is the first rank of Mana cultivators, known as Mages. They convert Essence into Mana through a nuanced refining process and release it through a true name of the universe.

A – Usually several hundred years are needed to attain this rank, known as High-Mage or High-Magous. They are the most powerful rank of Mages.

S – Very mysterious Spiritual Essence cultivators. Not much is known about the requirements for this rank or those above it.

SS – Pronounced 'Double S'. Not much is known about the requirements for this rank or those above it.

SSS – Pronounced 'Triple S'. Not much is known about the requirements for this rank or those above it.

Heavenly – Not much is known about the requirements for this rank or those above it.

Godly – Not much is known about the requirements for this rank or those above it.

Refining – A name for the method of separating essences of differing purities.

Rune – A *permanent* pattern made of Essence that creates an effect on the universe. Try not to get the pattern wrong as it could have... unintended consequences. This is another name for a completed Inscription.

Salt Village – The main location of Artorian's Archives one, where the majority of the story takes place. It is Located in the Fringe, and is a day's journey from the Lapis Village.

Salt Flats – A location in the Fringe. The Salt Village operates by scraping salt from the Salt Flats, a place where the material is plentiful. It is their main export.

Scar – Known as 'The Scar'. A location in the Fringe that includes the Salt Flats as one of its tendrils. It is rumored to be a kind of slumbering dungeon.

Sproutling – A title for a child in the Fringe who has not yet been assigned a name, and thus is not considered an adult. Until a certain key event, this includes the famous five: Lunella, Grimaldus, Tychus, Wuxius, and Astrea.

Skyspear Academy – An Academy present on the world's tallest mountain.

Socorro – A desert in the central-band, eastern portion of Pangea. It used to be a place for something important. Now there is only sand, and ruin.

Switch – A village Elder of the salt village in the Fringe region.

Tibbins – An Acolyte in the Choir. He has a deep passion for all things culinary, and possesses a truly unique expression.

Yvessa – An Elven name that means: 'To bloom out of great drought.' She is a choir-cleric going up the ranks, and holds incredible promise.

Made in the USA
Columbia, SC
15 September 2023

22940930R00264